RETURN ENGAGEMENT

By

Margaret McCarthy

Best wishes to Liz.

Many thanks for all
the efforts you used to help me.
I will be forever grateful.

Best regards
Marease Clay

AKA Margaret McCarthy

ISBN: 1-4033-6774-4 (E-book)
ISBN: 1-4033-6775-2 (Paperback)
ISBN: 1-4033-6776-0 (Dustjacket)

Library of Congress Control Number: 2002111793

This book is printed on acid free paper.

Printed in the United States of America
Bloomington, IN

1stBooks - rev. 09/19/02

Acknowledgments

It doesn't matter how many articles you have published or how often your poetry is read, when you attempt to write your first novel you set the foundation for a whole new venture. ***Return Engagement*** has been, still is, and probably always will be, my pet project. It took me years to write it, not on a full time basis, but a few hours every night after coming home from a two job work day.

Encouragement is the fuel every writer counts on to be successful. I will be forever grateful to Professor Eleanor Hope-McCarthy and Dr. Eugene Connolly who had faith in me when I didn't have faith in myself. They kept asking for more, and would tell me to clarify, specify and keep on writing.

Many thanks to Jean Brennan a faithful friend and A-1 critic who was always there with a pat on the back.

Thanks to Sue Smulski who could always alleviate job pressures and give me reasons to keep on writing.

Thanks to Judy Kelleher who never ran out of patience and always had time to read another page.

Many thanks to Mary Jane Sott whose keen sense of humor and quick suggestions were always there when I needed a lift.

Unending gratitude to Evelyn Tabberrah for all of her help and her infinite patience for all the times I "had to run something past her – just once more."

Chapter 1

The cab driver shifted his position, glanced over his shoulder at the two men in the back seat and asked, "You guys sure you want the Ballard Theater? Ain't no show there now, you know."

"We're sure," Bill Flanagan said and glanced at Dan Shaw for reassurance. Dan shrugged his shoulders and quietly answered, "I hope so."

The driver chomped on the soggy end of an unlit cigar and stopped the cab in front of the dark theater. "Good luck," the cabby grinned as he guided the vehicle back into traffic.

The stark whiteness of the barren theater marquee glared down on Bill and Dan like an angry challenge. Icy wind blew along 41st Street, leaving no doubt that winter in New York City can be cold and miserable. The two men turned up their coat collars against the wintry blast and crossed the sidewalk to the glass doors of the lobby area. The dark interior was as empty as the marquee over their heads.

This was their first attempt at auditions for anything as big as a Broadway show. Promising careers had been interrupted when Uncle Sam beckoned for World War II. The last two years of the war they spent a lot of time together. Two days before their final discharge Dan heard of a producer looking for talented ex-military personnel for the cast of a new Broadway musical that would highlight the problems of servicemen returning to civilian life. It didn't take him long to convince Bill to go to New York with him and try for an audition.

The bleak atmosphere of the empty theater began to raise a few doubts for both of them. Finally, Dan found what he was looking for in the area next to the closed box office. Space usually reserved for the playbill now held a sign that stated:

IN REHEARSAL

GENTLEMEN AGAIN

A new musical under the direction of
Brian Casey
Talented performers are invited to audition

Check with stage manager for times or appointments.

"This is the right place," he said, "All we have to do is figure out how to get in."

Bill tried each of the lobby doors and found them locked. "This is a fine way to start a career," he remarked. "The sign invites us in, then they lock us out! Do you suppose they're trying to tell us something?"

Dan grinned as he looked around and suggested they check the alley at the side of the building. "Maybe there's a back way in," he said.

From the sidewalk the alley looked endless. Hemmed in by windowless brick walls on both sides, its desolate appearance was nothing like the hustle and bustle commonly attributed to New York City and especially to the theater district. The only activity was scattered bits of paper that spun like whirligigs looking for shelter from the wintry winds that blew along 41st Street. At the far end of the alley they found a door marked, STAGE ENTRANCE – BALLARD. They buried their doubts, summoned their courage, and each took a deep breath.

"You ready?" Dan asked.

"Ready as I'll ever be," Bill answered. He stood up straight and took another deep breath. "Let's go," he said.

As they walked in an elderly security guard asked how he could help them.

"We would like to make appointments to audition," Bill said.

The guard pointed to a row of chairs to the right of the stage. "Have a seat over there and Mr. Casey will talk to you when the girls are finished." The seats gave both men a perfect view of the stage and the chorus girls rehearsing a dance routine. The director sat in the second row of the theater and tapped a steady rhythm on the back of the seat in front of him. Every step the girls took was perfectly timed to match his tempo.

Bill took one look at the chorus line and in long drawn out breaths remarked, "I've never seen that much gorgeous female flesh in one place in all my life."

Dan couldn't take his eyes away from the girls either. Through a slow intake of breath he managed to mumble a reply, "Tell me about it, they're more than beautiful!"

The girls finished their routine and the director picked up his notebook and walked toward the two new arrivals. He turned to the chorus line and, almost as an afterthought, said, "All right girls, take five." Some left the stage, others separated into small groups.

The four girls at the far end of the line looked at each other and breathed a sign of relief.

"Casey is a slave driver," Cass said. "I'm exhausted."

"I agree," Harriet added as she gently massaged her legs.

"You're right, Cass, he doesn't give us a break at all," Gracie, the third member of the group added. "It's easy for him to sit there with a cup of coffee and tell us to 'run through it one more time'." She glanced over her shoulder at the last girl in the foursome and asked, "What do you think, Jen?"

"What did you say?" Jen asked. All three of them looked at her. She wasn't paying any attention to them, she was fascinated by the two men talking to the director. Both were handsome, about six feet tall, one maybe an inch or two taller than the other. The shorter one had a more muscular build, but both were worth a second look.

"No wonder she didn't hear us," Cass said with a grin and rolled her eyes toward the director. "Look at the two guys talking to Casey. I hope they're here for auditions. I wouldn't mind working with either of them, on or off the stage."

Jen tried to hide the little traces of a smile and said, "You can have the taller one, Cass, I like the looks of the other one."

"They're both good looking," Harriet said. "I wonder what they do?"

Gracie casually glanced at the two men. "They look interesting but I can't make a judgment until I check their bank balances," she said. She was a talented dancer, but had no illusions of stardom. She admitted to putting up with the hardships of show business for the sole purpose of finding a wealthy husband.

"What a terrible thing to say," Harriet remarked and didn't try to hide the prim and proper New England background that was her way of life.

"Well, I mean it," a determined Gracie answered. "I'm not killing myself with these routines just for the fun of it. I'm not stupid enough to think I'm a Ginger Rogers or a Betty Grable. I'm me and that's it.

3

If I can't find a man with money in this business there isn't an available one out there."

Cass, Harriet and Gracie had a lively conversation about the new arrivals. Jen had not taken part at all, but found herself intrigued by the newcomers. When she realized she was staring and the shorter of the two men glanced in her direction she quickly averted her eyes. When he looked away she went right back to staring again. Something about him piqued her interest and her eyes wouldn't let him go. He looked her way again and this time made eye contact. She couldn't hide the blush that crept into her cheeks. He smiled, and she smiled back. She was embarrassed that he caught her, but couldn't seem to help herself.

Cass saw the eye contact between Jen and Bill. "Are you flirting," she asked? "You can only have one at a time, so if you get lucky share the other one with me."

All three girls were surprised that Jen was the first to notice the newcomers. She was the youngest of this foursome, not yet twenty. Sparkling deep blue eyes accentuated the perfect facial features of this pretty brunette. The girls had promised Jen's father they would take care of her. It was a condition he invoked when he agreed to let her move to the apartment they shared in Lower Manhattan. All three took their responsibility seriously.

"I'm not flirting," Jen assured them. "There's something about the shorter one that intrigues me and I can't seem to help myself. He must think I'm a nut, especially when I'm sure I never saw him before in my life."

Cass put a protective arm around the younger girl's shoulders. "Let's find out who they are," she suggested. "Maybe that will help clear up this fascination you have. Besides, it's a good icebreaker, and I'm curious, too."

Cass, like Harriet and Gracie, was a tall shapely blonde with a fantastic figure. Her rhythm and timing were perfect and she made every move seem effortless. She was the most outgoing of all four girls and although she joked about men, she was particular when it came to whom she picked for a friend.

The director finished his conversation with the two men and walked off the stage. It meant the girls would have a few more minutes of rest before going back to the dance routine. Most of them

4

made their way off stage. Jen, who was still trying to explain her fascination to Cass, Harriet, and Gracie, followed along and accidentally bumped into Bill. "Excuse me," she said and could feel the traces of blush coming back in her cheeks.

"It was my fault," Bill insisted and before Jen had a chance to get away he quickly added, "Do we know each other from somewhere?"

"I don't think so," she answered nervously.

"Are you sure?" he persisted. "I feel like I know you from somewhere. You look familiar and I would never forget such a pretty face."

"I don't think we've ever met," Jen answered. "But I have to admit, I had the same feeling. Maybe it was a long time ago and neither of us remember." She tried to look at him but each time she did she felt the blush return to her cheeks.

"I couldn't forget you, no matter how long ago it was," he said with a smile. "My name is Bill Flanagan, does that ring a bell with you?"

"Not really," she answered and smiled back at him. "I'm Jennifer Kelly, does that sound familiar to you?"

Bill was tempted to say yes and make up a story but this girl was different and he had to be truthful with her. "All Flanagans know lots of Kellys," he said. "If they don't know them, they would be letting down good Irish tradition if they didn't introduce themselves."

"That sounds reasonable," Jen answered as she smiled and nodded agreement.

The more they talked the more his interest grew. Jen Kelly was special and he was not going to settle for just a "hello."

"What's it like to work for Brian Casey?" he asked.

Jen thought for a minute. "Once in a while he can be difficult. He's a perfectionist and he wants each of us to be one, too. He expects a lot from us, but he puts in a lot himself. Everyone knows that Brian Casey puts on a good show." She was trying to make this encounter last, too, but she didn't want to be obvious or pushy. She was trying as hard as he was to make a good impression.

"That's nice to know," Bill said. He never met a girl who churned up feelings in him like Jennifer Kelly and he was going to make the most of this meeting. "Are you ladies finished for the day?" he asked.

"We're all tired enough to call it a day," Jen admitted, "but we'll probably be here for awhile. Casey usually wraps things up about 7 o'clock."

"What time do you start in the morning?" he asked in an attempt to prolong the conversation and keep her from leaving.

"About 9," she said and glanced over his shoulder at the daily callboard on the wall behind him. "Tomorrow we don't have to be here until 10:15. Probably because of your auditions."

"You mean thanks to us you can all get an extra hour of sleep?" Bill teased.

"I guess so," she conceded with a smile.

"Too bad," he said. "It would be nice to have you here for my audition. At least I'd have one friendly face in the audience."

"How do you know I'd be friendly?" she teased back. "I don't even know what you do."

"I'm a dancer."

"What kind of a dancer?"

"A good one."

"That's not what I mean," she said. "What's your specialty?"

"I don't have a specialty. Tap, soft-shoe, ballroom, you name it, I can do it. Or better still give me the music and let me work up my own routine. That's my real specialty." Before she could ask any more questions he added, "I know you would be friendly because you're a Kelly and I'm a Flanagan. Kellys and Flanagans have always been compatible. Besides, you're a dancer, too, and a good one. We were watching you."

"Thank you," she said and could feel the blush start in her cheeks again. Every time they looked at each other she felt it. I hope he doesn't notice, she thought, and tried to carry on the conversation by quickly adding, "I think you're prejudiced because I'm Irish."

"I didn't know you were Irish when I was watching you dance," he told her and quickly added, "but I'm glad you are."

"Why?" she asked.

"Because I'm Irish, too," he replied. There was no strangeness with these two. They seemed to know each other right from the start. Bill suggested they meet the girls after rehearsal and get a bite to eat.

"I'd like that," Jen told him, "if you don't mind waiting until Casey lets us go. We can't leave until he calls it quits for the day and I

6

have to let the other girls know who I'm going with and where I'm going."

"We don't mind waiting," Bill said and looked at his friend for confirmation. Dan, standing a few feet away was watching Bill's progress with this beautiful showgirl. He didn't want to be a third party if Bill was having any success. He agreed to wait if the other girls would join them.

"All three of them?" Jen asked.

"Why not?" Dan answered, "Everyone has to eat eventually."

"I'll ask them if they want to come," she said, surprised and pleased that all four girls were invited. "If it's all right with them, we'll meet you inside the stage entrance when Casey calls it a day, OK?"

"We'll be there," Bill assured her.

Chapter 2

Tuesday morning was rainy, but the cold gray skies didn't dampen any spirits. On the way to the theater the two men talked about the opportunities ahead if they could get a part in this show. Their auditions came so quickly it surprised both of them. They knew that to be part of a Broadway show was something most performers only dreamed about. This morning it could happen for them and they were excited. Dan wondered what it would be like to work in a major production, especially one that Brian Casey was directing. Bill wasn't even thinking about the show. His mind was on the girl he was with last evening.

"The girls say Brian Casey plays pretty fair," Dan commented.

"They also said he's a perfectionist who works the hell out of everyone in the cast," Bill added.

"That's all right with me as long as the finished product is top of the line," Dan said.

"Those girls are 'top of the line' as far as I'm concerned," Bill said with a grin. "If he hires us I'm really going to like working with this group."

"Are you sure it's the group that interests you?" he asked. "It looked to me as if Jen Kelly was the only one you were aware of last night."

"Was it that noticeable?" Bill asked with a grin.

"It couldn't have been more obvious," Dan answered. "I have to admit, you have good taste. She is a real charmer. All those girls are attractive." He paused for a minute and thought about what he said. "Attractive," he repeated, "Wow! What an understatement that is. All of them are raving beauties. We should get to know them better, whether we're hired or not."

They reached the theater a few minutes early and Bill scanned the empty seats. It was not like him to be nervous, especially when it concerned any aspect of dancing. He was good at what he did and his self-confidence carried him through any test of his talent.

"Calm down," Dan told him. "Brian Casey isn't God. If we don't make it here, we'll make it somewhere else."

"It's not Casey that bothers me," Bill said. "I'm wondering if the girls will show up. Last night Jen said they would be here." He couldn't hide his disappointment as he looked at the empty chairs on both sides of the stage.

Dan shook his head as he watched his friend. "I never saw a girl affect you like this. I think you're really hooked this time. All Jen Kelly has to do is reel you in."

Bill stopped his pacing, stood still for a minute and finally spoke. "I never felt like this about any girl in my life. Maybe you're right. I haven't been able to think of anything but Jennifer Kelly since I first saw her. I'm going to marry this girl."

Dan's quick intake of breath and surprised expression let Bill know his statement was a real shocker. He knew Jen made a big impression on Bill, but he had no idea how big.

* * * * *

Brian Casey came through the stage door and everyone shifted gears into a work mode. He was young for a director, but seemed to generate waves that put people into motion. "Can we get this show on the road," he hollered. Conversations came to an abrupt halt, coffee cups were set aside, and everyone focused on the task ahead of them. Casey called for the area to be cleared so he could give full attention to the two auditions scheduled for this morning.

Bill Flanagan and Dan Shaw watched the director's controlling moves and realized this audition might turn out to be a little tougher than they first thought. At exactly 9:45 Bill's name was called. He handed his music to the man at the piano, talked for a few seconds about special parts in the background that needed emphasis and was ready for his routine. He glanced around but there was no sign of the girls and he wondered if they would show up. He tried to hide his disappointment and focused on the job at hand as he started his routine. As he danced across the stage he turned and spotted the four girls on the opposite side of the theater. The pace of his routine quickened and the piano player had to adjust to his new mood and made the transition look like part of the arrangement.

The cadence of the dance punctured the stillness of the empty theater as Bill's feet tapped out feelings he didn't have the courage to say. As their eyes met, Jen knew he was dancing as much for her as he was to impress the director.

Cass was the first to break the spell. "Gee, Jen, he really is good. I thought he was just bragging last night, but he's better than good, he's great! I'll bet Casey signs him right away."

"I hope so," Jen answered.

Bill's dance rhythm echoed through the empty theater but couldn't keep pace with his heartbeat when he saw Jen. "She did come! She kept her promise! She does care! I'm going to marry this girl," he told himself. He ended his routine and returned to his seat next to Dan. He watched Brian Casey for the slightest hint of approval. Not a word was said, nor any reaction shown to what Bill considered the best performance of his life.

The director made a few notes on his pad and called for the next audition. Dan Shaw gave his music to the man at the piano and as he sang Bill noticed he was exceptionally good today, too. He must want this almost as much as I do, he thought. Dan ended his song and Casey still showed no reaction. Both men knew they put their best efforts into this audition. They glanced at each other as the director shuffled through his papers.

Jen, Cass, Harriet and Gracie were also watching Casey's expression for a hint of his decision. They could see all three men, but their seats were not close enough to hear what was being said. "Keep your fingers crossed," Jen pleaded. "He just has to sign both of them."

"He's crazy if he doesn't," Gracie commented. "These two are fantastic. Nothing like some of the stuff we've seen him audition. Did you see the stagehands stop what they were doing and watch them? I saw Casey notice it."

"I'd like to know them better whether he signs them or not," Cass suggested. "Besides having talent, they're nice guys."

"Casey will sign them," Harriet commented with her stoic New England manner. "Look at him, he's almost smiling, and lately that's rare for him."

Brian Casey put his papers in a neat pile and slowly inserted them into his notebook. He got up from his seat and turned to face the two men. "I don't make a habit of commenting on auditions but both of you have a lot of talent. You're good," he told them. He stopped for a minute and looked from one to the other and added, "damn good."

This director seldom indulged in compliments. He felt audiences deserved the best and he expected his performers to always deliver the best. To Casey good performances were unacceptable and excellent performances were routine. He looked at Dan Shaw and said, "I have a spot for you and it's yours if you want it." Before Dan had a chance to answer, he turned to Bill Flanagan and continued, "I'm going to make a place in this show for you, I like the way you work." Dan and Bill were too surprised to say anything but managed to mumble a "Thanks."

"Don't thank me yet," Casey warned them. "You never worked for me. I expect 110% effort 100% of the time. Give me that and we'll get along fine. I don't want excuses and I don't tolerate mistakes. I want performers who know what they're doing, who know how to take direction and who know how to deliver. If you're sure you want to be part of this production be here at four o'clock this afternoon and your contracts will be ready. If you don't want to play by my rules, say good-by now."

"We'll be here at four," Dan assured him.

"Good," Casey said, "You won't be sorry." For the first time since they met he showed traces of a smile. Everyone was satisfied with the arrangement and they shook hands to seal the bargain.

The girls watched Casey's every move. They saw the handshakes and knew both men were now part of *Gentlemen Again*. Jen couldn't control her excitement and since Cass was sitting next to her, Cass got a big hug. "Be careful of my hair!" Cass cautioned with a grin as she glanced at Jen. "You really are serious about this guy, aren't you?"

"Oh Cass, I can't tell you how serious I am."

Cass, Gracie and Harriet looked at each other and realized that this situation was a lot more than just a flirtation for Jen.

"Come on, Jen, you only met him yesterday," Gracie reminded her.

"I know," Jen answered. "That's the scary part. I'm so comfortable with him I feel like I've known him all my life."

"Oh boy!" Cass exclaimed anticipating good times to come. "Does this mean that we're going to introduce men into this tight little circle? I like that idea."

"Cass be serious," Harriet chastised. "Our agreement was to watch out for each other. Now we have to keep an eye on Jen until we know these men a little better."

"Harriet," Cass answered in a provocative way, "That is exactly what I had in mind. I want to volunteer to find out all about Dan Shaw. I promise to ask him all kinds of personal questions as soon as I can get him alone, OK?"

"You're impossible," Harriet said and tried to cover up the secret admiration she had for the way Cass handled every challenge.

The two newest cast members of *Gentlemen Again* invited the four girls to dinner to celebrate the signing of the contracts. Bill Flanagan thought it would be a good way to get to know the girls a little better. Dan Shaw quickly agreed, but knew that Bill only had eyes for Jen Kelly. "How do you expect me to keep up with three women?" he asked. Bill looked at his friend and smiled. "I know it will be difficult," he said with a grin, "But I'm sure you can handle it if you try."

Cass suggested they meet about 7:30 at Nick's Restaurant, a favorite gathering place for the little people of show business. Cast members who didn't qualify for star status, or whose names were not on any theater marquee, were always treated like headliners at Nick's.

The restaurant was near the girls' apartment in lower Manhattan. Gracie mentioned that by going to Nick's none of them would have to worry about a ride home. It would also give them a chance to introduce Bill and Dan to some of the other cast members who were sure to drop in before the evening was over.

The warm friendly surroundings at Nick's was a big part of its attraction. Double glass entrance doors opened to a carpeted lobby. A reservations desk and cashier's area occupied a small corner of the main room. A spacious dining room with a small dance floor offered a cozy, comfortable atmosphere. George, the very proper Maitre d' of Nick's had an air of total authority. His perfect manners and impeccable neatness always meant a sharp crease in his trousers and not one gray hair falling on the wrong side of his part. He took pride in calling many of his patrons by name and the future stars of Broadway enjoyed being in the limelight even if it was only for a few minutes. The ability to quickly sum up a situation made George a master of building self-esteem for those who needed a boost and capable of bringing others down a peg or two if inflated egos gave them a false sense of self-importance. He looked over the shoulders of those he referred to as his "seasonal crop of stars" and made sure they ate decent meals and didn't drink too much. He had no qualms about shutting them off if he thought they had one too many. His biggest concern was the friends they chose. George made himself a guardian to the cast of *Gentlemen Again* and many of the other Broadway shows. Everyone trusted him. His word was never doubted and no one ever argued with him. His reservations desk at Nick's had a commanding view of the dining room. He often used it to observe the habits, behavior and friendships cultivated by his latest "seasonal crop of stars."

On this cold, blustery evening the girls arrived a few minutes before 7:30. George greeted each of them by name as he helped them remove their coats. Gracie told him they were expecting two men to join the group for dinner. "Oh," he commented as he raised a critical eyebrow, "and who might they be?"

Cass was the first to answer. "Two good looking guys named Bill Flanagan and Dan Shaw. The newest members of our cast just signed on today. They're so good they even had Casey smiling this morning."

"What did they do to accomplish that?" he asked with a chuckle.

"Bill is the greatest dancer in the world," Jen stated, "and Dan has a voice that will be the envy of every other man on Broadway."

George noticed the particular way Jen described the men. "Jennifer, you sound very serious about these two. How long have you known them?" he asked.

"Not very long," she admitted. She tried to justify her enthusiasm as if she was explaining a new acquaintance to her father. "They're very nice. Wait until you meet them, you'll see."

"He won't have to wait long," Gracie said. "Here they are now."

Introductions were made and George led the group to three tables he had put together to accommodate everyone. Bill noticed there were extra seats and Jen explained that almost everyone from the cast came by Nick's and always stopped to say hello. "It will give us a chance to introduce you to some of the others and you won't feel like strangers at rehearsals," she told them. George retreated to his favorite spot at the reservations desk and scanned the dining room. He centered his attention on the four showgirls and their new friends. He intended to keep an eye on them until he knew a little more about the two men. He liked these girls and wanted to make sure the newcomers were aware of his protective role. He knew the girls did a lot of kidding among themselves but were careful about inviting others to join them. He made a mental note to check out the two new cast members. They had to be exceptional to be welcomed so quickly.

"Hey, look who's here!" Cass announced, as a thin, scholarly looking young man approached their table. "This is Alan Durling," she said as she welcomed the new arrival. "Alan supplied the music for both of you this morning." The men shook hands and Alan told Bill he didn't know many people who could change their rhythm in the middle of an audition. "You really surprised me," he added with a friendly smile.

"I'm sorry about that," Bill apologized. "I guess I got carried away this morning. You were so good on that piano the director thought it was part of the routine. I owe you one for that."

"You don't owe me anything," Alan told him with a chuckle. "We all need a hand now and then. We never worry about pay backs in this business. I'm glad Casey liked your routine. It looks like everyone did from what I've been hearing."

Bill was surprised. He knew he put everything into the audition, but he was trying to impress Jen Kelly. He never thought of all the other people who were in the theater this morning.

"Thank you, Alan," Jen said. "We told him how good he was but he thinks we're just being polite. Now that you said it, too, maybe he'll believe us."

"I've worked with Brian Casey before," Alan continued. "He's not easy to please. He never comments on anybody's good performance, but I noticed this morning he told both of you how good you were. You have to give him credit, he knows talent and he doesn't let the good ones get away."

"From what we've seen so far," Dan said, "This show seems to be loaded with talent."

"Now that's the truth," Alan agreed.

"You haven't seen it all yet," Harriet told them. "Wait until you hear Julian Brice sing. He has a voice that will send shivers up and down your spine. Every time he starts a song everyone drops what they're doing to listen."

"When Casey gets the whole cast lined up this show is bound to be a hit," Gracie added.

"He's particular about the people he hires. It makes all of us try that much harder."

"Yeah," Cass commented with a chuckle, "except for the times you would like to choke him for making you run through the routine – 'just one more time'."

The waiter arrived with menus and Cass nonchalantly remarked they would order a round of drinks. He said George's instructions were to serve dinner first. Bill and Dan noticed that no one objected to his suggestion. The girls insisted Alan join the party. That was fine with Dan Shaw. He thought Alan would even things up a little and he wouldn't have to keep three women happy while Bill concentrated on Jen.

The musician proved to be a wealth of information about show business in general and the Broadway stage in particular. He had worked with many big bands and his musical talent was well known in the entertainment world, but so was his alcohol habit. It was common knowledge this young man made many trips to the trough to quench an unquenchable thirst. What would have proven disastrous for others never affected this musician's fabulous talent. He was not an obnoxious drunk, not even a noticeable one. His quiet nature was the side of Alan Durling that everyone saw, no matter how much he drank. He was a musical genius and his alcohol level never impaired his talent. When his legs would no longer support him and his speech was slightly slurred, his fingers still fell on the right keys. If he played a song once it was etched in his mind forever. He always remembered where he heard it and who was involved. His total recall was envied by almost everyone. His musical talent was sought after by many of the big bands, but Alan didn't want to travel. New York was home to him and that's where he wanted to stay. When the big bands were scheduled to play in or around New York City, Alan Durling was the local talent requested to sit in. He felt he had the best of both worlds. He stayed in New York and still got to play with all the greats. His congenial manner and ability to put people at ease added to his popularity. Brian Casey thought Alan would be an asset to *Gentlemen*

Again. He knew Alan had the patience to handle the music for the most temperamental stars and also had the heart and understanding to cultivate the newcomers to the complex world of show business.

Drinks were served when dinner was over and they all enjoyed a dance or two. It was the beginning of exciting careers for Dan Shaw and Bill Flanagan. It was also the start of warm and welcome friendships with Alan Durling and the four girls who first introduced them to this new musical.

It was much more for Bill Flanagan and Jen Kelly. They danced every dance and sang every love song to each other. They treasured the closeness the slow dances encouraged. It was a wonderful night.

"If you guys need an apartment, I know where there will be a vacancy that might fill the bill," Alan told Dan. "It's a nice place and it's not far from the girls."

"We're interested," Dan quickly replied. "I'm not crazy about the hotel we're in now." Alan gave him the address and promised to put in a good word with the owner. An evening that started out as a contract signing celebration turned into a very productive night. Both men were glad to be accepted into this close knit group of regulars from what everyone was sure would be one of Broadway's memorable hit shows. Even George, the self appointed Guardian Angel for the girls, gave his stamp of approval.

Dan Shaw had a fantastic time. Bill Flanagan had and even better time. Bill was in love – and it showed.

Harriet, Cass and Gracie weren't going to take any chances. They didn't know Dan Shaw or Bill Flanagan well enough to make a judgment. They seemed to be nice but the girls made a promise to watch out for each other and they meant to live up to their agreement.

Jen was mesmerized by all the attention she was getting from Bill. He seemed honest and sincere, but Harriet, Cass and Gracie were going to make sure. Love, they explained to Jen, had a funny way of shutting out all the bad things and just letting you see what you wanted to see. Each of them tried to talk her into going a little slower in her relationship with Bill, but their efforts fell on deaf ears. She couldn't get him off her mind. She knew he was everything she wanted and she wasn't going to be persuaded otherwise.

Dan listened as Bill talked about his feelings for Jen Kelly. "I'm going to marry her," he insisted. "I can't offer her very much now, but if this show is a hit and I can see a decent future for us, there will be a wedding. You can bet a bundle on it.'

"You don't waste any time, do you?" Dan remarked.

"When you find someone like Jen you'll know how I feel," Bill explained. "I can't put it into words. I don't know how to describe it. The one thing I am sure of is that there is no other feeling in this world that can come close to it."

Dan was not trying to discourage him, just slow him down a little. "I realize Jen is pretty special to you, but all of these women are special," Dan told him. "They were the first ones to welcome us to the cast. They made sure we met everyone from the show. They treated us like we belonged before we were hired. That makes them special to me." Bill had not looked at him through the whole discussion and Dan wondered if his advice was being ignored. He figured he had gone this far so he may as well finish what he had to say. "I would love to see you marry Jen. Just make damn sure it's what both of you want before either of you make a commitment."

Bill finally looked at him and in a quiet but determined manner said, "Dan you and I have been friends for a long time. We know each other pretty well. We've been out with a lot of women and we've had lots of fun. Jen is different," Bill continued. When he mentioned her name his voice mellowed and a soft look came into his eyes. "I'm not looking for a one night stand or a trip to the nearest motel. This is the girl I want to marry. I want to share my life with her. I want her to have my children. I want to love her and be loved by her for the rest of my life. What more can I say?"

"Nothing," Dan answered with a grin and gave his friend a pat on the shoulder to reassure him he understood his feelings.

* * * * *

Jen encouraged Bill to try new dance routines. She seemed to bring out talent that even he didn't realize he had. They were good for each other. Bill thought he had been given a little piece of Heaven. He was in love with a beautiful girl and she was in love with him and to top it all off, she was Irish! His mother would love Jen and his father would be delighted. Jen thought everyone should love Bill as much as she did. In her eyes he had no faults at all. The Irish factor was a big plus for her, too. Her parents were born in Ireland and for her to fall in love with a man of Irish ancestry would be the ultimate satisfaction as far as they were concerned. She couldn't wait for the first day of no rehearsals so she could take Bill to meet them.

Jen was the middle daughter of Walter and Molly Kelly. With the help of Cass, Gracie and Harriet she convinced her parents to let her move to New York City. The girls would share an apartment and watch out for each other. Walter was not sure it was a good idea, but Jen's companions promised him they would take good care of her.

"I never should have listened to them," Walter told his wife. "Jenny was only living in New York City a few weeks and now she wants to bring a man home for us to meet. They told me they would take good care of her. I don't call it taking good care of her when they let her get starry eyed over the first guy that comes along."

Molly listened to her husband and suggested maybe he was being a little too quick in his judgment. "Why don't you wait and see what the young man is like?" she said. Walter appeared to have already made up his mind. "Maybe they thought they would win me over because he's Irish. Well, that's not going to work. This is my Jenny who's involved, so this young fellow had better be something special, Irish or not."

Walter liked Bill as soon as he met him, but was still determined to run him through every test possible to find his strengths and weaknesses. Bill was in show business and that was not easy to explain to the stevedores who worked for Walter. Being a dancer was even harder to explain. Walter insisted on dropping in to the local pub with Jen's new friend. Bill was introduced to some of the hardiest human beings he had ever encountered. After the second round of drinks he took Walter aside and told him that was his limit. "I don't want to hurt any feelings by saying 'no thank you' to any of these men," he said, "but I'm driving today and I've got Jen in the car with me. I don't want anything to happen to her because of a stupid move on my part." He was afraid Walter wouldn't understand, but instead of dimming his chances to impress this man it worked just the opposite. "I admire a man who knows his limit," Walter told him. "I admire you more for having the good sense to fall in love with such a wonderful girl as my Jenny."

18

Bill's honesty had completely won over the man who could have been his severest critic.

Chapter 3

Patience was not one of Brian Casey's big attributes. After his morning meeting with the producers he couldn't hide his anger. He was being forced to accept a headliner he didn't want and more important didn't like. He had nurtured this show since its conception and he resented the intrusion on what he considered his sacred territory. He had agreed to direct *Gentlemen Again* with the understanding he would have control of the hiring and firing of the cast. "I know what this show needs," he told the producers, "and I know talent. If you give me a free hand, I'll give you a hit musical." Both producers agreed to stay out of the way and let him handle things. Now, six weeks into rehearsal, they changed the rules and informed him the headliner would be Jack Boyd.

Brian Casey knew of Boyd's talent as well as his reputation for causing trouble. He had carefully assembled a cast that would make any director proud. Most of them were newcomers to Broadway and he didn't want to subject them to someone like Boyd because of a last minute decision of the producers. Without someone to control the situation, Jack Boyd's caustic humor and inflated ego could undermine the entire cast. Brian Casey was not going to let that happen.

He left the producers office and headed back to the Ballard Theater. He decided to walk, hoping he could vent some of his anger. He needed time to figure out how to handle this situation. He couldn't let it affect the novices he had trained so carefully. He felt sure he could count on Alan Durling. The likable little musician was wise to the ways of Broadway and had helped him over a lot of the roadblocks he ran into since rehearsals began. Brian also knew Alan was familiar with Jack Boyd and his reputation for mayhem. He had a sinking feeling when he realized Alan might leave when he heard Boyd was joining the cast. He couldn't let that happen. He needed Alan now more than ever. It was Monday. Boyd was scheduled to show up on Wednesday. Brian wanted everything covered by then. He decided to talk with Alan as soon as he reached the theater.

His mind was not on where he was walking, but rather on solving the chaos he felt sure Jack Boyd would cause when he joined the cast.

Boyd was a maverick and would not take direction from anyone. In other shows many good routines had been scrapped because Jack Boyd insisted on changes. Well, Brian thought, he's in for a surprise this time. Not one single change will be permitted. This time it will be play by the rules or get out of the game. He was so wrapped up in his thoughts he walked right past 41st Street, and had to retrace his steps to the theater. He asked the security man at the stage entrance if Alan was there.

"He went to the deli for a sandwich five minutes ago," the elderly guard said.

"I want to see him the minute he gets back," Brian instructed. "Tell him to stop by my office as soon as he comes through the door."

"I'll tell him, Mr. Casey," the guard replied.

"By the way, John, I hear you're going to retire, is that true?" Brian asked.

"It sure is," the guard told him with a smile. "I'm going to be 70 years old on Friday. I'm tired of punching a clock. So Friday is the last day I'm going to do it."

"I hope you won't be a stranger," Brian told him. "Everyone here likes you. I hope you will stop by and see us once in a while."

"Thank you, Mr. Casey, I sure will," the guard said.

The director's office was a small cubicle off the main corridor. The door was always open to let the cast know they had access to the director at any time. A cluttered desk filled most of the tiny office. Brian was sitting at the desk and doodling around the edge of a pad when Alan knocked on the open door.

"Hi, Brian, John said you wanted to see me the minute I got back. What's up?"

Alan knew something was wrong before Brian said a word. The director was usually full of enthusiasm and energy. This morning they were talking about how lucky he was to sign up so much new talent and have everything fall into place so perfectly. Now, Brian looked worried. The enthusiasm and energy had been replaced with doubt.

"Alan," Casey confided, "We have a problem – a big problem. At the meeting with the producers this morning they told me they have the headliner for *Gentlemen Again* all signed up. He'll be here Wednesday."

"What's the problem?" Alan asked with a shrug of his thin shoulders. "The material is all set."

Brian watched the musician's reaction as he continued. "They didn't go with our man, Phil Bender, they insisted on Jack Boyd." He noticed the troubled look that came over Alan's face at the mention of Boyd's name. "I couldn't get them to change their minds no matter what I promised. Jack Boyd is the last person in the world I want to work with and he definitely doesn't fit in with this cast. That's why I said we have a problem." Brian wanted to let the musician know how important he was to the cast, but he didn't want to put him in a position where he would be forced to stay. "Boyd is nothing but trouble," Casey continued. "These kids haven't come up against the likes of him yet." He shrugged his shoulders and looked back at the pad he had been doodling on as he added, "We have a cast of Broadway virgins and I don't want any of them to get hurt. Everybody Boyd encounters gets trampled sooner or later. How am I going to protect these kids?"

Alan had never heard Brian Casey sound so desperate. He couldn't hide the empathy he felt for the young director. He knew Jack Boyd and the unsavory reputation the comedian enjoyed. The thought of constant hassles upsetting the camaraderie of this cast bothered him. He didn't envy the decisions Brian would be facing. Rehearsals were going very well. There was noticeable improvement every day. Alan had no trouble visualizing great futures for some of these young performers. He leaned against the door frame and ran his hand through his hair. Brian watched him carefully silently praying he would stay with the show. Alan bit his bottom lip as if it would help him find a solution to this predicament. Finally, he exhaled a long slow breath and looked at the director.

"Brian, if anyone else was directing this show and told me what you just said, I'd hand in my notice. But when it comes to *Gentlemen Again* I feel the same as you do. It's good! It's damn good! Julian Brice is going to surprise the hell out of every audience that hears him sing. Bill Flanagan will have them dancing in the aisles, and you can bet Dan Shaw isn't going to be far behind either of them. I'm not willing to give all that up because of Jack Boyd."

"Thanks Alan, I needed that," Brian said with a lopsided smile and an audible sigh of relief. "If you walked out on me now, I don't know what I'd do. I couldn't handle it by myself."

"I don't think you will have to," Alan told him. "These kids may be young and new to this business, but they catch on fast. Julian is a couple of years older than the rest of them and he's a deep thinker. He may turn out to be a good leveling influence. Dan is quiet, but he's probably the smartest one of the group. I think if we can explain the circumstances to them, they'll be more than willing to help. If they know what to expect, that may stabilize the whole situation."

Brian listened to Alan's idea and after a few seconds of heavy thought said, "OK, sounds like a good start."

Instead of the usual 7 o'clock quitting time, the director called a halt at six. Alan passed the word to the group to be at Nick's at 7:30 for an important meeting with Brian. No one knew what to expect, but some of them had noticed the young director was quiet all afternoon and seemed to be worried about something.

* * * * *

Alan Durling and Brian Casey were the first to arrive at the restaurant. They let George know the whole group would be on hand tonight with the possibility of a few extras stopping by.

"What are we celebrating?" the maitre d' asked.

"We're not celebrating anything," Brian told him. "We're trying to keep the show healthy."

George gave him a puzzled look and with his usual air of authority said, "I wasn't aware you were having any problems."

Brian told him about the situation forced on him that morning. George listened intently but showed no reaction. Then he looked directly at Brian and said, "I know your cast, and I know your work. I also know Jack Boyd. If at any time you need me, remember, I am always here to help."

This statement surprised both men. George never took sides in an argument, he was always the impartial mediator. He didn't wait for a response, just turned, walked into the dining room and enlisted the help of two of the waiters to put a few tables together to make room for everyone.

23

Bill Flanagan and Dan Shaw were next to arrive and Alan commented it was rare when Bill and Jen were not together. "She'll be along with the girls," Bill said. "You sounded so serious about this meeting we didn't want to be late so we decided to meet everyone here."

Julian Brice came in the front door and was followed a few minutes later by Cass, Harriet, Jen and Gracie. Alan took a quick head count and was satisfied everyone he had contacted was there. Brian explained the problem and told them what had happened with other shows when Jack Boyd was a member of the cast.

"I never expected this," he confided to the group. "Frankly, I'm at a loss as to how to handle it. Avoiding problems with this man will take a miracle. My main concern is the effect he can have on all of you. This cast has worked hard to put together a good show and I want to keep it that way." Brian Casey was rarely this straight forward with his problems. He was accustomed to solving them himself. Asking for everyone's help, as he was doing now, was difficult for him. "I can't figure out why the producers are doing this," he said. "Until I can figure it out I want everyone in this cast aware of what to expect from Jack Boyd."

Now was the time for some protective strategy and the young director looked around the table and tried to encourage ideas. "The object of this meeting is to put all of your good brains to work on a solution to this dilemma."

Julian was the first to speak. He cleared his throat and in his distinctive manner of carefully choosing each word, he began. "This Boyd person has been painted as an ogre. Had this been done by anyone else I would have walked away from the conversation. But, Brian, I consider you a charter member of this group so your word and your judgment are sufficient for me." He glanced at the serious faces around the table. He wanted to tell them this was not a new situation for him. A black man in a white world runs into adversity every day. He knew that did not apply to these people. To each of them he was a talented singer and as much a part of this group as everyone else. His unique quality was his tremendous voice. The color of his skin wasn't even a consideration. "From what I have heard here tonight," he continued, "It seems that Mr. Boyd operates under the influence of an over active ego. Proper treatment may be to deflate it. Perhaps that way he may learn the advantages of cooperation. I would suggest we ignore Jack Boyd. Work with him on stage and completely ignore him off stage. That means no dates with the girls, no socializing of any sort, no arguments or fights, no matter what he does or says. We must smile at him a lot and avoid him even more."

The girls looked at each other and seemed puzzled. "How can we smile at him and ignore him at the same time?" Cass asked.

"It takes a little practice," Julian told them. "If this is the route we decide to take I shall teach you."

"Whatever we decide, he's not going to go away and putting up with him on a daily basis won't be easy." Alan warned. "This guy is a real pro when it comes to insulting people. The worst part of it is, he doesn't care who he insults. All the girls will have to be extra careful because he has been known to be free with his hands."

That bit of information seemed to light a fire under Bill, "He had better not pull any of that stuff on the girls in this cast," he said. "Headliner or no headliner, he touches one of these girls and he won't make the next performance."

"Maybe he'll be smart enough not to try," Dan said in an effort to defuse Bill's temper.

Julian's plan was the most sensible and the easiest to implement. The girls agreed to talk to the other members of the chorus line, fill them in on what to watch for, and how to handle any unwanted advances. Dan, Bill, Julian and Alan would talk to the men in the cast and Brian volunteered to speak to the stagehands and grips to let them know what to expect.

By Wednesday morning everyone was ready. Brian Casey was determined to keep things on a business as usual basis and cover his anxiety as much as possible. At the meeting on Monday the producers said Boyd would be at the theater on Wednesday. Brian was so angry he didn't ask what time Wednesday. He scheduled the routines the same as he did every day and stuck to his format.

A few minutes after eleven Alan Durling got up from his seat at the piano and walked over to the director. "Maybe we got a break and he won't show up," he said.

"No such luck," Brian replied disgustedly. "He's timing things to make a grand entrance. He'll want everyone to know when he gets here."

"Maybe he'll get a surprise," Alan chuckled. "This time everybody is ready for him."

Brian signaled for the next rehearsal segment to begin and Alan went back to his seat at the piano. He started the music for the chorus line number they were having a little difficulty perfecting. A couple of the steps the girls had to maneuver were tricky and seemed a little awkward to the director. The girls were half way through the number when there was a commotion at the stage door. Brian and Alan looked at each other as if to say, "Boyd is here," but not a word was spoken. The chorus line continued uninterrupted and everyone's attention was focused on the stage. The girls completely ignored the racket off stage.

Jack Boyd had pushed past the elderly guard and in a boisterous voice said, "Get out of my way old man. I am the star of this show." The guard stayed right behind him until Boyd walked on stage while the chorus line number was in progress and loudly announced, "Jack Boyd has arrived!"

Two burly stagehands followed the comedian on stage and carefully put a hand under each of Boyd's arms, lifted him off the floor and carried him to the wings. Boyd protested loudly and although his feet were moving they never touched the floor. By this time he was screaming at the two stagehands who simply looked at him and smiled as each held an index finger over their closed lips. All through this episode the chorus line danced to perfection and never missed a step. These kids are all right, Brian thought, when they can perform under that kind of pressure there's not an audience in the world that will scare them.

Jack Boyd was furious. His grand entrance had bombed and instead of being the center of attention he was completely ignored. This had never happened to him before and he didn't know how to handle it. The angrier he became the more the stagehands smiled at him. "What's going on here?" he shouted. "I demand you get Brian Casey up here this minute."

The stagehands, who had not left his side, looked at him and the shorter of the two, who towered at least a foot above Boyd, very politely said, "Mr. Casey will see you when he's ready." The comedian was so mad you could see his eyes bulge. He glanced at his guardians and decided their size was a factor to be considered and chose to be quiet.

At the conclusion of the chorus line number Brian Casey took a few minutes to thank the girls for doing such a good job. He glanced at Boyd, waiting in the wings, and wanted to delay the encounter as long as possible. No need to worry about the self proclaimed "star of the show" going anywhere, he thought. The two stagehands had total control over Jack Boyd's every move. The director picked up his papers and carefully tucked his daily routine sheet inside his notebook. Better get this over with, he thought, and looked for the simplest way to handle the problem. He remembered Julian's words from Monday night, *"no arguments or fights, no matter what he does or says."* He saw the wisdom of those words when the chorus line refused to be interrupted and the stagehands so aptly handled the intruder. Now it was his turn. He walked to the area where the two sentinels were keeping vigil over the disruptive comedian. He ignored Boyd, looked at the two burly watchdogs and said, "Thank you, gentlemen." He turned to Jack Boyd, who by this time had built up enough steam to cause a volcanic eruption. Brian looked directly into the face of the comedian and in the calmest of tones said, "Don't you ever attempt to interrupt any routine again. In this production we all play by one set of rules and anytime you don't want to play by those rules, don't let the door hit you in the ass on the way out! Do we understand each other?"

The comedian was in a state of shock. No one had ever talked to him like this. He always had the upper hand. Now a total stranger, a director who was obviously several years his junior was giving him orders. The great Jack Boyd was at a loss for words. Brian could see his confusion and decided to take full advantage of the opportunity.

"You may be billed as a headliner, but you are not **THE** star of this show. Every single member of this cast is a star in my book and deserves to be treated like one, by you, by me, and by every other member of this company. That's another one of our rules, so get used to them, Mr. Boyd. If you intend to be around here for awhile you're going to have to learn to play by them."

The mighty Jack Boyd was clearly overwhelmed. He couldn't even muster an answer for the young director. He looked at Casey as if he still couldn't believe anyone would have the nerve to talk to him with such authority. Brian Casey started to walk away and as an after thought looked over his shoulder and said, "Ask the stage door man to show you where to find your dressing room."

This put the stunned comedian in a position where he had to go back to the same man he so carelessly abused when he first entered the theater and ask for directions to his dressing room. The elderly guard enjoyed every minute of it and smiled broadly through the whole episode.

Jack Boyd was not a handsome man. He stood five feet ten inches tall in his stocking feet. His habits of self-indulgence resulted in a weight gain that made him look short and fat. Slicked down black hair gave him a patent leather look as if his hair was polished rather than combed. His ego was big enough to cover all his drawbacks and let him go on believing he was the greatest of the great. On stage he was funny. He had an effective delivery and a fantastic sense of timing. Off stage he was offensive and disagreeable. He considered himself indispensable and unequaled in talent and charm. He thought it was clever to belittle the stagehands or make off color remarks to the chorus girls. Trouble was something he enjoyed causing almost every time he opened his mouth. It was one thing he excelled at.

On his first full day with the cast Boyd tested his charm on Gracie. She tried to ignore him and when that didn't work she politely refused his overtures and told him she had strict rules when it came to men friends. Boyd ignored her put downs and persisted with his unwanted advances. Alan noticed her predicament and came to her aid. Gracie was forever grateful and his rescue attempt endeared him to every member of the cast. They were all aware of the biting humor of this so-called comedian and Alan became his prime target. Boyd reminded everyone of the musician's drinking habit by referring to him as Broadway's answer to Prohibition. He called Alan "The John Barleycorn of the Great White Way." Alan didn't bother to answer. Instead he followed Julian's original plan, smiled a lot and ignored Boyd completely. It drove the comedian crazy!

Everyone tried to ignore Jack Boyd as much as possible. He was not included in conversations. No one invited him anywhere or welcomed his company. Even this treatment didn't put a dent in the egotistical comedian's inflated ego.

Chapter 4.

Bill Flanagan, Dan Shaw and Alan Durling were leaving the theater and Boyd overheard them say they were going to meet the girls at Nick's and he immediately invited himself to join them. They didn't want him and they knew the girls didn't want him but they didn't want to say anything to him that would create a problem.

As they walked out the stage door Bernie Goldman was on his way in. Bill grabbed Bernie's arm as if he was greeting an old friend. "Where in hell have you been?" Bill demanded. "We waited for you and now we're all late. Come on, don't waste any more time, get in the car and let's get going."

Poor Bernie was flabbergasted. He had been trying to make friends with these people for weeks and couldn't get past the security guard. Now, they were hustling him off somewhere and he didn't even know where. Before he could ask, Bill pushed him into the back seat of Dan's car and shut the door. Alan was already in the back and motioned him to be quiet. Bill and Dan got into the front and they drove off before Boyd could get out the door of the theater.

"Nice work guys," Alan said and breathed a sigh of relief. "I didn't want to spend the rest of tonight listening to that big mouth tell us how good he is at everything."

Bill glanced over his shoulder at the two men in the back. "Thank your friend back there," he said and pointed to Bernie. "He showed up at just the right time."

A surprised Alan looked from Bernie to Bill and said, "What do you mean, 'my friend' I thought he was your friend."

All three men looked at Bernie who just shrugged his shoulders and said, "The name is Goldman, Bernie Goldman. I'm everybody's friend, except that Boyd guy. I'm not part of your show. I'm a salesman – socks, stockings, belts, suspenders, you name it, I got it."

Bernie knew if he wanted to stay with this group he had to put his salesmanship into high gear. "I appreciate what you guys just did for me. The last time I was at the Ballard, Boyd had the guard throw me out. Today kind of frosted his cookies." He enjoyed outsmarting Jack Boyd, no matter how it was done. He grinned and said, "Now he thinks I know you guys. Well, I feel like I do. Before he was part of the show I watched you work a lot. *Gentlemen Again* is a good show. Too bad you have to put up with the likes of Boyd to have a comedian, but you take the good with the bad, I guess." He shrugged his shoulders again and looked from one to the other wondering what was going to happen now.

Bill, Dan and Alan solved one problem but created another. They managed to evade Boyd's attempt to join them, but none of them knew Bernie Goldman. Now they didn't know what to do with him. They knew Boyd overheard their plans and it would be typical of him to show up uninvited. They decided to take a chance on Bernie and keep an eye on him until they knew a little more about him. At least with Bernie as part of the group it added up to four couples and there was no room for Jack Boyd.

Bernie Goldman proved to be excellent company and fit in with the group better than any of them expected. Even George, the paternal maitre d', reluctantly gave a temporary stamp of approval. Cass was instantly attracted to Bernie. She thought he was cute. This shy little salesman, who was trying his best to please everyone, was a complete opposite of the men Cass usually dated. She decided she was going to be Bernie's partner for the evening and coaxed him into dancing, even though he insisted he couldn't dance a step.

"You can't be a part of this group if you don't know how to dance," she told him and led him toward the dance floor as she said, "I'll teach you."

He was a quick learner, but it was the general consensus that his fascination with Cass helped considerably. Bill, Dan and Alan came to the conclusion they had struck it lucky with Bernie. Little by little this circle of friends was growing and each individual included in it was fully acceptable to all the others. No one worried about what was said. No feelings were intentionally hurt and doubts were never left unanswered.

Jack Boyd was never included in their plans. His efforts to force his way in were always ignored or discouraged. That didn't stop him from showing up uninvited and causing problems or discomfort for one or more of the group. This night was no exception and as usual the comedian made his noisy entrance. The group tolerated his bragging until they were all at the end of their patience. As if on cue,

George came to the table and announced, "Mr. Boyd, there is a phone call for you at the reservations desk."

"Who's bothering me now?" Boyd blustered. "Can't you handle it? Must I do everything myself?"

George had confrontations with this obnoxious comedian before and was very capable of giving back everything Boyd could dish out, but he chose not to this evening. "I'm afraid I can't help with this one," George answered. "The gentleman on the phone said he was from the Police Department. He also said the call was urgent."

"All right, I'll take it," the unfunny funnyman said impatiently as he left the table and headed for the telephone.

"Is everything all right, George?" Dan asked the maitre d'. "Is there anything we can do to help?"

"There's not a thing you can do, Dan. Everything is under control," George assured him as he turned and walked back to his reception desk with just the slightest trace of a sly smile at the edges of his mouth.

Boyd was furious when he returned to the table. The police told him someone had broken into his apartment and he was needed at Headquarters to identify the stolen articles. He told them he would be there in the morning but they insisted it had to be done right away. There was a matter of booking the thief and they needed positive identification of the stolen property. Boyd was incensed that anyone would have the audacity to invade his apartment. He was also angry at the police for disturbing him during his leisure hours.

"You people will have to carry on without me," he told the group in his usual demeaning manner. He turned to Dan Shaw and said, "Since you are the only one with a car handy I suppose I will have to let you drive me uptown."

Before Dan could answer him, George came back to the table and interrupted the conversation by announcing, "Mr. Boyd, your cab is here."

"What cab?" Boyd asked brusquely.

"I couldn't help overhear some of your conversation and you seemed so upset I took the liberty of ordering a cab for you. Of course, if you would rather not use it I can dismiss him."

32

"Well, if the cab is already here I'll use it," Boyd said in his overbearing pompous style. "Forget the ride, Shaw. You can take me next time."

"Thanks," Dan quietly remarked to Jack Boyd's back as the comedian hurried out of the restaurant. No one at the table said a word. Finally Alan commented, "I'm sorry his apartment was robbed but I'm glad to see him leave."

Bernie chuckled and said, "Too bad we don't know who the burglar is we could hire him on a regular basis, if it would guarantee to get rid of His Highness that quick."

"What a nice idea," Alan said with a smile. "Bernie, I'm going to like having you around."

"Did we miss some excitement?" Bill asked as he and Jen returned from the dance floor.

"Nothing important," Alan told him. "The police called Jack to tell him someone robbed his apartment and they want him down at headquarters to identify the things that were stolen."

Bill gave them a puzzled look and asked, "How did they know he was here?"

They all looked around the table at each other and finally Dan said with a laugh, "To be truthful, Bill, none of us thought to ask. We were all so glad to get rid of him we weren't concerned with the specifics." Not another thought was wasted on Jack Boyd. The group turned their attention back to having fun.

* * * * *

Dan and Alan were kidding Bill about being a perfectionist like Brian Casey. They watched as he changed from street shoes to tap shoes for a dance routine rehearsal. All of a sudden the dressing room door was jerked open and a furious Jack Boyd confronted them.

"You guys think you're pretty damn smart, don't you? One of you set me up last night and I won't forget it," he almost shouted. "You all knew there was no robbery at my place and you let me go running out of that crummy little bistro in a near panic. Not one of you offered to lift a finger to help. No one does that to Jack Boyd and gets away with it. I'll fix each and every one of you, you'll see."

The three friends looked at each other and tried to keep from laughing as the distraught comedian left the dressing room in a rage.

"Do you think he will ever calm down?" Bill asked as he tried to stifle a laugh.

"You haven't heard the best part of it," Alan told them. "I heard him talking to someone on the phone this morning. It seems the cab driver didn't know where Police Headquarters was and the first precinct he found was somewhere in Harlem. Boyd insisted it was the wrong place and wouldn't get out of the cab. The cabby took him to three other out of the way precincts before he got the right one. By then he was so mad he wasn't making any sense and the cops almost arrested him. In the meantime, the cabby took off and he couldn't find another one and had to walk home. He didn't get home until almost five this morning."

The more Alan told them the harder they laughed. It was finally payback time for Jack Boyd and it gave them all a feeling of satisfaction to see him on the receiving end of the dirty tricks for a change.

"I'd like to know who made that phone call," Dan said. "We know it was none of us, we were all together at the table. Except for you, Bill. You were dancing with Jen."

"I wish I could take credit for it," Bill said, "But this time I have to plead not guilty."

"It had to be someone who knew he was there," Alan added. "We weren't even sure he was going to show up."

"At least I can thank George for getting me off the hook by calling the cab so quickly," Dan commented. They looked at each other and almost at the same time realized that George was the only one who could have pulled off such a scheme so well.

"Boy, we owe him one for that," Alan remarked.

"I'm willing to bet a bundle George will deny knowing anything about it," Bill said.

"He may deny it," Dan said, "But I could swear I saw him smile when Boyd went to answer the phone. Almost as if he knew what the outcome would be."

"He couldn't have made the call himself," Alan reasoned. Then added, "George is on a first name basis with almost every actor on Broadway. All he would have to do is hint at what he wanted and any one of a dozen guys would have done it for him, no questions asked. He probably had the cabby working for him, too. Why else would anyone cart that big mouth all over town at two in the morning?"

"I have a lot of respect for George," Bill said as he tried to control his laughter, "But he just went up ten points in my book."

Chapter 5.

An opening night on Broadway is a spectacular event. Theaters are spruced up, audiences are catered to, and the cast of the show is honed to razor sharpness. It was that kind of night at the Ballard Theater as the performers listened closely to the last minute instructions from Brian Casey. This was the night they had all worked so hard to perfect.

Day after day they had rehearsed and polished each routine in the show. Tonight they would show a critical first night audience how good they really are.

The chorus line inspected each other and made last minute costume adjustments and make-up touches. The signal came to take their places on stage as the orchestra began the Overture. Spirits were high and hopes were higher as the curtain opened, the show became a reality and *Gentlemen Again* made its Broadway debut.

Brian Casey's skill in choosing the girls for the chorus line was evident. The difficult first night audience showed their appreciation by loudly applauding the first number.

"That applause is for each and every one of you," he told them as they made their way off the stage. "You people are the greatest! Listen to that audience. They can't get enough of you! Keep this up and we'll have a hit on our hands!" His enthusiasm spread to every one in the cast. It erased any traces of nervousness and inspired perfect performances.

This show was not considered a major opening because most of the cast members were new to Broadway. The only big name on the marquee was Jack Boyd. Before this night was over there would be many other names that would be remembered for a long time.

Julian Brice began to sing and an absolute silence came over the audience. As the last notes of his song drifted through the air a wave of thunderous applause followed. Oohs and aahs echoed through the theater as Bill Flanagan danced to the delight of all the first nighters. He was a hard act to follow, but Dan Shaw was up to the challenge. He put his heart into each of his songs and the audience loved it. Jack Boyd gave an exceptional performance. His timing and delivery were perfect and his material hilarious. Everyone roared with laughter, even the cast, who despised him, applauded.

Brian Casey was ecstatic! "I knew you people could do it!" he said, as each scene ended. "You are the answer to any director's prayers."

As the curtain closed on the last act the entire first night audience was standing. Everyone in the Ballard Theater had a good time and no one wanted to leave. After the third curtain call the chorus line was brought on once more. As the girls filed on stage Gracie and Cass left the line and each hooked an arm of Brian Casey and escorted him on stage.

Jack Boyd walked to the center stage and reached into the orchestra pit for a microphone. "Ladies and gentlemen," he said, "If you enjoyed what you witnessed here tonight, this is the man who made it all happen, our director, Brian Casey." Brian got his own standing ovation.

It was quite a night at the Ballard Theater. The biggest shock of the evening was Boyd's short but effective introduction of the director. Until that night there had been very little dialogue between them and it was common knowledge that Brian would have dumped Boyd in a minute if the producers would allow it. The entire cast wondered what was behind Boyd's impromptu message to the first night audience. They knew he always had an ulterior motive. Everything he did or said was done for a self-serving purpose. This time he had everyone puzzled.

"Perhaps he is learning the advantages of cooperation," Julian commented.

Alan knew the comedian a lot better than Julian and wasn't ready to accept any conciliatory moves by Jack Boyd. "Maybe he's looking for ways to zing us and is using nice tactics to get us to drop our guard a little," the musician suggested.

"That sounds more like his style," Julian agreed, "but I would like to give him the benefit of the doubt. There is no denying, it was a gracious gesture."

Bill was listening to the conversation and looked at both of them. "Gracious or not," he said, "I agree with Alan and I'm still not inviting him to our wedding. This is going to be the most important day in my life and I don't intend to spend one minute of it worrying about whether Jack Boyd will start any trouble."

"That could be why he's being so nice," Dan commented with a grin. "He's looking for his invitation."

"He's not getting one," Bill stated emphatically. "He's not even being told when or where it will be. I'm not taking any chances." Everyone laughed at Bill's extensive precautions, but they all understood how necessary they were.

* * * * *

Gentlemen Again opened to surprisingly optimistic reviews by the critics. It was the first original musical of the season to be acclaimed a smash hit. The interesting thing noted by the critics was the introduction of so many talented new young performers. Julian Brice, Bill Flanagan and Dan Shaw were all mentioned in the reviews and the girls were making a name for themselves as the most beautiful and talented chorus line since the Ziegfeld Follies.

Brian Casey was experienced with the fickle ways of the public and since he brought this cast to the pinnacle of success he was determined to keep after them until they proved to the world they were worth the attention. The only day Casey didn't work was the Sunday Bill Flanagan and Jen Kelly married.

Jennifer Kelly was a gorgeous bride and William Flanagan a handsome groom. He waited patiently with his best man, Dan Shaw, just outside the altar rail in St. Catherine's Church as the wedding party came slowly down the aisle. A proud, but humble, Walter Kelly offered his middle daughter his arm as they took their first steps down the aisle toward a new life for Jen.

The church was packed to the rafters as the folks from Bayonne, New Jersey turned out to witness the Kelly-Flanagan nuptials. It wasn't every Sunday that the cast of a hit Broadway show made personal appearances in New Jersey. The absence of Jack Boyd went unnoticed.

"Wow!" Bernie remarked to Brian as he looked around the crowded church. "Look at this turnout. This cast plays to standing room only – even in church!"

At the reception Brian Casey turned out to be the life of the party. He was an excellent dance partner and made sure he had at least one dance with every girl there. Cast members plied him with more than his share of liquor and encouraged him to sing several songs. His vocal talent surprised and delighted everyone. He sang *Mother Machree* for the parents of the bride and *Galway Bay* for the parents of the groom. His dialect rendition of *Danny Boy* had everyone on the verge of tears. He put them right back in the party spirit with a very funny version of an old Irish folk song. Hilarious lyrics painted a vivid mental picture of the ancestral Irish mourners stealing ice from around the corpse to put it on the beer. Brian Casey was a great entertainer and the cast of *Gentlemen Again* saw their director in a very different light. It was a wonderful celebration.

* * * * *

Brian arrived at the theater late Monday afternoon and slowly walked down the alley to the stage door. Before he opened the door he put his back against the wall and using the outside of the building as a prop forced himself to stand up straight. He had a good time at the wedding and he added to everyone else's good time, now his body was paying for it. He was determined to set a good example for the cast and not let anyone see how he was really suffering. He took a deep breath and with perfect posture walked through the stage door.

"Hello John," he said to the security guard and was surprised when the answer came back, "I'm not John, I'm Fred. John retired a few weeks ago." Oh boy, Brian thought, I'm really off to a good start.

As the cast members arrived the director noticed they all seemed to be suffering from an overdose of Irish Wedding. He sympathized with them, but this was show business. The world of make believe. And on Broadway nothing interfered with a performance. The show went on as scheduled. When the orchestra struck up the Overture and the curtain opened, new life seemed to flow through the whole cast. Headaches and hangovers were forgotten and this performance was the only thing that mattered.

Jack Boyd was furious that he had not been invited to the wedding. He intended to get even in his own vindictive manner. He could see that the entire cast was affected by their Sunday celebration.

It was the perfect time for him to ad-lib, mess up their cues and interfere with their timing. In spite of hangovers, headaches, and unsolicited ad-libs by the resentful comedian, the performance went well. Jack Boyd underestimated the talent he was up against and even Brian Casey was surprised.

"These kids are fantastic!" he told Julian. "They can handle anything and anybody. There's not an audience in the world that can intimidate them."

"Brian, you have brought out the best in all of them," Julian concluded. "It is obvious many from this cast are destined to leave their marks on the history of the theater."

Chapter 6.

Josh Golden, a five foot seven inch rotund bundle of energy, owned The Aurous Agency. He spent fifteen years building a solid reputation and was well known as one of New York City's most outstanding ticket brokers. He knew every important person who lived, worked, or visited New York City. It didn't matter if they were in show business, politics, industry or visiting dignitaries, if they were prominent Josh knew them. Most of them made a habit of calling on him when they needed tickets for a show, sporting event or other activity in the City.

Josh never seemed to run out of steam. He often had half a dozen things brewing at once and it was common practice for him to carry on two phone conversations at the same time. He loved the business he was in. He was an advocate of New York City and Broadway was his cherished domain. When a box office posted Standing Room Only signs The Aurous Agency could always find good tickets.

Marianne Gordon worked for Josh Golden. She was young, but he liked her. He admired her ambition, was aware of her good sense and appreciated her honesty. He wanted to help her reach the goals she had set for herself and tried to include her in many of the Agency's activities. He knew she would pick up on any opportunity for ticket sales and they would both profit. He tried to convince her that a full time job with his agency would be a smart move. She liked the job she had during the day and her present set up with Aurous suited her fine. There was no salary involved. She worked entirely on commission. The more tickets she sold for Josh the more money she made for herself. She didn't spend much time at the agency. Most of her sales she handled on her own. Josh had to agree it had its advantages for both of them. She was a real asset to his agency and even though there was more than twenty years difference in their ages, she was one of the few people Josh Golden really trusted.

Marianne wasn't a pushy salesperson. She was young, ambitious and determined to be successful. She had the ability to size up a customer almost immediately and had little difficulty separating the serious buyers from the comparison shoppers. Josh noticed she was seldom wrong in her judgments. She would give her opinion if asked,

41

but she liked to encourage her clients to do their own choosing. She thought it gave the customer the feeling they were in control of the transaction. Marianne was more interested in a profitable trip to the bank than who was in control of the situation.

The producers of *Gentlemen Again* invited several columnists, promoters, ticket brokers and others who could keep ticket sales on the top level, to a backstage party at the Ballard Theater. This was the type of occasion Josh Golden enjoyed. It gave him a chance to meet the cast members he referred to as "the little people" of show business, the ones not featured on the theater marquee, but an integral part of the show. He firmly believed every good show was built on "the little people" in the cast, and someday many of those "little people" would be big names in show business.

Marianne agreed to accompany him to the Ballard party as long as they didn't have to stay very long. "Kiddo," he assured her, between puffs on his cigar, "You have my promise we will leave within the hour,"

She teased him about his continuous cigar smoking and often referred to his good Havana cigars as "El Ropos." It didn't bother Josh. He would just light up another one. Marianne tried to keep a watchful eye on him whenever she accompanied him to theater events. She was aware of his reputation of being a pushover for beautiful women, especially blondes.

"You better stay right next to me," she told him.

"What's the matter, Kiddo?" Josh teased. "Don't tell me you're nervous. These people are just a bunch of actors. Don't let them intimidate you."

"I don't know any of them," she said, "and remember, this wasn't my idea."

Marianne thought many of the people Josh had to deal with were pretentious and full of their own importance. When she reminded him of this, he tried to convince her the cast of this show was different.

"They're all newcomers, just regular people," he said. "They haven't been on Broadway long enough to be affected. So meet them now, and you can at least like them for a little while." He glanced at her from the corner of his eye as he flicked the ashes from his cigar. "It's not often you can go to a party where everybody is going to be famous someday. Think of all the fun you can have when you look back on this in thirty or forty years. Something you can tell your grandchildren about," he told her and shrugged his shoulders as he grinned and seemed to enjoy her uneasiness.

"You're not making me feel any better," she told him as she parked the car across from the theater and they went back to the stage entrance. Marianne reminded him again that she was only doing this as a favor to him. "The sooner we get out of here, the better I'll like it," she told him.

Josh Golden was greeted like the whole affair was in his honor. He loved all the attention, but Marianne didn't enjoy being in the spotlight. She knew Josh's reputation for always being seen with a beautiful woman and she didn't want any part of that. Her relationship with him was strictly business. She wondered how many of the people they met today would be aware of it. Probably none, she thought. One reason she had agreed to accompany him was because he said they would only stay for a few minutes. "Just long enough to say hello to everyone and let the competition know I'm still alive and kicking," he assured her. "Today is your birthday and I want to take you to dinner. This is just a stopover on the way. After all, I owe you something. You're my top sales agent. Even my wife told me, 'Josh take her out to dinner', and you know my wife. She never says things like that."

Marianne didn't know whether to believe him or not, but decided to make the best of it. From time to time she had accompanied Josh to openings, sneak previews of new shows or affairs where he could gain a little insight on what to expect in the coming theater season. These occasions were strictly business. Josh knew that, but more important, Josh's wife knew it. When he was with Marianne he knew he wouldn't have any explaining to do when he got home.

Josh was surprised when he met Bernie Goldman at the party. "What are you doing here?" he asked.

"My girlfriend is in the chorus line," Bernie replied. He knew Josh Golden was a good contact for anyone in show business. "Let me introduce her. You'll love her. She's a beautiful blonde and the best dancer in the show"

Josh took the cigar from his mouth and looked at Bernie skeptically. He flicked the cigar ashes into a receptacle and raised his eyebrows in curiosity as he smiled and said, "Where is this lovely lady? I would like very much to meet her."

"I'll be right back," Bernie said and disappeared toward the dressing rooms.

The backstage area was crowded. It looked like everyone was talking at once and no one seemed to be paying any attention to anyone else. Show people, Marianne thought, were a breed all their own.

Josh Golden was on a first name basis with many of them. He knew all the other brokers and introduced Marianne to them, but never mentioned that she worked for him. He knew his competition well and was an expert on how to handle them. She watched as he shook hands with a few of his biggest competitors. She wondered how he could be so cordial to them when he knew they would undersell him in a minute. He was neither deceitful nor vindictive and would never be part of any underhanded deals. He didn't mind taking chances when it could mean dollars in his pocket but he wasn't greedy. Josh Golden was a good man to know in New York City. To Marianne, he was the first five steps up the ladder of success, but what was more important, he was a good friend.

Josh unwrapped a fresh cigar and Marianne made a face at him. "Do you have to smoke those disgusting El Ropos?" she asked.

"I don't smoke them, Kiddo. They're a status symbol," he said with a laugh as he touched a match to the end of the cigar. She shook her head and turned the other way in time to see Jack Boyd brazenly pat the backside of one of the showgirls as she passed him. The girl turned and gave him a look that would cut down any normal man, but she didn't say a word. When she walked by them Marianne quietly asked, "Why didn't you smack him?"

"I would have if there was no one around," the girl replied, "He loves it when you make a scene and I won't give him the satisfaction."

"I wouldn't mind smacking him for you," Marianne offered joking.

"If he does it again I'll call you," the girl said with a friendly smile.

Josh warned her about Jack Boyd and his pompous, arrogant attitude. "He thinks he's God's gift to Broadway," he told her. "He's more like a 'get even' than a 'gift.' No way would God do that to us, no matter what we did."

She thought Josh was exaggerating and didn't like the comedian. After watching how Boyd treated the other cast members she realized her boss was pretty accurate. Jack Boyd was a very obnoxious person. "I'd still like to smack him," she whispered.

"Marianne, be nice," Josh scolded with a grin. "Remember, all these people are going to be famous someday."

"Wow!" she answered sarcastically, "Does that mean they will lose their anonymity?"

Josh gave her a surprised look as he raised his eyebrows and asked, "My God, Kiddo, where did you get that word?"

"I've been saving it to use on you in a situation like this," she told him.

He realized she was not very comfortable in these surroundings and tried to put her at ease by reassuring her they would be leaving shortly. She knew his 'shortly' could mean anywhere from ten minutes to two hours.

Bernie Goldman finally returned with the most beautiful girl Marianne had ever seen. "Josh," he said proudly, "I want you to meet Cass." Even Josh was surprised. He took the cigar from his mouth, his chin fell and his mouth hung open as he gazed at her in awe and exclaimed very slowly, "God – you're – gorgeous!"

Cass was embarrassed by this unexpected flattery. "How do you do Mr. Golden," she said in a quaint little girl voice.

"Call me Josh, honey, please call me Josh," the broker said. Marianne watched amused as his eyes brightened and his interest grew and he tried to make a good impression.

"Bernie said some very nice things about you and I'm happy to meet you." Cass told him in an effort to salvage the conversation. Josh was still mesmerized and Marianne knew she would have to keep a close eye on him now. He never passed up a chance to make points with a beautiful woman and this show had plenty of them.

Cass was friendly, cheerful and pleasant and made a very good first impression on Marianne as well as Josh. There was nothing phony or pretentious about her. If the rest of this cast is anything like Bernie's blonde girlfriend maybe this will turn out to be a good stop after all, Marianne thought.

Josh introduced Marianne to Brian Casey and she wondered why he was back in the wings directing instead of on stage in front of an audience. He was young, handsome, and had a contagious smile that brightened his whole face. Casey, as the cast referred to him, made sure Josh and Marianne were introduced to any cast members Josh didn't already know. Marianne couldn't help notice how he, too, avoided Jack Boyd. Her curiosity finally got the best of her and she asked Josh how Boyd got in the show when everyone disliked him so much.

"It's a difficult situation to explain," he told her. "Let's say it was a package deal. If they wanted enough money to produce the show Boyd had to be included, so here he is."

Marianne wrinkled her forehead in a look of disbelief, "That's lousy," she said.

"It happens often," he told her. "Sometimes it works. Most of the time the mistake is rectified before opening night and the backer's pet is replaced by the director's choice. Boyd's case is different. On stage he's good. Off stage he's a shetekhn." Marianne had no idea what that word meant but she knew Josh had a habit of substituting Yiddish words when he was angry about something.

"Someday I'm going to make you tell me what those Yiddish words mean," she warned.

The portly little broker laughed and said, "Forget about Boyd. There are a lot of good people in this show. Brian Casey is young, but he has a reputation for picking new talent like you wouldn't believe. Some of the people you meet here today will be real big names someday." He looked at Marianne and tried to stress that this was something he really meant. "I'm not kidding," he added. "Have I ever lied to you, Kiddo? Would I give you a bum steer?" She knew he was trying to put her at ease and she laughed and tried to relax a little.

They mingled with the crowd and she tried to enjoy the party even though she was still uncomfortable. As they made their way toward the center of the backstage area Josh leaned toward her and said, "Now here are two boys you are going to hear a lot about." He grabbed the arm of one of them and introduced him to Marianne.

"This is Bill Flanagan. He's Fred Astaire and Gene Kelly all rolled up in one. His buddy here is Dan Shaw. Crosby, Sinatra, Como and the whole bunch are going to have to move over for him."

This time Marianne was the one who was caught off guard. Josh had just introduced her to two of the handsomest men she had ever seen.

"We both need an agent like you, Josh," Bill said with a laugh. He looked at Marianne and winked. "Don't believe a word he says. He lies a lot."

"Well, Josh," Marianne commented with a satisfied smile, "At last I found someone who knows you as well as I do."

Josh grinned and shook his head. He asked Bill and Dan if they would keep her company for a minute or two. "I have a little quick business and I'll be right back. I can't leave her alone. She's looking for an excuse to smack Boyd and I'd rather not get involved with him today."

"We'll take good care of her," Bill promised as Josh hurried off to catch one of the producers.

Marianne was amazed at the down to earth attitude of almost everyone in this cast. Except for the egotistical comedian they were just what Josh said they would be – regular people. She was surprised when she realized she did like them. Cass was gorgeous, but not a bit artificial or phony. Bill Flanagan and Dan Shaw were two more examples of nice, and they, too, seemed unaware of their good looks. Brian Casey surpassed them all in the looks department. If his black curly hair and bright blue eyes didn't win you over, his smile was sure to do the job.

Josh kept his word and returned in just a few minutes. "OK, Kiddo," he said, "Let's go."

As they left the Ballard Theater, Marianne looked at him and smiled. "You really are something," she told him.

The portly little broker looked at her and wrinkled his brow. "So all of a sudden I'm getting a compliment?" he questioned. "What do you mean, I'm really something?"

She cast him a sideways glance and said, "When there's a beautiful blonde female involved you take your good natured time. When I get a chance to spend a few minutes with two good looking guys you pop right back in a flash. I can't win."

Josh laughed, "They are good looking guys," he said, "and just as nice as they are handsome. Bill married one of the girls from the chorus line last month. She's a sweet heart, a real story book romance." He tilted his head and glanced at her from the corner of his eye. "You should get to know the other one – Shaw. He's talented, available and a good catch."

Marianne rolled her eyes as she said, "Stop your matchmaking, Josh. I was only kidding." In spite of her protests he continued with his advice. "This show has a lot of good people. They're young, they have lots of talent and they're going to go places. You should get to know them better. They're a great bunch. You could learn to have fun with them. They'll teach you how to have a good time." He looked at her as he added, "Just stay away from Jack Boyd."

Marianne knew he was trying to tell her more than just what he put into words. Sometimes Josh was deeper than she realized. He was well known for his attentions to beautiful women, but Marianne also knew she didn't fit into that category. She wasn't the glittery showgirl type. She had a good figure and carried it well, but to her style and fashion were not important. Her prime concern was making a success of the sales opportunities that came her way through Aurous Ticket Agency. Josh always treated her with respect. They had built a good, solid friendship and he never attempted to overstep it. Once in a while he would offer what he called "fatherly advice" but there was never a come on or an advance of any kind. There was plenty of mutual respect.

They waited for a break in the traffic so they could cross the street to the car. "Josh," she said, "I have an idea for a sales promotion I would like to run by you. Maybe we can talk about it over dinner. If you think it will work we can get it started with tickets for *Gentlemen Again*. That's a good show. It has a beautiful cast and the music is catchy. It's got a lot of good selling points and people like it."

The broker frowned and shook his head, she never stops working, he thought. He had invited her to dinner because it was her birthday. He knew she spent most of her time working and seldom took an evening off for fun. Several times he introduced her to young men, but she politely brushed them off and didn't seem interested. That never stopped Josh from trying again.

"If you want to talk business we should go downtown to eat. That way we won't be disturbed every five minutes," he said. "Unless you prefer someplace in particular," he quickly added.

"Who's paying?" she asked, "You or me?"

"I am," he said, "It's your birthday."

"OK," she said, and handed him her car keys. "As long as you're paying, you pick the place and you drive."

"Fine, we'll go to Nick's. It's quiet, the food is good and I think you'll like it." He nosed the car into the line of traffic and headed downtown.

The atmosphere at Nick's was a welcome change from the confusion and noise at the Ballard Theater. Josh greeted the maitre d' like an old friend and Marianne wondered if he knew everyone in New York City. It certainly seemed that way.

Josh did the ordering and while they waited for their food she watched the broker scan the dining room for familiar faces. She thought this might be a good time to discuss her sales idea. "You know I sell a lot of tickets to groups and clubs. Lately I find that some of my customers are having a little difficulty with transportation and it upsets the plans they have for a good night out. If they take the train into the city it means getting cabs from Penn Station to a restaurant. If they drive, they have to worry about parking, moving the car after dinner and getting out of the lot before it closes. It's a pain in the neck for most of them. I think I can put together a package deal by supplying buses for transportation and making dinner arrangements, then the theater, and possibly a night club for a couple of hours afterward."

Josh noticed the enthusiasm she had for this new project and he liked the interest she showed in a business that was special to him.

"The Brisbane Hotel has an attractive dining room," Marianne continued, "and there is a separate facilities room if the group is big enough. The food is excellent and the service is good. Dinner could be taken care of with plenty of time left to get to the theater. I know the maitre d' there and I think I can work something out with him. Transportation won't be a problem. I can hire the buses. If the Brisbane can handle arrangements for dinner, and the theater is taken care of, the only snag left is the night clubs. That's where I need your help. You know all of those people. You can tell me who to talk to and who to avoid. Better still, you can talk to them. You know them. The important thing here is to keep this whole thing affordable or it will never sell."

Josh liked what he heard. He thought it had all the elements of a good, workable, profit making plan. "I'm all for it, Kiddo," he told her. "It sounds like a winner. I know people in almost every worthwhile club in town and I think they will be glad to work with you. Let me make a few phone calls Monday morning and see what kind of a response we get. If it looks favorable, we'll try it." He sounded genuinely interested and Marianne was glad she had discussed it with him. If anyone could make it work, Josh Golden could.

"What time is it?" she asked as she looked around and noticed the restaurant was filling up.

"Why? Are you in a hurry to go someplace? Do you have a heavy date that I don't know about?" he teased.

"I thought I might take in *Gentlemen Again* tonight," she said. "If I'm going to start this sales promotion with it I had better know what it's all about."

"Good idea," he agreed. "Always know your product before you try to sell it to someone else."

Marianne looked at Josh and grinned. "Besides," she said, "birthday dinners are a drag. Your obligation is over now and you can go back to your usual Saturday night philandering."

Josh laughed and told her she was more than a birthday obligation to him. He didn't trust many people but he did trust her. He admired her ambition and could remember when he was her age and work was the most important factor in his life. He appreciated her honesty and straight forward opinions. "Even if they hurt sometimes," he added with a grin. "I have twenty-five years more experience than you, so listen to me, Kiddo," he said, as he shook his index finger at her. "Don't spend all your time making money. Learn to live a little, enjoy yourself. Have some fun. That's what life is all about." Josh's sermon was interrupted by the waiter with their dinner.

Marianne looked at the concerned expression on the broker's face and said, "Josh this is not the time to become a philosophical playboy. I know what you're getting at and I'm ignoring your suggestion. I'm happy with what I'm doing. Getting involved with some guy now would mess up my plans. I'll make my money first and do my playing around later."

"You take my advice and get to know some of the people you met this afternoon. You saw for yourself they're a good bunch. They'll show you how to enjoy life."

"OK, Josh, I get your message," she conceded and tried to change the subject from her social life back to the project they had discussed. "I have to stop at the agency for a ticket, I hope there's a decent one there."

"Not a chance," he said. "That show is sold out. Standing room only. Don't let that stop you. I'll call Brian. You go in the stage door and ask for him."

"Thanks, Josh, I appreciate that," she said. Now, she knew for sure that he was trying to get her interested in the people in this show and he would go to any lengths to get what he wanted. Not a bad idea, she thought, not a bad idea at all.

"Can I drop you somewhere on my way uptown?" she asked.

"You go ahead, Kiddo. I'll get a cab."

On her way back to the Ballard Marianne thought about what Josh said and had to admit he was right, again. She did worry about making money, not solely for the sake of a dollar, but it was something she had to do. She could remember her father telling her and her brothers they were born on the wrong side of the tracks and they would never amount to anything. Her goal in life was to prove him wrong. "Well," she told herself, "Maybe I can include some fun in the process."

Chapter 7.

Marianne parked across the street from the theater almost in the same spot she had when she and Josh were there earlier. She asked the stage door guard where she could find Brian Casey.

"Wait here, I'll get him," he said and headed for the tiny backstage office of the director.

Brian Casey greeted her like an old friend. "Josh called and said you were coming back. I'm glad you did. Now you can meet the rest of the cast and we can show you how this production works."

It pays to have someone like Josh Golden to open doors for you, Marianne thought. She explained her sales promotion to Brian, and told him she was looking for a few good selling points. She liked to tell her customers to watch for specific things. Not the advertised features, but special little things that will pique their interest. "I would like to watch the show tonight," she told him, "but I don't want to be in your way."

"You won't be," he assured her and suggested she spend some time with the girls from the chorus line. "They know everything that goes on around here."

Marianne told him she met Cass at the party that afternoon. "That's a good start," he said, "She knows everybody. Let me locate her and she can guide you through the rest of the cast."

Cass remembered Marianne from the party earlier. "You disappeared in a hurry," she said. "Bernie and I looked for you and Bill told us you left. What happened?"

"Josh and I had a dinner obligation and a new business plan to work out," Marianne told her. She wanted it to look like she had a good reason for coming back tonight, so she explained a little about the new sales project and was surprised when Cass showed as much interest as Brian.

"It sounds like a good idea," the showgirl said. "If you can eliminate a lot of the problems people can have a worry free night out."

"I thought this show would be a good one to get it started," Marianne continued. "It has good music, a timely subject, lots of laughs and a beautiful cast. You can't ask for more than that." She watched Cass for any reaction to the comments about the show. There was a look of satisfaction and Marianne knew it was sincere. "Right now, I would like to get as much information as I can. I'm looking for special little things you girls do that I can tell my customers about."

Cass gave her a puzzled look and said, "I don't pay much attention to gossip."

"I didn't mean gossip," Marianne said. "I meant some of the superstitions or habits the cast may have. A lucky charm they always carry or anything that's unusual.

"Gee, I'll have to think about that," Cass said. "I'll let you know."

Cass made sure Marianne met all the girls in the chorus line and introduced her to a few cast members she had not met earlier. She explained how some of the girls pooled their resources to stretch their small salaries. "Gracie, Harriet and I share an apartment downtown," she said. "Jen was with us for awhile, but she married Bill Flanagan a few weeks ago. Now it's just the three of us."

"Josh introduced me to Bill and Dan Shaw this afternoon," Marianne said. "He told me about Bill's romance and it sounds wonderful."

"It really was love at first sight," Cass told her. "Boy, that wedding was fabulous. We all had a great time. I think the whole town turned out to give the bride away and then stayed around to celebrate. Almost everyone from the show was there." She smiled as she recalled the good time she had. "This show has a great cast," she continued. "The only one you have to watch is Jack Boyd. He's probably all right, too, but he's so full of his own importance he doesn't give anyone a chance to find out. Most of the guys ignore him and the girls try to stay as far away from him as possible."

In appearance Cass matched the stereotype of a dumb blonde. The high pitch little girl tone of her voice added to the misconception. In reality she was the opposite. She knew how to use every one of her attributes, especially her looks. She had good sense and lots of brains to go with those good looks. Most of the girls from the chorus line were as attractive as Cass and just as knowledgeable. Marianne wondered how Brian Casey managed to collect such an array of beauty, charm and brains. Josh is right again, she thought. Casey is very good at what he does.

As curtain time approached the pace of the backstage activity increased. Cass had to join the rest of the chorus line for make-up and costumes. Marianne watched as scenery was checked and props positioned for easy access. Everyone had a job to do. Brian suggested she stay with him while the performance was in progress. That was fine with her there wasn't a better seat in the house.

When the curtain opened Brian Casey focused entirely on the performer on stage. He really is good, Marianne thought, and admired his style as he gently prodded his entire cast through another perfect performance. No wonder they all like him so much, she thought, he's trying to make stars out of every one of them and it looks like he's going to succeed.

Marianne watched the show unfold and she could see why the critics gave it rave reviews. She could also visualize the prospects of a real money maker if she used this timely musical to introduce her new sales promotion. The more she saw of this show, the better she liked it. She could see how everyone in this cast enjoyed what he or she was doing. Josh predicted that many of the "regular people" from *Gentlemen Again* were destined for bigger things in show business and no one knew this business better than Josh Golden.

Casey asked her if she would like to join the group after the performance. She hesitated a minute and he assured her there were no strings attached.

"Strictly business, if that's the way you want it," he told her. "It's one way to get to know this group a little better. You'll have fun and probably find some of those special qualities you said you were looking for. What have you got to lose, except a couple of hours of your time?"

Marianne wondered if this was his idea or something Josh suggested when he called about her coming back to the theater. She decided to go anyway. "You talked me into it," she conceded. "Where do I meet them?"

"If you don't mind waiting a few minutes after the final curtain we can ride downtown together," he said.

"That's fine with me," she answered, "as long as there are no strings on the offer." Brian Casey looked at her and a funny little lopsided grin turned into a beautiful smile as he said, "Marianne, you couldn't be in safer hands." She wondered why he put so much emphasis on her being safe with him. He was nothing like the obnoxious Jack Boyd, and he didn't resemble the big brother type but he was convincing and she believed him. She didn't want to mislead him and let him know that this was strictly a business venture.

She was surprised to see their late night get together was at Nick's, the same place she had dinner earlier with Josh.

"This maitre d' is going to think I'm really playing the field," she said with a nervous laugh as she explained to Brian about the birthday dinner.

"Don't give it a second thought," he said. "Everybody in show business comes to Nick's. George is noted for two things, his powers of observation and his total discretion. Nothing surprises him."

Brian Casey was an excellent partner, attentive but not overpowering. He made sure she knew everyone there and she was pleasantly surprised at the warm welcome. Casey explained what Marianne was trying to do with the new sales promotion. They all thought it was a good idea and offered to help if they could. It looked like the entire cast wanted this show to be around for a long time.

"It's like a comfortable habit," Alan Durling told her. "We all like what we do and who we do it with. You can put a lot more effort into something when you enjoy doing it." She had to keep reminding herself these people were in show business. There didn't seem to be one phony in the whole crowd.

Marianne was amazed at the talent in this group. Cass was beautiful, talented and smart. Bernie was a salesman who Cass described as "the world's best." Bill and Jen Flanagan were fantastic dancers, Jen with the chorus line and Bill in a featured spot. Gracie was another chorus line dancer who had the peculiar habit of asking and answering her own questions. Herb, her constant companion was an insurance broker. He was as quiet and laid back as Gracie was talkative. They seemed to be a perfect pair.

Alan Durling, the director's right hand man, supplied the musical accompaniment for rehearsals. Marge Crawford, his faithful companion, took care of the wardrobe headaches for the show. Brian Casey was a young, enthusiastic perfectionist they all referred to as "the best director on Broadway."

When Casey had to leave he asked the group to make sure Marianne had everything she needed. "Don't worry about a thing," Alan assured him. "She fits in just fine."

In spite of her attempts to keep this evening strictly on a business basis, Marianne found herself having fun. She had danced with Alan, Brian and Bill and enjoyed each of them.

"This is our way of unwinding after a long day," Jen explained. "We don't do this every night, but the days that have matinees are usually more trying than others. We like to relax a little before we go home."

"This is only part of our regular group," Alan told her. "Harriet Wethersfield and Julian Brice are usually here and so is Dan Shaw. Once in a while a few others join us but most of the time it's just the regulars. Brian comes by often and sometimes we're blessed with the presence of Jack Boyd. That doesn't happen too often - if we can help it."

"That's good to know," Marianne said. "From what I've seen so far, he doesn't appear to be very well liked."

"We never encourage him," Alan explained, "but sometimes it can't be avoided, he invites himself."

"I know why he was hired," Marianne said. "Josh explained the package deal process. What I don't understand is why you people put up with him at all."

"It's a complicated situation," Alan answered and seemed hesitant about saying any more. Marianne didn't want to push for an answer. She liked these people and didn't want to pry into things that were none of her business. She thought it best to drop the whole subject of Jack Boyd. Perhaps, when she knew this group better, someone would enlighten her a little more about their feelings toward the comedian. Boyd wasn't here tonight, so why pollute the atmosphere with conversation about him.

She started this evening as a stranger but it didn't take long for this group to make her feel like a regular. Jen Flanagan encouraged her to stay after Brian Casey left. She explained that everyone was not welcomed so quickly. "You look like you're having a good time so why not stay and enjoy yourself for awhile. We're a good bunch but if we don't like you or you don't fit in we don't encourage you to stay." Jen smiled as she continued, "It's an old fashioned quality we all have called – honesty. It helps us to be ourselves with no put ons. After all, we're on stage almost every day and we don't want to keep the curtain up when we're not getting paid for it." Their conversation was interrupted when Dan Shaw arrived.

"Where have you been?" Jen asked him. "Bill was very evasive when I asked him why you weren't here tonight. Do you have a secret romance going on that none of us know about? You can't hide things from this group for long. We'll find out all your secrets sooner or later."

When Jen attempted to introduce Marianne, Dan said he met her at the theater that afternoon. "I was hoping to see you again," he said, "But I didn't expect to see you tonight."

"I didn't expect to be here," she told him. She was surprised he remembered her. They had only spoken for a few minutes that afternoon. She didn't have a problem remembering him. He was one of the reasons *Gentlemen Again* caught her attention. When Josh introduced them at the Ballard party Dan seemed like the quiet one. Bill Flanagan did most of the talking. Dan didn't say much, but he had a magnetic attraction. She remembered thinking at the time that she would like to know both of them a little better. Dan Shaw seemed to fascinate her. It was a strange new feeling, unfamiliar and disconcerting. It was too strong to ignore and left her uneasy and unsure of how to handle it. The same feeling came back again when Josh mentioned she should get to know Dan better. Maybe some day, she thought, but not now. I'm too busy to be sidetracked right now. She reminded herself that he was in show business and she had her doubts about show people. She thought they were pretentious, overbearing and saw themselves as great stars to be idolized by an adoring public. Jack Boyd was the perfect example of show business conceit. After a few hours with this group she realized she was wrong. Jack Boyd was the exception. All the people in this group were good at what they did. They liked their work and were proud of it, and there was no conceit in any of them.

The time seemed to fly by tonight and Marianne wondered if she would get a chance to do this again. She had fun with this group and she especially enjoyed the dances and conversation with Dan Shaw. When the group left the restaurant they split up into twos and threes and headed their separate ways. Jen and Bill said good night and Jen made a point of asking Marianne to come again whenever she wanted to join them. Dan insisted on walking her to her car. They said good night and he gave her a quick wave as she pulled away from the curb and headed home to New Jersey.

Chapter 8.

Ticket sales were usually slow in the beginning of the week. Marianne didn't go to the Agency on Monday or Tuesday nights unless she was working on something specific. Josh agreed the new sales project they had discussed was a good idea and she was anxious to get started on it. She hoped he had contacted some of the people he said he would talk to about getting the plan off the ground. He promised to talk to them on Monday and today was Monday. She wondered if he had done his homework.

This evening 47th Street was quiet. Marianne parked about three doors down from the Aurous Agency. Josh was surprised to see her. "I'm glad you came by," he told her. "I called your office and they said you already left. I called your aunt and she said you were not home yet. I thought for sure you had something going on the side that I didn't know about," he teased.

"I wouldn't tell you if I did," she chuckled. "What's so important that you have to chase all over to find me on a Monday night? Did you get some good responses on our package plan?"

Josh ignored the reference to work and said, "You had a phone call I thought you should know about." She gave him a puzzled look and tried to figure out who would call her at the Agency number. She couldn't even guess and finally asked, "Who called me here? I never give anyone your number."

"Dan Shaw called about four o'clock. He asked me if I had a number where he could reach you." He glanced at her with an impish grin that seemed to say, "See, I knew you could have fun with these people."

"Did you give him my number?" she asked.

Josh looked at her like he didn't believe she would ask such a question when he was the one who suggested she get to know the singer better in the first place. "Did I give him your number?" he repeated. "I gave him your home number, your office number and even directions to your door. Am I a good friend or what?" he asked cheerfully.

Marianne shook her head and had to laugh at the pudgy little broker who was trying so hard to be a matchmaker. She wondered if she should tell him about the good time she had Saturday night, then decided against it. If something went wrong she didn't want to have to explain what happened. Leave well enough alone, she thought, for now anyway.

She put her small briefcase on the edge of the desk, opened it, and took out the notebook she used to record her orders. She could see that Josh was getting fidgety and she was enjoying his uneasiness. Finally he couldn't keep quiet any longer and asked, "Aren't you even going to call him back?"

"No," she said casually, "If he wants me he'll find me."

Josh was clearly unnerved by her indifferent attitude. "He's probably calling all over creation looking for you," he said. "You could help a little and at least call him back."

Before Marianne could answer him the phone rang and Josh automatically reached for it. She could only hear the broker's end of the conversation but it sounded like someone was looking for a favor.

"That's impossible," Josh told his caller. "That show has been sold out for weeks." He put his hand over the mouthpiece and instructed Marianne to get on the other phone and call the Biltmore Theater. "Tell Amy I need two tickets for tonight. Good tickets, for a visiting VIP." Marianne did as she was told and had the tickets secured in no time. Josh was still talking to his caller when she gave him the OK. He glanced up at her and winked as he continued his conversation. "Listen, Judge, I just thought of something. A friend of mine has two tickets for tonight. Let me call him and see if I can get him to give up his seats. I'll call you right back. Better still, hold the phone and I'll get him on the other line."

Marianne couldn't believe what she heard him say. "Josh, I already have the tickets on hold for you," she whispered.

"I know," he said, "but I don't want to let him know it was that easy. Let him sweat for a minute." It was at least five minutes before Josh went back to his caller. "You're in luck, Your Honor," he said as if he had done the judge the biggest favor in the world. "I'll leave the tickets at the box office for your friend. What name should I put on them?" He wrote the name of a visiting dignitary on the small pad in front of him. "By the way, you owe me one for this. These tickets are impossible to come by now. You're lucky you picked the right night."

He smiled as he put the phone back on the receiver. He was satisfied with his performance.

"You old faker," Marianne said as she frowned at the broker.

Josh smiled and remarked, "It's good to have a judge owe you a favor. You never know when you'll need it."

She watched him reach into the desk drawer and take out a fresh cigar. He sat back in the chair and began to remove the cellophane wrapper as if he was getting ready to celebrate his victory.

"Why do you smoke those awful things?" she asked.

"Hey, Kiddo, I have to have one vice," he said with a grin.

"All kidding aside, Josh, did you do your homework today?" she asked. "I really am anxious to get this package deal started."

Josh grinned at her as he puffed away on his cigar. "I not only did my homework, I made such a deal for you, like you wouldn't believe possible." He knew she was excited about the new project and he continued to puff on the cigar, just to tease her. Finally he put the cigar in an ashtray and sat back in his chair. He had teased long enough, now even he couldn't wait to tell her of his success.

"I talked to several people today. I explained what you had in mind and believe it or not, there was not a scrap of objection. Everyone I spoke with was interested. Most of the clubs will be happy to accommodate you with just 24 hours notice. Not bad, huh?"

"Josh, that's wonderful," Marianne beamed. "Now how about the expense end of it, any tips on how to handle that?"

"I have a suggestion that may solve the problem and make a few bucks for you, too. In your package include transportation, dinner, and the theater. Do not include the nightclub charges. After all, you don't know if your customers will want to eat or just have a couple of drinks or whatever. So eliminate the problem by having them take care of their own nightclub tabs. That helps in two ways. If the nightclub price is included all your beer drinkers will switch to scotch that night. If they pay their own tabs they will be a little more conservative and go home sober. They will still have a good time and probably want to do it again. Sound good so far?"

"It certainly does," she said and was happy to accept Josh's suggestion.

"You haven't heard the best of it yet," he added. "I worked it out with the clubs so that each customer you give them will have a fifteen percent gratuity added to their check, seven and a half percent for the waiter and seven and a half percent for you. You pick up a check once a month. Now how good does it sound?"

"Josh you're terrific. I knew I could count on you. You never let me down." Before she could say anymore they were interrupted again by the telephone.

"I can't see how you ever accomplish anything in this office," she told him. "That phone would drive me crazy."

Josh laughed and reached for the receiver. She went back to her order book so it wouldn't look like she was listening to his conversation. She heard him say, "Your timing is beautiful. She's just coming in the door now. Hold on, I'll get her." He put his hand over the mouthpiece and said, "It's Dan Shaw. Here," he said, and held out the receiver, "Take the phone and YOU BE NICE!"

Marianne laughed at him as she reached for the phone. "Hello," she said.

"Hi Marianne. It's Dan Shaw. Remember me?"

"Sure do," she answered. He hesitated for a minute as if he didn't know what to say and finally asked, "We were wondering if you would like to join us after the show tonight?"

"I hadn't planned on it, but if this is an invitation I can always change my plans."

"Please consider it an invitation," he said and before she had a chance to reconsider he added, "Do you want to come by the Ballard or meet us at Nick's?"

"I can come by the theater. If anyone needs a ride they can ride down with me."

"See you about eleven," he said.

"OK," she answered and hung up.

Josh was still sitting at the desk, but now he was avidly puffing away on his victory cigar and grinning like the cat that ate the canary.

"What's so funny?" she asked.

"Not a thing, Kiddo," he answered, as he continued to puff away and make clouds of smoke in the office.

"Well what are you sitting there grinning at?" she asked.

"Nothing at all," he assured her, still sporting a big grin. It was easy to see he was more than a little pleased with himself for getting her started on this route in the first place. Good thing I don't smoke cigars, she thought, or I'd probably be puffing right along with him.

Chapter 9.

Marianne found it hard to believe this group welcomed her so quickly. There were no questions, no inquiries, simply trust. She had been introduced to them only four weeks ago but their speedy acceptance made her feel like she had known them all her life. She never had time for many friends her main interest had always been focused on work. She enjoyed the good natured teasing by everyone and noticed how they relied on each other for almost everything. With this group there was always a friend available. She thought "The Crew" was a tailor-made nickname for them because they were always there for each other, like the crew of a well run ship.

Dan Shaw and Marianne Gordon were the only ones in the group who didn't have a steady partner. They didn't mind and they enjoyed each other's company and usually ended up together. They liked the same music, were excellent dance partners and found that many of their likes and dislikes were similar. Dan seemed a little on the quiet side but Marianne thought it was because she didn't know him very well. His conversations were interesting and he knew how to listen when someone else had the floor. She especially liked the fact that he was impressive but not overpowering. He hardly ever mentioned his family but that didn't seem unusual to her for she seldom spoke of her family either. She knew he had recently been discharged from the Army, but that was the past and they weren't interested in the past, they were only concerned with the present. They were comfortable friends who could relax and have fun with each other without making commitments neither of them wanted right now.

* * * * *

Gentlemen Again was selling out night after night. The Standing Room Only sign seemed to be a permanent part of the playbill. The cast had settled into the good feeling of being part of a hit show. The theater party package Marianne had suggested was proving as successful as the hit show she chose to initiate it. The sweet smell of success was in the air for the entire Crew, including it's newest member.

Jack Boyd had been a problem since he came on the scene, but the cast no longer thought of him as a threat. They treated him as a challenge and learned to ignore his jibes. He never stopped trying to create problems, but Julian's original suggestion worked so well it became standard practice for everyone.

Brian Casey put a lot of effort into being a good director. He kept reminding his cast the public was fickle and if another show came along that could top what they were doing their show would quickly lose its audiences. He kept his performers primed to perfection and never allowed their standards to slip an inch. He would join the Crew at Nick's once in a while, but he never stayed very late. There were no binding ties with this group. Everyone came and went as they pleased and did what made each of them comfortable.

Josh Golden was delighted with Marianne's new social life and followed each step with the interest of a concerned father. "Remember who introduced you to them," he would remind her. He never passed up the chance to tease her by asking, "Are we having fun yet?" As the weeks went by he noticed that each time he mentioned Dan Shaw's name it brought a little touch of color to her cheeks.

* * * * *

New York City was not a comfortable place on a hot, sticky, July afternoon. Bad moods caused tempers to rise as fast as the temperature. One cure for the problem was to get out of the city but that was not easy to do when your profession kept you on stage every night.

At the Ballard Theater all rehearsals were kept to a minimum. Wednesdays and Saturdays had matinees, but other days the cast was on their own until 7 p.m. It wasn't that easy for Marianne. During the day she worked in an office that had no connection to Broadway. Her evening hours were devoted to Aurous Ticket Agency and for the last two months her activities with the Crew.

After the performance on Wednesday night Cass spoke with Marianne. "Tomorrow we're getting out of this steamy city and spending the day at the beach. This means you, too, no excuses," she said.

"I can't go on a Thursday," Marianne told her. "The only way I can get out of the office on a weekday is to call in sick. I can't do that. Every time I lie I get caught."

"Come on," Cass pleaded. "Bernie is taking the day off. You can, too."

Marianne wondered what Bernie was taking the day off from. She never associated him with any kind of physical work. He was a hustler, and a good one. If you wanted to buy something Bernie Goldman could get it for you "wholesale." If he had agreed to go to the beach it probably meant a sale to concession owners for "wholesale" something or other. He never passed up an opportunity to make a dollar.

"I'm not a beach lover," Marianne told her and hoped it was a good enough excuse. "You people go and I'll see you after the show."

"Oh no," Jen said, "You're not getting off that easy. A Crew is not a Crew unless it's complete and we're not going without you. So call in sick or do whatever you have to do and come with us."

Marianne sighed and shook her head as she conceded defeat and agreed to go along. "I guess I have no choice," she said. Even though she protested she enjoyed the feeling that she was a real part of this group.

The weather was still hot and sticky when they gathered at Bill and Jen's apartment a little after nine the next morning. Dan Shaw and Herb Preston had the driving chores and the entire Crew headed for Coney Island.

It looked as if everyone in New York's five boroughs had the same idea, go to Coney Island for the day. It was still morning but the beach was crowded. Finding an empty spot on the sand was almost impossible. Alan Durling had the right idea. "It's too damn hot out here for me," he said and headed for the first watering hole he could find.

"It's too hot to go back to the city," Bill said. "As long as we made the trip out here we may as well make a day of it." He suggested they try some of the rides in the amusement park before going back to the hot city.

"I don't want to sound like a poor sport," Marianne told Jen, "but I'm scared to death of those rides."

"Don't worry," Jen promised, "Dan will take good care of you. He won't let you go on anything without one of us right next to you."

"I think I would rather just watch," Marianne said and knew she would never get out of it that way. She found it easier to give in than listen to the teasing from the whole group.

The last ride on the midway was a thriller called The Parachute Jump. Two people were strapped in a seat and carried to a platform high above the midway. At the top their seat was connected to a large overhead parachute that opened as it descended to give the effect of a parachute landing.

Marianne couldn't understand how so many people could enjoy a ride that to her seemed to put their lives in jeopardy. She had given in to the group's persuasion on several of the less sensational rides, but this monster was something else.

"NOT ON YOUR LIFE!" was her emphatic comment. No amount of persuasion was going to change her mind on this one. "I won't even set foot in an airplane and you expect me to jump off something with a parachute? NO WAY! Just forget it!" She couldn't convince them she was really terrified of this thing.

Cass tried to convince Marianne that the frightened feeling she had was similar to the stage fright they all experienced and it would disappear when she got on the ride.

"We all have it every night," she told her. "Once the curtain goes up the feeling goes away."

This was not enough to persuade Marianne. She watched as Julian and Harriet were strapped in and took the first ride.

"They're absolutely nuts," she said. "Out of their minds entirely! You will never, and I stress the word NEVER, get me on that thing."

Her adamant refusal didn't stop the rest of the Crew from coaxing her. "It's just a fun ride," Cass said as she took her turn with Bernie. Marianne was still not convinced and watched as Marge and Alan (along with Alan's trusty flask of picker-upper power) followed them. Gracie and Herb took their turn and Bill and Jen were next. Marianne still held back.

"It only takes a couple of minutes," Dan told her as he put his arm around her shoulder to reassure her he was there if she needed support. "Let's go and get it over with," he suggested.

She gave him a desperate look and was almost pleading with him as she asked, "You're going to stay right next to me, aren't you?"

"I certainly am," he assured her.

"OK," she conceded, "I'll go, but I'm doing this against my better judgment."

Somehow Dan Shaw could reach her when no one else could. She trusted everyone in the Crew, but Dan was special – she trusted him a little more.

An attendant strapped them in. The motors started, the cables moved and they were carried to the top. Dan put his arm around her. He knew she was nervous and thought it might help relieve some of her tension. He watched her squeeze her eyes shut trying to block out what she thought was in store for them. He was glad to have an excuse to put his arm around her, until today it only happened on the dance floor. As they started to descend Marianne reached for his other hand and held it so tight he couldn't pry her fingers loose. It surprised him. For the first time since he met her, Marianne seemed vulnerable. She needed him. He was concentrating on her and not the ride when they came to a sudden jolting stop. Dan tightened his grip on Marianne and she clung to him.

Everything stopped. No cables moved, no motors sounded. Even the crowd below was quiet. The seat they were strapped into swayed back and forth and came to a sudden stop in a tilted position halfway to the ground. Neither of them dared to move. Dan held on to Marianne and in a soft, reassuring voice said, "Just stay calm and try not to move."

"Danny," she whispered, more terrified than before, "I'm so scared right now that I won't even move my eyeballs."

"There's nothing to worry about," he told her in that same smooth, calm manner. "They'll have us down from here in no time."

She wanted to look up at him but was afraid to turn her head. "I'd like to believe that," she said, "but you're going to have to be a little more convincing."

"I'll never let anything happen to you," he told her as he tightened his grip even more.

"Right now you're in no position to make that kind of promise," she said.

"I'll make it anyway," he said, "And when we get down from here I'll say it again, OK?"

Marianne had the feeling he was enjoying this situation. She couldn't understand how anyone could dangle in mid air, high above the Coney Island boardwalk and not be scared to death. It didn't seem to bother Dan that much, but she was petrified and clung to him with every bit of strength she could summon.

The ride attendants scurried around on the ground below, but all their efforts were in vain. The cables didn't move an inch. The police arrived in minutes and the sound of their sirens attracted more spectators. The crowd below grew bigger and doubled by the time the Fire Department ladder truck arrived and moved into place under the ill-fated ride. The longest ladder available would not extend far enough to reach the dangling seat and its stranded occupants. Hopes of an early rescue faded as they watched the firemen fold their equipment and move out of the way.

"Danny," Marianne said with a disgusted sigh, "I think we're destined to spend the rest of our lives hanging in mid air in this miserable amusement park"

"It's OK with me," he said calmly, "as long as we're together."

His comment surprised her and for a minute she didn't know how to answer him. Finally she said, "I was only fooling."

"I wasn't," he told her in that same calm manner he used to quiet her earlier fears.

"Dan Shaw, cut that out. I can't argue with you with all these people looking at us."

"I didn't think you would," he told her with a smile and tightened his grip just a little bit.

Minutes stretched into hours and finally a new cable was put in place. After three and a half hours the seat was lowered safely and they were back on solid ground.

Marianne remembered the confident way Dan promised not to let anything happen to her. "I owe him one for that," she told herself. "What a terrific guy to have around in an emergency. On second thought, what a terrific guy to have around – anytime!"

The Crew barely made it to the theater on time, but the audience never knew of their hectic afternoon. As the final curtain came down

Bernie walked in the stage door with the early edition of the Daily News under his arm.

"Some people will do anything for a little publicity," he joked as he came over to Dan and Marianne.

"What does that mean?" Dan asked.

"Take a look at the early edition," Bernie said and handed Dan the newspaper.

Coney Island Tragedy Averted was printed in big letters under the half page picture of Dan and Marianne stuck in mid air on the amusement park ride.

"Oh no!" Marianne exclaimed as she looked at the picture. "I called in sick this morning. If my boss sees that picture my job is a memory. See, I told you I can't tell a lie, I always get caught." Dan chuckled at her dilemma. She looked up from the newspaper and asked, "Are you making fun of me?"

"No," he assured her, "I'm not."

She remembered his calm reassuring attitude and how it saved her from what could have been a life threatening disaster. She also remembered that there was a point during their harrowing experience when she had the feeling he was enjoying himself. "There's something I have to ask you," she said and watched for his reaction. "When that cable broke this morning, for a minute or so I had the feeling you were enjoying it, were you?"

Dan looked at her and held his breath for a second or two before answering. "That takes a little explaining," he said. "Your feeling was right. In a way I loved it. I didn't enjoy knowing you were in danger, but I loved having a reason to put my arms around you. I loved holding you close all the time we were stuck up there. To me it would be worth doing all over again just for that."

It was then that Marianne realized there was a lot more than just friendship between them. Dan finally let her know his real feelings and she was surprised when she discovered she felt the same way about him.

Wouldn't Josh be pleased, she thought, if he knew how well his match making was succeeding.

Chapter 10.

It was a wonderful summer for Dan Shaw and Marianne Gordon. Like the other couples in the Crew these two were good for each other. Marianne was very conscious of Dan's tremendous talent. She was convinced there was stardom in his future. Dan's steady, patient disposition was perfect to keep her ambition under control.

The Crew teased them about taking so long to discover what everyone knew was there all along.

"You two were destined to be together," Jen told them. "We could see it start the first night you danced with each other at Nick's."

"None of us had a chance once Dan showed up," Alan added. "One dance with him and I think she forgot the rest of us were even there."

The teasing continued for weeks but it didn't bother Dan or Marianne.

* * * * *

They left the theater and walked down the dimly lit alley toward 41st Street where Marianne had parked the car. Dan reached for her hand but she quickened her step and it was just out of his reach. He glanced at her and wondered if she was angry at something. She didn't seem to be yet she managed to keep that sliver of distance between them. Sometimes he couldn't figure her out. They reached the car and she handed him the keys. "Where are we off to tonight?" she asked.

"It's been a long day for everybody," Dan said. "I think most of the Crew are pretty tired. No one mentioned anything about going anywhere, but we can drop by Nick's for a while if you want to."

"I don't mind skipping it tonight," she told him. "Have you had any supper?"

"Not really," he admitted. "I shared a sandwich with Bill earlier but that was all I've had. I'm still not very hungry."

"Why don't we stop by the deli and get some salads and cold cuts," she suggested. "We can take them to your place and I'll put a couple of sandwiches together and you can make the coffee, OK?"

71

"Sounds good to me," he agreed. "I feel pretty confident tonight. I think I can beat you at Gin Rummy. Are you up to a good game?"

"You're on," she said.

* * * * *

"That deli makes the best salads in the city," Marianne commented as she cleared the dishes from the table and gave the plates a quick rinse. How nice it is to have someone like Dan in her life, she thought. He's really one of a kind. I hope nothing ever happens to spoil this relationship. She watched Dan deal the first hand of cards and noticed he was quiet tonight. We can play a couple of hands and let him unwind a little then I'll say good night and see him tomorrow, she thought. Her Gin Rummy luck was holding true and she won the first game. The second game took a little longer, but finally she put her cards on the table, looked at Dan and said, "Gin."

"Impossible," he said as he looked at the cards she placed face up on the table. She grinned at him and still had her hands on the cards. He reached over and took her hands in his and asked, "Marianne, why are you afraid of me?"

She tried to pull her hands away but he held on to them. "What do you mean by afraid of you?" she asked quickly. "What makes you think I'm afraid of you? Would I be sitting in your kitchen at midnight if I was afraid of you? What gave you that idea?"

The unexpected question shook her up and Dan knew right away that he had struck a nerve. "Every time I try to get close to you, you brush me off," he said. If I reach for your hand you take it away. If I put my arm around you, you change position. Even on the dance floor you always make sure there is space between us. Don't you realize that what we have is more than just friendship and I would never do anything to jeopardize that? I love every minute we can spend together, but sometimes you confuse me."

Her reaction surprised him. Instead of the casual attitude she usually had, Marianne started to cry. "I'm sorry Danny," she said. "I'm sorry if I hurt you. That was never my intention." She looked at him and wondered if she should tell him what had been on her mind for so long. If he understood, it would be wonderful. If he didn't she would be hurt all over again. But this was Dan Shaw and she knew he was different. She decided to start from the beginning and tell him everything.

"There are some things about me that you don't know and I think it's about time I did some explaining." She closed her eyes and shook her head as if she couldn't believe she was talking about this. "This is my problem and I shouldn't dump it on you, but I have to be honest with you."

Dan didn't expect this reaction. He had never seen her cry. She always seemed to have control over her emotions. Marianne was the best thing that had ever happened to him and he didn't want to see her unhappy. He also wanted to show her that she didn't have to shut him out of her feelings or build any barriers between them. He wanted to put his arms around her and hold her but he was afraid to let go of her hands. He thought she would pull them out of his reach and he would lose the ground he had already gained. Still holding both of her hands he stood up and said, "Let's go sit in the living room and talk. If you have a problem, go ahead and dump it on me. Between us we'll find a solution." He let go of her hands and put his arm around her shoulders. She didn't resist or try to pull away. This time she was ready to accept his support and above all she hoped he would understand.

"I shouldn't tell you any of this," she repeated. "It's my problem and I'm the one who has to live with it."

"If it concerns you I want to share it," he said. "Come on, talk to me. We don't have to hide anything from each other."

"All right," she answered, "But please hear the whole story before you make a judgment. I don't want anything to interfere with the good start that we have and I don't want to mislead you, either. I don't know where to begin," she confessed. "I've never talked about this to anyone, so please be patient. I'll get it all out eventually." She took a deep breath and began. "My mother died three weeks after my thirteenth birthday. I was left alone with my father, a man who had nothing buy contempt for all children, especially his own. The feeling was mutual. For years I saw how he treated my mother and I had no respect for him at all. After my mom died we lived in the same house, but there was very little communication between us. I couldn't leave, I was only thirteen years old and I had no place to go anyway. So I tried to make the best of a bad situation.

I stayed out of his way as much as I could. I was in school all day and after school I had a job in a neighborhood store. I didn't see very much of him and that was fine with me. When we did come face to face I tried to be agreeable. I really tried to get along with him, but that wasn't what he wanted. The only thing that seemed to please him was when he could get me upset. He was not happy until he had me in tears.

A couple of times he made off color remarks and I didn't know what he meant. I was so naïve when I was a kid that I didn't even know what all the items were in a drug store window. When I asked him to explain he said, 'Didn't your mother ever tell you anything?' Resenting him as much as I did, I thought it was clever to give him a smart answer like. 'She didn't have time, she died, remember?'"

"When he worked a late shift I went to bed before he got home. That way we didn't see each other at all and it meant no fireworks. It was what I usually did to avoid confronting him. I heard him come in and I pretended to be asleep so there wouldn't be an argument. I heard him moving around in the kitchen and I finally dozed off. Next thing I remember, he was sitting on the side of my bed. I remember asking him what he wanted. He just sat there smiling, but it wasn't really a smile it was more like a sneer. He said he was going to show me all the things my mother never told me about. I tried to get away from him but he was too strong for me. I was a thirteen year old kid, he was a big strong six footer who was just as quick as he was big. He got what he wanted. He finally succeeded in breaking my spirit. It was the worst night I had ever lived through and I'll carry the memory of it with me the rest of my life. I couldn't shake off the feeling of him touching me and I didn't know what to do. I couldn't tell anyone. Who would believe me? He was my father. I felt trapped. I was so ashamed I never left the house for almost a week. I thought, in some way, I was to blame. I was sure that if I left the house everyone who saw me could tell what happened. I couldn't face anyone. He loved my embarrassment. He said I'd learn to like it and we could do it again. I told him if he ever touched me again I'd kill him. He must have believed me, because he never so much as mentioned it again. But that didn't take away the pain or the shame."

"Danny," she continued, "I've never told this to anyone before, and I have no intention of ever repeating it to anyone else. You're the exception. I have to be honest with you no matter what it costs. Think about what I've told you and if it affects your feelings toward me in any way just say so and I'll understand. I wouldn't want to continue building what we have on a false foundation."

Dan listened to everything she said. He didn't attempt to interrupt or stop her. Once she started to talk he wanted her to get it all out in the open. He could see how hard it was for her to tell him. He knew how difficult it was to cope with memories that you wanted to bury forever. He remembered the awful night he got the news of his parents accident and how he wished there was someone he could have talked to then. He couldn't imagine how Marianne managed to endure this horrible experience all by herself and not say a word to anyone for more than five years. He was glad she finally talked to him about it. He moved closer to her on the sofa and gently put his arms around her. She didn't resist as he rested her head against the front of his shoulder.

"Go ahead and cry if you want to," he said. "You've earned it. Don't blame yourself for that situation, you're not the cause, you're the victim. I wish there was some way I could make things right for you, but I don't know how. I do know that I love you very much and this is not going to affect that, except to make me love you more. As far as you and I are concerned the bedroom will be off limits until you say otherwise." Dan's compassion and understanding caused the tears to flow even more, but it was just what she needed.

For more than five years she had burdened herself with a guilt that she didn't deserve. She had put up a protective barrier around herself, and Dan Shaw was the first person she allowed inside that barrier. After her confession she knew that her trust in Dan was well placed. He reminded her that they had agreed the past was behind them and now they both felt they had a future they could share.

* * * * *

It was almost the end of August and summer was reluctant to let go of its sweltering strangle hold on New York City. There wasn't a breath of fresh air anywhere. The energy it took to breathe caused perspiration. Marianne handed Dan the car keys and got into the front seat next to him.

"We have to find some place that's cool and get a little relief from this heat," she said. "My clothes are all stuck to me and I'm sweaty and uncomfortable. This is the worst day we've had all summer."

She didn't usually complain about the heat and Dan wondered if there was something else bothering her tonight.

"I felt so bad for the whole cast tonight," she continued. "Those stage lights must have been murder."

"You got that right," he said. "They'll warm you in the winter and cook you in the summer."

"We can take a ride to the beach," she suggested. "At least it will be cooler there and we don't have to worry about a sunburn at midnight."

"Do you really want to go to the beach at this hour?" he asked as he started the car.

Marianne could tell by the way he asked the question that he wasn't too thrilled with the idea, but he never said 'no' to her. "Do you have a better suggestion?" she asked.

"We can pick up something from the deli and take it to my place," he said. "I set up two new fans so they cool the whole apartment. It's very comfortable. How about it?"

"Every time you invite me to your place you have a hidden chore that has to be done. What's your ulterior motive this time?" she asked. "Do you have a sink full of dirty dishes?"

He could usually tell when she was joking, but tonight her off hand comments sounded serious.

"How can you be so sure of an ulterior motive?" he asked with a grin. "Am I that deceptive?" Before she could answer he added, "Maybe I want to get you alone on my territory so I can make mad passionate love to you."

"Or you can try again to beat me at Gin Rummy," she teased.

"We may be able to squeeze in a game or two," he agreed. Dan turned the car into Seventh Avenue and headed downtown. "We can go right to the apartment and I'll get the fans going. You can stay comfortable while I go for the food," he told her.

"Wait a minute," she said. "We can stop by the deli on the way downtown and you can forget about going out again tonight, OK?"

He glanced over at her and wondered why she gave in so easily. He noticed she was edgy and he was curious about what was causing it. He thought it was the unbearable weather, or a bad day at the office or maybe both.

"Are you sure that's what you want to do?" he asked.

"No," she answered, still in a state of confusion, "but it will do for starters."

* * * * *

Dan emptied the deli bags on the kitchen table. "You bought enough food to last all week," Marianne said. "Would you like me to make sandwiches or would you rather wait a little while?"

"I'm not very hungry, but if you want to eat now it's all right with me," he answered. He started the fans and tried to cool the apartment or at least circulate the air a little. The kitchen didn't get much of the breeze but the living room and bedroom were comfortable.

"You're quite the engineer, Mr. Shaw," Marianne said as she watched the breeze from the fans ruffle the pages of the magazine on the coffee table. She put two cold drinks on the table next to the magazine and sat next to him on the sofa. "I put the food away for now and decided to enjoy the breeze."

He put his arm around her and she rested her head on his shoulder. Not a word was spoken. After a few minutes she turned and looked at him. "Well?" she said.

"Well what?" he asked.

"Well, is this your idea of mad passionate love making?"

"No," he answered with a chuckle. "I was just waiting for you to get comfortable."

She kicked off her shoes and tucked her feet underneath her on the sofa. She glanced up at him and said, "There, I'm comfortable. Now what?"

She was doing a good job of getting him confused tonight and finally he said, "Marianne, what's bothering you? You've been on edge ever since you picked me up. I don't know how to please you. What do you want me to do?"

Without the slightest hesitation she said, "How about a demonstration of the mad, passionate love making you talked about in the car."

"I can handle that," he said and kissed her with an intensity she never realized was in him. She pulled away and looked at him with a surprised expression. "Wow," she teased, "I think you've been practicing, haven't you?"

"Yes," he answered with a grin, "But not nearly enough." He kissed her again and this time really set her heart pounding. He didn't let her go and it surprised her that at last he was being a little forceful. "You take your homework seriously, don't you?" she teased.

"When it concerns you I do," he told her and gently but firmly pulled her closer to him. "I love you, Marianne," he said as his lips brushed her ear. He had said this to her many times before and she always came back with the same answers, "I know you do," or "I love you too." It was said somewhat reluctantly and he wondered if she really meant it. Tonight was different. She looked at him and with a quiet but determined tone said, "Don't say that unless you're sure you mean it."

"You know I mean it," he said.

She looked directly at him to see his immediate reaction as she said, "If you really mean it let's go to bed."

"WHAT?" he almost shouted and didn't believe what he knew he heard. "Don't tease me like this. It's hard for me to control myself now, but when you say things like that I may just lose it, even though you're only joking."

"I'm not joking, Danny, I mean it," she told him.

He couldn't believe what he was hearing and when he realized she did mean what she was saying he looked at her and exclaimed, "JEESSUUSS KEEYRHIST!!!!! Maryanne, you never cease to amaze me. What brought this on all of a sudden?"

"Danny, you told me the bedroom was off limits until I said otherwise," she reminded him. "Well, I'm saying it now. From now on we play by a whole new set of rules." She could see the beads of perspiration on his forehead and wondered if they were caused by the hot weather or by what she had just proposed. "A few minutes ago you said you loved me, I know you do, I love you, too. More than you will ever know. It hasn't been easy for either of us, so maybe it's about time we handled it differently."

"Are you finally telling me that you'll marry me?" he asked.

"Not yet," she answered as if she was unsure of her real feelings. "You have a very important career to be considered first. You're so talented and so good on stage I know you're going to be famous. A wife will only hinder your chances for success. I can put off the marrying part, but I can't put off the loving you part……..

Now he understood why she had been nervous and edgy. This was what she had on her mind and she didn't know how to approach him with it. He wondered if she really wanted things to progress this way or was she doing it just for him. He put his arms around her and held her close to him. "I don't care about any career, and being famous doesn't interest me either. All I care about is you. Without you none of it means anything. Think about this," he cautioned, "Is this really the way you want it?"

She stood up and looked at him. "For now it seems to be the only way we can have it," she answered with a subdued sigh. He was still seated on the sofa and she leaned over, kissed him lightly on the lips. Reached for his hand and calmly led him into the bedroom.

The room was dark and the only sound was the whir of the fan in its attempt to circulate the humid summer air. As they lay next to each other Dan asked her again, "Are you sure this is what you want?"

"I'm sure," she whispered. "Isn't this what you want, too?"

"Oh, God, yes!" he responded. "You can't imagine how much. My concern is that you don't have any regrets later on."

"Danny, I love you with all my heart," she told him and the depth of her feeling for him could be felt in every word. "The only thing I regret is that it took me so long to realize where my priorities should have been."

He put his arms around her and the feeling of her body against him was almost more than he could stand. "I love you," he said over and over again. "I know you do," she answered. "I love to hear you say it. I love you, too."

His touch was gentle and considerate. She was firmly convinced nothing in this world could compare to this. She couldn't believe anything would ever make her feel better than the touch of this very special man and she was glad she made this decision.

Dan had always given in to anything she wanted. Now it was her turn to give in to him. He tried desperately to keep the situation under control and proceed slowly, but both of them got caught up in their

79

emotions and the waiting was over. All control was gone. Dan didn't want to let her go. He gently nuzzled the side of her neck and said, "Only God knows how much I love you."

"I know, too," she said and just above a whisper added, "Almost as much as I love you."

They spent every last bit of energy on lovemaking and in spite of the muggy heat she fell asleep with her head on his shoulder. He could feel her contented breathing and hesitated to move for fear of waking her. He was a very happy man tonight. What pleased him more than anything was that this was Marianne's suggestion. He realized how much it took for her to make such a decision and how much more to carry it out so perfectly. This is more than love, he thought, this is the perfect relationship. With those thoughts uppermost in his mind and Marianne held securely in his arms, he closed his eyes and fell asleep, too.

*   *   *   *   *

Dan was in that limbo of half asleep and half awake as he turned on his side and suddenly realized the other side of the bed was empty. "Marianne," he called as he sat up and put the light on.

"I'm here," she answered from the living room.

He reached for his robe on the back of the chair and went into the living room. She was sitting in the corner of the sofa, wrapped in his big terry cloth shower robe. He sat beside her and gently took her hands in his. "Regrets already?" he asked.

She looked at him and slowly shook her head. "I have no regrets," she assured him.

"Then what are you doing out here?" he asked.

"It's very late," she said. "I should go home."

"No," he said as he put his arms around her, "Not tonight, Marianne. Let this be home for tonight. Don't leave now, please." He gently put her head against his chest. "This is a very special night for both of us. If you're worried about explaining anything I'll go with you in the morning, but don't leave tonight. Come back to bed, put you head on my shoulder and let me hold you for the rest of the night. Let's worry about tomorrow when tomorrow comes."

Marianne closed her eyes and thought, – God, I love this man. "Danny, you have a way of wording things that make them sound so sensible and so right. I have a feeling it's going to be very difficult for me to ever say 'no' to you again." He put his hand under her chin and turned her face toward him as he leaned over and kissed her softly on the lips. He reached for her hand and this time he was the one who led her back into the bedroom.

Chapter 11.

I hate third floor walkups, Marianne thought, as she climbed the stairs to the tiny apartment Bill and Jen Flanagan called home. In his haste to convert a storage loft to living quarters the landlord overlooked some important amenities. The Flanagans apartment did not have a bathroom. Toilet facilities were an afterthought and a lavatory was hastily installed in a small room, no bigger than a closet, in the hall. Bill knew he couldn't do anything about the location, so he built a throne around the john and put a sign over the door that said, *Throne Room*. It served its purpose and was the first thing a visitor saw when they reached the third floor landing. It was always good for a laugh, even when you were in the lowest of moods, as Marianne was now.

She trusted everyone in the Crew, but in the discussions about marriage they all sided with Dan. She wanted an honest opinion from someone she thought would understand her feelings. Marianne had always handled her own problems but this time it affected Dan, too, and she had to talk to someone. She called Jen and asked if she could stop by.

"Anytime," was Jen's quick response. "Bill will be out all afternoon. If you can come by today we can have a good old fashioned gab session."

By the time she reached the third floor Jen had the apartment door open. "I've got a problem and I really need to talk to someone," Marianne said.

"Hey, what are friends for?" Jen answered as they went into the kitchen. "A serious discussion in an Irish kitchen needs a cup of tea to go with it," she said as she filled the kettle. "I knew something was bothering you. I was hoping you would talk to me, but I didn't want to pressure you. Whatever is on your mind seems to be causing you enough trouble."

Marianne sat at the kitchen table. She was having second thoughts about whether she should have come here. As much as she liked everyone in the Crew it was still difficult for her to share her problems. "I don't know where to begin," she said and sounded completely lost.

"The beginning is always a good place," Jen suggested as she tried to lighten the atmosphere and relieve some of the tension.

"I'm so mixed up I don't know where the beginning is anymore," Marianne admitted.

"Let me make it easy for you," Jen said. "Are you feeling guilty because you spent a couple of nights with Dan?"

Marianne had no idea anyone knew about their nights together. "How did you know?" she asked. "I didn't say anything to anyone. Did Dan say something to Bill?"

"I don't think so," Jen answered. "If he did Bill would have told me and he hasn't mentioned it. He did say he thought something was bothering Dan and we all noticed the change in you in the past two weeks. You have all of us concerned. Cass asked me yesterday if you were all right. I told her you were not getting very much sleep, and you were probably tired, but I don't think she believed me."

Marianne sighed and shook her head. "You're right, Jen, I do feel guilty," she confessed. "Not because we've done anything wrong," she insisted. "I feel guilty because I pushed Dan into doing something I wanted. I was so sure it was what he wanted, too, that I talked him right into it. Just like he always does, he tried to keep me happy and went along with it."

Jen glanced at her friend and said, "Do you really expect me to believe that?"

"It's the truth, that's exactly what happened," Marianne stated firmly. "Before we did anything he asked me three times if I was sure it was what I wanted."

"Was it?"

"Yes."

"Are you sure?"

"I'm positive."

"Well then, why do you feel guilty?"

"I just told you, I pushed him into doing something he didn't want to do. It wasn't his idea it was mine."

"Marianne," Jen said patiently, "I don't think you have one problem, I think you have several. First of all, there is nothing wrong with sex between two people who love each other. It's not something we should be ashamed of anyway. It's normal, natural follow up to emotions and feelings that build up inside of us. It was definitely something Dan wanted, probably more than you. He held back because he thought it would offend you if he mentioned it. No amount of persuasion could have talked him into it if he thought for a minute it was wrong for either of you. He loves you too much to let that happen. I can't figure out why you won't marry him. He certainly has asked you often enough."

"That's another thing that's bothering me," Marianne said. "He wants to get married now. But I think that would mess things up for him. Before we became so involved I could always reason with him and show him how much better off he'll be if he stays single for a while. Now he doesn't see it that way. He said the couple of nights we had together prove how good we are for each other. Jen, I just don't know how to get through to him. He has so much talent I know he's going right to the top. A wife will only hold him back and I don't want anything to get in his way. I sell plenty of tickets to a lot of shows and I know what my customers are looking for. I know who they want to see. Believe me, when they go to see *Gentlemen Again* they are not interested in Jack Boyd. Sure, his name is on the marquee, but you know as well as I do, Julian, Bill and Dan are building reputations that are going to take them right to Hollywood."

Jen could see that Marianne was deeply concerned about interfering with Dan's success. As she watched her friend struggle with the problem, she wished she could convince her that success wasn't as important as happiness. With Marianne, success was an obsession. Jen knew it would be useless to try to persuade her otherwise. Perhaps Dan could do it, she thought. Right now Marianne has a few other problems that might be more in her field.

"Your success theory is fine, if that's what you want to believe," Jen said. "I think Dan Shaw will be a success at anything he does. The difference is, if you two were married he would be a happy success – and so would you." Jen carefully watched Marianne's reaction as she continued, "I think another big part of your problem is that you've lived in a sheltered atmosphere. You and I were taught the same values. Our Catholic school background taught reading, writing and arithmetic, but the problems of the real world were never touched. We had to learn a lot of things the hard way." She wondered how much of her advice was getting through and tried to make eye contact, but Marianne chose to stare at her teacup. "I hate to admit it, after all I'm supposed to be a worldly showgirl, but I never even knew what a penis looked like or how big they can get. It's a good thing I fell in love with Bill. He was patient, gentle and understanding, otherwise I think I would still be in a state of shock."

Marianne almost choked on her tea. Jen never said anything like this before but it was exactly what was needed and Jen knew it. "I like to think Bill and I are still in the learning stage. We make our own rules and do what's right for each other. Maybe you and Dan had better start thinking along the same lines. Forget about other people and do what's best for both of you. While you're at it put your guilt feelings on hold until you do something to deserve them."

By the time Marianne was ready to leave the Flanagan apartment she was rethinking a lot of her concerns. The only thing she couldn't seem to shake was her consuming obsession with success. It didn't matter whether that success was for her or for Dan, it was something that had to be achieved before she would be satisfied.

Jen knew some of the things she had suggested this afternoon would mean big changes and they would take a lot of thought before Marianne could be comfortable with them. She was also aware of the depth of the feelings between Marianne Gordon and Dan Shaw and she was certain he would be there whenever Marianne needed him.

The two women walked out into the hallway and as Marianne started down the stairs Jen leaned over the rail and said, "By the way, if you don't want anyone to know you're at Dan's don't leave your car in front of the house all night. It stands out like a sore thumb when it's the only one left on the street in the morning."

* * * * *

Marianne loved Sundays. It meant she could spend the whole day with Dan. There was no performance to worry about and their time was their own. They went to Dan's apartment after leaving the Crew at Nick's on Saturday night. It was one of those times when neither of them wanted to say good night – so neither of them did. They slept late Sunday morning and while Dan was in the shower Marianne made coffee. She took the milk from the refrigerator, poured some in her coffee and made a face as she watched it curdle to the top of the cup. She could hear Dan singing as he moved around in the bedroom.

She called in to him and said, "Hey, Mr. Shaw, when was the last time you opened this refrigerator?"

"I don't know," he answered. "I don't use it very much. Why?"

"There are some funny little fuzzy green things growing in there and the milk is sour," she told him. "You really need help with your housekeeping."

"I know," he answered, "I've been telling you that for over a month." He came into the kitchen and looked over her shoulder into the refrigerator. "You're right," he said, "it definitely needs a woman's touch."

"That's easy to fix," she said, and grinned as she gave him a quick glance. "Hire a cleaning lady."

"That's not what I had in mind," he said and chuckled at her attempt to evade his hint.

"Don't look at me, Danny," she quipped. "House cleaning is not one of my specialties." She hurried past him through the bedroom and into the bathroom to take her shower.

Dan emptied the refrigerator into a trash container. When Marianne returned to the kitchen he was sitting at the table swishing his coffee around in the bottom of his cup.

"You're lucky you can drink your coffee black," she commented. "I have to have a little milk in mine." He didn't answer and she noticed the serious expression on his face.

"What's the matter Dan, are you disappointed because I'm not the domestic type?

"Oh no, that's not a problem," he answered, "but I do have something important I have to talk to you about."

"Now?" she asked.

"Right now," he said and she could tell by the tone of his voice that this was serious. "I should have told you a long time ago, but I was afraid you wouldn't understand."

"What do you mean, 'I wouldn't understand'? If you have a problem it's my problem, too," she told him. "What's the matter? You're not sick are you?"

"No," he answered quickly, "It's nothing like that. It's a money problem."

Marianne breathed a sigh of relief. "Is that all that's bothering you?" she asked. "Don't worry. I have money in the bank. It's yours if you need it."

"Wait a minute," he said, "You don't know how much money is involved. Let me explain."

"You don't have to explain anything. If you have a money problem and I can help, I want to. I don't care how much is involved. There," she said. "Problem solved, right?" She started to walk into the other room and Dan reached for her arm to stop her. "Where are you going?' he asked.

"To get my bankbook, it's in my pocketbook," she answered.

He took her hands in his and pulled her toward him. He didn't want her money he was trying to tell her about his. When he said money problem she assumed he needed it. He didn't expect that reaction and now he was at a loss for words. He put both arms around her and held her close to him. "Marianne, there is something I have to tell you and I want you to listen and promise you won't interrupt. Please let me finish before you say anything, OK?"

"OK," she answered, "But you don't have to explain any ......"

"Marianne," Dan interrupted as he put his index finger over her lips. "You promised to listen, now listen." He told her how his grandfather had started a pharmaceutical business many years ago. His grandfather retired and his father took control of the business. It doubled and then tripled and continued to grow. When his parents were killed in an automobile accident the business was left to him and his older sister. He had been close to both of his parents and their deaths hit him hard. At that time he didn't want any part of the business. He left college and joined the Army. His half of the inheritance was put in a trust that paid him a yearly allowance until he was twenty-five. Then the bulk of the money would be turned over to him. "I'm going to be twenty-five soon," he told her. "I have to make some decisions and I need your help."

"How can I help? She asked. "That has nothing to do with me. They're your decisions."

"No, they're not my decisions," he said, "They're our decisions. I'm talking about our future. You're a very important part of that future, so these decisions are not mine they're ours."

"Dan Shaw, you don't play fair," she said. "You know perfectly well how I feel about your career. I've told you many times what I hear customers say when they order tickets for your show. Yes, Danny, I said your show and I meant your show, yours, and Julian's and Bill's. Oh sure, Jack Boyd is the big headliner, but the packed houses aren't for him and you know it. The audience wants to see you and Julian and Bill. Every single review has specifically named all three of you. Believe me, Danny, people know that what they see in *Gentlemen Again* is just the tip of the iceberg as far as your talent is concerned. Like it or not, Mr. Shaw, you are a star!"

He told her many times that his career was not the most important thing in his life. Now she wondered if he was looking for a way out of it. "If you want to put fame and fortune aside and go back to Ohio and run your father's drugstore, that's all right, too. Just as long as you are sure it's what you want and you give it your best shot. There is one other little provision there, too," she added. "Please don't leave me out, I haven't got a thing against Ohio."

Dan could tell by her reference to his father's drugstore that Marianne didn't have the slightest idea he was referring to the Shaw Pharmaceutical Corporation – one of the biggest in the country. He was completely overwhelmed at how she thought his reference to money problems meant he needed it and how quickly she offered him everything she had worked so hard to save without asking for any sort of explanation. He remembered a conversation he had with Bill Flanagan many months ago. *"When you find somebody like Jen you'll know how I feel,"* Bill had said. *"I can't put it into words, I don't know how to describe it. The one thing I am sure of is that there is no other feeling in this world that comes close to it."*

"How right you are, old buddy," Dan told himself, "now I know exactly how you felt."

Chapter 12.

Traffic on 41st Street was worse than usual. Cars lined both sides of the street and there was no place to park. As she edged the car slowly toward the Ballard Theater Marianne noticed several police cars parked in front of the entrance. She wondered why when there didn't seem to be any sign of a problem. Something serious must have happened in the area, she thought, and made a mental note to ask Fred, the security man at the stage door, what was going on.

The traffic only moved inches at a time and she was getting impatient. She watched a man cross the street and get into a parked car. She let him pull out and take her place in traffic and she maneuvered her car into the parking spot. What a lucky break, she thought as she locked the car and crossed the street to the alley that led to the stage entrance.

"Hi, Fred," Marianne said to the guard, "Why are the police cars out front?"

"Evening Marianne," the guard answered and leaned toward her to whisper. "They're here because of Jack Boyd."

"Oh great!" she said disgustedly. "Who did that nitwit insult this time?"

"A lot worse than that this time," Fred told her. "Somebody killed him. Shot him twice sometime late last night. The lady who cleans his apartment found him when she got there this morning."

Marianne was shocked by this unexpected news. "Wow!" she said. "Who did it?"

"Nobody knows," the guard told her. "The police have been here for almost an hour. They're talking to everybody in the show."

Jack Boyd was rude and insensitive. He enjoyed making people angry. Marianne couldn't think of one person who liked him, but that was an image he created for himself. He had no friends among the cast members, but they would never cause him any physical harm. They chose to ignore him and got a charge out of deflating his ego a little at a time. To most of the Crew he was a challenge and it was a game of wits to see how well they could avoid him. Everyone connected with *Gentlemen Again* knew the comedian was good on stage. He was an essential part of this production and the important thing to this cast was the success of the show.

My God, Marianne thought, what is this going to do to the show? Brian Casey must be half crazy trying to get a replacement.

"Are any of the Crew here yet?" she asked the guard.

"A few," he told her. "Dan, Bill and Alan are here. They're in their dressing room talking to a couple of detectives. Jen and Marge came in a few minutes ago. I think they went to the girl's dressing room. Some of the other girls are here, but that's all of your Crew, so far."

She would see Dan when the police were finished. In the meantime, she decided to ask Brian Casey if there was any way she could help. "Is Casey here?" she asked Fred.

"Yes he is," Fred answered and motioned toward the director's office. "He's been in that little office of his with the door shut ever since he got here."

"Thanks, Fred," Marianne said and left the security man with a friendly pat on his shoulder. She headed for the director's office and knocked softly on the closed door.

"Come in," Casey said. A little too quickly Marianne thought, as she opened the door just enough to poke her head inside. "It's only me, Brian. Can I talk to you for a couple of minutes?"

"Anytime, Marianne, anytime," he answered tensely. He was nervous and jumpy, very unusual for this young man. She went into the cramped office and closed the door.

"You look terrible, Brian. Are you all right?" she asked.

"I'm OK," he answered. "For now anyway."

This show revolved around the steady, guiding hand of this young director. Today that steady hand shook so much he couldn't hold his coffee cup. She wondered why this unfortunate incident would unnerve him so completely. Everyone knew there was no love lost between Jack Boyd and Brian Casey. Brian's dedication to the show would eliminate the possibility of him doing anything that would interfere with the performance.

"Are you stuck for a replacement?" she asked.

"That's not a problem," he said with a shrug of his shoulders. "I expected trouble from Boyd all along. I thought he might pull a no show and I talked with Phil Bender weeks ago. Phil agreed to sign on anytime Boyd didn't show up. He knows the whole routine and would have been better for the part right from the beginning but the producers wouldn't budge from their decision to go with Boyd. I think Boyd put up a good part of the cash involved. That's why they were so insistent about him staying in the show."

She was surprised that he was talking so freely, but thought it was a good way for him to release some of his tension.

"That's all in the past now," Casey said soberly. "I called Phil Bender as soon as I heard the news and he's ready to go on tonight." To Brian Casey the show always came first. Everyone in the cast knew this, but Marianne wondered if the police would understand it as they did. Brian seemed to know what she was thinking and asked, "How is this going to look to the police? They'll think I had this all set up and I killed him to get him out of the show. I didn't even know about it until the police came by my place this morning." He looked up from his seat at the cluttered desk and asked anxiously, "You don't think I had anything to do with this, do you?"

"Of course not," she said and was astonished that he would even think she would connect him to the crime. She reached for his hand and was surprised to find it was cold and clammy. She remembered that Brian Casey didn't know she was aware of his unusual promiscuity with a select group of male friends. She realized his efforts to cover it up now might really put him in a questionable position. The police wouldn't consider his feelings and she didn't want him hurt or embarrassed. Maybe it was time to let him know his habits were no secret.

"Jack Boyd had a million enemies," Marianne told him. "I don't think he had one friend. That has nothing to do with you. Sure you wanted to get rid of him, we all did. Look at how he persecuted Alan. Ever since the first day he arrived here Alan was his prime target. That doesn't mean that Alan did it either. In fact, Alan was with the Crew until early this morning. As far as you are concerned, I know where you were, too."

"I was with all of you until a little after midnight," he told her. She wondered if he was trying to establish an alibi, or if he was having a problem telling her where he really went when he left Nick's.

"I mean after you left us," she said.

91

"You do?" His startled expression told her he was caught completely off guard.

"Sure I do," she said. "The whole Crew knows where you go and who you go with."

"Oh my God!" Brian moaned as he put his elbows on the desk and dropped his forehead into the palms of his hands. "I thought I was being so careful."

"You were," she assured him as she patted his shoulder. "You were also very discreet and considerate. Remember, Brian, we're your friends. We're kind of an extended family. Your preferences are your business. Your success and happiness are what we care about."

He was still shaky and nervous and she knew he had to calm down and think clearly or he would talk himself right into getting arrested for something he didn't do. She wondered if Jack Boyd knew about Brian's friends, and if so, did he taunt the young director about it? It would have been a typical Boyd tactic to threaten exposure if he thought no one else knew.

"How much have you told the police?" she asked.

"Nothing really," he answered. "They didn't ask me very much this morning. I think they came by my place because there was no one here and they didn't know anyone else to contact. I gave them the name and address of Jack's ex-wife, but that was all I knew.

I told them there was information at the office and I offered to come and get it, but they said they would be here this afternoon and would get it then. When they left I called Dan, but there was no answer. Bill wasn't home either and I didn't want to say anything to the girls over the phone. I've been sweating it out in here waiting for them to knock on the door since four o'clock." Marianne was still holding his hand and he confided to her that he was worried.

"I'm sure everyone is worried," she told him. "I haven't had a chance to see Dan or any of the Crew yet. Fred just told me about this. He said the police are talking to Dan, Bill and Alan now. They'll probably be over here next." Seeing the shape Brian was in, Marianne knew he needed help. "Pull yourself together and go over last night's events so you know what to tell them. You have nothing to worry about. You can account for your time. The whole Crew was at Nick's until early this morning. We were there until they closed and that was four o'clock. You left a little after midnight. Did you take a cab to 23rd Street?"

The mention of 23rd Street made Brian flinch. She remembered he didn't know how much they knew of his after hours activities. "No," he replied. "My friend, Calvin, picked me up."

"Why didn't he come inside?" she asked. "At least someone would have seen you leave together."

"He did go in," he told her. "He asked George to tell me he was there. That's when I left."

"Did anyone see you at 23rd Street?" she asked.

"I don't know," he answered, still confused. "I never pay any attention to who is there. When we got there a party was going on and neither of us felt like staying. We met a couple of other friends and went back to my place."

"Are you telling me that all four of you left together, went to your place and stayed there until this morning?" she asked.

"Yes," he said. "They were still there when the police came by." He looked at her with the expression of a child caught with his hand in the cookie jar. "I know what you're thinking," he said, "and I really should explain ....."

Marianne interrupted him, "No you don't know what I'm thinking and you don't have anything to explain. Besides the Crew you have three witnesses to where you were all night long. You don't have a thing to worry about. Just make sure you let the police know the four of you were together. You can give them names, can't you?"

"Sure," he answered, "But I don't want to if I don't have to."

"Then don't volunteer any information. When the police question you answer them and tell the truth. If they catch you in a lie it will really look bad. As far as the people here knowing that you walk to the beat of a different drummer, who cares? We certainly don't. That's your business. As far as every one of us is concerned you are still the one and only Brian Casey. Personally, I love your smile, I like to dance with you and once in a while I would appreciate a hug," she added with a smile.

Brian leaned back in his chair and Marianne could almost see the tension drain from him. His voice steadied and his calm demeanor slowly surfaced. He was relieved that the cast and especially the Crew knew about his activities and didn't let it influence their affection for him. He rubbed his chin and glanced up at Marianne. "How long have you known?" he asked.

"The first night you asked me to join the group at Nick's you stressed that I couldn't be in safer hands," she said. "At the time I wondered what you meant. Then I noticed little things here and there, and a month or so later Dan confirmed my suspicions. He said the Crew had been aware of it all along. You didn't say anything and they thought you didn't want to talk about it, so no one mentioned it."

Brian shook his head, "Thanks, Marianne," he said. "I know what you're trying to say, and I get your message." He smiled and added. "I like dancing with you, too, and anytime you need a hug, look me up."

She was relieved when she saw that contagious smile spread across his handsome face. He'll be all right now, she thought, at least he's thinking clearly.

"By the way, Brian," she said as she started through the door of the tiny office. "You have to move to a real office. This place isn't big enough to be a closet. This is the first time since I've known you that this door has been closed. Can I leave it open now?"

"You sure can," he answered, "and thanks again, Marianne. You tell Dan Shaw he's a lucky guy."

"You tell him," she replied with a smile. "He never believes anything I say."

As she left, Marianne pushed the door back as far as it would go. The best director on Broadway really needs a bigger office, she thought.

Two detectives were leaving the dressing room that Dan, Bill and Julian shared. They thanked the men for their cooperation and said they would be back if they had any more questions. It was said in a way that let all three men know they would be back as soon as they could find an excuse. They wanted to talk to Brian Casey and Alan walked them over to the director's office. Instead of asking them to come in, Brian chose to come out. Wise move, Marianne thought.

Dan told her what he knew of Boyd's demise. She told him what she had found out from Fred and what was discussed in Brian's office.

"Thank God you got to Brian before those detectives," Dan said. "They can't wait to give him a bad time. They asked us what we knew of his activities and none of us made any fuss about the fact that he does things a little differently. They couldn't understand that it didn't matter to us." He sighed and shook his head as he continued, "You should have seen the looks they gave us when Julian came in and Bill told them he shared the dressing room with us. You know Bill, he can't leave well enough alone. When he noticed they were shocked to see a black man sharing our dressing room, Bill told them Julian was actually the star of the show, but the producers let Boyd keep his name on the marquee for old time sake. I think Bill really enjoyed their confusion. I don't know if they believed him, but he certainly was convincing."

Dan suggested that Marianne talk to the girls and make sure they knew what Brian was up against with these detectives. He thought if the police realized the rest of the cast knew about Brian's habits they might not put so much pressure on him. "It certainly was a stroke of luck that you came by when you did. At least now Brian knows where we all stand. I hope he doesn't worry about it. It's never been a problem as far as we're concerned."

"He knows that," Marianne said. "It might be a good idea to encourage him to join us at Nick's tonight, even if it's just for a little moral support."

"I'll make sure he gets the message," Dan promised.

Brian Casey put all his efforts into making *Gentlemen Again* a memorable hit show. He had taken raw talent and worked hard to cultivate it until it was as close to perfect as possible. Young show business newcomers who had never been on a Broadway stage were now performing nightly to the delight of standing room only audiences. Casey had a fantastic knack for bringing out talent that even the possessor was unaware of having. He was often referred to as "a master of his art." Unfortunately the police didn't look at him the way real artists did. The hard line detectives questioning the cast about Boyd's murder considered the young director odd. They referred to him as "the queer". They were not accustomed to dealing with people in show business, especially people as unique as this group.

Julian expressed everyone's feelings when he let Brian know he was a charter member of the group and his word was all that was needed for him to be believed. That same trust held true for this situation. Although Jack Boyd was known to have caused dissension in previous shows, there was not a speck of internal trouble with this cast. They treated the odious comedian like a challenge and every one of them was capable of meeting that challenge. It was useless to try to explain these circumstances to the police. You had to witness it to understand it. Not one of the detectives who were so quick to refer to Brian Casey as "queer" knew Jack Boyd. How could you point out to them that he was much more tolerable as a corpse than as a human being. No one could – so no one tried.

Chapter 13.

Tribune reporter Paul Gray shook his head in disbelief. He ran his finger slowly down the list of calls on the logbook at the 51st Precinct. This must be one of the reasons you always hear sirens in this city, he thought, and wondered how such a small area could spawn so much trouble in just a few hours.

"Doesn't anyone in this city ever go away on vacation?" he asked the desk sergeant.

The policeman grinned at the remark and in a distinct Irish brogue replied, "Somebody in this city is going away for a long time when we unravel the murder of comedian Jack Boyd. It's unbelievable how many enemies that guy had."

Paul listened and wondered if it would be worth his time to look into this one. Boyd was a well known comedian but no one seemed to know much about his personal life. The murder was front page news and Paul thought a look into this man's private life might make good copy. Even if he didn't get a good story out of it he might get to meet some of the beautiful showgirls from the chorus line of *Gentlemen Again*. It would be worth a shot, he thought, then quickly reconsidered the use of the word "shot" and changed it to "try." That sounds a little better, he thought, and grinned as he left the police station and headed for the Ballard Theater.

* * * * *

Everything backstage at the Ballard was in turmoil. Police had been at the theater all day. Everyone had been questioned, some of them two and three times. Brian Casey felt sorry for the two detectives who talked to him. It seemed like everyone they questioned added to their confusion. One of them mentioned it was incredible that Jack Boyd could be so good on stage and so disliked by everyone off stage.

"He was a good actor," was the only comment Brian would offer them.

Paul made no attempt to hide the fact that he was a reporter. His *Tribune* press card didn't impress the security man at the stage door.

97

He had orders not to admit any unauthorized people. There was too much confusion and the director didn't want to add to the problems.

"I understand," Paul told the guard, and said he would contact the director at another time and get clearance for some interviews. He wanted to cooperate with the guard. He thought the security man might be a good source of information – but not tonight.

As he turned to leave he bumped into Marianne Gordon on her way in. She recognized the reporter right away, and was surprised and pleased to see him.

"Hi, Paul," she said.

"Marianne Gordon," he exclaimed and couldn't hide his surprise. "What are you doing here?"

"Right now I'm on a mission of mercy," she told him. "A lot of the people in this cast are friends of mine. With all the confusion here today and police all over the place, no one has had a chance to get anything to eat. While the cast is taking care of makeup and costumes I went to the deli for some sandwiches. What about you?" she asked. "What are you doing here?"

"I'm working," Paul told her. "I'm still with the *Tribune* and right now I'm on the police beat. The Jack Boyd incident caught my eye and I thought I would follow up on it for some human interest stories, but I can't get past the security guard."

Marianne hesitated a minute then said, "Gee, Paul, I never thought to get in touch with you. Let me talk to Brian Casey and see what he can work out. You wait here with Fred. I'll be right back." She headed for the director's office and even though the door was wide open she knocked anyway.

"It's me again, Brian," she said. "Can I bother you for a minute?"

"Come on in," Casey said, and quickly added, "Marianne, you're never a bother. I owe you big time for your earlier visit today. It helped a lot. What can I do for you?"

"I know you said no visitors backstage, but there is someone here who may be worth making an exception for tonight. He's a reporter with the *Tribune* and he's also a friend of mine. He's a good reporter, but more than that, he's ethical. Not the type to look for sensationalism to make a story. It might help all of us in the long run. I'm sure the Crew won't mind talking to him, and I can make sure he stays with me all the time he's here."

Brian hesitated and Marianne wondered if he understood what she was trying to do. Finally he said, "That might be a good idea. If we have to make the papers we'll be much better off to have coverage by someone we can trust. If he's a friend of yours he must be all right. Why don't you bring him in here first. I'd like to meet him." He stood up and looked around the cramped office and reconsidered. "Better still, why don't I come out with you and let Fred know it's OK for him to come in."

"Thanks, Brian, you're a sweetheart," she said as they left the office.

"Don't say that too loud," he told her, as he put his arm around her shoulder. "People might get the wrong impression and think I play both sides of the fence."

Marianne was glad Brian Casey finally realized he had nothing to hide anymore.

She introduced the two men, and Brian told Fred it was all right to admit Paul, but no one else. "Just the regulars tonight," he instructed, "No strangers, no matter who they are."

"Why don't you two talk for a few minutes," Marianne suggested. "I have to get this food to the Crew before they faint from starvation." She took the bag of sandwiches she was carrying and headed for the dressing room area. After a few steps she stopped and turned back toward the two men. "Brian, if you don't mind, please bring Paul over to the dressing room after you show him around. I'll be with him during the performance and we'll stay out of everyone's way, OK?"

"Sure," Brian answered. "Give us about ten minutes."

Paul did a quick visual appraisal of this young man and immediately liked what he saw. He was surprised that Brian Casey was so young. The reporter was under the impression all directors and producers were over the hill show people who could no longer perform. Brian laughed when Paul told him and explained that he loved to sing and dance as much as some of the cast but he had a terrible time trying to control what was commonly referred to as stage fright.

"Performing before an audience terrifies me," he said. "I decided to try directing. That way I wouldn't have to deal with the audience factor and could still be a vital part of the show. I like it better than being on stage and I'm better at it, so here I am."

He showed Paul how some of the scenery changes took place and how props were placed for easy access. He explained how they used signals and cues and how important timing was to all of them. Paul was amazed at the complexities involved and could understand the importance of having everything work on cue.

"I never realized it took all this effort to put on a show," he admitted. "There's a lot more to it than just a few songs and dances. You people make it look so easy it never dawned on me there was so much work involved."

"We earn our money," Brian assured him. "I know that's not what concerns you the most tonight. Your interest is in Jack Boyd and what happened to him, isn't that right?"

"You're partially right," Paul answered. "I'm interested in Jack Boyd, but not the performer. I want to know about the personal side of the man. Can you help me with that?"

"That's difficult," the young director replied, as he rubbed his chin and tried to think of an answer. "Jack Boyd was like two different people. On stage he was funny and did an excellent job. Off stage he was a complete opposite. He seemed to go out of his way to make people dislike him. I don't think he had any real friends. The cast tolerated him, but only because he was important to the show. It's a miserable way to go through life, but it didn't seem to bother Boyd. He acted like he enjoyed it. He had two ex-wives that I know of and he wasn't very nice to them, either. He enjoyed fighting with them, especially in public. Other than that I don't know of any family. He lived up near Central Park, I'm not sure where, but I can get the address if you need it."

"Don't go to any trouble," Paul told him. "I can get it from the police report or the paper will have it. I was interested in what kind of a person he was off stage. How did he spend his time? Who were his friends? Who were his enemies? In Boyd's case it seems like the enemies outnumber the friends."

As they went through the backstage area Brian introduced the reporter to some of the other members of the cast. Paul wondered how someone like Jack Boyd landed a part in this show when the comedian didn't fit in with these people at all. He asked Brian about it and was told the producers insisted Boyd get the part and since it was their money that backed the production their word was law.

"In the beginning we argued about it," the director confided, "but they wouldn't budge from their position. If I wanted the show to open it had to be with Boyd as the comedian.

It was difficult at times but as long as he did his job on stage I couldn't protest too much. I have to admit, as obnoxious as he was personally, he was excellent on stage."

Paul wondered if Boyd was acting when he was on stage or if the life style he chose for himself off stage was the real act. It will take a little looking into, he thought, and made a mental note to follow up on it later. When they reached the dressing room area Brian said he had to get back to work. Phil Bender was taking Boyd's place and even though he knew the routine as well as Jack Boyd, the prevailing circumstances may make him a little nervous. He left Paul with Marianne and went back to his office.

She introduced the reporter to the Crew and he couldn't help notice the special way she introduced Dan Shaw. It was plain to see these two were a lot more to each other than just friends. Marianne explained the role each of them had on stage and the family they became to each other outside of the theater. Bernie Goldman and Herb Preston were not members of the cast, but were regulars with this group. Bernie and Cass were a steady pair and Gracie didn't go far without Herb.

"Why don't you join us at Nick's tonight?" Marianne asked Paul. "You've met almost everyone in the group and it will give you a chance to get to know them a little better."

"We can tell you about some of our experiences with Boyd and perhaps supply some of the material you'll need for your story," Dan suggested.

"We guarantee you'll have a good time," Bill added. "We always do."

The invitation was a surprise. Paul didn't want to impose on these people but he didn't want to pass up a chance to get to know them better. "I'd love to go," he said, "if you're sure I won't be in the way."

"We're sure," Marianne said, and explained that the Crew was a close knit group who took good care of each other. They listened to problems and helped when they could. They smoothed each other's rough spots, built up low esteems and once in a while deflated a puffed ego. Everyone in the Crew knew there was always someone there for them, whether they needed a prompter to feed them cues, a partner to dance with or a shoulder to cry on.

Chapter 14.

Paul Gray was quiet and unassuming with a deep concern for accuracy in a job he was dedicated to doing well. Like any good reporter he paid close attention to bits of information that were often dropped inadvertently. He made sure every detail was checked thoroughly before he put it in print. Scandalous news never interested Paul, but interesting news fascinated him. The Boyd murder fell into the interesting group and the reporter was determined to find out all he could about the comedian who enjoyed making enemies of everyone he met.

Paul and Marianne had both been students at St. Monica's High School and even though he was two years ahead of her they had worked together on the school newspaper.

He recognized the same qualities that Josh Golden picked up on a few years later. She had ambition, quick wit, and the ability to make accurate judgments of people. He often wondered if it was luck or skill. He had not seen her for a few years and accidentally ran into her at the Press Photographers Ball the previous year. Neither of them wanted to be there. Both had been pushed by employers to attend. When they ran into each other things turned around and Paul thanked her for saving him from an uncomfortable evening. They promised to keep in touch, but never did. Now, another chance meeting and she came to his rescue again.

He spent some quality time with the Crew before the performance that evening. Information he gathered from other cast members led him to believe Brian Casey was accurate in his description of the departed comedian. Everyone seemed to characterize Jack Boyd in the same way. Paul thought it was strange all the opinions were so close in every detail. It looked as if Boyd had purposely set it up that way. If that was true, he wondered what the reasoning behind it could be. Why would anyone want to alienate himself so completely? He tried not to ask too many questions. Sometimes more information came from listening than prying. Everyone knew he was a reporter and why he was here. Marianne helped by letting the cast know he was her friend.

As curtain time grew closer she suggested they wait in the wings and he could see how Brian Casey guided his whole cast through each performance. She knew you had to witness him in action to realize what a good job he did.

Phil Bender was new to the show but with the special touch of this director and a little help and encouragement from the cast he did very well. To everyone's surprise he was a lot better than Jack Boyd in several of the routines. Boyd had the nasty habit of putting in ad-libs and sometimes it threw the timing off for the other performers. Phil Bender stuck with the script and made life easier for everyone on stage.

Police seemed to be everywhere and confusion was rampant. Brian Casey's dedication to perfection pulled them through and the show went off without a hitch. It was a long, tedious day and everyone in the Crew was looking forward to a little relaxation at Nick's. Marianne was glad Paul had agreed to go along. She introduced him to George and watched for a reaction from the maitre d' when she told him Paul was a reporter. George didn't act a bit surprised and she wondered if he knew Paul like he seemed to know everyone else in this city.

Jack Boyd was the main topic of conversation. Paul listened carefully and tried to remember who said what and when. It was a very interesting evening and after an hour or so with the Crew at Nick's he realized what a close knit group they were. He had gone to the Ballard Theater and had run into an old friend. Before the night was over he felt as though he had gained a dozen new friends. They treated him as if he had always been a part of this group. It was a nice feeling and he could understand why Marianne felt so strongly about these people. He liked the way they watched out for each other. If any member of this group was responsible for the crime the police would have their hands full trying to prove it. They all seemed to be open and honest about everything. He was annoyed at himself for even thinking any of them could be involved.

Marianne was positive no one in this group was responsible for any part of the crime. On the night of the murder the Crew was together until the early hours of the morning, but that was their regular routine. She knew Paul Gray was looking for the guilty party and wondered how long it would take him to realize no one in the Crew had anything to do with it.

*****

Paul was looking for information on Jack Boyd's background and asked Vinny Malzone, the young man in charge of the *Tribune's* archives to find any stories the paper had concerning the murdered comedian. He was surprised when less than thirty minutes later the phone on his desk rang and he was told his material was ready.

"Boy, Vinny, you're good," Paul said as he looked through the stack of items the researcher handed him. "You even included the ads from Boyd's old shows. This is great."

"You said you wanted everything," Vinny reminded him, "so I gave you everything."

He shrugged his shoulders and started to walk away then added, "Everything that was in the paper."

Paul began to thumb through the material and stopped when he realized what Vinny had said. "Do you know something about Jack Boyd that wasn't in the paper?" he asked.

"Forget I said anything," the researcher answered quickly as he scanned the room to see if anyone was within hearing range. Paul could see that Vinny didn't want him to forget it. He seemed anxious to tell what he knew, but was uneasy about sharing it with anyone.

The reporter leaned across the waist high counter that separated the main room from the archive files. "Vinny," he said quietly, "if you know anything about Boyd that will help me figure out this mess, don't hold back on it now."

Still reluctant to say anymore, Vinny replied, "Maybe it has nothing to do with the murder."

"Why don't you tell me what you know," Paul suggested. He wanted every scrap of information he could gather but he didn't want to coerce anyone into talking. Vinny knew Paul Gray's reputation, but he was wary about getting involved. Paul didn't pressure him any further, but waited silently for an answer.

"I need my job here," Vinny told him as he busied himself with a stack of papers and glanced around the room again. "If it ever got out that I told you anything I'd probably get in trouble. I can't afford that." He was apprehensive, but he knew he could trust this reporter, and reconsidered. "If I tell you what I know will you promise never to tell how you found out?"

"You have my word on it," Paul promised.

Vinny was still nervous and glanced around again to make sure no one could overhear. He leaned across his side of the counter and began his story. "About twelve years ago my father was a grounds keeper at Belmont Academy. You know, that fancy boys' school upstate where all the rich kids go. There was a big fuss there about some boys getting mixed up with other boys." He looked at Paul to see if he needed to explain any further and seemed embarrassed to say more. "You know what I mean, don't you?"

"Homosexuality?" Paul asked.

"Yeah, that's it," Vinny said, relieved that Paul said the word for him. "Jack Boyd was a student there and he was up to his eyeballs in it. The kids involved came from rich families and their money got the whole thing squashed real quick. It never made the papers. Most of the help got fired and were replaced by people who didn't know about the problems. My father lost his job and so did a lot of other good people who worked there. I guess the school was afraid they'd tell somebody and the whole scandal would come out. I don't know how the scheme worked, but Jack Boyd was one of the kingpins and he got kicked out of the school. A couple of years ago my father saw an ad for one of Boyd's shows and recognized his picture. He didn't know the name because in school he wasn't Jack Boyd, he was Boyd Jackman."

"Holy Jesus!" Paul exclaimed in wide eyed surprise. "Are you talking about the Jackmann Hotels and Resorts people?"

"You got it," Vinny acknowledged.

"Wow!" Paul said with a low whistle. "The more I find out about this guy the sorrier I am I ever started digging."

"Just remember, Paul, you promised you didn't hear any of this from me," Vinny reminded him.

"Don't worry," Paul assured him. "You've got my word on it." He knew Vinny was worried and thought maybe he could approach this from a different angle. He wanted another way to get the facts he needed and not involve Vinny at all. "Would you mind if I talked to your father?" he asked. "I don't want to get you in the middle of anything and I won't mention knowing you. I'd like to find out more about this school scandal and I think your father may be able to supply the information I need. Why don't you tell me how I can get in touch with him?"

"I don't know about this," Vinny remarked and Paul thought he asked the wrong question and may have shut off his source. "My father would probably love that," Vinny said. "He'll talk to anybody who will listen to him. Just don't let him know that you know me."

"Thanks," Paul said, "Don't worry. I won't mention you. I owe you big time for this."

"You don't owe me anything. Let's call it a 'get even' for my father." Vinny told him.

Paul left the office with a phone number for Antonio Malzone, Vinny's father, tucked in his pocket. He intended to call and ask if he could see him. He didn't want to explain too much on the phone. He liked to watch the reactions of the people he interviewed. Sometimes he got more from their body language than from their conversation. He was sure this was a side of Jack Boyd that no one knew and he wanted to find out more about it.

Antonio Malzone lived in a small cottage in a quiet section of Staten Island. The ferry ride from New York City to the Island gave Paul time to go over the material he already had. He liked the idea of opening a new door to Jack Boyd's past. He was certain there was more to this man than what the public saw.

The former grounds keeper was happy to talk to Paul. He told him about his job at Belmont Academy and his confusion with the stage name that Jack Boyd was using. "I saw his picture in an ad and at first I thought it was a coincidence," he said, "So I went to see the show and there he was, big as life, right there on the stage in front of me." The former groundskeeper said he felt sorry for the youngster when he was at school. "He was a real loner. No one ever came to visit him and he never went home, not even on the holidays. It seemed like his family wanted a place to put him where he'd be taken care of, but out of their way." He shook his head as if to say he still felt sorry for this kid who was left out of everything.

"I wish I could say he was a nice kid, but he wasn't," he told the reporter. "He got into one mess after another. His family would send someone to straighten it out and then it would start all over again with something else." He was not sure how this final episode worked, but he knew that Boyd Jackmann was the brains behind what went on and it was serious enough to have the boy expelled. "Even the Jackmann money couldn't buy him back in," he said.

Paul asked if he could remember any of the other students involved. The old man wrinkled his brow, and after a little thought came up with a list of names. He said there were a lot more, but he was positive of the ones he gave the reporter. Paul was amazed at the prominent names on the list and asked how he could remember all of them so well.

Antonio Malzone sat back in his chair and lit a funny little Italian cigar. "I loved my job at the Academy," he said. "I was there almost ten years. As long as I was an employee I had a little house right on the grounds. It was a good place to raise a family. I had special flower beds and I even grew vegetables in my back yard. It was the best job I ever had and I didn't like losing it because some punk kid couldn't stay out of trouble."

He talked for more than an hour about his experiences at the school and mentioned many of the people he met while he was there. He seemed to enjoy the nostalgia and the chance to talk to someone who would really listen to him.

Paul thanked him for all his help and said he would check into it and see what he could find. Mr. Malzone gave him names, addresses and phone numbers of other people who worked at Belmont Academy and lost their job when he did. The reporter scanned the list but none of the names were familiar.

On his way back to New York Paul couldn't help thinking the more he found out about Jack Boyd or Boyd Jackmann or whoever he was, the more complex the case became.

* * * * *

It was close to 11 p.m. when Paul got back to Manhattan. The performance at the Ballard would be over. He thought he might find the Crew at Nick's so he headed for the restaurant. As usual, George was at the reservations desk. Paul asked if any of the Crew would be there tonight.

"They're here often, but not every night," the maitre d' said. "Occasionally, if the group is going to be large, they will call and let me know so I can have tables ready. So far tonight I haven't heard from anyone, but you are welcome to wait if you wish."

"Maybe I will," Paul said, "For a little while anyway. I'd like to talk to Marianne tonight." He noticed the concerned look on George's face and quickly added, "We're old friends from high school days."

"Really," George commented with a raised eyebrow and a touch of skepticism in his voice. Paul picked up on the implication right away and explained that he knew Marianne from a few years back. In high school she regarded him as one of her brothers. "Dan Shaw is a lucky guy. I hope he realizes it."

"I'm sure he does," the maitre d' said. This news seemed to melt his frosty, strictly business attitude toward the reporter and he invited Paul to join him at the desk for a cup of coffee. George left to show some new arrivals to a table and Paul sat in the chair behind the desk.

"Can we have a table for four?" a familiar voice asked. He looked up to see Dan Shaw, Marianne Gordon and Bill and Jen Flanagan.

"Did you get tired of your job at the *Tribune*?" Marianne asked.

"Not yet," he answered with a grin as he got up from the chair to join them. "I wasn't sure you were going to show up tonight. It was too late to go to the theater and I wanted to talk to you about a few things I found out today. Do you mind?"

"We're glad to see you," Dan told him. "We're all anxious to compare notes, but we're all hungry, too. Let's order something first, then we can talk. If you want to wait a few minutes you can fill everybody in at the same time. The rest of the Crew will be along within a half hour."

Paul watched the faces of the people around the table as he filled them in on his progress. The better he got to know this group the more certain he was that none of them was directly involved. Four days had passed since Jack Boyd was killed. The police were no closer to solving the crime now than the day it happened.

"It seems like everybody he met wanted to kill him at one time or another," the reporter said. "Too many suspects are worse than none at all. The police aren't saying much. They won't even release the time of death. Nobody knows if it was Thursday night or Friday morning. The cleaning lady found him about eleven Friday morning. No one had seen him since the performance Thursday night. That's what has the police puzzled. They can't find anyone who saw him leave the theater. So they're not releasing much information. I thought if we could pool what we know we might be able to come up with something worth a second look"

"I'm tired of even talking about Jack Boyd," Jen said. "I hate to be disrespectful of the dead, but this show is better off without him."

"We all agree," Bill added, "but if we can help clear up this mess everyone will be relieved."

Herb and Bernie thought Paul was closer to finding the culprit than the police. Paul cautioned them to be aware that the police are not telling all they know.

"They'll wait and try to trip someone up on a detail or question them a second time and compare their answers with the first time around," he told them. "Murder investigations are complicated and the police are experts at nit picking."

He told them what he learned from Antonio Malzone about Jack Boyd's problems at Belmont Academy. Boyd's real name was a surprise to everyone.

"With a reputation like that I don't think I would want to be on the stage," Herb said.

"That's one of the problems with this case," Paul told them. "Boyd spent his life doing what everyone else would shy away from. It doesn't make any sense at all."

Marianne had been listening to all the theories passed among them and had not commented on any of it. She leaned over and quietly whispered in Dan's ear, "I have to talk to you – right now – dance with me, please."

Dan gave her a surprised look and wondered what was wrong. All of a sudden, in the middle of an important conversation she decided she wanted to dance. She must have a good reason, he thought.

When they reached the dance floor Marianne quietly told him she was worried and didn't want anyone to overhear what she had to say.

"No one can hear us from here," he assured her.

"Paul just said the police are not releasing the time of death. They're not telling anyone when Boyd was shot. Not even saying whether it was Thursday night or Friday morning. Did I understand him correctly?" she asked.

"That's the way it came across to me," he answered.

"Danny," she said, "I know when he was shot."

"What do you mean, 'you know'? How could you know? You were with me?"

"Somebody told me. That's how I know."

"Who?" he asked with concern.

"Fred," she answered.

"Fred who?" Dan asked and couldn't hide the feeling Marianne might know something that could put her in danger.

"The security guard at the stage door," she said.

"How would he know?" Dan asked, and couldn't hide the concern in his voice.

"That is exactly what I was wondering," she said. "When I got to the theater Friday night I asked Fred why all the police cars were out front. He said they were there because of Jack Boyd. I thought Boyd had insulted someone again and they were making a fuss over it like the time he pinched that lady and she turned out to be married to some ambassador. When I asked who he insulted this time, Fred said, - and these are his exact words – 'Seems like somebody killed him. Shot him twice sometime late last night.' If the police are not releasing the time of this thing, how did Fred know it happened late Thursday night? And why did he say 'shot twice'? Why didn't he just say somebody shot him and let it go at that?"

"That's a good question," Dan replied and held her a little tighter as if he wanted to protect her. They were quiet for a minute and subconsciously kept in step with the music.

"Marianne," Dan asked, "how much do you trust Paul?"

"What do you mean, how much do I trust him? What kind of a question is that?" she asked.

"We don't know how to handle this kind of information," he told her. "We don't even know what to do with it. This is the kind of thing Paul deals with all the time. Do you trust him enough to ask for his help in clearing it up?"

"I trust Paul completely," she answered, "but I don't want to point a finger at Fred. I don't know if he did anything wrong. I certainly don't want to cause him any trouble. I don't remember ever seeing him even talk to Jack Boyd."

"I think we should let Paul know about it and see what he says," Dan suggested. "He's been digging into this for a couple of days and he knows more than he's telling anyone."

They left the dance floor and went back to the group at the table. Marianne told the reporter about her conversation with Fred on Friday.

"The time frame could have been something he assumed," Paul told them, "But I'm not so sure about the 'shot twice' statement." He explained that in his business you learn never to take anything for granted. He took out a small notebook and asked for Fred's last name.

"I don't know what it is," Marianne said and looked at Dan for help.

"I don't know it either," Dan said. "I just know him as Fred."

Paul asked around the table and none of the Crew knew the guard's last name. Even Cass, who knew everyone at the theater, had to admit she had never heard anyone mention it.

"Brian will know," Marianne said. "He should be here any time now."

"Where is he?" Paul asked.

Marianne told him the police asked the director to drop off several notes Jack Boyd left for him at the theater. They wanted to compare Boyd's handwriting with some papers they found at his apartment.

"I hope that's the real reason," Paul said doubtfully. "From what I hear the police think Brian is holding out on them."

"Brian Casey is no more guilty than I am," Marianne said angrily. "Every one of us knows where he was and if Fred is right about the time, Brian was right here with us."

"I agree with you," Paul said. "I don't think he had anything to do with it either. The police can be hard to convince on something like this. It's a good thing he told them the truth and didn't try to hide anything when they questioned him Friday or they would have crucified him by now. He surprised them and let the air out of their theory when he was so open about his friends." The reporter chuckled as he said, "You people sent the police into a tailspin when you let them know you all knew about Brian's habits. The detectives I talked with were sure Boyd was threatening Brian with exposure if he was ever replaced in the show. You know that's not true. It was the producers who kept Boyd in the show. Brian would have dumped him in a minute if he could."

It was after midnight and Brian Casey had not arrived yet. Twelve-thirty came and there was still no sign of the director. Cass couldn't stand the waiting any longer and went to George with the problem.

"Do you know anyone you can call to make sure the police are not giving Brian a hard time?" she asked.

"Let me see what I can do," George said and picked up the phone on his reservations desk. Twenty minutes later Casey joined the Crew at Nick's. Cass rewarded George with a grateful hug and everyone agreed the maitre d' blushed, then quickly regained his aplomb and denied any participation in the young director's quick exit from Police Headquarters.

Paul quickly filled Brian in on the information he had gathered, including the incident with Fred and the time frame. "Do you know Fred's last name?" he asked. "Sure," Brian told him, "It's Covington."

The reporter took out the lists that Antonio Malzone supplied and scanned the names of the employees who had lost their jobs. There was no Covington on the top list and they were all disappointed.

Before putting the papers away Paul glanced quickly at his other list of names, students who had been involved with Boyd. The fifth name on the list was Stuart Covington. It was not a common name and although the names were the same he still had to find a connection. He realized not much could be done at one o'clock in the morning and promised to have more news for them after the next show. He suggested they meet again the following night. If he found anything significant before then he would call Dan. He cautioned all of them not to mention a word to anyone about Marianne's disclosure. He wanted to talk to Dan about the position she was in, but he didn't want to scare them. When he got the chance he quietly said, "I know you have a performance tonight, but I don't think it's a good idea for Marianne to be alone until we can clear this up."

Dan agreed with him, "I've been thinking the same thing since she told me about her conversation with Fred. She doesn't realize the danger she could be in."

"We may not have a thing to worry about," Paul said. "Fred may be completely innocent. Until we know for sure we can't afford to take any chances. If he's guilty and he remembers what he said, he may be scared enough to do something foolish."

"Don't worry," Dan told him. "I won't let her out of my sight. Better still, we'll all make sure she is not left alone until we hear from you."

Dan explained his concerns to Marianne and she agreed to stay with him. She could see he was worried and she didn't want to cause him any more concern so she went along with his suggestion. As Dan unlocked the apartment door Marianne looked at him and said, "This is stupid, I don't have clean clothes for tomorrow or anything to sleep in tonight. I really should go home."

Dan was not going to lose this argument. "Please go along with me on this. Fred may not be guilty of anything, but we're not sure. There's too much coincidence here, and I don't want to take any chances where you're concerned. The same last name as one of the students, making the remark about the time of the killing, and saying Boyd was shot twice, is a little too much. If Fred comes from a family who can afford to send a boy to Belmont Academy what is he doing working as a security guard? It doesn't add up and I don't want you out of my sight until we have some reasonable answers."

She knew he was right but she didn't want him to know how frightened she really was. She tried to put a little humor in her tone as she said, "Do you expect me to stay here tonight and wear the same clothes tomorrow? Or do you have something I can borrow to wear to the office?"

"What I would like you to do," he said, "is to stay here for the rest of tonight. In the morning we can drive over to Jersey and get what clothes you may need in case you have to stay here for a day or two. I'll explain to your aunt what's going on, and I'm sure she will understand. For tonight grab a pair of my pajamas from the second drawer. We'll take care of tomorrow in the morning."

She had to admit Dan had a good argument. She was concerned, too. She was also afraid she was putting him in danger and was furious at herself for telling him what Fred had said to her.

Dan laughed when he saw her standing in the bedroom doorway in his pajamas.

"I admit they are a little big," she said, "but I didn't think they looked that funny."

He looked at her, shook his head and laughed. He noticed her attitude had softened and he breathed a sigh of relief. "You could roll up the legs a little," he said with a chuckle. Every step she took added a comic touch to the situation. The legs were so long they covered her feet. The top wasn't a much better fit. The sleeves hung down over each hand. She padded across the living room, sat on the edge of the sofa and he helped her roll up the legs of the pajama pants.

"That's better," Dan said. "At least now you can move around without breaking your neck."

"My hero," she teased as she rumpled his hair. When she sat down she noticed the extra pillow and blanket on the end of the sofa. "What's this for?" she asked as she pointed to them.

"You take the bed, and I'll sleep out here," he said.

"I thought the idea behind me staying here tonight was so you could keep an eye on me?" she questioned.

"It is," he assured her.

"Well, how can you do that from out here?" she asked. "You had better put these back in the closet," she told him as she patted the extra pillow, "and come into bed where you belong."

"Good idea," he agreed, and smiled as he thought, sometimes it really pays to let her have her own way.

Chapter 15

Paul Gray knew George was more than just a headwaiter. As far as the Crew were concerned he was a fountain of knowledge with extraordinary connections throughout the city. The reporter lingered after the others had decided to call it a night. He had broken the ice with George earlier in the evening, and thought he could get more information if he talked with the maitre d' after the late customers had gone. Since his position with Marianne was clarified and George was sure there was no romantic intent, he welcomed the reporter's company.

Paul told him about matching the names on the two lists and George didn't seem surprised. Jack Boyd's real name didn't surprise him either. When Paul asked him about it, he was told it was common knowledge in the theater district. The reporter wrinkled his brow in disbelief and said, "None of the Crew knew a thing about it."

"The Crew," George explained, "is a very unique group. They pay no attention to names or social standings or even worldly assets. They all possess remarkable talents. However, that is where their appraisals end. If you fit with the group you are immediately accepted. If you don't fit, no amount of money or influence can buy your acceptance. It's as simple as that," he stated.

He noticed Paul's inquisitive look and remembered this reporter was new to the group.

"Allow me to explain," he continued, and seemed to enjoy sharing his observations. "Each of them has a different background, but *Gentlemen Again* gave them a common bond that unites them closer than many families."

"Harriet is from a wealthy old New England Puritan family. Jen's father is a stevedore on the Hoboken docks. Cass has been an orphan most of her life. Gracie is the only daughter of a Midwestern farmer. Marge is worldly and in many ways, street wise. Of course you are familiar with our young friend, Marianne, the workaholic of the Crew."

George couldn't hide the traces of a discreet smile when he noticed Paul's renewed interest in a group he thought he knew. "As for the men," he continued, "They are as varied as the girls. Alan is a musical genius, unaffected by his fabulous talent or his overindulgence. Before he became part of this group his only family was his piano. Julian is the son of a Southern sharecropper. His voice is worthy of the Metropolitan but he prefers Broadway. Herb is an honest man in a difficult field, but his good judgment and stability promise an excellent future. Bernie is a born salesman. No matter what the product, Bernie will find a buyer for it. However, his claims of a Kosher background are doubted each time he enjoys a ham sandwich. Bill is extremely talented. His Irish heritage has instilled a compulsion for independence. I'm sure you know who Dan is," he concluded.

"How would I know who he is?" Paul asked, "I just met him a few days ago."

"You don't recognize the name?" George asked surprised.

"No, I don't," Paul admitted. "Should I?"

"Dan Shaw and his older sister are the only heirs to the Shaw Pharmaceutical fortune. Need I say more?" the older man asked as if to imply the name didn't need explaining.

"HOLY JESUS!" Paul exclaimed as his chin dropped and his mouth hung open. He couldn't hide the surprise that came with this disclosure. "He must be worth millions," the reporter commented. When the total shock subsided he looked at the older man, who was very amused at his astonished expression, and asked seriously, "Does Marianne know who he is?"

"Oh, I imagine she does," George answered casually, "but knowing her it wouldn't make any difference. To all of them he is just another one of the Crew. I told you they were a very unique group," he concluded with a chuckle.

"I never dreamed they were that unique," Paul said as he tried to digest all George had told him. His job as a reporter was interesting, but since the investigation of Jack Boyd's death began he was exposed to a totally different aspect of how some people lived. As he sat across the table from this prodigious, gray haired man, he wondered how it was possible for him to know so much about everyone when he always seemed to be at the restaurant. He certainly must have his connections, Paul thought.

While George was saying good night to a few of his late customers, Paul tried to match faces with the facts he had just learned.

Every face in the Crew seemed to match the character description that was presented. Every one, except Dan Shaw. Paul could only picture him as the quiet, easy going singer from a hit Broadway musical. It was impossible to imagine this soft spoken, down to earth young man as the controlling factor in a corporate dynasty. Looks can be deceiving, he thought, and wondered if Marianne knew about Dan's background. He made a mental note to find out. He tried to sort out what he had learned in the past twenty four hours and realized each piece of information he uncovered generated another set of questions.

He wondered if Dan had persuaded Marianne to stay with him. If not, where did she go? He wanted to call Dan and ask, but thought if he did he would be interfering. When he thought about Dan Shaw his brain kept reminding him who this talented young singer really was. He had a hard time trying to connect the two personalities. That was not an important issue now, he thought. The Covington connection was the thing he should be concentrating on. The answer to that might be the solution to Jack Boyd's death.

Paul's body was telling him he needed sleep, but his mind was so full of information it wouldn't let him rest. He decided to go back to the *Tribune* and see if he could piece together some of the information he collected. Things that didn't make any sense yesterday made a whole lot of sense today. He had to find a common thread that would tie them all together. He intended to talk to Vinny Malzone as soon as the researcher arrived at the office. Maybe Vinny could find something that would connect the names. He had a lot of information and thought some of it should be turned over to the police. He wasn't sure how far he could dig without getting in the way of their investigation, and he didn't want to create any unnecessary problems. He wanted to locate a detective he could trust and get some input on how to sort out what he already knew. The self righteous attitude the detectives displayed toward Brian Casey annoyed him. Paul was positive the young director had nothing to do with the murder but two of the detectives investigating the case seemed intent on connecting him to it in some way. He knew he could trust Mac McCarthy, the desk sergeant at the 51st Precinct. He wasn't sure if Mac would be working tonight, and decided to try the police station before going to the paper.

As the reporter walked into the station house, the booming voice of the desk sergeant announced, "Look who blessed us with his presence! Did the show business kings and queens tell you to go back to your own neighborhood?"

Paul laughed and said they were jealous because he was having a good time with the beautiful showgirls from the chorus line of *Gentlemen Again* and they were stuck looking at each other.

"What brings you back to these humble surroundings at five in the morning?" the sergeant inquired.

Paul shrugged his shoulders as he sat down opposite him. He waited until the other two policemen left the room and leaned over toward the sergeant. "Mac, I have a problem," he confided. "I have to talk to somebody assigned to the Boyd case, but I don't know who I can trust. Some of the detectives working that case are pretty hard to convince when it comes to telling them something they don't want to hear. Is there anyone you can recommend?"

The sergeant pushed aside the papers he was working on and looked at the reporter. "What's bothering you, Paul?" he asked.

The reporter gave him the facts he had learned so far. He was careful not to mention any names or sources of information, and Sergeant McCarthy had to smile at the reporter's discretion.

"Most of what you said is already old news here," the policeman told him. "I'm not so sure about this Covington angle. That's a new one on me. That Boyd character had so many enemies it will take the homicide boys forever to check them all." Mac McCarthy frowned and ran the palm of his hand across his chin. He looked at the reporter and said, "I know one of the boys assigned to that case. Maybe you should talk to him. If he thinks it's worth anything he'll tell you how to handle it."

"Thanks, Mac," Paul said, relieved that at last he could get some help with the mass of information he had uncovered. While the sergeant made a phone call, the reporter flipped through his notebook.

The sergeant motioned for him to come over to the desk. "He wants to talk to you," he said.

Paul looked at the officer with a worried expression as if to say, "Can I trust him?" Mac sensed his uneasiness and told him to talk freely, the detective was his nephew, Mark McCarthy.

Paul repeated the information he had given the desk sergeant. He told the detective he intended to see what the archives of the paper had about the Covingtons, but couldn't do it for another hour or two. They decided to meet at the *Tribune* and go over everything together.

* * * * *

The reporter and the detective were so engrossed in the material Paul accumulated they didn't notice the other people drifting into the newspaper office a few at a time. They didn't see Vinny Malzone until he came by the desk and said, "Good morning."

"Hi Vinny," Paul answered. "You're the guy we're looking for. This is Detective Mark McCarthy. We need some help if you don't mind."

"I don't mind," Vinny assured him. "How can I help you?"

Paul said they needed any information he could find in the archives about the Covington family.

"I remember something about a Covington who died a few years ago," Vinny said.

"Give me a couple of minutes and let me see if I can find it." He left the two men and disappeared among the shelves of the indexed material.

"If there was ever anything in print about any Covington, this guy will find it," Paul told the detective.

In less than ten minutes Vinny reappeared with a stack of newspaper articles. Paul smiled and said, "I told you he was good."

As they started their search Vinny handed them one more item. "This is the latest thing we have," he told them, and handed Paul an obituary notice for Stuart Covington. They read the item and noticed the young man was only twenty-three years old when he died suddenly at the family's summer home in Maine.

Mark said that the term 'died suddenly' was a polite way of evading the cause of death in obituary notices. It was often used to cover questionable deaths like accidents, suicides or anything out of the ordinary. Let me make a phone call and see what this Covington 'died suddenly' really means."

"Before you make that phone call look at this," Paul said as he handed the detective the newspaper clipping. In addition to his parents, the obituary stated, the young man was survived by his grandfather, Frederick Covington, retired President and former Chairman of the Board of Cove Industries.

"Do you have any idea who these people are?" Mark asked. Before Paul could answer he added, "We're talking about BIG – and I mean BIG business, BIG money and BIG influence. If this man is connected to Boyd's case in any way we're going to have one hell of a job trying to make anything stick." The detective was not happy about this discovery but he intended to follow it regardless of how much influence was involved.

"Keep poking through that material until I can get some more details on this obituary," he instructed. "You'll probably find a lot more, now that we have a tie in."

The detective made a series of calls while Paul sorted through the research material. "Now we have to wait for answers," he said. "Shouldn't take more than twenty minutes or maybe a half hour. In the meantime we may as well see what we can learn about the Covington family."

Vinny's thorough research gave them a pile of information. There were items on everything from family weddings to corporate mergers. By the time the detective's calls came back he was familiar with many of the Covington holdings.

Mark's partner at Headquarters had contacted the Chief of Police in the small Maine town where the Covington summer home was located. The Chief told him the young man's death was a suicide. He also said Stuart had been the grandfather's favorite since he was a baby. He went to a fancy boys school for a couple of years and when he came back he had changed considerably. He became nervous and depressed. The family tried everything from psychiatrists to quacks to help him but he got worse instead of better. When young Covington died the grandfather had a breakdown and was hospitalized. The money and influence of that family hushed the whole thing up quickly. For the last couple of years everything about them has been on a low key basis. They still have the summer home, but seldom use it. The Chief said he would check the place out and call back in an hour or so.

The detective also contacted the security company where Fred Covington was employed as a guard. His fingerprints were on file, but there was very little other information. The company had checked for any police record and as long as there was none they didn't ask any other questions. They gave the detective an address for the guard and that was all they had.

"Paul, I think we've gone as far as we can here," the detective told him. "I'd like to take what we have back to headquarters and see if there is enough to bring Covington in for questioning. In the meantime, caution your friends to be careful and above all, to keep quiet about this until we can pick this guy up. You did a great job in digging up all this material. Now, I want to see if we can make some sense out of it. I'll keep in touch and let you know if and when we get him. If you come across anything else, give me a call."

When the detective left, Paul couldn't subdue the yawn he had been holding back for quite some time. He realized how tired he was and decided to go home for a few hours of much needed sleep. It felt like he had just put his head on the pillow when the telephone next to the bed shattered the silence of his room. Only half awake he fumbled for the receiver. "Hello," he muttered and tried to blink the sleep from his half opened eyes.

"Hi Paul," Detective Mark McCarthy said. "Sorry to wake you but I promised to keep you up to date on this Covington matter and a lot has been happening down here."

The reporter shook himself awake and stifled a yawn as he listened to the detective. The material they had put together earlier was substantiated during the day and there was enough to bring Fred Covington in for questioning.

"They found him in his summer place in Maine," the detective said. "He didn't put up any resistance, in fact, he told the Maine officers all about the murder. He said he got the security job so he could watch Boyd until he had a chance to shoot him. It seems he had been planning this thing since his grandson's suicide. It started years ago when Stuart Covington was in school. He got mixed up with Boyd in some kind of a scheme that caused his grandson endless problems. The old man kept repeating that Jack Boyd killed his grandson and he killed Boyd before he could hurt anyone else. The Maine police could see he needed help. He was completely out of it. They notified his family and are keeping him in protective custody there until they see whether he goes to jail or to a hospital. I'm betting he doesn't spend an hour in jail. As far as we're concerned the case is closed."

"Wow!" Paul exclaimed. "That's terrific. All our work really paid off."

"It sure did," Mark agreed. "I wanted to say thanks for all your help. You supplied a lot of information that tied things together enough for us to make a case. If you ever need a favor just let me know."

"I need one now," Paul said. "I need an exclusive on this story."

"You've got it." Mark assured him.

"Thanks," Paul replied, "It was nice working with you." He chuckled as he added, "I'm sure our bosses will appreciate the cooperation between the paper and the police."

He hung up the phone and sat on the side of the bed trying to figure out his next move. He had to get to the paper and get his story in right away. First, he had to let Dan Shaw know that Marianne was out of danger. He called the number Dan had given him and couldn't get an answer. He glanced at the clock and saw it was after seven. The Crew would be at the theater getting ready for the performance. He called the theater and left word for Dan to call him at the paper as soon as possible. After a quick shower he dressed and headed for the *Tribune*.

When Dan returned his call Paul relayed exactly what the detective told him. He said there was no longer anything to worry about as far as Marianne being in danger. Fred was in custody and probably didn't remember talking to her at all.

"I think we did the right thing in taking the precautions," he said. "You never can tell in this kind of a situation."

Dan thanked him and breathed a sigh of relief. "That's great," he said. "Will we see you after the show tonight?"

The reporter hesitated for a minute then said, "I can't make it tonight, I have a lot of material to get ready for the paper. The *Trib* is still my bread and butter and I have to stick with this until it's completely wrapped up. I'll see you at Nick's tomorrow night, OK?"

"Fine," Dan answered, "Then we can get all our questions answered and put this mess behind us. I'll let the rest of the Crew know what's happened and we'll count on seeing you tomorrow."

Dan didn't say a word to Marianne about Paul's phone call. He told Bill and Julian and said he wasn't going to tell her. "If anything goes wrong I don't want her in the middle of it. Let's keep it to yourselves until I get her out of here tonight, OK?"

Bill and Julian looked at each other and then looked at him and smiled as they both answered, "Sure."

Dan and Marianne left the theater less than ten minutes after the last curtain call. "I feel like I'm being kidnapped," she joked.

"Pretend we're eloping," he suggested.

"What?" she asked.

"Never mind," he said with a chuckle. "Let's call it a necessary precaution." He wondered if somehow she knew about the arrest. If she asked him about Fred he'd tell her the truth. He wouldn't lie to her, but he wasn't going to volunteer any information that would encourage her to go home. He had convinced her to stay with him until Fred was either cleared or arrested, and as far as he was concerned he was going to continue it for as long as possible. She didn't seem to mind and he wondered if her initial protest was real or to let him think he had won an argument. Either way it gave him a legitimate excuse to prolong the arrangement. He loved the time they had together and knew she did, too. He also knew she would never admit it.

Bill and Julian told the rest of the Crew about Paul's phone call. They also told them Dan was not telling Marianne until tomorrow.

"Chalk one up for Dan!" Cass said with a grin, "Good for him."

"Remember," Julian cautioned, "We will all have to keep his secret."

The following night Paul was welcomed like royalty when he arrived at Nick's. He told the Crew everything that had happened and gave them all the details he knew.

"We're all relieved this Boyd situation is finally over," Herb said. "We weren't even aware that Fred knew Jack Boyd. He certainly was a good actor."

"Under the circumstances," Bill added, "He was probably a lot better than any of us."

"I'm glad the whole thing is behind us," Jen commented. "Now maybe we can go back to our regular routines without having to look over our shoulders all the time."

Marianne listened to all the comments about the bizarre case and finally asked, "When did the police arrest Fred?"

"A little before six last night," Paul said. He saw the looks on the faces of everyone around the table and realized that Dan must not have told her about the arrest. He quickly added, "but he wasn't formally charged until early this morning."

She looked at Dan, who seemed to be waiting for her next question and asked, "Did you know about this last night?"

"Yes," he admitted, "but I didn't want to say anything until I was sure."

"Oh," she said, "Just when did you plan on saying something?"

Dan could tell she knew he purposely delayed giving her the news and he didn't want her to be angry. He glanced at her from the corner of his eye and said, "Probably tomorrow morning."

"Tomorrow?" she questioned. "But I can go home tonight."

"I know," he said quietly. "That's why I was going to tell you tomorrow."

Marianne shook her head but didn't say anything. She noticed the smiles on every face around the table. She pushed her chair back and stood up. Dan thought she was angry until he saw her smile.

"How about a dance, Mr. Shaw?" she asked and watched Dan's face as the corners of his mouth curled upward and the little lines next to his eyes crinkled together in a happy pleased smile.

"Absolutely," he quickly agreed.

As they walked between the tables to the dance floor Bill remarked that it was nice to see Dan win one once in a while.

"What do you mean, 'once in a while'?" Jen asked. "I think Marianne does a good job of keeping him happy. Look at them, can't you tell."

The Crew watched as Dan and Marianne enjoyed the closeness of a slow dance. He held her secure and protected in his arms, and she knew this was one place she would always be safe.

"I guess you're right," Bill conceded. "They both look pretty contented." He reached for his wife's hand and they joined the other couples on the dance floor. Things were finally getting back to normal with this group.

Paul wondered if some things a reporter discovers would be better off left as unknowns. Like the once buried scandal of Belmont Academy. Who would it help to bring it all out in the open? It wouldn't bring back Stuart Covington, or undo the damage his suicide did to Fred, his grandfather. It wouldn't change the miserable reputation Jack Boyd had built for himself, or even restore a job for Vinny Malzone's father. Why not leave it all buried.

A reporter walks a tight rope. If he prints everything he discovers people get hurt. If he doesn't print it people still get hurt. He wondered if he had the right to publish secrets kept hidden over the years to guard an identity or rectify a mistake?

George knew all about Dan Shaw's background, his family and the extent of his wealth. But a secret was always safe with George. On the other hand, was this really a secret? The whole Crew knew about it. Paul was still not sure if Marianne knew, and if not, should he tell her? Maybe he should talk to Dan and let him be the one to tell her. He saw Dan handle other troublesome problems with no apparent difficulty. He could probably deal with this one, too. Maybe George was right, he thought, it wouldn't matter anyhow.

Paul also knew how to keep a secret. He knew George had a son, a very talented son who was in show business. A son who suffered from stage fright so badly he gave up acting and turned to directing. A son named Brian. It's amazing the things a good reporter uncovers.

Chapter 16.

Bernie Goldman and Herb Preston sat next to each other at one end of the three tables George put together for the Crew. Bernie spun the half empty glass around and watched the ice cubes bump against each other in the remnants of his high ball.

"I feel like a father with a house full of kids," he said. "Do you know how many romances we have suffered through with this group?"

Herb set his drink back on the table and glanced at Bernie. "We're probably the last two who should say anything," he commented. "Bill and Jen are the only ones with sense enough to get married. I haven't been able to talk Gracie into it and you don't seem to be doing much better with Cass. Maybe we should take a few lessons from the younger ones," he said with a laugh.

Bernie swished his drink around again and looked at Herb, "Maybe it's about time this whole crowd went to another wedding," he said. "Every once in a while we have to be reminded there's life outside the Ballard Theater and Nick's Restaurant."

"That's a fine idea," Herb agreed as he looked around the table for a candidate. "Who do you nominate?"

"Don't look at me," Bernie said as he shook his head. "I sure as hell would like to, but I'm living on a shoe string. I want more than that for Cass. She deserves a lot more than promises."

"You echo my sentiments exactly," Herb agreed. "In the meantime I hope Gracie doesn't find the millionaire she's looking for."

This comment brought a snicker from Bernie and he asked, "You don't think she's still looking, do you?"

"Not openly," Herb said, "but I think it's still somewhere in the back of her mind."

"I haven't heard her mention it in a long time, and I thought she forgot about it," Bernie said.

"I wish she would," Herb commented with a smile. "I can't compete with that kind of a rival."

"What kind of a rival?" Alan asked as he pulled out the chair next to Herb and sat down to join them. Herb filled him in on the conversation and Alan agreed they needed another wedding like Bill and Jen's to give them all an excuse to tie one on. "We must be getting old," Alan told them. "Not too long ago all we needed for an excuse was a holiday."

"Yeah," Bernie chuckled, "and you weren't fussy about what holiday it was. You celebrated everything from Ground Hog Day to Chinese New Year."

"Now let's get serious here," Herb said with a grin. "We have to look for a prime candidate for the altar."

Their planning session was interrupted when Cass, Gracie and Marge returned to the table. "Has anyone noticed that Julian and Harriet have been missing a lot lately?" Gracie asked. "They haven't been here in over a week. Do they have a problem of some kind?" she asked. Then, in her own peculiar manner, before anyone had a chance to answer, she continued with the questions. "Does anyone know if something is bothering them?" What's going on anyhow?" Before she could ask any more questions Bernie said they had noticed the absence. Cass asked Harriet if anything was wrong and was told everything was fine, but she wasn't very convincing. Cass thought the answers came a little too fast and Harriet was pretty evasive about specifics. She didn't want to share the problem, so Cass didn't press the issue.

"Maybe we should ask Bill or Dan to talk to Julian in the dressing room," Bernie suggested. "He wouldn't hold back on them. He'll tell them if anything is bothering him."

Herb agreed that was a good idea. "Julian is always ready to give everyone a hand, but he doesn't like asking for a favor for himself. The dressing room idea is probably the best way to handle it."

* * * * *

Bill sat on the little round stool and put his left foot into his shoe. Dan was standing next to him, buttoning the top buttons of his shirt. Julian, dressing quietly on the other side of the room, glanced up to see them looking at him. "Is something the matter?" he asked.

"Now that you asked, Julian," Dan answered as he crossed the room toward his troubled colleague, "There is something wrong. We have a friend, a very good friend, who has something bothering him and he doesn't trust us enough to share it so we can help."

No further explanation was needed. Julian knew immediately what he meant. He turned to face them and forgot he was in the middle of dressing. The usually impeccable Julian, with half of his shirt tucked in and the other half hanging over the waistline of his trousers, was overwhelmed by the concern of his friends. In his very distinct manner of pronouncing every syllable of every word he said, "Oh my good friends, what have I done to you? In my moments of self pity I have not considered the way I have mistreated you. Please accept my apologies."

"It's nothing that can't be fixed," Bill said as he put on his other shoe. "All you have to do is let us in on what your problem is and maybe we can put our heads together and help solve it."

"It is not fair for me to burden you with an unsolvable problem," he told them.

"The only unsolvable problems are the ones we create for ourselves," Dan said.

In a subdued voice Julian replied, "I'm afraid mine is one that society created."

"Julian, talk to us please," Dan urged. "If we can't help you solve it at least let us share it with you. That's why we formed the Crew in the first place. We've all had to depend on each other now and then. You've always been there when one of us needed help, now let us help you."

"Is there trouble in Paradise?" Bill asked as he glanced up from the stool. "Are you and Harriet having problems?"

"Oh no," Julian quickly assured them. "My love for Harriet is immeasurable and hers for me is the same, I am sure. My problem is with society. I want desperately to marry this wonderful woman and she longs to pledge her love to me. But society frowns on the union of a black man and a white woman. Even our families will not accept such an arrangement. I am 'uncivilized and socially unacceptable' by the standards Harriet's mother has proclaimed." He looked at Bill and Dan as he concluded, "That, my friends, is why I am troubled."

Both men were accustomed to Julian's way of speaking. Now they had the urge to shake him to make the words spill out a little faster, but there was no rushing Julian.

"We have pleaded our case with Harriet's mother," he explained. "She threatens to disown her only daughter completely if we do not discontinue our relationship. We are not willing to do such a thing."

With each fragment of information he related, the frustration surfaced a little more. "I thought I could make it up to her by sharing my family with her and proving that we are not guilty of breaking any divine laws, but that is not to be," he sighed. "My mother, too, shuns the affection we have for each other. I am reaching beyond my realm, she tells me. Now, neither of us is a welcome visitor in either home." Julian ended his explanation and slowly shook his head as he turned back to his task of dressing. He started to tuck the rest of his shirt in his trousers and quietly asked, "Now, my friends, can you still say we do not have an unsolvable problem?"

"Well," Dan answered as he rubbed his hand across his chin, "it's a little tougher than I expected but there has to be a solution." He frowned as he added, "I thought Harriet's family liked you? They always seemed to welcome your visits."

"Oh yes," Julian replied, "I was welcomed as a coworker or a friend, but when the subject of marriage came up it opened a floodgate of opposition."

Dan looked at Julian and asked, "Can we share this with the rest of the Crew? They're all worried about you two." Julian didn't answer for a minute and Dan continued, "I don't want to take anything away from Harriet's family, or your family, either. I know how important they are to you. But don't ever forget you have a concerned family right here who cares very much about both of you."

Julian looked surprised for a minute and then seemed to light up with enthusiasm as he said, "Daniel, you are wise beyond your years. I deeply appreciate your concern." A broad smile replaced the frown he had been wearing for the past week or more. "I will talk to Harriet immediately, and be happy to share our decision with the Crew." He almost ran from the room and headed for the chorus line dressing room, completely unaware that his shirt was only tucked in on one side, and he was in his stocking feet.

"What the hell did you say to him?" Bill asked. "I didn't hear you come up with any solution."

Dan scratched his head and looked as confused as Bill. "I'll be damned if I know," he said. "Whatever it was worked, so don't knock

130

it. Just remember when you have an unsolvable problem bring it to Dr. Dan and he'll find a magic solution." The two men looked at each other and grinned. "We must have come up with something," Dan added, "Or he never would have left this room until he had every button buttoned and every hair in place. He'll be in a state of shock when he realizes his shirt tail is out and he has no shoes on."

"I don't think he cares," Bill said. "The only thing on his mind right now is Harriet."

Julian headed straight for the chorus line dressing room. He didn't stop to knock, just barged through the door and across the room to where Harriet was standing. Shrieks, hollers and screams echoed all through the room as the tall black man bolted past the half dressed chorus girls to the woman he loved. Girls grabbed for anything handy to cover up quickly. This was one area of backstage territory that was only for females.

"What's wrong?" Harriet asked.

"Nothing is wrong!" he almost shouted and made no attempt to hide his excitement. "Now," he emphasized, "nothing is wrong." He put both arms around a surprised Harriet and in his very meticulous manner told her, "Daniel has offered the perfect resolution to our dilemma. It was there all along but we were too involved with self pity to see it."

"Julian, calm down and tell me what this is all about," Harriet said as she tried to help him regain his composure. He took a deep breath and held her at arms length so he could watch her reaction to his news.

"As I was dressing," he began, and suddenly realized he never finished dressing, his shirt was still out and he was in his stocking feet. "Oh," he said and smiled sheepishly while trying to hide his embarrassment. "Please excuse my state of disarray." He started to tuck the shirt tail in with one hand and hold on to Harriet with the other and finally decided the shirt was not important, but Harriet was. He ignored his half dressed condition and continued his explanation with a correction. "As I was attempting to dress, Daniel asked what was bothering me. I explained what happened with each of our families. He was sympathetic, but also quick to remind me we have another family who cares very much about us. This family does not restrict us with unbearable conditions, and is interested only in our

131

happiness. Shamefully I must admit we did not consider the Crew. As for me, they are all the family I will need, but the ultimate decision rests with you." He was still holding her at arms length and watching her expression. He wanted her to agree, but he wanted it to be her decision.

She looked up at him and he could see tears fill her eyes. "I knew you would find a solution," she said. Julian's arms closed around her and she cried softly with relief.

Dan explained to the rest of the Crew why Julian and Harriet had been so troubled. He told them of the ultimatum put down by Harriet's mother and the shock to both of them when Julian's family took a similar stand. No one could understand the reasoning behind such a decision, and Bernie was furious.

"What does she mean, 'uncivilized'?" he wanted to know. "Julian is so civilized that half the time even I don't understand him."

No one in the Crew ever thought of Julian as being different. To all of them the most outstanding thing about him was his tremendous voice. The color of his skin had never been an issue.

Herb explained that Harriet's mother was the product of old New England Puritan stock and very set in her ways. "She has no room for change or progress and is very content to live by the rules of her ancestors. We're from a different generation and we'll probably never bridge the gap that separates us."

Bernie was still mad about anyone referring to Julian as uncivilized or socially unacceptable. "Someday she's going to be very sorry she ever thought that way. Julian is in a class all by himself, a gentleman in every sense of the word." It would be impossible to describe Julian any better.

It looked like the Crew would have good reason to celebrate, and Herb and Bernie would get their wish. Julian and Harriet were going to get married. Julian's family sent regrets. They didn't know when the wedding was going to be, but they were sure they could not be there. Harriet's family also refused to attend. The attitudes of both families put a damper on the party spirit, but only temporarily.

"Those people could use a few lessons on how to be a real family," Bernie remarked.

"Don't get so upset," Cass told him. "Right now Harriet's mother is not important. We should be more concerned with Harriet. We can't change her mother's mind and neither can she, so we had better concentrate on making sure she gets through this wedding without any scars. After all, weddings are supposed to be happy times. Let's think about making this a happy time for both of them"

Harriet knew she made the right decision, but she couldn't shake the empty feeling when her family refused to attend. She wanted her wedding day to be the happiest day of her life. Now, to marry the man she loved, she had to forfeit the rest of her family.

"The Crew is the only family who really cares about us, and as long as you will attend we will celebrate," Julian declared.

After Tuesday night's performance they gathered at Nick's to help plan for an occasion to remember. Julian was nervous and worried. Again he had to be coaxed into sharing his problem. "I met with the Judge this morning," he stated. "He says I must appear with my bride-to-be and two witnesses at 10 a.m. on Friday."

"Those instructions are easy enough. What's the problem?" Bernie asked.

"Harriet and I have ten dear friends and we find it impossible to choose two from the ten," Julian explained. "It is unfair to expect us to make such a decision."

"Don't worry about hurting any feelings," Herb assured him. "We all understand. No matter which two you choose they will represent every one of us. So in spirit we will all be there."

"That does not satisfy me," Julian answered in his distinctive fashion.

"How can we make you feel better?" Jen asked.

"I will be happy if I can have all ten of you," he said, "but the Judge says only two."

Marianne watched him struggle with his problem and asked, "Does the law say only two, or is this the Judge's idea?"

"I never thought to ask," he replied. "I think the Judge is trying to keep this as quiet as possible, but I am not willing to hurt the feelings of my treasured friends in the process."

Bill turned to Bernie and asked if he knew someone who could help.

"I don't know anybody," Bernie answered, "But Marianne does. Josh Golden has more political pull than the mayor. In fact, the mayor is a good friend of his. He looked across the table and asked, "Marianne, will you mention it to Josh?"

"Sure," she said, "I'll talk to him first thing in the morning."

Josh listened to her problem and agreed that something should be done. He reminded her of a conversation they had a few months earlier. "Do you remember when you called me a faker because we stretched the truth a little on a couple of tickets for a Judge?" He asked.

"I sure do," she answered.

"Well, Kiddo, it's time to call in the favor he still owes me."

"Thanks Josh," Marianne said with a chuckle as she hung up the phone.

Friday morning at 10 a.m. Julian Brice and Harriet Wethersfield were married with ten legal witnesses. Everybody was happy — especially Julian.

* * * * *

"Hi Mike," Marianne called to the man behind the desk as she went in the stage entrance to the Ballard.

"Evening Marianne," the security man answered as she walked toward the hallway to the dressing rooms. Before she could knock, Julian opened the door. She could see by his expression he was upset. This is unusual. He never lost his composure. He was always even tempered and a perfect gentleman.

"What's the matter?" Marianne asked.

"I feel like Peter, Peter, Pumpkin Eater, had a wife and couldn't keep her," he said. "Unless I want to keep her in a hotel room for the rest of our married life, which is totally unacceptable. We have tried a hundred different apartments and no one will rent to a black man with a white wife. They view us as oddities that should be on display in a carnival. I knew the future would present many strange and intolerable conditions, but I was unaware of how widespread the inequity had become."

Marianne stared at him and wondered what brought on this sudden outburst. "Wait a minute, Julian," she said. "You lost me in that speech somewhere. Are you telling me you are having a problem trying to find an apartment?"

"Exactly," Julian answered. "My bride does not complain, but I want her to have more than four walls and a bathroom. That is not my definition of a home."

Marianne didn't answer him right away. She gave him a quick glance and said, "hummm. Maybe Dan and I can help. I have an idea that may work," she told him. "Let me talk to him about it tonight and see what he thinks."

Dan listened and liked her idea. She suggested they accompany Julian and Harriet on their search for an apartment. Julian would keep quiet and let Dan do the talking. If the rental agent thought Dan and Harriet were the prospective tenants it would work out fine. They would look until they found the right apartment and take their chances from there. Once Julian's name was on a lease, the apartment was his. Dan thought it was worth a try and Julian was so desperate he was willing to do almost anything.

They looked at the first apartment at 9:30 Friday morning. It was a terrible place and they passed it up quickly. The next one on the list was no better. The third apartment was beautiful. Dan took Harriet's arm and followed the rental agent through the place. Each of them asked questions. When Julian had a question he directed it to Dan. The rental agent was trying hard to give the impression of a building manager with total control. She kept referring to Dan and Harriet as the "happy couple". She pointed out the amenities of her apartment building and assured the "happy couple" they could enjoy life as her tenants. So far, so good, they thought.

The four of them were still in the apartment when the agent took the rental lease from a large envelope she had with her.

"Shall we get these annoying details out of the way right now?" she asked with a voice so syrupy sweet the words almost slid out on their own. She crossed the room and handed the papers to Dan. He studied them with great care and decided everything was in order. He was looking for a way to slip them to Julian, but the agent never moved more than a few feet from his side.

Marianne looked at the agent and asked. "Did you say there were no pets allowed in this building?"

"Oh, I did, I did," the roly poly little agent responded in that same syrupy sweet voice.

135

"They are just too difficult to control," she continued. "Pets are not meant for apartment living. They get confused by so many people, and elevators are devastating to some of them."

"Does that mean only new tenants are restricted or is that rule for everyone?" Marianne persisted.

"That has always been our policy," the agent replied. "Why do you ask?"

Marianne casually shrugged her shoulders and said, "I just saw a man go by the apartment with a dog on a leash, and I thought I heard you say 'no pets'."

"Just now?" the agent asked in a shocked tone and dropped all pretense of the syrupy sweet attitude that was there a few minutes before.

"Yes," Marianne answered.

"Which way was he going?" the agent asked.

"Toward the elevator," Marianne replied.

"Excuse me a minute. I must check into this," she said and almost ran out of the apartment.

Dan handed Julian the lease, he signed it and handed it back. Julian and Marianne were in the living room and Dan and Harriet were in the dining area when the agent returned.

"I apologize for the interruption," she said. "I wasn't quick enough to catch them. The elevator was almost to the street floor before I got to it. I will look into this matter, believe me, I will."

Marianne stole a quick look at Dan and he looked back at her. He bit his bottom lip to stifle a grin and Marianne had to look the other way. Both of them were sure she would look into the dog matter.

"The lease is signed," Dan said and handed her the agreement. "My secretary also has a substantial deposit for you. If anything else is required, just call her and she will take care of it.'

"Thank you very much," the agent said and quickly added, "I'm sure you will be happy here."

Dan was enjoying his role as chief executive and decided to exploit his position a little.

He looked at Marianne and in his best executive fashion said, "Leave a number where you can be reached if they need any more information." He took Harriet's arm and guided her out of the apartment.

136

Julian, Harriet and Dan were waiting at the elevator when Marianne left the apartment with a very happy rental agent.

"You be sure and let me know if there is anything else I can do for you," she said and the syrupy sweet voice was back again.

"I will," Marianne assured her and entered the waiting elevator.

They didn't dare look at each other all the way to the street floor. They managed to control themselves pretty well as they crossed the lobby and headed for the car.

"Is this lease legal?" Julian asked as he examined the copy Dan gave him.

"Certainly," Marianne said. "You signed it. No one told her Dan was going to rent the place. We said Mr. and Mrs. Julian Brice. She never asked who was who. In fact, she never referred to anyone by name. She kept saying "the happy couple". It wasn't our fault if she assumed wrong."

"Besides," Dan added, "she'll see us around the place so often she won't know who is who."

Julian scratched his head as he laughed and said, "You two are too much."

"You better be careful, Julian," Marianne cautioned with a grin. "Dan said I was his secretary, he probably said you were the chauffeur. Make sure you never answer the door in your underwear." They all laughed at the thought of the rental agent's confusion with who was who and the outcome when she finds out which two are the "happy couple". Julian's frustration was gone and now they could all relax.

"We were lucky that man went by the door with the dog when he did," Harriet said.

Dan and Marianne looked at each other, then turned and looked at Harriet. At the same time both of them said, "What dog?"

* * * * *

Bill and Jen needed a bigger apartment. The three tiny rooms they had on the third floor wouldn't be enough when the newest Flanagan arrived. A second floor apartment would be ideal, accessible, yet away from prying eyes at street level. If one could be found with a real bathroom it would be like stealing a little piece of Heaven.

Bernie Goldman found the perfect place. Five big beautiful airy rooms on the second floor and no other tenants to share hallways, porches, parking spots or anything else. It even had a real bathroom! Another advantage was a big, bright loft area on the other side of the stairway that Bill could convert to a dance studio. The landlord agreed to let the Flanagans have the loft as part of the lease in exchange for a little maintenance work from Bill. Now he could give private dance lessons and pick up extra cash.

Bernie managed to work out excellent terms on the lease and when he was praised for his efforts all he would say was, "We were lucky." The apartment had been vacant for a long time. It needed cleaning, painting and general sprucing up, but everything essential worked fine.

Herb's insurance office was replacing their reception room furniture and he made a deal with his boss to take the old furniture off his hands. It looked fine in the Flanagan's new dance studio.

Bernie Goldman showed up with a new washing machine. "An absolute necessity for all new mothers," he told Jen.

On moving day everyone came to lend a hand. Alan Durling arrived in the middle of the moving process, slightly under the influence. He leaned against the door frame at the bottom of the stairs and called for some help with his contribution. On the sidewalk in front of the door was a fine looking upright piano. Alan announced to everyone it was his gift to the Flanagans. He had already consumed half a day's allotment of his liquid power supply and he was certain he couldn't handle the piano on the stairs by himself. After lengthy questioning it was evident to everyone that Alan did not have the foggiest idea where the piano came from or how it got to the front door. Since there were no police or irate piano owners chasing him, the instrument was moved upstairs and adopted by Flanagan's Dance Studio #1.

Chapter 17.

It was a chaotic week. Wednesday and Saturday matinees were sold out completely and standing room only crowds filled the theater every night. The entire cast knew Hollywood scouts were in almost every audience. Tension was getting to all of them. Herb Preston suggested that some diversion would be a good stabilizer. Bernie Goldman said the Village Barn had an excellent show and a late performance at midnight. The Crew thought it was a good idea and they liked the idea of sitting back and letting someone else entertain them for a change.

Herb made reservations for Thursday night. Last curtain call was at 10:50. By 11:15 make-up was off, costumes changed for street clothes, and everyone was ready to go.

Dan parked the car a half block from the Village Barn. As they walked back to the entrance they saw Julian and Harriet pull up, and Gracie and Herb were right behind them.

Bernie and Cass came in as they were checking their coats. Marge and Alan were the only ones missing, but that was not unusual. Costumes were Marge's responsibility and she was meticulous about checking them after each performance. It often meant she was the last one to leave the theater. Alan always waited for her and was rewarded for his patience by a stop at the first watering hole.

The table reserved for the group was one row in from the dance floor. It was an ideal spot to view the show and convenient for those who wanted to dance. Bill and Jen Flanagan were already on the dance floor. Dan leaned over Marianne's shoulder and asked if she had eaten supper.

"No, I haven't," she said.

"Let's go across the street to Nick's and get a steak," he suggested. "This place has a great show, but Nick's has the best food."

"Do you want to go now?" she asked with a puzzled look.

"Sure," he answered. "We can leave our coats here and run across the street. We'll be back in time for the show and no one will even know we're gone."

"OK," she said, "let's go."

139

It started to snow lightly as they ran across the avenue to Nick's. George greeted them just inside the door and asked why they were not wearing coats. Dan told him the rest of the Crew was at the show across the street. "We ran over here for dinner," he said. "We know who has the best food."

George smiled and asked if anyone else was going to join them.

"I don't think the rest of them know we left," Dan told him.

"In that case," George said, "may I suggest a nice quiet booth by the window?"

They had barely settled into the seats when their waiter appeared with two steaming cups of coffee, a pitcher of fresh cream and a basket of hot rolls. George knew how to take care of his regular customers.

Dan ordered for both of them. As they sipped their coffee the flashing lights of police cars filled the window next to their booth. They watched in amazement as uniformed officers hurried into the Village Barn and began to escort people to the waiting police vans.

"What's going on?" Dan asked the waiter.

He shrugged his shoulders and in an unconcerned way explained, "Every once in a while the police raid the Barn for an indecent floor show. Don't worry, it will be back on tomorrow night."

They started to laugh until Marianne remembered their coats were still in the checkroom across the street.

"We'll get them tomorrow," Dan said.

"That's fine for you," she said with a trace of a laugh still evident. "You live around the corner. I have to drive home to New Jersey and it's freezing out there. How am I supposed to explain going home without my coat? It doesn't sound good to say the place where I checked it was raided by the police and I had to come home without it."

Dan laughed as he reached across the table and took her hands in his. "You can stay at my place," he suggested, and smiled as he welcomed the excuse to have her stay with him again. "Then you won't have to explain anything to anyone."

"Not tonight," she replied quickly.

"Why not?" he asked.

"Lots of reasons," she said, "but mostly because I have an early day tomorrow and I have no clothes with me." She was beginning to

140

wonder if she should have joined him for dinner. Lately she had been careful and tried to make sure they spent very little time alone. She was afraid the serious feeling they had for each other was going to interfere with his career. She was determined that would not happen.

"That little show of force by New York's finest certainly messes up our plans," she said. "Since we don't have our coats it looks like it's going to be an earlier night than we figured on."

Dan was not ready to give up yet. "Why not stay here and have a few dances and a couple of drinks. We can talk just as well here as we can across the street."

The waiter appeared with their order and began to set the dishes on the table. The aroma of the food reminded them how hungry they were. Dinner was excellent, the atmosphere friendly and the music pleasant. They danced and talked and felt a familiar closeness. As they danced Dan's lips brushed Marianne's forehead.

"What are you doing?" she asked.

"Falling in love with you all over again," he answered. "It happens when I dance with you, when I look at you and every time I think about you."

She didn't resist when he held her a little closer. Her head told her to stop, push him away, get a little breathing room between them. At the same time her heart told her to hold on to him and never let him go. She listened to her head and said, "It's just the drinks."

"No its not," he answered quickly.

"Sure it is," she chided. "You always fall in love again after the second drink." She knew it wasn't the drinks – she had the same feelings. She listened to her head again and was determined that impulsive passion was not going to interfere with what she was sure would be a fabulous future for him. Dan Shaw had remarkable talent. He was a big part of a hit Broadway show. Serious romance in his life now would be a big mistake. She convinced herself she was wrong to have let her feelings go this far. Look at Bill and Jen, she thought, they're married a little over a year and struggling already. Worries seemed to come with a marriage license, a package deal of some sort. She was not going to let that happen to Dan. No matter how much she loved him, his career had to come first.

They had talked about love on other nights and she always managed to evade definite answers. This night was different. There

141

was only the two of them, no one else to draw into the conversation and no way to change the subject. Even her attempts at humor weren't working tonight. "Shall we order one more drink before we leave?" she asked.

"Not for me," he said, "I have a couple of things I want to talk to you about and I don't want you telling me it's something I always say after three drinks. I'll stop at two tonight."

Marianne could hear the orchestra playing *It Had To Be You* in the background. I'm fighting a losing battle, she thought, even the music is on his side tonight. Songs like that will keep him in a mellow mood and I'll never break the spell.

"Danny, I've been having such a good time tonight I forgot our coats are still in the checkroom across the street. It's cold outside," she said. "We're going to have to get home in a hurry."

Maybe this would be the excuse she needed to avoid what he wanted to discuss. They had been over it all before and it was always left unsettled. It was getting more and more difficult to convince him that now was not the time to look for the country cottage with the white picket fence. Maybe I'm wrong, she thought, maybe Dan doesn't care about his career as much as he should. He has so much talent it would be a sin to stifle it. She convinced herself that she couldn't be that wrong about anything.

Dan's thoughts were going in a different direction. This was the first time in more than two weeks that he had a chance to spend some time with Marianne alone. He was going to make the most of this opportunity. Tonight he was going to tell her exactly how he felt and he would make her listen.

The music stopped but he still held her close. "I don't ever want to let you go," he told her. She reluctantly pulled away and quietly said, "Come on Danny, let's go home."

They left Nick's and headed for Marianne's car parked a half block away. The light snow had stopped and turned to slush underfoot.

"Can I have your keys?" Dan asked as they walked down the avenue toward the car.

"That's OK, I'll drive," she answered. "I'm just going to drop you off and head for home."

Dan stopped and reached for her hand. "Marianne," he said firmly, "Please don't do this to me tonight. This is the first chance we've had to be alone in weeks. We have some serious talking to do. Give me one hour, please."

She had always been able to coax or joke him out of a sentimental mood. She knew she couldn't do it this time and she didn't try. "Neither of us have a coat, it's freezing outside, and we can't talk in the car," he continued. "Let's go to my place. Give me one hour, please, that's all I'll ask for."

"Danny," she sighed, "I can't say 'no' to you. I shouldn't do this, but I'm going to." She handed him her car keys and said, "You drive."

Dan's apartment was less than ten minutes from the restaurant. Marianne took off her wet shoes and put them under the hot radiator in the kitchen. "Maybe I can dry them out a little before I leave," she said as she glanced over at him. "Remember, Dan, one hour and then I have to go home." She was still trying to avoid what she was certain he wanted to discuss. Now she would have to listen and give him an answer and that was something she didn't want to do.

"All right," he said, "If I only have an hour, let's skip the preliminaries. You know how I feel about you and I know you feel the same way about me." He sat next to her at the small kitchen table and put his hand under her chin so she had to look at him. "You keep telling me this damn career is so important. Well, it isn't! Not to me it isn't! If I can't have it with you I don't want it without you."

She sat at the table in stunned silence and looked at him. He had never come on this strong before. He's right, she thought, I love him more than anything but I can't get in the way of his career no matter what he says. I can't jeopardize the good start this show has given him. I can't hurt him either. Oh, God, what do I do now?

"Danny," she said, "You're right, I do feel the same way. I know I've kept you at a distance these last couple of weeks but it was not because my feelings for you have changed. It was only because I didn't want to interfere with any opportunities that were offered to you. I love you, Dan Shaw, I always have and I always will. I think you know that but I don't mind telling you again." She watched his face as the corners of his mouth curled upward and the little creases next to his eyes crinkled together in a happy, pleased smile. "Right now," she continued, "I think our timing is off, and in this business timing is very important." Before she could say another word the phone rang.

"To hell with it," Dan said, "Let it ring."

The persistent ring continued and Marianne said, "You'd better answer it. One of the Crew may be in trouble."

He heaved an impatient sigh and reached for the receiver. "Hello," he said sternly.

"Hi, Dan, it's Alan. I'm glad you finally got home. I've been calling everybody but no one answers."

"What's the matter, Alan?" Dan asked abruptly.

"Well it seems like I'm kind of lost," the little musician replied. Dan knew right away what happened. Alan Durling was having a running battle with the New York City subway system. Every time he attempted a ride, no matter which direction the train was headed, he ended up in Brooklyn. After a few more drinks he would get enough courage to try another ride and again end up in Brooklyn.

"Alan, did you get on the subway?" Dan asked. "I'm afraid I did," Alan admitted, "this time I had the directions written down and I followed them to the letter. Now, I don't know where in hell I'm at."

Dan knew Alan had to have quite a few drinks before he had enough courage to get on the subway. It was evident by his unsuccessful efforts to sound sober that he had more than his share tonight.

"Listen to me," Dan said in a calm but firm manner. "Look around and see if you recognize anything. Is there a sign anywhere near you?"

"Sure," Alan answered quickly.

"What does it say?" Dan asked.

"Exit," Alan answered.

Dan put his forehead in the palm of his hand and shook his head. "Alan, if you want me to help you I have to know where you are. Look around again. Are there any other signs that you can see?"

"No more signs," Alan slurred, "but there's a flight of stairs with a guy's name on it."

Dan knew Alan was trying to be coherent and he patiently asked, "What do you mean 'a guy's name'? What does it say?"

"Ken Arcy," Alan said as he squinted to read the letters.

"Ken Arcy?" Dan questioned.

"Yes," replied a bewildered Alan. "This guy must be pretty popular. His name is all over the place."

"Spell it for me, Alan," Dan coaxed.

"K-E-N A-R-C-Y" Alan answered.

"Look again, that doesn't sound right," Dan insisted and tried to be as tolerant as possible.

"I'm sorry, Dan," Alan apologized. "There's stuff written everywhere here."

"Don't read the chalk writing," Dan told him. "Look for a printed sign."

Alan wanted to answer the questions sensibly and sound as sober as possible but he wasn't being very successful at either. He looked around carefully and finally spotted the sign he wanted. "I see one, Dan," he said cheerfully, "It say CANARIES. Is that what you mean?"

Again Dan patiently asked him to spell it.

"C-A-N-A-R-S-I-E," Alan answered.

"Jeessuuss Keyrhist, Alan, you're in Brooklyn again," Dan almost shouted at him. "That's not someone's name and it's not birds either, it's a subway stop."

"No kidding," Alan slurred. "Am I really in Brooklyn, again?"

"I know where you are," Dan told him. "Sit on the bench at the foot of the stairs and I'll come and get you. Don't you move off that bench. I'll be there as quick as I can." He hung up the phone and looked at Marianne who had been listening to the whole conversation.

"Good thing you answered it," she said. "He can get in real trouble out there."

"I guess so," he reluctantly admitted. "But our conversation is far from over. I love you and you love me and I'll be damned if I want to put everything on hold for an uncertain future." He had been watching her reaction closely and realized that Alan's untimely phone call had upset the balance of his argument.

"We'll talk about it tomorrow," Marianne promised as she reached under the kitchen radiator for her shoes. "Right now, if you lend me one of your coats, I'll put my shoes on and we can go get Alan."

It had been a long night and a lot was left unsaid. She was grateful for the reprieve but she knew the same questions would come up again and she would have to have some valid answers.

They rescued a stranded Alan and took him back to Dan's apartment. By the time they got there it was almost dawn. Marianne dropped them off and headed for home. As she neared the house she shut the motor off and coasted in next to the curb. She didn't want to wake anyone at this hour. Time went by so fast tonight she didn't realize how late it was until she saw the first traces of daylight peek through the darkness.

She got out of the car and held the latch in on the door handle so she could close it as quietly as possible. She crossed the porch and as she put her key in the lock she slipped her shoes off and put them under her arm. She was halfway across the living room when her aunt came in from the kitchen.

"Good morning," the older woman said cheerfully. "I didn't know you were up already. Would you like some breakfast?"

"Just a cup of coffee will be fine," Marianne answered and headed for the bathroom. She leaned on the inside of the closed bathroom door and breathed a sigh of relief. Because she wasn't wearing her coat her aunt thought she was getting ready to leave instead of just getting in. This was the second time tonight circumstances got her out of a tight spot. Someone up above is on my side tonight, she thought.

Chapter 18

Gentlemen Again was an established success. The cast had settled in to the familiar roles they were so comfortable with and performed so well. A few had some problems but most of them could handle their potential star status. None of the crew had any difficulty because they had each other to rely on. If egos were inflated they could be deflated just as fast. More important, the low spots were recognized and handled. There were no egotists in the Crew and there were no failures.

* * * * *

Steven J. Broderick owned Broderick Enterprises, a talent agency that exploded on the Hollywood scene with the introduction of three of the biggest overnight box office attractions the movie world had ever seen. Broderick was a rotund, self-centered, ostentatious individual whose height and waistline shared identical numbers. Money was the bottom line in all of his dealings and the deciding factor in Steven Broderick's world. Many of his methods of gaining lucrative contracts for his clients were questionable – but always had monetary rewards. The more money he got for his clients, the more he made for himself.

Broderick sought out Dan Shaw at the Ballard Theater before Tuesday's performance.

Dan listened politely to the agent's offer and tried to hide his excitement. He said he would get back to him within forty-eight hours with an answer. Before he would commit to leaving the show for California he wanted to make sure Marianne would go with him. He told Bill Flanagan and Julian Brice about the agent's offer and how he put him off for two days.

"Wise move to delay, Daniel," Julian said. "Many of his clients become successful, but few of them stay happy for very long. Weigh your decision carefully. Your future happiness may depend on it."

Dan was puzzled by Julian's comments and lack of enthusiasm but he didn't question it. Bill was as excited as Dan. "Broderick's made some fantastic deals for his clients," Bill said. "I guess you do have talent if you impressed him, but I'll be damned if I can find it," he added with a grin. "What does Marianne think about the offer?"

"She doesn't know about it yet," Dan said. "That's why I put him off for awhile. I want to talk to her first. If she doesn't want to go with me, I'm not going."

"Are you serious?" Bill asked.

"Of course I'm serious," Dan replied. "This is a decision for both of us, not just me."

"Oh boy, "Bill commented with a quick intake of breath, "You're going to have one mad female on your hands if you tell her that. You know how important your career is to her."

"I'll talk to her after the show tonight," he said. "Maybe I won't get an argument this time."

"How do you feel about the offer?" Bill asked. "Do you want the California contract?"

"Sure I do, but it won't mean anything if she won't go."

Bill shook his head as he cautioned, "That's asking a lot. She has a lot at stake here. If she decides to go with you she'll have to quit her job and give up her business. That won't be an easy decision for her. Josh Golden says she is doing great things for his agency and he thinks she's on her way to a big bucks future."

"She'll never have to worry about money. That's one thing I am sure of," Dan said. "I wish I could convince her of that. Sometimes she's so damned independent it's impossible to reason with her. Maybe this time she'll see things my way."

* * * * *

Jen Flanagan suffered through the early stages of her pregnancy and was beginning to show some of the signs of approaching motherhood. Before her condition became noticeable she left the chorus line. Bill thought it was a good idea, too. He wanted her to get away from the strenuous routines and the nightly performances. The transition was a difficult one for Jen. Some of the Crew made it a point to spend as much time at the Flanagan apartment as possible. Most nights Jen would accompany Bill to the theater and help the girls with makeup or lend Marge a hand with costumes. It was a struggle for her to sever her ties with this popular musical when so many of the Crew still had a performance every night.

This Tuesday Marianne spent the evening with Jen. Bill and Dan would join them after the performance. Bill tried to think of a way to give Dan and Marianne some time alone so he could tell her about Broderick's offer. The best idea he could come up with was to order Chinese food and he and Jen would pick it up.

"You can tell her about Broderick while we go for the food," he suggested.

"If you think it will work we can try it," Dan said.

"You're going to have to be pretty convincing," Bill told him. "She's not going to be happy if she finds out you may pass up this offer."

"Don't hurry with the food," Dan told him. "Give me as much time as you can, OK?"

When Dan explained Broderick's offer to Marianne she surprised him. "Danny, that's wonderful," she said. "It's the best news you could tell me." She put her arms around him and said, "This is what you've been working so hard for all this time. Finally someone who matters saw how good you really are. This is your big break! Now watch what happens. Everybody in the world is going to get a chance to see you. This is great!"

"Wait a minute," he said with a little laugh as he tried to tone down her enthusiasm. "I'm not finished."

"There's more?" she asked as she looked up at him.

"Broderick agreed to wait forty-eight hours for a decision. If I take him up on this offer we'll have four weeks to finish things up here before we head for California."

She let go of him and took a step backward, "What do you mean 'we'?" she asked. "You're the one Broderick is interested in. He made you the offer, I wasn't part of it."

He expected opposition from her but he thought she would tell him to hold out for something better. He didn't expect this reaction and it shook him for a minute.

"Marianne, you're part of everything I do," he told her. "Remember, we talked about decisions and our future? Decisions that were 'ours', not mine, and a future that was 'ours' together. I thought that was settled."

"I thought it was, too," she said, "But look at what you have here. Steven Broderick made you a promising offer and he did it for several reasons. First, because of your tremendous talent. Second, you are the handsomest guy in the cast. Third, you're young, and fourth, and probably more important than all the rest you're still single." She made a point of emphasizing – single. "If you show up in California with a wife you're going to blow your chances of a movie career right out the window. Broderick is looking for someone who will be a good box office draw. A married man won't fit that category. No matter how much talent you have, you need that extra leverage to get started. You worked hard for this chance. You earned it. Go for it."

Dan held her at arms length and in a soft, but firm voice said, "I'm not going to California, or anywhere else, without you. If you don't go, I don't go."

"That's foolish," Marianne shot back at him. "You're the one with the talent, not me. I didn't have anything to do with it. This is your chance for a movie career. Your whole future could rest on this offer. Don't mess it up." Here we go again, she thought, he just won't recognize how important his career is. "I don't think I should go, not right now," she continued, "but that shouldn't have anything to do with your decision."

"It has everything to do with my decision," he argued. "This contract is important, I admit that, but you're more important. Without you it's not worth a damn."

"You don't mean that," she said. "Right now you're excited and not thinking of what's best for your future."

Dan was adamant at this point and he wasn't going to give an inch. He was determined to convince her that she was more important to him than any career. "Sure, I'm excited," he admitted, "who wouldn't be with an offer like this staring him in the face? But it's not the most important thing in my life, you are! There's nothing more to discuss. If you don't go, I don't go."

"Dan, this contract is a once in a lifetime thing. You may never get another chance like it. What I want to do is not important, your future is." She wasn't getting through to him and she knew it. Quiet, easy going, Dan Shaw, who always gave in to her when she wanted something, was finally taking a firm stand.

"Can you give me one good reason why you don't want to go?" he asked. "Jen would go if Bill asked her."

"You want one good reason," she replied quickly, "I'll give you two." She held up two fingers of her right hand. "First, we're not married yet, and second, I'm not pregnant. Jen is both."

He was not going to let her walk away this time. He held her firmly by both shoulders and made her look at him. "If that's all that's holding you back," he said seriously, "I can fix both of those reasons."

Marianne knew he was not going to give in this time. She realized this argument was getting out of control and they were saying things that should never influence their decisions. Neither wanted to hurt the other but neither would give in to the other's point of view.

"Danny," Marianne pleaded, "let's compromise. Take Broderick up on his offer. You go to California......"

"Will you go with me?" he interrupted.

"Let me finish, hon, please," she said. "Try it for a month. If you find it's not what you want, come back. If it works for you, I'll join you, OK?"

"No, it's not OK," he said and stood firm on his decision. "I want you to go with me or I'm not going."

"What do you mean, you're not going?" she said angrily. "Isn't this the break you've been hoping for all along? Isn't this what you have been knocking yourself out for? How can you stand there and say you're not going?"

"Let me spell it out for you," he said, and now he was angry, too. "I will not go to California or anyplace else – without you. This contract doesn't mean a damn thing to me without you by my side. Marianne, I can't make it any plainer than that."

She had never seen him angry. He had always gone along with anything she wanted, but this was different. "Think about this, Dan," she reasoned. "If you go, we can call each other every day. We can write some steamy love letters. It's your chance to become rich and famous," she teased as she winked at him and tried to lighten the atmosphere. "It will probably do us both good to have a little breathing room for awhile. Besides, you'll be so busy the first few weeks you won't have time to think of anything but work. I'll be the furthest thing from your mind."

Dan still wouldn't budge. No matter how hard she tried she couldn't change his mind.

"Marianne, you know very well money has nothing to do with any of this. As far as being famous is concerned, it's not that important either. I just want to be happy, and you make me happy. Can't you understand that?"

"Danny, for more than a year I've listened to you say you wanted to make it on your own. Well, if you meant it, this is your chance. A chance like this may never come along again. Don't pass it up. We have lots of time. We don't have to rush into anything. Do you think I would ever take a chance on losing you? I love you. I'll always be here for you. All you ever have to do is pick up a phone….. "

This was not what Dan wanted to hear. No amount of persuasion was going to change his mind. He knew what he wanted and he was not going to settle for anything less.

Marianne tried reasoning and persuasion. Neither worked. She could think of only one other thing that she hadn't tried. If she could make him mad enough she was sure he would sign with Broderick. Every other argument had been exhausted, so she reverted to what she regarded as a last resort.

"You have to remember," she told him, "I have a good job and a good business. I don't want to part with either of them right now."

"In that case," Dan calmly conceded, "I'll tell Broderick I'm not interested and we can stay right here in New York."

His unexpected concession caught her off guard. She quickly regained her composure and fired back with, "That's the dumbest thing I ever heard you say."

"It's no dumber than your argument," he replied. "You know you never have to worry about money. It isn't even a consideration."

"It certainly is," she said. "Just because you have a healthy bank balance doesn't mean the rest of us do. Personally, I don't give a damn about your money. It never was important to me, you know that. I can't understand why you keep bringing it up, unless you're just rubbing it in."

"Marianne, I don't want to argue with you," he said. "Please see my side of this for a change."

"You have no argument this time," she told him. "You've been knocking yourself out waiting for this break, then when it comes you don't know how to handle it. Maybe you're not ready for it yet, or maybe you didn't really want it at all."

She could see he was angry and even worse, he was hurt. She wanted to reach out to him, hold him as tight as she could and tell him she didn't mean any of what she was saying, but she couldn't do that now. She was close to tears and she didn't want Dan to see her cry. "I've heard enough of this," she said. "I'm going home. Call me when you come to a decision." She picked up her pocketbook and headed for the door.

The ride home to New Jersey was frightening. She could hardly see through her tears. She wanted Dan to be famous. She wanted the whole world to know how talented he was. She wanted to see him in the movies, but she didn't want him to go to California this way. She tried every reasonable argument she could think of and none of them worked. Dan wouldn't listen. She knew if she went with him it would be a setback for his career. She didn't want that to happen. If he passed up this chance he might never get another and perhaps he would regret it forever. She had convinced herself it was right for him to go. She knew she would miss him terribly, but she was determined she was not going to stand in the way of his success.

Dan Shaw signed a contract with Broderick Enterprises the following Monday and left for California on Tuesday morning.

153

Chapter 19.

Marianne was miserable. She was certain she did what was best for Dan's career. Now she was lost without him. Jen disagreed with her reasoning but it didn't interfere with their friendship. They phoned each other every day. Marianne wanted to know the minute anyone heard from Dan. She felt sure he would keep in touch with Bill. At least that way she would be sure he was all right. She arranged for two weeks off from work because she didn't want to explain her actions to anyone. She knew she could never justify those actions to Josh Golden. He would let her know in no uncertain terms that he disapproved of her decision. He probably would revert to using strange Yiddish words that she wouldn't understand, and she would get mad at him, too.

She didn't tell her aunt the real story either. Instead, she said she was tired and needed the time off. She told both Josh and her aunt that Dan went to California with the possibility of a movie contract in the future. She didn't tell them the circumstances behind his leaving.

By the second week boredom was setting in. She wanted to get back to the routine of the office and the activity at the agency. She missed Dan tremendously. No matter how hard she tried she couldn't stop thinking about him. When he was not around there was a big gaping hole in her life. She missed being with the Crew, but didn't want to be there without Dan. She did keep in close touch with them and made it a point to talk to Jen or one of the girls every day. She was concerned about not hearing from Dan and anxious to know if any of them heard from him. She was disappointed he had not phoned or written but she realized he was very angry when he left. He would need a little time to think things through, she thought. Then, he would understand her reasoning and finally agree with her, like he always did.

The transition from Broadway to Hollywood was a big one. He would have to get used to a new set of rules with lots of changes. She convinced herself Dan needed a little more time but she couldn't help worrying when Jen told her none of the Crew heard from him either, not even Bill. She set the following Wednesday as the deadline. If there was no word from him by then she would ask Josh Golden to look into it. Josh knew people everywhere and could usually get answers when he needed them.

Saturday's mail included the latest edition of Variety, the show business trade paper. Marianne thumbed through the first few pages when a column headline caught her eye.

Broderick Newcomers Tie Knot In Reno. The story went on to say that after a whirlwind courtship, Dan Shaw, who made a name for himself in the hit Broadway musical *Gentlemen Again*, married Broderick Enterprises' newest starlet, Jane Blanchard in a quiet Reno, Nevada ceremony. The newlyweds were both under contract to Broderick Enterprises and were being seriously considered by several major studios.

Marianne couldn't believe her eyes. This has to be a mistake, she thought. It has to be wrong. Dan wouldn't do this, no matter how mad he was. It would hurt too many people and he wasn't the kind of a person who could knowingly hurt anyone. This story had to be a mistake, it just had to be!

She was so upset she could hardly manage the phone. It took three tries before she could get her trembling fingers to dial the right number. The first one she called was Jen.

"I don't believe it," Jen told her. "No one else in the Crew will believe it either. Dan couldn't and wouldn't do anything like that." Jen promised to call her back as soon as she could find out more about it.

Marianne was anxious to get some answers and called Josh Golden for help. When Josh came to the phone she had a difficult time trying to keep her voice under control.

"What's the matter, Kiddo?" he asked. "Are you all right?"

"No, I'm not Josh, I've got a problem and I need your help," she told him. She explained the article in Variety and asked him to check into it.

"I'll get right on it," he promised. "Don't worry, Kiddo, it has to be an error. Dan would never do that."

"Don't be too sure," she answered. "He was pretty mad when he left."

"Mad," Josh repeated after her. "What do you mean 'mad'? Did you two have a fight?"

"Well, sort of," Marianne admitted. "But I didn't mean any of it, Josh, I faked an argument so he would take Broderick's offer. It was for his own good. I just wanted what was best for him."

Josh listened quietly and Marianne waited for him to explode. She expected a barrage of Yiddish words describing how stupid she had been. At this point she didn't want to be reminded. Instead, Josh said, "I still think it's a mistake. Give me half an hour and I'll have the answers for you. Stay by the phone, I'll call you back."

"Thanks, Josh," Marianne said and hung up. She felt numb. She wanted to cry, but she couldn't. She didn't want to believe what she read but she had a nagging feeling that something was very wrong. If the article in Variety was true, maybe this was the reason Dan had not been in touch with any of the Crew.

She watched the kitchen clock and was amazed at how long it took the second hand to make the complete circle around the face and how much longer it took the bigger of the two hand to pass just six numbers. A half hour went by and then forty minutes and still no call. She wondered what could be taking him so long. If it is a mistake he should know by now. Her thoughts were interrupted by the shrill ring of the phone. She almost knocked it off the table as she grabbed for the receiver.

"Hello," she answered tensely.

"Hi Kiddo," Josh replied in a subdued tone. She could tell by his voice it was not good news. "I can't believe it," he said, "but my sources tell me it's true and I know they're reliable." He sounded as if he didn't want to believe what he had to tell her. To reinforce this feeling he thought he would add a glimmer of hope. "Don't give up yet. I have a call in to Dan at the studio and he damn well better answer me."

"Cancel the call, Josh," Marianne said. "Dan is a big boy. He knows what he's doing. If that's what he wants it's OK with me." Josh knew it wasn't OK with her. He had never heard her sound so down and he never knew her to give up without an argument.

Now she sounded totally defeated.

"Cancel the call," he shouted! "What do you mean cancel the call? This situation stinks out loud and I want some answers. I'm so mad I bit through my cigar!" He was so excited he could be heard all the way into the other room. "Dan is a good boy," he continued to shout.

"Something happened that triggered this mess and I intend to find out what happened and how. So don't tell me to cancel the call. You get yourself in your car and get over here. I want you here when these answers start to come in. Do you hear me?"

"Josh," Marianne said, "I could hear you even if you weren't on the phone." He was still shouting at her when she quietly hung up the receiver.

She went up to her bedroom and put a few clothes in a suitcase. She couldn't stop thinking of Josh's words, "Something happened that triggered this mess." He's right, she thought, it was my big mouth that triggered it. I pushed Dan too far this time. I never should have said any of what I said. I didn't mean it and Dan didn't deserve it. But it had been said and she couldn't take it back now. She could only regret it.

She explained a little to her aunt and told her she was going away for a week or so. She said if anyone from New York called to tell them she wasn't there and get a name and number and she would call them when she came back.

"Where are you going?" her aunt asked.

"I don't know," she said, still in a state of confusion. "I honestly don't know. I just know I have to get away from all of this and straighten out my thinking and then I'll be back. In the meantime, I'll call you and keep in touch, so don't worry."

"What shall I tell Dan if he calls?"

"Tell him the same thing you will be telling everyone else. You don't know where I am." She looked up from her half packed suitcase and added, "I don't think you will have to worry about Dan calling. He has more important things on his mind right now."

She squeezed her eyes shut to hold back the tears. At this point she would have welcomed a large black hole to swallow her into oblivion but she knew that wouldn't happen. She left the house and headed into town. She couldn't go back to the Crew. She couldn't even face Josh Golden. She felt like a complete failure and wanted to disappear completely. Her first stop was at the bank. She told them to close out her account. She wasn't going to leave any traceable loose ends behind. She left the bank and drove to the railroad station. She had an idea where she would go but she didn't want to make any phone calls from home. She just wanted to hide and she couldn't do that if they knew where to find her. She wanted to disappear without leaving any trail. She went inside the depot to the pay phones. Her friend, Betty Whalen, lived on a secluded farm in the mountains of Oregon. The perfect place to go if you wanted to escape the world.

Betty was surprised when she got the phone call.

"I need a favor," Marianne told her. "I have a problem and I'm looking for a place to go where no one can find me." She still had a hard time trying to control her feelings and make her voice sound normal.

"What's the matter?" Betty asked.

"It's a long story," Marianne told her. "If it's all right with you I'll explain when I get there."

"You come on out," Betty said without a moment's hesitation. "This is one place where even God couldn't find you. Just answer two questions for me, first, are you pregnant? And second, would this be something involving the police?"

"The answer is 'no' to both of them," Marianne said.

"It doesn't matter," Betty assured her, "I just wanted to be prepared. Do you want us to meet you somewhere?"

"No, I think I'll drive. I really need the time alone to think through this mess."

Betty was surprised at her friend's confused and evasive state of mind. Any loss of composure was completely out of character for Marianne Gordon.

"You be careful," she warned. "Call us from your over night stops so we can keep track of your progress. I promise I won't tell a soul where you are. We'll be on edge until you get here, but we'll be glad to see you when you do."

Marianne hung up the phone, left the depot, got back in her car and headed for the seclusion of the mountains of Oregon.

It was a long, lonesome ride across the country. Marianne cried herself to sleep at every overnight stop. Sometimes she doubted the circumstances and other times she doubted her sanity. What happened to the promises they made to each other, she wondered? She tried to convince herself that now she had to face the facts. Dan had married someone else. Josh confirmed it, and his sources were the best. This was not the way she intended things to turn out. Fate had twisted things around and now she had to accept it as the truth. By the time she reached the small town of Rankin, Oregon, there were no tears left.

She arrived at the Whalen's farm with so much bottled up inside of her she was ready to explode. She tried to tell them what happened with Dan. It was difficult to explain it to someone else when she still couldn't believe it herself. She wasn't looking for sympathy. She wanted to be understood, not pitied. She was sure it was all her fault. Dan was not to blame for any of it. He had taken enough grief and put-offs from her to last a lifetime. She knew she had carried her stubbornness one step too far, and now it was too late.

Betty suggested several times that Marianne contact someone in the Crew and at least let them know she was all right. Marianne wouldn't budge on her intent to be isolated. She told them there was no room in the Crew for a loser. Besides, she reasoned, Dan was one of the originals in the group. She was one of the last ones they really accepted as part of their self-made family. She wouldn't think of causing problems for any of them by creating a compromising situation should she run into Dan. The isolation of the Oregon mountain farm was made to order. Marianne hoped it would solve her dilemma. Now all she had to do was convince herself.

Betty and Bob Whalen bought the farm a few years earlier when it was a run down little place that needed everything. There were very few modern conveniences, no indoor plumbing, electricity, or central heat. They took on each project in the order of its importance to running a successful farm. What seemed like an absolute necessity to a city dweller was not a priority to the Whalens unless it made farming more efficient. The telephone was the first thing to be installed. Things like crops, animal care and chicken houses took precedence over creature comforts. Since they were working with limited funds, almost all the labor fell to the two of them.

Marianne explained that she didn't want to be treated as a guest. She wanted to keep busy any way she could to keep her mind occupied during the day and at night be so tired she would fall asleep before she had a chance to think about Dan Shaw or the Crew or anything related to her life in New York. She had the feeling they thought she couldn't handle farmyard chores and that made her all the more determined to do a good job at anything they chose to send her way. They teased her by calling her "city girl" and they did it in a way

159

that made her want to learn as much as she could about country living. She was a quick learner and the Whalens were good teachers. Almost every day turned into another challenge for the "city girl."

Rural life in Oregon was very different from New York City, and worlds away from the fast life of Broadway There were no Monday to Friday work weeks on the farm. Things were done when they had to be done. Deadlines didn't mean very much. You worked until you couldn't work any more and then you continued until you finished what had to be done before the sun set.

Bob showed her how to stack wood for the kitchen stove. When the pile was neatly in place he advanced her to splitting some more to add to it.

"Me? Chop wood?" she exclaimed.

"Sure," he answered. "You're the one who wants to be a farmer. You have to start somewhere and you can't mess up firewood."

The first few pieces were a disaster but she caught on quickly. Once she got the knack of it she split the logs like a pro. The effort she put into chopping the wood was a perfect outlet for her frustration. She learned to do a lot of things, some successfully and some not so well, but at least she tried.

The absence of indoor plumbing was one thing Marianne knew she could never become accustomed to, no matter how hard she tried. When the Kidney Express beckoned in the middle of the night, you had two choices, get to the outhouse in the dark and wonder what you were sitting on, or carry a lantern and signal every bug, bat, or night creature that you were about to be in a vulnerable position. This farm had given her the isolation she wanted but she had to admit rural living had its drawbacks.

Almost a year on the farm had changed a lot of things for Marianne Gordon. She learned to deal with life with a completely different attitude. Success no longer meant being at the top of the heap. She learned it could also be measured by the degree of happiness achieved or the amount of satisfaction gained. Her days were full of activity and new experiences. There was always a new challenge on the farm.

The nights were a different story. When the sun went down loneliness moved in as her constant companion. Sometimes she would awaken in the middle of the night firmly convinced she had heard

Dan's voice. Then she would remember where she was and why she was there and reality would close in again. She missed his soft voice, his easy manner and his unending patience. She dreamed of being back in his arms and often thought of the wonderful nights they spent together in his apartment. She missed everything about him and often wondered how long it would take to heal the wounds of separation. She knew she could never put him out of her mind completely, even though she told herself there was someone else in his life now. She was sure there would never be anyone in her life who could ever take his place. She treasured her memories and tucked them in a special corner of her heart that would always be just for Dan Shaw.

* * * * *

Josh Golden slowly peeled the wrapper from a fresh cigar as he glanced across his desk at Dan Shaw. It was hard to believe that only five days had gone by since Marianne's desperate phone call asking for his help. As he thought about it, he was sorry he had been so truthful with her. He wished he had talked to Dan before he called her back. He could see that Dan was hurting and he wanted to help but didn't know what else to do.

They had tried everything possible to find Marianne. There wasn't a trace of her anywhere. They both talked with her aunt in New Jersey and were convinced she was sincere when she said she didn't know where Marianne had gone. They went to the police for help and were told she couldn't be listed as a missing person since she left of her own accord. Dan was so angry at their lack of concern he hired a private detective in New Jersey to locate her. Josh hired another one in New York City. "Just to make sure they don't miss anything," he said.

Dan had not slept for days. Worry and concern were etched in his face and Josh noticed the deep circles under his eyes. "Sometimes this can be a lousy business," Josh told him.

Dan knew how true that statement was. Josh had phoned on Saturday morning and questioned him about the item in Variety regarding his marriage.

"Not true!" Dan had exclaimed. "It was only a screen test that Steve Broderick set up for Jane Blanchard." He told Josh what had taken place in Reno and Josh figured out the scheme right away. Dan was the one who was "set up." Now they were trying to undo the damage done by the deceptive press release given out by Steven Broderick. In spite of their efforts they weren't being very successful. Dan's private little world was falling apart all around him. His aspirations, hopes and dreams melted right before his eyes and there was nothing he could do to stop it.

Weeks turned into months and all his efforts to locate Marianne failed. In desperation, he turned his back on show business and concentrated on the business interests inherited from his family. He intended to fill every hour with enough work to keep his mind so busy that he would not have time to even think of her. It worked for awhile, but the memories would occasionally seep through the outer shell he had built around his feelings and every now and then he would give in to deep bouts of apathy and depression.

At such times the Crew proved to be invaluable. Someone always had a plan that needed his attention or an idea that required his business sense to make it work. They never let him down and he always responded to their efforts even though he knew most of the emergencies were manufactured for his benefit.

The Flanagans convinced Dan to stay with them. "We need your help with the business end of this dance studio," Bill told him. "It's growing a little too fast for us to handle by ourselves."

When Dan couldn't find a way to say no, the Crew breathed a sigh of relief. Now they could keep an eye on him and make sure he didn't do anything foolish. He had threatened to even the score with Steven Broderick and they were concerned that he might carry out his threat.

He seemed to settle in with the Flanagans and felt more at home with them than anywhere. He refused to talk about Marianne with anyone, but Jen and Bill Flanagan knew that she was never far from his thoughts. He was determined to keep busy and he put all his efforts into one business venture after another. It was almost to the point where work became an obsession with him. The Crew began to refer to him as Midas as one opportunity after another turned into a success story. He not only made money for himself, every member of the Crew seemed to benefit, too. As time went by the Crew became closer than ever. They were bonded as a family through caring, love and concern for each other. They were tied together financially through multiple business ventures engineered mainly by Dan Shaw and aimed at putting each of them in the millionaire category.

Marianne's situation evolved differently. She returned from the West Coast almost a year after their separation. It was a very different Marianne Gordon who returned to New Jersey. Her aunt had retired to Florida and she found herself virtually alone. She used a good deal of her savings during her stay in Oregon. Now it was time to go back to work for real. She wasn't anxious to build friendships with anyone. She was determined she would never leave herself open to be hurt again. Once was enough, she thought, and turned her attention to work in an attempt to bury herself in responsibilities.

Marianne didn't have the closeness or support of the Crew to rely on. Several times she thought about contacting Josh Golden. Maybe she could even go to work for him again. She was sure he would welcome her back and it was an appealing idea. She thought about it but couldn't force herself to do it. She was afraid she would run into one of the Crew or come face to face with Dan. She didn't think she could handle that. She still considered herself the world's greatest loser and New York, especially Broadway, was no place for losers.

Loneliness haunted her and no matter how many hours she put in or how hard she worked, it still greeted her when she went home. She had only been on the job a short time when one of her coworkers introduced her to Bobby Clemens. There were no dynamic sparks between them but they were comfortable when they were together.

After three months of being good friends they both realized they could fill a void for each other.

Marianne was honest with Bobby right from the start. She told him about Dan and she made it clear that she could never love anyone again as she had loved him. It didn't matter to Bobby. He had been through a messy divorce and all he wanted was physical fulfillment. As long as Marianne was willing to handle that he would settle for a marriage of convenience. She was not sure that was the answer to her loneliness, but she was willing to try.

It was not a marriage built on love, but it gave both of them the stability of a home and family atmosphere. Two years later their daughter was born and as far as Marianne was concerned the baby made up for everything the marriage lacked. A few years later there was another baby, this time a boy. Beth and Tim put meaning back into life for Marianne and she focused her attention and love on both of her children.

Over the years the wounds slowly healed. Neither Dan Shaw nor Marianne Gordon ever completely recovered from the scars of separation. It was impossible to quiet a love as deep and meaningful as theirs had been. Ten years – twenty years – thirty years had passed and although they were both unaware of it the flame of that initial love still smoldered silently in its own private corner of each of their hearts.

PART II

Margaret McCarthy

Chapter 20

Bill Flanagan listened to Melanie McCambridge rattle on for almost an hour. She was a pushy little real estate broker, but she knew her business. She showed him three properties he had no interest in at all. The fourth one was a former grade school building. He didn't want her to know how much he already knew about this property so he listened to her sales pitch. He knew the building was structurally sound with plenty of light, high ceilings and good floors. A minimum of renovations could turn it into an excellent dance studio. If all went well it would be a chance to expand his studios to another state and open up a whole new territory for his ever growing business. "Where does the time go?" he asked himself. It was hard to believe that forty years had passed since he struggled with his first studio in lower Manhattan.

Bill didn't want to seem too anxious and politely listened as the broker droned on about the advantages a city like this could offer his business. She suggested they stop by her office and pick up the listing sheet for the school property so she could explain all the details. That was fine with Bill, now he was ready to get serious.

The phone rang as they opened the office door. Bill didn't want to eavesdrop on her conversation so he sat on the other side of the room and thumbed through the local paper. An article on the second page caught his eye. St. Monica's High School Class of 1945 was planning to celebrate the 45th anniversary of their graduation. A list of classmates they had been unable to reach was included in the article. Bill glanced down the list and spotted one name that grabbed his attention ..... Marianne Gordon (Clemens). "Is it possible," he asked himself. "Could this be the same Marianne who was a part of their Crew so many years ago?" This was her home town and the Class of '45 would be the right time frame. The article directed anyone with information to contact Ruth Cairns at 201-555-3288. That name struck a familiar note, too. "Ruth Cairns?" he asked himself, "Didn't Marianne have a friend named Ruth?" It was so long ago he wasn't sure, but the name struck a familiar chord. It couldn't be a coincidence that both names were in the same article.

The broker finished her phone conversation and noticed his interest in the newspaper. As she hung up the phone, Bill asked where he could get a copy.

"That's yesterday's paper. You can have that one if you want it," she told him, then quickly added, "Is there a problem?"

"No problem," he answered, "Just an article that may interest my friend."

He carefully tore the article from the page, folded it neatly and put it in his wallet. He told the broker he had seen enough for today but was very interested in the school property. He made an appointment to see her again and asked if she could arrange for him to view the inside of the building.

"I'll handle everything," she assured him.

He closed the office door behind him and headed for the nearest pay phone. He grinned as he patted the pocket that held his wallet with the newspaper article inside.

He called his home number and waited impatiently for Jen to answer.

"Hello," she said.

"Hi beautiful. Is Dan there yet?"

"It's way too early for him. You sound excited. What have you been up to?" she asked.

"I am excited," he answered. "I'll explain it all to you when I get home. If Dan gets there before I do have him wait for me. Don't let him get away, Jen. It's important that I talk to him today."

"Why don't you call him at his house?" she asked.

"Because I want to see his reaction to what I have to tell him," he answered.

"Bill Flanagan," she demanded. "Don't you dare keep me in suspense. What are you up to?"

He grinned and was glad she pushed for an answer. He wanted to tell her, but he wanted her to coax him into it. It didn't take much. It never did with these two. "You won't believe this," he said and expected her to brush it off as not possible. "I may have found a way to locate Marianne."

"Are you serious?" she asked.

"Before I go any further I want to find out how Dan feels about it," Bill continued. "That's why I want to talk to him in person and not on the phone. This might be just what he needs to put a little meaning back in his life."

"Be careful, Bill," his wife cautioned, "Dan doesn't need any more disappointments. Maybe Marianne won't want to see him. You never know."

"I'll talk to him first, I promise. If he doesn't want to check into it we can drop the whole thing." He didn't want to think about that. Right now he was all keyed up about his new clue. "This is the best lead we've had in years and I think he'll be more than just a little interested."

"What time will you be home?" she asked.

"I'm leaving here now and I should be home about 3:30."

"Don't worry," Jen told him, "Dan doesn't usually come by until after four o'clock so take your time. If he gets here early today I'll make him stay around until you get home and I won't give away your surprise."

"Mrs. Flanagan," Bill teased, "your husband is one helluva lucky guy."

"I know that," she answered and laughed as she hung up the phone.

Tunnels, traffic and tolls were each doing their part to slow Bill's ride home. Any other day it wouldn't have bothered him at all. Today was different, he couldn't wait to tell Dan about his discovery. He crossed the last bridge to Long Island and settled in for the rest of the ride. He smiled as he thought about the newspaper clipping tucked safely in his wallet. If he could persuade Dan to try again to find Marianne it would be a real break. Maybe it was wishful thinking on his part. He wasn't even sure they could locate her. At least now they had a starting point and this time it looked like a good one. For many years Dan wouldn't talk about her. Bill noticed lately it was just the opposite he spoke of her often. The more he thought about this the more convinced he was the newspaper item would generate interest. How many times in the past had Dan said the biggest mistake he ever made was letting her walk out of his life. "Well old friend," Bill said to himself, "maybe we can do something about that at last."

* * * * *

Jen wondered when Bill was going to mention the newspaper clipping. She wished he would hurry up. She was anxious to see Dan's reaction, too. Finally, Bill asked, "Do you remember when we were at the Ballard Theater?"

"Sure," Dan answered with a smile. "They were the best years of my life. I guess we all did pretty well back in the good old Ballard days," he added with a touch of nostalgia. He looked at Bill and asked, "Why?"

"I came across an article in a newspaper today that might interest you," Bill said as he took the folded paper from his wallet and handed it to his friend. Dan's reaction was instant. He had a quick intake of breath and tried to cover it up by clearing his throat and asking, "Where did you get this?"

"I was looking at a piece of property in New Jersey this morning," Bill said, and explained how he found the article in a newspaper at the real estate office. "The broker is probably wondering what happened to me," he continued with a chuckle. "After I read that I couldn't get out of there fast enough." He watched closely as Dan read the article again. He wasn't sure if it struck a nerve or not.

"Have you called anyone?" Dan asked and tried to keep his anxiety from showing, but his voice faltered slightly and now Bill noticed his hands were shaking.

"Not yet," he said with a trace of a smile. "I wanted to talk to you first." He knew Dan was interested but he could see a tinge of doubt there, too. "I think we should," he added.

"Why?" Dan asked. "She's probably married and content with her life and doesn't need any interference from us." He folded the newspaper clipping and instead of giving it back to Bill he put it in his own shirt pocket.

"You don't know that," Bill persisted. He could tell from Dan's attempt to cover his feelings that this was something he did want to follow up. Bill knew his friend well enough to know it would take a little more convincing before he would allow himself to believe he could ever find Marianne.

"If we find that to be the case, we can back off and no one will know we even tried to find her," Bill continued. "We should at least take a shot at it."

"Bill, do you realize it's been forty-three years since I've seen Marianne. That's a lifetime for some people. I wouldn't know where to start looking."

Bill pointed to the shirt pocket where Dan had put the clipping. "That article has a phone number for Ruth Cairns," he said. "Let's start there. At least she can tell us if anyone has heard from her."

Dan was still unsure about this. "Ruth will never remember who we are," he said.

"She may not remember me," Bill told him, "but I'm willing to bet a bundle she'll know who you are."

"Well," Dan said reluctantly, "we can try, I guess."

Bill was right. Ruth did remember Dan. She told him the article in the paper was wrong. Marianne's name should not have been on that list.

"Oh," he said, and tried to hide the disappointment in his voice. "I was hoping you could tell me how to get in touch with her."

"I can do that," Ruth told him. Marianne and I are good friends. I saw her last summer and she'll be back for our Class Reunion some time in late October." She gave him the phone number he was looking for and went on to say that after Marianne's husband died, nine years ago, she decided to move from New Hampshire back to Massachusetts and has been there ever since.

This unexpected news sparked new enthusiasm for Dan Shaw. He thanked her for all the information, especially the phone number. He hung up the phone, turned to his friend and with a satisfied smile said, "Bill, after all these years, I finally know where she is. Now all I have to do is get up enough nerve to call her."

Jen had been quiet through the whole conversation. Now, she sipped her coffee and looked at the two men. It was hard to tell which of them was happier with the outcome.

Chapter 21

The 11 o'clock news had its usual amount of rape and murder with an extra helping of dire political forebodings. Marianne clicked off the television, picked up her Mary Higgins Clark novel and headed for bed. She was startled when the phone rang. Can't be anything but a wrong number at this time of night, she thought, as she picked up the receiver and said, "Hello."

"Hi Marianne," Ruth Cairns answered.

"Ruth," Marianne responded, surprised when she recognized her friend's voice. "I never expected to hear from you at this hour."

"I never expected to be calling you at this hour either," Ruth said. "I had an interesting phone call that I thought you should know about."

Ruth Cairns was one of the few people who knew Marianne from what they referred to as "the good old days." They had been classmates in high school back in the 1940's. After graduation Ruth enrolled in Nursing School and Marianne went to work in an office. Ruth became a Registered Nurse and Marianne struck a deal with Josh Golden.

Their lives headed in different directions but the friendship was still there. They saw each other now and then and a few times Marianne invited Ruth to join her and the Crew at Nick's. Ruth was impressed with all of the Crew, and was glad to see Marianne so happy with Dan Shaw. Like the Crew, Ruth lost track of Marianne, too. Twenty years later an accidental meeting renewed the friendship and they kept in touch ever since.

"Is everything all right?" Marianne asked with concern.

"Oh sure," Ruth assured her. "It's all good news, I hope. I had a very surprising phone call and I thought you should know about it."

"Wow," Marianne said. "It's almost midnight and you're calling long distance to tell me about a phone call. That must have been some call."

Ruth told her about the mistake with the names in the newspaper. "A very interesting man called looking for a way to contact you."

"Me?" Marianne said with a laugh. "Ruth, cut it out, I don't know any interesting men. Who was it?"

"Dan Shaw," Ruth replied. The name caught Marianne completely by surprise. She couldn't believe what she knew she heard. "Who did you say?" she asked.

"You heard me," Ruth said. "Dan Shaw called here and asked me if I knew how he could get in touch with you."

"Are you sure it was Dan Shaw?" Marianne asked, still doubting what she heard.

"Of course I'm sure," Ruth answered. "Do you think I would be calling you at midnight if I wasn't? I've been trying to reach you all day, but I couldn't get an answer. I know you work crazy hours and I was scheduled to go on duty at the hospital from three to eleven, so this is the only time I could get back to you. I wanted to tell you before he called you."

"What makes you think he'll call me?" Marianne asked.

"I gave him your phone number," Ruth told her. "I also told him Bobby died nine years ago."

"Why did you tell him that?" Marianne asked.

"I don't know," Ruth admitted. "I guess I remembered how you two felt about each other when you worked in New York."

"That was over forty years ago." Marianne said with a chuckle. "The last time I heard anything about Dan he was married and living in Ohio. As far as I know, he still is."

"I didn't ask him why he wanted your number," Ruth continued, "but I have a feeling he's going to call you."

Marianne laughed and reminded Ruth she had always been an old romantic. "You can't stop playing Cupid, can you?" Even though it was a long time ago, Marianne couldn't control the feelings she had churning up inside. They were the same feelings she had when Josh Golden first introduced her to Dan. Familiar, disconcerting, magnetic attraction, all those feelings came rushing back now. "I appreciate your call, Ruth, but I think you're mistaken this time. I'll be very surprised if Dan Shaw calls me. If he does, I'll let you know, OK?"

"You had better," Ruth told her. "I want to keep track of you this time."

Marianne carefully replaced the phone on its cradle but her thoughts were a million miles away. She looked at the clock and couldn't believe that almost three hours had gone by since Ruth called. Sleep was impossible. There was too much running through

173

her mind. Forty years, she thought, no, forty-three to be exact, since she last saw or heard from Dan Shaw. She could remember it as if it was yesterday. Why would he call Ruth for my phone number? she asked herself. Why would he want to get in touch with me after all these years? So many questions and they all added to the confusion. No sense in stirring up any more old emotions until she found out what this was all about. She shut off her memories and tried again to go to sleep.

* * * * *

Marianne wished Ruth had never told her about Dan's call. Now, every time the phone rang her heart skipped a beat. This is foolish, she thought, if Dan was going to call he would have called yesterday. In spite of her sleepless night she put the thought in the back of her mind and tried to follow her regular Saturday routine. She had almost convinced herself it would never happen, when the phone rang and shattered her composure altogether. She swallowed her anxiety and reached for the receiver. In the calmest voice she could manage she said, "Hello."

"Hi Gram," a peppy little voice answered.

Marianne breathed a sigh of relief as she realized her grandson was the caller.

The youngster tried to sound serious and grown up as he said, "How would you like to go on a date with me?"

"What did you say?" she questioned with a laugh.

"How about a date, Gram?" he repeated. "You drive and I'll pay."

"Let me think about it," she teased. "Where would you like to go on this date?"

"I know where there is a good movie that you would like. How about it, Gram?"

"OK," she agreed. "I'll pick you up at five o'clock. Maybe we can get a burger before we go to the movie, OK?"

"Sure Gram, thanks, see you at five," the youngster said all in one breath and hung up.

Marianne smiled at the thought of a nine year old asking his grandmother for a date. Her mind was still on her grandson's call when the phone rang again. She reached for the receiver and said, "Hello."

"Hello Marianne," said a familiar male voice from the past.

She tried to cover her uneasiness by asking, "Who is this?" when she knew very well who it was. She would have recognized Dan Shaw's voice even if Ruth had not called.

"This is Dan Shaw," he said. "Do you remember me?"

God, she thought, how could anyone ever forget that voice? All night long she had practiced what she would say if he called. Now she couldn't say any of it. She tried to answer him but no words would come out. She wanted to say, "Ruth called last night and prepared me for this," then decided against it. She wanted to say, "God, Dan, do I ever remember you. I've thought about you every night for years and years." She had second thoughts on that one, too. Instead she covered her anxiety by stalling for time. "Well — uh – I did know a Dan Shaw, but that was a long time ago."

"We met in 1947," he said, "the place was the Ballard Theater in New York City and the occasion was a backstage party for the cast of *Gentlemen Again*," he continued. "If I remember correctly you came in with a portly little ticket broker named Josh Golden."

"That's some memory," Marianne said and knew that sounded foolish as soon as she said it. She wanted to say something clever, but her mind wouldn't function. She was afraid anything she said would sound stupid, so she let Dan do the talking.

"Do you want me to describe the surroundings? Or tell you who else was there, or have I convinced you I am who I say I am?"

"You've convinced me," she said and sounded confused as she asked, "Why are you calling me now?"

Dan wondered if he had made a mistake by making this call. He didn't expect to be greeted with open arms, but he did want a chance to explain. Marianne's question added to his worry. She really doesn't want to talk to me, he thought. She's just being polite.

"I guess I could make up a story," he said. "But I don't think I could fool you for long. I have to be honest with you and tell you that after all these years I finally found a way to contact you and I would like to know how you are and what you have been doing with you life?"

175

She listened to his familiar voice and felt like the forty-three intervening years were slowly melting away. He sounded the same as he did when they spent countless hours with each other and made promises they never kept.

"The first part of your question is easy to answer," she said, "I'm fine. The second part takes a little more explaining. I can't answer it in a sentence or two." What a loaded question, she thought. Do I tell him I'm old, I'm tired, I'm ready to throw in the towel on this miserable life..... or do I do the happy face routine and hit him with the same question? Happy face won and she asked him, "What about you?"

"Oh I'm fine, too," he said a little too quickly.

Neither of them knew what to say next. How do you carry on a conversation with someone you haven't heard from for forty-three years? Do you ask them what's new? How do you feel? How is the weather where you are? Just what do you say? Dan was the first to pick up the slack. He told Marianne about the newspaper article concerning the class reunion.

"I called Ruth to find out how to contact you. She gave me your number. I hope you don't mind."

"I don't mind at all, I'm glad to hear from you," she said. Then thought to herself, you don't know how glad I am to hear from you. "Actually," she confessed, "Ruth phoned me last night and told me about your call."

"She did?" he said. "And you let me go through that whole explanation. You haven't changed a bit," he told her with a chuckle.

The first five minutes of conversation was difficult for both of them. Dan wasn't sure if she would want to remember him, and if she did would she want to talk to him after all these years.

Marianne was having trouble with all those in-between years, too. She wanted to ask why he was calling, why now and why her. She decided to wait and see where this conversation would go.

Once the initial worries were past, the conversation came easier. Little by little the tensions eased and they realized they could let their guard down and relax. Not a word was said about their separation. Neither of them wanted to talk about it. They each had questions, more than forty years of questions, but now the questions could wait. They were old friends looking to renew an old friendship and it was working fine for both of them. It was not fair to expect forty minutes of phone conversation to bridge almost a half century of life. That seemed to be what they were trying to do. Dan asked about Bobby, and Marianne told him of Bobby's valiant but losing battle with cancer. "That was nine years ago, but sometimes it feels like yesterday," she said.

"Time certainly doesn't stand still for any of us, does it?" he commented. "Jane died in 1984."

Marianne waited for him to explain a little more, but he never mentioned it again. They talked of happy times, of memories and dreams and friends and fun.

"Dan," she said, "this has been wonderful. I hope we don't have to wait another forty years before we do it again."

"Not if I can help it," he answered. "If it is all right with you, I'll call you again next week." Just the tone of his voice let her know he was sincere.

"That's fine with me," she said.

"I'll be in Chicago early in the week and back here next weekend. Is Saturday morning a good time to call?"

"It's the best time," she said. "I'm not home from work before 10:30 at night, but I'm always here on Saturday morning."

"I'll remember that," he said and ended the conversation with a promise to call the following week. Marianne knew he would.

Dan slowly placed the receiver back on the telephone as the corners of his mouth curled upward and the little lines next to his eyes crinkled together in a very happy, pleased smile. He was glad he listened to Bill and called Marianne. He was already looking forward to next Saturday. All of a sudden the world was a much better place.

For so many years Marianne wondered if there would ever be anyone special in her life again. Now here he was as if he had been there all along. She stared at the telephone as if she couldn't believe what had just taken place. These things only happen in the movies……….. In real life they never happen to people like her………. She was afraid that she would wake up and find it was just another dream ……….

Chapter 22

All the way home from work Wednesday night Marianne told herself this was the longest week in history. It was only the middle of the week and Dan said he was going to call Saturday. She wondered how she would get through the next few days and cautioned herself not to expect too much. She thought of their phone conversation and was amazed that he remembered the things that were special to her so many years ago. Next time he calls I'll be prepared, she thought, and tried to focus on questions she would ask him.

As she put her key in the lock she could hear the phone ring. It was on the third ring before she could answer it. "Hello," she said, and quickly added, "If you are selling something I don't want any. If you have the best vacation paradise in the world, I'm not interested and if you are a computer I hope you blow a fuse."

"Hi Marianne," Dan Shaw answered. He laughed as he said, "Honest I'm not selling anything, there is no vacation paradise involved and I'm not a computer."

"Hello there," she said and tried to cover her impulsive reaction by casually asking, "Is it Saturday already?"

"I couldn't wait until Saturday," he told her.

"That's good news," she said with a chuckle. "When I heard your voice I thought I missed a couple of days this week."

Dan laughed and remembered how Marianne could always come up with an answer. She knew how to make him laugh when he was feeling low. She also knew how to bring him down a peg or two when he needed it. "Saturday seemed like such a long time to wait, I thought we might try to shorten the week a little," he said.

"At the rate I'm using up my weeks I think I want to add a few days to each one instead of shortening them," she told him. She remembered she had just complained to herself about this being the longest week in history and reconsidered. "I have to admit this felt like a long week to me, too," she added. "I'm glad you didn't wait."

Conversation came easier to both of them now. As they talked they remembered things from the past that would jog a memory or create more unanswered questions.

Like their first call the conversation was limited to small talk. Mostly reminiscing and a lot of memory prodding but no serious matters were mentioned. Dan told her he kept in close contact with several of the original cast members of *Gentlemen Again.*

"Do you remember what we named the old crowd?" he asked

"The Crew," she replied almost automatically. "Some things you never forget. They were the best group of people I've ever known. I'm sorry I lost contact with them but sometimes circumstances don't let you do what you want to do"

"I know the feeling," Dan agreed. He told her that since their phone conversation last week he had spoken with most of the Crew and they were all anxious to get together.

Jen Flanagan asked for an address and said she wanted to write a long letter. "I didn't think you would mind if I gave it to her."

"That's fine with me," Marianne said. "I'd love to hear from any of them."

Dan told her Bill and Jen were the parents of six Flanagans. Julian and Harriet were doing well and still lived in New York City. Cass was married to Bernie and they are as comical as they always were. Gracie stopped looking for her illusive millionaire and has been happily married to Herb for forty years. "I'm sure you remember Alan Durling," he said.

"He was one of my favorite people," she said.

"Alan married Marge but insists he doesn't remember doing it. Marge says it was all his idea. Alan gave me a message for you. He said to tell you he hasn't proposed to a single woman since you left." "Danny," Marianne said with a laugh, "Alan never did propose to 'single' women. He made sure every woman he asked to marry him was already married. He wasn't as out of it as most people thought. He covered up a lot of his feelings by drinking, but he was still one of my favorite people."

She was the only one who ever called him Danny. She didn't realize that she had said it, but he caught it right away. A spark of their old feeling was still there, he thought, and it made him feel pretty good.

"Everyone wants to see you," he said, and almost added – especially me – but thought he had better not, not yet. "When can we get together?"

"That's hard to say," she told him. "I haven't traveled very much in the last ten years."

"We can come and get you," he offered.

"From Chicago?" she asked a little surprised.

"No," he said with a chuckle, "probably from Long Island, or even Chicago," he added quickly. "It doesn't matter. We'll come and get you from anywhere."

"You make me feel pretty special," she said.

"You were always special to me," he said without a moment's hesitation.

She heard what he said and liked what she heard, but she was afraid to believe it. She couldn't understand why this was happening to her now and she didn't know how to cope with an unfamiliar situation. She tried to hide her confusion by asking, "How are you going to come and get me?"

"Bill and I do a lot of flying," he answered. "There must be an airport close to you."

"Wait a minute," she said, "You aren't seriously thinking of me getting into an airplane, are you?"

"Why not?" he asked. "We're both certified pilots and we'll take very good care of you."

"I've only been in a plane once in my life. For a week after that trip my hands were shaped like the armrests. Does that tell you something?"

"My guess would be that you don't care much for airplanes," he said.

"Good guess," she answered. "Let's put that suggestion on hold for a little while."

Dan wasn't going to be put off that easy. "Ruth Cairns mentioned that you intended to go to a class reunion in October. Is there a chance of coming a day or so early and spending some time with us?"

I'd love to, she thought. I'd love to see him again. I'll bet he hasn't changed that much. I'm afraid he would run the other way if he saw me now. All those in between years have taken their toll. "I'm not sure I can go to the reunion this time," she told him. "October is a busy time at my office and it may be difficult to get time off."

"Everyone here is anxious to see you," he persisted. "Let's try to work out a specific date."

"We'll find a way, I'm sure," she told him, but didn't seem to be in a hurry to do it.

He thought he was expecting too much, too soon. Maybe he would have to settle for a phone call now and then—temporarily. "I apologize for calling you so late, but I wanted to talk to you again," he told her.

"No need for an apology, I'm glad you called. It's been a long week for me, too." She wanted to tell him it had been a long forty years. She wanted to say a lot of things to him but she was still unsure of herself. This was like a fairy tale and she didn't believe in fairy tales. "There is so much I would like to talk to you about that I don't know where to begin. Yesterday I had a million questions, everything I was going to ask next time you called. Now I can't think of any of them."

"It's nice to hear that you were thinking about me yesterday," he said and wondered if his phone call last week awakened the same feelings in her as it did it him.

"Danny," Marianne said, and this time he knew she used the name intentionally, "I haven't been able to think about another thing since you called last Saturday. What I can't figure out is WHY you called?"

She heard Dan clear his throat and in a voice filled with emotion he answered her. "Many years ago I fell in love with a woman who loved me more that I deserved. She put her own feelings aside because she thought it was more important for me to be a success than for her to be happy." He hesitated for a minute, took a deep breath and continued. "Because of some foolish mistakes, I lost her. I hope I have found her again and I hope I can show her I've learned by those mistakes. That's WHY I called."

She didn't expect such a straight answer. "Dan Shaw," she said, as she brushed away the tears with the back of her hand, "if you were trying to make me cry you've succeeded."

Dan could tell she was crying. He didn't intend for that to happen. She asked why he called and he had to be honest with her. Now he wanted to wipe away the tears but with so many miles between them all he could do was convince her he still cared.

"That's the last thing in the world I wanted to do," he told her. "I would much rather try to make you happy."

"I don't believe this is happening," she said through the tears. "Things like this don't happen to people like me, they only happen in the movies. I'm going to wake up and find it was just another dream and I'm going to be disappointed all over again."

"You're not dreaming," he said. "I'm the one who is reaching for a dream. I didn't want to say these things to you on the phone. I wanted to tell you in person. These telephone talks have been great, but we have to get together. Can I see you this weekend?"

"You're right, Danny," she conceded, "we have a lot to talk about but I don't think we can do it in a weekend. Let me see about getting some time off from work. Next time you call we should be able to make some firm arrangements."

For the next three weeks the phone calls came almost every night. Marianne scolded him for calling so often. The expense of the long distance calls that always lasted the better part of an hour seemed staggering to her. She had learned over the years to budget and stretch from one payday to the next. Dan didn't seem to mind the expense, but money never was a worry for him.

Every plan they tried to make hit a snag somewhere. Finally Dan came up with a workable idea. He suggested they meet over the Thanksgiving holiday weekend. Marianne had four days off and anything he had to deal with could be rescheduled.

"That should give us time to work out any arrangements we need," he said. "Do you think we can count on that?"

"We can try," she answered. "Right now I have one big problem. I haven't mentioned anything about you to my daughter or my son. I should have," she continued, "But I didn't think we would get beyond a few phone calls. You surprised me. You kept coming back for more. I don't think either of us realize the changes that have taken place over the years. I'm sure the image you have of me is a self-assured, independent female with a decent shape who was ready to go dancing five nights a week." Oh my God, she thought, what time has done to stamp out that image. "Once upon a time that was true, but that was a long time ago. Times change and people change. Today, I'm very different. The self-assurance has been replaced with uncertainty and the independence has given way to servitude. I learned a long time ago I wasn't as important as I once thought. Life goes on whether I'm included or not. We have to remember we're not youngsters anymore.

I'm sixty-two years old with a lot of gray hair. The shape you once admired has slipped in many different directions and although I hate to admit it, I haven't been on a dance floor in over twenty years. Not a good record, for sure, but I have to be honest with you, too."

Dan didn't say a word but his thoughts took him back to New York City and the Ballard Theater days. She may look different, he thought, but I know she is still the woman I fell in love with a long time ago.

Marianne thought she had really dampened his spirits. In spite of her doubts she continued, "Let me talk to Beth and Tim over the weekend. Call Monday night and if you still want to get together we can plan from there. Just keep in mind, I'm a sixty-two year old, gray haired grandmother with a shape like an apple." I've given him every chance to change his mind, she thought. If he doesn't call Monday I'll know it's over.

"Marianne," Dan said, "I never thought I would have to be "explained" to anyone. I understand your position. Talk to your family and I'll call you Monday night. Let me give you a thought to keep in mind until then ..... I love apples. Good night." The click at the other end of the phone line let her know she had no chance at rebuttal and she smiled as she replaced the receiver.

Somehow problems got solved. Time slipped by faster than ever. Thanksgiving was only a week away. Marianne was nervous about the coming holiday yet she was looking forward to it. Mixed emotions, crazy turmoil, second thoughts, were all there. Scared was the best way to describe her feelings. Now it was too late to back out.

Dan made plans to come to Massachusetts on Thanksgiving Day. Marianne had agreed to go to a reunion with the Crew in Connecticut on Friday. Finally things seemed to be working out. Any doubts she had were erased by the eagerness in his voice each time he called. Both of them were looking forward to the holiday weekend.

Chapter 23

Dan was scheduled to arrive at the airport at ten o'clock on Thanksgiving morning. Marianne was there a little before ten so she could see his plane come in. He told her to watch for a twin engine silver Cessna with a blue stripe.

"I have no idea what a twin engine Cessna is," she said.

He laughed and described it as a medium size silver plane with a motor on each side. That still didn't mean much to Marianne. To her all small planes looked alike. She watched as a new arrival set down at the far end of the runway. The plane slowed and came almost to a stop. An attendant guided the pilot to an empty space near one of the hangars.

She saw the pilot leave the plane and cross the tarmac toward where she was standing.

Oh God, she thought, that's Dan. A rush of memories cluttered her mind and she found it difficult to control her emotions. Her first sight of Dan Shaw rekindled feelings she was sure she had buried many years ago.

He carried a small suitcase in one hand and a suit bag in the other. She watched him go into the office building and a few minutes later he came through the gate where she was waiting. As he walked toward her she noticed the changes that had occurred over the years. He was a little heavier around the middle, silver rimmed glasses were an addition and the wavy brown hair she remembered so well had turned a soft white. He was still a very handsome man.

She couldn't move from the spot where she was waiting. Her palms were sweaty and her mouth was as dry as unbuttered toast. She took a deep breath and tried to think of what to say but her mind was a total blank.

Dan dropped both of the bags he was carrying. He took her hands in his, looked directly into her eyes and smiled as he said, "I'm really glad to see you."

She smiled back at him but all she could manage to mutter was, "Me too, Danny, me too." His touch was electric and Marianne felt like someone had just turned her life back on. As they hugged each other both of them realized that their old feelings were still very much alive. Dan said this would happen and she didn't believe him. She thought too much time had gone by, now she knew she was wrong. She tried to hold back the tears. After a minute or two she could feel them working their way out of the corners of her eyes and running down her cheeks.

"Danny," she said softly, "Everyone is looking at us."

"Good," he answered, "I hope they can all see how happy I am." He slowly released his hug, picked up his bags with one hand and held on to her hand with the other as they crossed the parking lot to her car.

"I hope this weekend is as special for you as it is for me," he said. "I have so much to say to you and so much to hear from you." He looked at her and thought, I have forty-three years of missing you to fill in, where do I start? I can't rush this. I'm not going to take a chance on losing you again. "For now" he said, "let's not ask a lot of questions or look for too many answers. We can do that when we're ready. This weekend let's just enjoy each other. Is that OK with you?"

What a relief, Marianne thought, I was afraid he was going to begin the conversation by asking what happened to us? We do have serious questions that need answers, but they've gone unanswered this long, they can wait a little longer. "That's fine with me," she agreed as she started the car and backed out of the parking space. "Now let's go home. I have a family waiting anxiously to sit in judgment of you, so be on your guard."

"If you're trying to scare me off it won't work," he said with a half hearted smile. "If you're using reverse psychology to reassure me, that's not working either."

"Stage fright?" she asked. "I find that hard to believe."

"You can't imagine how nervous I am," he confessed. "I have more butterflies now than any time in my life."

Stage fright was something they often joked about many years ago. Everyone's mistakes, nervousness, anxieties, and ailments, from a hangover to indigestion, were blamed on stage fright. They knew everyone who stepped out on a stage suffered from it at one time or another. Now she wanted to put him at ease.

"If it's any consolation," she offered, "you'll be playing to a very receptive audience who really wants to like you. No one will be looking for any faults." She looked at him and quickly added, "Of course, the fact that you're a good looking old guy doesn't hurt one single bit."

Dan smiled and seemed to relax a little. She hasn't changed he thought, she still knows how to get me over the rough spots.

She knew he would be comfortable with everyone. She also knew he would have to find that out for himself. There was no way she could convince him of it. It would be an interesting afternoon, she thought.

Ten minutes after meeting Marianne's family Dan's butterflies were under control and all signs of nervous tension disappeared. He was Mom's friend and Gram's friend and that made him their friend, too. He was welcomed and right from the start treated like one of the family. Now he could understand why Marianne didn't want to miss Thanksgiving at home. It was easy to see how important *family* was to all of them.

* * * * *

Dan was looking forward to Marianne's reunion with the Crew. She was nervous about it but he knew those fears would disappear as quickly as his did when he met her family. He reminded her the Crew was still her family in spite of her long absence.

Fairfield, Connecticut was a three hour ride and Marianne wondered what they could talk about for three hours. He tried to convince her the trip would be quicker and easier if they went by plane. She would have no part of it. This time the automobile won over the airplane. Once they were on their way neither of them worried about conversation. Being together seemed to be all they needed.

"You went to a lot of trouble for this weekend, didn't you?" she asked.

"It will be worth it," he answered with a smile, "you'll see. The Crew has been looking for a reason to celebrate for a long time. When you agreed to the reunion it was all the excuse any of them needed."

"Jen's letters have been a big help. They filled me in on a lot of things I had missed," she told him. "They also raised a million questions. I'll never get all the answers in one weekend."

"Are you saying I can count on doing this again?" he asked with a grin.

Marianne laughed and said he was an opportunist. "I wasn't hinting," she told him, "I was commenting."

"Oh," he answered as the corners of his mouth curled upward and the little lines next to his eyes crinkled together in a happy smile. He wanted to reach across the seat, put his arm around her and pull her close to him. He suppressed the urge and continued the conversation. "The Crew has always been a close group. You were the only one who wasn't there and everybody wants to see you. I'm not the only one who missed you."

The little after thoughts Dan added to some of his comments were having a strange effect. They made Marianne feel young again, a lot like she felt many years ago. This man has a way of reviving feelings and emotions she thought were lost forever. He seemed unaware of the effect he had on her and she wondered if it was wishful thinking on her part or if he, too, had buried emotions that were creeping to the surface a little at a time. We'll see, she thought, as she listened to Dan say, "It's a break for us that everyone will be coming to Gracie and Herb's in Connecticut. It will save a lot of traveling and you can answer everybody's questions at the same time." Before they realized it they were on the outskirts of Fairfield. As Dan turned the car into the Preston's long curved driveway Marianne began to feel uneasy.

"Now I know how you felt yesterday," she said. "I think I caught your butterflies. All of a sudden I'm not sure I want to be here."

"Relax," he said in his calm reassuring voice as he took her hand in his. "I promise you this will be one of the most memorable weekends you will ever have." At the same time he promised himself he would make sure of it.

As Dan parked the car Gracie and Herb Preston came out of the house to greet them. Both of them were at the car door before Marianne could put a foot on the driveway. Gracie hugged her and asked, "Where have you been all these years? – Everyone has been looking for you." She continued to talk in her own distinctive manner, asking and answering questions before anyone else had a chance. "Finally this old guy tracked you down – well good for him –What took him so long? – Now we can find out all about you – You look wonderful – We're so glad to see you – Aren't we, Herb?"

Herb Preston had listened to his wife's chatter for more than forty years. Instead of answering her he acquired the habit of just nodding his head. When Marianne looked at him he smiled broadly and winked. From her past recollections of Herb's outward emotions the wink was a grand gesture.

The men each took a suitcase and Gracie took Marianne. As they walked toward the front door she noticed that Gracie was as beautiful now as she was forty-three years ago. Aside from a few small facial lines she had aged very well. Her hair was neither blonde nor white, but a perfect blending of the two. She had a trim figure and moved with the symmetry of a dancer. She never lost her habit of constant chatter and talked every foot of the way into the house.

People change over the years, especially when it has been so many years since the last contact. Hair turns gray or hairlines recede, wrinkles become more prominent, hips tend to broaden, muscles turn to flab and joints stiffen, but eyes don't change. Eyes are a window to the inside that show true feelings. Gracie and Herb had sparkle in their eyes. They both seemed to say, "Welcome back old friend."

A quick tour of this gorgeous home was interrupted by the arrival of Bill and Jen Flanagan and Marge and Alan Durling. There were smothering hugs and lots of happy tears. There were endless questions and everyone trying to talk at the same time. It was total confusion, but what a delightful state of confusion to be in, Marianne thought. She was amazed at the greetings. She never dreamed of a reception like this. She thought they had all forgotten her years ago. She wondered if Dan might have engineered it. Never! She told herself. One thing everyone in the Crew had in common was honesty. They were all good at what they did when they were on stage, but all pretense was always left in the theater.

Gracie finally called an intermission and suggested they give their old friend a chance to catch her breath. She took Marianne upstairs to freshen up and Jen and Marge went along to "catch up on the gossip".

"This is just like old times," Jen commented as they walked along the upstairs hall. Gracie showed Marianne into a beautiful big bedroom with an adjoining bath. Her suitcase stood beside Dan's against the bedroom wall. She started to ask about them but was sidetracked by the splendor of this beautiful home. She remembered when Herb first proposed to Gracie and she wouldn't consider him because, in her words, "he wasn't a millionaire." She made it plain that her objective in show business was not stardom but finding a millionaire to marry. At the time Herb didn't qualify, so she wouldn't give him an answer. The whole Crew sided with Herb the night he proposed, but all Gracie would agree to was a "maybe." He told her someday he would be the millionaire she wanted. A glance around this magnificent Fairfield home proved how right he was.

"Don't you dare get dressed up tonight," Gracie instructed. "Stay comfortable it's probably going to be a long night."

"How long?" Marianne asked.

"Who knows," Jen commented with a mischievous grin. "Everyone will be here, no one has to drive anywhere, and now that you're back we intend to celebrate all night long."

"Maybe even into tomorrow," Marge added happily.

"Or Sunday, if we last that long, "Jen continued with a laugh.

"Remember when we did this every weekend?" Marge reminded them with a touch of nostalgia in her voice.

"And loved every minute of it," Jen added.

"Nothing can come close to the good times we had when the Crew was all together," Gracie commented. "Now that you're back, Marianne, we intend to pick up where we left off."

"It's been a long time since I did any celebrating," Marianne said and wondered if Dan had mentioned anything about what they discussed in their phone conversations. "I don't know if I can keep up with you people. Remember, I've been away from New York for a long time."

"You may be a little out of practice," Marge said, "but once the music starts you'll be right out there like you always were."

"I don't know about that," Marianne said doubtfully. "It's been more than twenty years since I've been on a dance floor."

They could see her uneasiness and Jen tried to calm her fears by commenting with a half hearted grin, "You know there are some things we never forget, like driving, dancing and – uh – uh –"

"Sex," Marge volunteered with emphasis. "God Jen," she added with a chuckle, "this crowd is getting so old our imaginations are wearing out."

"I don't feel old anymore," Gracie said. "Somehow this weekend turned back the clock for me."

"If you think your clock is turned back," Jen commented, "take a look at Dan." She looked at Marianne and said, "His clock started ticking again after your first phone conversation. I haven't seem him like this in years."

"He's beaming like a newlywed," Marge teased. "Marianne, is there something we should know that you're holding back?"

"Not much of a chance of that," Gracie said. "With you two no one has any secrets."

Marianne could feel the beginning of a blush as she answered, "We're still at the hand holding stage. Some things are a little awkward, but we're working on it."

"If that's the case," Marge said with a chuckle, "We'll have to have a good heart to heart talk with both of you."

"Remember," Jen added, "we're not twenty years old anymore. At our age we can't afford to waste much time on preliminaries. We have to get right to the objective or we miss it altogether."

Marianne turned to face Marge and Jen who were sitting on the end of one of the twin beds. "All right," she asked, "What do you want to know?"

"Everything," Marge said as she shifted to a more comfortable position and waited for all the intimate little details of a very complicated relationship.

"How can I explain it to anyone when I don't understand it myself?" Marianne admitted. "A long time ago Dan and I had a beautiful thing going. You all know that. Somehow we managed to botch it up. Now we have a second chance and this time we're going to be very careful. We talked a lot on the phone but there is still a lot to be said and some of it has to be done face to face. We have a lot of questions for each other but we are not going to ask any of them this weekend. This weekend is just for fun." She was surprised at their unwavering attention and realized they were not prying, they were trying to help make sure this relationship would last. She looked from Jen to Marge to Gracie and could see by their expression they expected a lot more than she told them. "We agreed to put all serious questions on hold for now," she added. "Does that satisfy your curiosity?"

Marge shook her head, "Doesn't even come close," she said. "We want to know how you feel about Dan after all these years. We all know how he feels about you – how he has always felt about you."

There were the little after thoughts again, this time from Marge. Marianne reminded them that yesterday was the first time she and Dan had seen each other in over forty years. "There have been a lot of changes for both of us," she said. "Yesterday and today have been filled with activity. We haven't had a chance to do any serious talking and we have lots of questions to be answered." She knew these women were Dan's family and concerned about him just as her family had been concerned about her. She also knew they were there to help if she needed them, but they were not going to overpower her with their suggestions. They deserve more of an explanation, she thought, and began again.

"When I first saw Danny at the airport yesterday morning I knew that what we had years ago never died. It may have been smothered for a lot of years, but all it took was that first few minutes together to show both of us those feeling were still alive." She choked up as she talked and tried to swallow her emotions and continue. "Dan said that would happen but I wasn't so sure. He was right," she admitted. "He was very right."

She had to pause for a minute to regain her composure. "No words can describe how I felt when he walked through that airport gate." Her lower lip started to quiver and she felt her emotions getting the best of her again. She quickly shifted the tone of the conversation. "We know it's going to take time to get back what we had before but we also realize we're in a better position to appreciate each other now. Much more than when we were young. There are so many years to cover it seems like an impossible task. Dan hasn't talked about himself at all and there are a lot of questions I would like to ask. I haven't told him anything either, but only because we haven't had time. This weekend we intend to have fun and enjoy everyone. We'll get around to questions and answers when we're both ready for them."

That explanation seemed to satisfy them a lot more. Marge glanced at Jen and Gracie then looked at Marianne and said, "I would have loved to have seen you at that airport meeting. You description gives me chills. God, you two are lucky you found each other again."

"I think Bill described it best," Jen told them. "He says it's destiny."

Chapter 24.

Herb suggested their dinner start with a toast. As he raised his glass he looked at Marianne and said, "Welcome back old friend. Never run out on us again." Short and to the point, Herb was a man of few words but those words were always well chosen.

Bill followed Herb's toast with one of his own. "If there was ever a time when fate brought two people together this is the time," he said and raised his glass as he looked at Dan and Marianne. "The circumstances are unbelievable, the odds phenomenal, and looking at you two tonight I would say the outcome looks beautiful. Welcome home."

Alan's toast seemed to express everyone's feelings, "Here's to a successful return engagement."

Marianne looked around the table and remembered the last time she was with this group. It was a long time ago but now the in-between years were only a blur. Elegance was everywhere yet there was not a trace of pretentiousness with anyone. This was evident as Marianne watched Alan carefully mix his peas with his mashed potatoes. He glanced across the table at her as if he knew she would be watching. He grinned and said, "I still hate to see them roll off my fork." Nothing has changed with any of them, Marianne thought. They're the same now as they were forty years ago, a little older, a little wiser, a lot wealthier, but their basics are the same as they always were.

Julian, Harriet, Cass and Bernie had not arrived yet, but Dan assured her they would be along before the night was over. Julian was the oldest member of the group and although his pride would never allow him to admit it, driving from New York City to Fairfield, Connecticut would be a chore for him. Bernie suggested he and Cass would pick them up and they could make the trip together. Halfway to Fairfield Bernie wisely chose to stop for dinner. "We can join the Crew for dessert and coffee," he told his passengers.

Julian smiled graciously and shook his head. "Bernie," he said, "You are a thoughtful man and a very good diplomat. I am aware of your ulterior motive and I deeply appreciate your finesse." After more than four decades as a family all of these people could read each other pretty well.

Julian's distinctive voice was the first one Marianne heard as the four late arrivals joined the group in the dining room. "At last our boat floats with a full Crew once again," he said. Although he had aged, the same as everyone else, the beautiful, resonant tones that had carried many a show tune to success were still as active as ever. He was often called upon to dub his voice for other performers who were less endowed. He didn't have to sing, just to listen to him speak was a pleasure. Harriet was still a very beautiful woman. These once troubled lovers were living proof that real love and understanding was a solid core for a good marriage.

Cass and Bernie Goldman were complete opposites of Harriet and Julian Brice. The Brices were happy and content in a world of their own. The Goldmans were dedicated to making everyone a part of the happiness they enjoyed with each other. Cass still had the flirtatious manner she used so perfectly in the chorus line, but now she was Bernie's greatest cheerleader. In her eyes he could do no wrong and was the greatest salesman on earth. Her enthusiasm pushed the shy little salesman to unbelievable heights. To him Cass was always his "blonde beauty" who deserved the best of everything and he spent the major part of his life giving her what he thought she deserved. The years had been good to Bernie. His salesmanship had expanded his bank balance beyond his wildest dreams. His good living had expanded his waistline to similar proportions. His good natured, let me do you a favor, attitude never changed.

Gracie suggested everyone move into the recreation room for some music and dancing. The "rec" room, as she called it, was made for parties. Special attention went into the décor this weekend. It was a perfect replica of Nick's Restaurant, the favorite gathering place of the Crew so many years ago. The transition from the elegance of the dining room to the memorable setting of Nick's was so fantastic Marianne expected George, their paternal maitre d', to suggest he put a few tables together to make room for everyone.

"We need some music," Jen suggested, "so we can all go dancing just like we did in the good old days."

Marianne was nervous about that suggestion.

194

"Don't worry about a thing," Dan assured her. "The first dances are all reserved for me and by the time I let you go you will have had plenty of practice."

She looked at him with a doubtful expression and asked, "Have you forgotten that many of the people here are professional dancers? That scares me a little."

"I'm not a professional dancer," he said.

"Well, you're a lot better at it than I am. I'm not even sure I remember how to dance. I've been away from it for a long time," she said.

"You'll remember," he assured her. "Years ago we knew each other's rhythm and style and that always made us look good. We'll do it again, you'll see." He took her hand and said, "Come on, let's try it and I'll show you what I mean."

Till Then by the Mills Brothers was playing on the old fashioned juke box in the far corner of the room. Would the rhythms he spoke of still be there she wondered? She would give it a try, if she goofed it up there were plenty of pros here to help her remember. She didn't forget. She followed Dan's lead perfectly. Maybe those in between years weren't there after all, she thought. Dan held her close and didn't leave any space between them this time.

"See," he said, "I knew you would remember."

The décor of the room, the memorable music, the familiar voices mingled in the background and the secure, safe feeling of Dan's arms around her brought back a flood of memories. If I dared to close my eyes we would be back in Nick's just like the old days, she thought.

Till Then was followed by *Sentimental Journey, I Don't Want To Walk Without You,* and *You Made Me Love You,* all the old favorites they had danced to so often in their earlier, happier days. Each dance helped Marianne realize she did remember how to do a lot of these things. Dan's reassuring way convinced her she had not lost any of her old dexterity. By the third dance she was enjoying herself and not giving any thought to keeping up with any of them.

Julian was the first to break the spell. "Daniel," he said, "may I steal your lady for just one dance?" The vibrant tones of his fabulous voice brought Marianne back from her reverie.

"I reserved the first ten," Dan told him and seemed reluctant to let her go. "If Marianne is willing we'll make an exception for you, Julian."

At first she was uncertain about dancing with anyone else, or letting go of Dan. He had given her the support and assurance she needed to pick up some of the pieces of the past. He helped her regain enough of her self confidence to try the dance floor with him. Now the rest of the Crew would do their share and Julian was first. She hesitated for a minute and looked at Dan. He gave her a quick wink and a nod of approval.

"I would love to dance with you," she told Julian as he took Dan's place on the dance floor. He was a smooth dancer and Marianne found it easy to follow his lead.

As they circled the floor he told her how glad he was to have her back. "I am pleased to see Daniel so happy tonight. He has been sad for far too long." When Julian spoke she noticed he still pronounced every syllable of every word. Like so many other things about the Crew, this had not changed, either.

"When Dan is happy it makes me feel good, too," she said. "We're really enjoying this weekend. I was surprised everyone remembered me. It's been a long time since we've all been together."

"Much too long a time," Julian said as he held her at arms length and tilted his head as he spoke. "Timing was an important factor in your case. You came into our lives when we each needed confidence and self-assurance. Budding careers, such as ours, required constant applications of both. You were a profound influence on each and every one of us."

"Julian, you're going to give me a big head if you keep talking like that," she said with a grin.

"I doubt that very much," he answered. "From what I have observed in our short hours of reunion you are older and wiser, but still the same Marianne of long ago. The only ability you seem to have lost is you proficiency to hide your love for Daniel. Tonight it shines like a beacon."

Marianne laughed at his comment and said she didn't think it was that obvious and quickly added, "I can't help it if it shows."

"Look around you at the happy faces in this room tonight," he said. "Believe me, there are no objections. This is long overdue."

Their conversation was interrupted when Bill tapped Julian on the shoulder. "Excuse me sir," he said with exaggerated politeness, "Are you ever going to give the rest of us a chance to dance with this lady. We're all looking for a turn. You were the only one with enough nerve to ask Dan to let her go."

"I surrender to your request," Julian answered, "Only because you are younger and stronger. But I warn you I will be back for more."

"Thank you," Bill said with a grin as Julian relinquished his dance partner. Marianne's doubts about her dancing came to the surface again and she said, "Remember I'm not a professional dancer like Jen. No fancy steps with me, please."

"OK," he answered with a grin, "no fancy steps. Jen tells me you haven't been on a dance floor in twenty years. I can't imagine that, and you certainly haven't forgotten anything."

"Flattery will get you everywhere," Marianne replied.

"What I really wanted was a few minutes to talk to you," he said.

"Oh," she answered, "is something wrong?"

"No," he said, "just the opposite. You know Dan and I go back a long time. He's been my best friend for more years than I can remember. We're closer than a lot of brothers. In all that time I have never seen him as happy as he is tonight. Thanks, Marianne."

"For what?" she asked. "I haven't done anything."

"You're here, and that's what counts. Dan isn't the only one who missed you."

The mood set by the music brought back pleasant memories for everyone. They danced, sang and enjoyed the old songs they all remembered so well.

"This has been such a fantastic night. I don't feel like I've ever been away," she told Alan as they finished a dance. He looked at her and smiled. "What's more important is that you're back," he told her. "To hell with the past, let's look at the future."

"Good idea," she agreed. Alan could always be counted on to put the party spirit in any occasion.

Dan tapped Alan on the shoulder and asked, "Can I have my partner back now? You guys have all had your turn and I'm the one she came with." Alan pretended to ignore the interruption and asked Marianne, "Did you hear something?"

"Uh — I think so," she said.

197

"Oh well," Alan sighed, "I can take a hint." He stepped aside and let Dan take his place. As he walked away he looked back and gave Marianne a big happy wink as he headed straight for the piano.

The jukebox stopped and Alan ran his fingers across the keyboard. Everyone's attention was captured when he played the Overture from *Gentlemen Again.* Bill and Jen were coaxed into doing one of their old dance routines. They were still as good as they ever were, but tonight their audience appreciated them a whole lot more. Julian sang two songs that originally put him in the limelight and by the time he finished there was not a dry eye in the room. Gracie, Jen, Harriet and Cass attempted a chorus line number but ran out of steam about halfway through it. Everyone had a good laugh but they were also reminded the years had taken a toll. Alan's musical talent and total recall took them all back to the Ballard Theater and an hour of songs and music from their original Broadway success.

"What about a song from you, Dan?" Bernie asked. "You had some of the best music in that show."

"I'd rather not tonight," Dan answered. "I'm afraid I'd have a job remembering some of the lyrics." Dan was uncomfortable with Bernie's suggestion and Julian came to his rescue.

"Very understandable, Daniel, I can see where lyrics would not be among your priorities tonight."

"Thank you," Dan replied with a nervous laugh. Marianne couldn't help notice the relief in his voice. That's odd, she thought, he always loved to sing. He was singing all the time. When he didn't know the lyrics he would make them up. He was so good at it sometimes we doubted the real lyrics when we heard them. She made a mental note of another question to be answered later.

Alan was enjoying himself at the piano and Marianne watched as his hands moved with smooth precision across the keyboard of the marvelous old upright. This was his spot in the universe and only he could fill it. He reached for his drink with his left hand and his right hand took up the slack. He never missed a note. The man was an absolute musical genius.

"Alan," she said, as she put a plate of assorted snacks on the small table next to the piano. "I haven't seen you eat a thing since dinner and that was hours ago. I brought over some munchies to share with you."

"If you share my piano bench, I'll share your munchies," he replied. He slid to one side and made room for Marianne to join him. She was fascinated as she watched his fingers dance across the keys. It seemed as though the instrument welcomed his graceful touch.

"How I envy your talent," she told him. "I wish I could play the piano like you do."

Alan looked at her over the rim of his glasses and with a whimsical frown said, "Marianne, you don't have to play music, you cause it." He began to play *Because of You* and she wondered how he always managed to connect to a heartstring. He was a gentle person who looked at the good side of everything. No wonder Marge loves him, she thought.

Marianne put her arm around his shoulders and said, "Someday I want to do something that will make you feel as special as you always make me feel."

"Do you really?" he asked, as he glanced at her and quickly turned back to the keyboard.

"Sure I do," she said.

"Be good to Dan," he told her. "Be real good to Dan. That will make me feel good."

His response surprised her and she looked at the little musician with a puzzled expression. "Alan, you're serious, aren't you?" she asked and realized this was not just party conversation, Alan meant what he was saying.

"Yes, I am," he said in a solemn tone. "He's had a lousy life since you left."

"How can that be?" she asked. "He was married to Jane for a lot of years."

"Correction, dear lady," Alan interrupted, "Jane was never married to Dan. Jane was married to Dan's money." He was still playing the piano, but now Marianne didn't hear any of the music.

"Oh Alan, you don't mean that," she said and wished she had not heard what she knew he said.

"Oh yes I do," he said emphatically. "She was a first class bitch. She trapped Dan out in California and he paid for it for years."

Marianne could feel the color drain from her face as the shock of Alan's statement hit home. She hoped no one noticed her reaction. Jen had mentioned that there were problems between Jane and Dan but she didn't go into detail. Marianne thought it was something Dan would explain when he felt the time was right. It was not one of the things they had discussed in their many phone conversations. She never asked any questions about Jane and thought maybe that was the reason Dan had not said any more about her. This weekend was so full of activity they didn't have a chance for any real discussions. She couldn't believe what Alan said. This was a man who could always see the good in everyone. He gave Satan credit for keeping Heaven warm. Could it be that he had changed over the years? Dan said he hadn't. "A few gray hairs, but the same old charmer he always was," were Dan's words. Perhaps there were a few things she still didn't understand. She knew this was something they should have talked about but purposely avoided. Neither of them wanted to say anything that would trigger a negative reaction. Perhaps this was not the time to say anything. Maybe it would be better to keep quiet and see if Dan said anything before the night was over.

"I never suspected anything like that," she admitted. "I appreciate you telling me. I promise you I will be good to him. He's pretty special to me, too. You know that, don't you?"

"If I wasn't absolutely positive of that point I wouldn't have said a word to you," Alan stated. He stopped playing the piano, turned to face Marianne on the bench and said, "If this night goes by and Dan does not ask you to marry him, will you marry me?"

Marianne laughed and said, "Alan, I'd love to. Just make sure it's all right with your wife. I'd hate to do anything that would make Marge angry." Dan's voice brought the both of them back to reality. He put an arm around each of their shoulders and asked, "Has this old flirt proposed to you again?"

"Uh, oh," Marianne said. "Looks like we've been caught."

"Certainly does," Alan sighed. "Every time I get a good thing going somebody interrupts. It's the story of my life," he lamented as he shrugged his shoulders and turned back to the piano.

"There's something I want you to see," Dan said as he took Marianne by the hand and led her through the living room and into Herb's office area. "Where are we going?" she asked.

"With all the activity tonight I thought you might appreciate a little quiet time," he said. "Herb has a special place he calls his peaceful room. I'm going to show it to you."

200

They crossed the office and he opened another door. This one led to a beautiful glassed in area that ran the length of the south side of the house. It was like walking into a tropical paradise. The only sound came from a small fountain in the far corner. It wasn't a drip or running water, but more like the occasional small splashes a little brook makes as it travels through the woods.

"This is where Herb comes to get away from the outside world," Dan told her. "I think he also uses it to get away from Gracie's constant chatter. She's a wonderful woman and I love her dearly, but she never stops talking. I often meant to ask Herb if she talks in her sleep."

"This is fantastic," Marianne said as she glanced around the beautiful collection of flowers and plants. "If you didn't show it to me, I wouldn't have known it was here."

"Plants are Herb's hobby," he explained. "He's very proud of these." He put his arm around her shoulder and pointed to the antique porch glider at the other end of the room. "Let's sit here for awhile and pretend we're back in the days of the Ballard Theater," he suggested.

"I don't like to go back in time," she said. "There are a lot of things in the past that I wouldn't want to relive. I don't even like to think about some of them. Let's just sit here and not pretend anything."

He agreed and wondered if she was referring to the same things he had in mind. "We also have some great memories," he reminded her. "I remember the first time I met you," he continued. "Do you remember that backstage party at the Ballard? You came in with Josh Golden. Bill and I thought it was the biggest mismatch in history. We didn't know you were Josh's number one sales agent. We thought you were another one of his girlfriends."

"Don't pick on poor Josh," Marianne laughed. "He was always good to me. Ours was strictly a commercial relationship and as long as I worked for him he never overstepped the bounds. There was never even a hint or suggestion on his part, and I was always teasing him about his girlfriends."

"Maybe Josh only liked blondes," Dan teased. "You had red hair when we first met."

"You're right, I did," she agreed with a chuckle. "Boy, that was a long time ago. There is still a trace of red in there somewhere," she told him as she ruffled up her hair. "Now you have to poke around in the gray to find any of it." She raised her head from his shoulder and looked at him. "How come you remember it so well?"

"I guess there was something there right from the start," he said. "Josh told us it was your birthday. When I asked you how old you were, you said, 'forty' and I wondered what it would be like to go out with an 'older' woman." They enjoyed the memories conjured up by reminiscing but each carefully avoided asking any of the serious questions that could put a damper on this weekend.

The spell of nostalgia was broken when the door opened from the office area. "So this is where you two have been hiding," Herb said. "I should have known. Everybody is afraid Marianne is going to disappear again. You had better not count on any privacy this weekend."

Neither Dan nor Marianne realized the sun had risen on a new day. They were so preoccupied with their memories time slipped right past them.

"We want to reserve this spot, Herb," Dan said. "We have a lot more reminiscing to do."

Marianne agreed it was a good idea. "Right now we should get back to the party before it's all over," she said.

"Not a chance of having it end until at least midnight," Herb told them. "This crowd has real cause to celebrate and they all intend to take full advantage of it. Tomorrow we will all suffer, but tonight we celebrate."

The party had moved into the main part of the house. Alan preferred the baby grand piano in the living room. He liked to watch the reactions when he played a favorite song or remembered something that awakened old memories. It seemed like everything he played jogged a memory for someone.

The food supply had been completely restocked, but this time it was for breakfast. Marianne wondered how these women could all consume so much food and keep the trim figures they had forty years ago. Gracie laughed and said it was a trade secret.

"That's a crock," Marge added. "We don't do this very often, so we're skipping the bran flakes and bananas this morning and living dangerously. The last good party was when Bill and Jen's youngest daughter, Kathy, got married. That was five years ago.

Now it takes me that long to recuperate from one of these all nighters. It's not like the good old days when we could party all night then work all day with no sleep."

"We certainly did cram a lot of living into a few short years," Jen commented.

"I wish we could do it all over again," Marge added.

"I wouldn't mind doing it again if I could pick out the times I wanted to repeat and leave out the ones I didn't like," Harriet suggested.

Memories, Marianne thought, we all have them and we all rely on them once in a while. She never realized what a big part memories played in her life. This weekend awakened many she was so sure she had buried forever. Memories she thought were hers alone were also part of Dan's and many were shared by the entire Crew. If we could only dip into our memories and fix all of our mistakes, she thought, or change things so all our memories came up pleasant.

Chapter 25

It was almost noon on Saturday. Time was going by too fast, Marianne thought. There is too much to talk about in one weekend. Then she remembered it didn't have to be done in one weekend. This was not intended to be a one time reunion. It was the reuniting of old friends and the renewal of an interrupted relationship. There were lots of blanks to be filled in before either of them could hope to pick up the pieces. She felt uneasy about discussing some of the things that bothered her. She wanted to wait until she could talk with Dan. She knew any of the Crew would answer her questions if they could. She felt certain Alan could help her. She saw him get up from the piano several times but each time she tried to get his attention someone called her or distracted him.

Finally he motioned to her to come over to the piano.

"Were you looking for me?" he asked.

"Yes," she said, "I'd like to talk to you if you don't mind."

"It will be my pleasure," he assured her as he pointed to the piano bench next to him.

"Have a seat."

She didn't want to talk at the piano. She wanted someplace where there wouldn't be interruptions.

"Can we take a walk?" she asked.

"Walk?" Alan questioned. He thought it was common knowledge that his total capacity for physical exercise was entirely in his fingers.

"OK," Marianne conceded. "Let's forget the walk. Can we sit somewhere and talk for a few minutes?"

"How about the kitchen," Alan suggested. "It's the last place anyone would look for me."

"Good idea," she agreed.

Like everything else in the Preston's fabulous home the kitchen was far from ordinary. This one had everything Marianne ever dreamed could be in a kitchen. This is a cook's paradise, she thought and glanced at Alan as she motioned toward the table.

"Here?" she asked.

"No," he said and pointed to a small area off the main kitchen, "over there."

Like Herb's peaceful room, you had to know it was there or you would miss it altogether. It was a small, comfortable alcove that almost invited you to sit and have a cup of coffee. Alan took two mugs from an overhead cabinet and poured coffee from a fresh brewed pot on the counter. As they sat across from each other he rested his elbow on the table and cupped his chin in the palm of his hand. Marianne noticed, this time he didn't add anything to his coffee.

"I have the distinct feeling I am about to be third degreed," he said.

She didn't want to put Alan on the spot, but she needed some blanks filled in quickly.

"I don't want to ask any embarrassing questions," she said, "but remember, I've been away a long time and a lot has happened that I don't know about."

He tilted his head and looked at her over the top rim of his glasses. "Have you asked Dan?"

"Yes and no," she answered evasively. "We agreed not to get into the serious questions this weekend. I know we'll get everything straightened out eventually but I don't think Dan is going to say too much right now. He's having fun this weekend. I'm having a good time, too, and I don't want to mess it up by saying the wrong thing. I feel like I'm walking on eggs. I hope you understand."

"Sure I understand," he said as he slowly sipped his coffee. "You have to promise me that anything I tell you stays between us, all right?"

"That's a promise," she answered.

"You know about the rotten deal Broderick tried to pull on Dan when he went to California, don't you?" he asked.

"Not all of it," Marianne said. "Jen wrote to me after Dan's first phone call. She told me Broderick set up a marriage ceremony with Jane Blanchard, supposedly for a screen test and it turned out to be a legal wedding. She didn't explain very much about it. She probably thought Dan would tell me."

"That was only part of it," Alan told her. "That miserable mess in California was a set up from the start. Broderick knew all about Dan's family, how and when his parents were killed and everything about them including their financial background. He had contract offers for Dan before he even tried to sign him. That wasn't enough for that greedy bastard. He wanted some of what Dan already had. He tried to match him up with one of his girls, but that didn't work. That's when the phony screen test took place. In those days nobody could afford bad publicity. So Broderick would "arrange" a quiet settlement to avoid a scandal that would screw up those contracts. Stevie Boy would get a bundle of money and that little bitch would clean up, too. Dan wasn't supposed to know anything about that. Josh Golden dug up the dirty details." Alan shook his head as if to say these memories were things he would rather forget.

"When Josh told Dan about the press releases the first thing he thought of was you," Alan told her. "Dan was afraid you would believe the story because of the argument you had before he left New York. He couldn't find you to explain. None of us could. Dan nearly went nuts looking for you. He thought you were still mad at him. Julian finally got it across to him that the argument you two had was an act you put on to make him do what was best for his career. He was frustrated because he couldn't find you. He was mad at himself because he didn't realize what you were trying to do. When he found out about Broderick's scheme he was furious. It was the only time I ever remember seeing Dan Shaw really mad. He wanted to kill Steve Broderick. For the next couple of weeks we made sure he was never alone. In his frame of mind, at that time, he probably would have gone after the bastard and we weren't going to take any chances. Bernie came up with the idea of putting Broderick Enterprises out of business," Alan continued. "It cost Dan a small fortune, but he didn't care. As long as there were no more Hollywood contacts, there was no more Broderick Enterprises. That's when Continental Casting was born. Dan had a score to settle with Steven Broderick but he didn't want any of the legitimates who had signed with him to get hurt. Bernie took care of the business end and Julian screened the talent. Dan still owns Continental. Broderick never got another chance to get back in the business. He tried but every time he got a toehold Dan squashed it. He was determined to make sure Broderick never hurt anyone else."

Marianne listened intently to everything Alan was saying. Each new bit of information added to the already overwhelming regrets she felt for her impulsive actions so many years ago. She had been so sure she knew what was best for Dan that, in a way, she aided in setting him up for the biggest disappointment of his life.

My thickheaded, know it all, stubbornness has caused him a lifetime of unhappiness, she thought. I really have some making up to do.

Alan took a sip of his coffee and studied Marianne for a few seconds. He wondered if he was saying too much. She had not interrupted or tried to stop him. She just listened. I hope I'm doing the right thing, he thought, and picked up where he left off.

"Broderick was gone and Jane still tried to pull off her divorce scam. She got a big surprise. Dan told her to go ahead, but she wouldn't get a cent and she would probably go to jail. She threatened to start a messy scandal and he told her to go ahead with that, too. He had twenty million bucks to back him up and he was itching for a fight. Instead of wiping her out in court, he decided to make her pay for her part in the scheme. He told her there wouldn't be any divorce. She was married to him and would stay married to him. She could give up her plans for an acting career and move to his house in Cincinnati but if she ever fooled around with anyone, she would be out with nothing. It was either move to Ohio or go to jail. She picked Ohio. After what she put Dan through it was nice to see her squirm. That was the arrangement and that's what Dan stuck with for years. He figured as long as there was no divorce she could never marry anybody and as long as he was legally married to her he would never get trapped into anything like that again. He never paid any attention to anyone else that I know about. We all tried to match him up from time to time, but he wasn't interested. Then Bill found the article in the paper and you know the rest."

Alan knew that Dan Shaw was a very patient man and thought everything through before he made a move. He sympathized with Marianne's predicament and wanted to eliminate any obstacles in the way of these two staying together this time. He was sure Dan would eventually explain everything in detail. Now all he wanted to do was ease her worries a little. He wasn't sure if he had answered her questions or confused her more.

Once the information started to flow it was like a faucet had been opened. Alan had a lot more to say and he thought now was as good a time as any to say it. Twice he refilled the coffee mugs and Marianne noticed again, he drank only coffee, no additives. She wondered if his liquid power supply was depleted or if he didn't need anything extra now. What a nice compliment, she thought, Alan trusts me enough that he doesn't need reinforcement to talk to me. Dan was right again. Every one of these people were glad she was back — so was she.

"After you left, Josh Golden came by all the time to see if anyone had heard from you," Alan continued. "He told us how all those club tabs were paid. It came off your commissions, didn't it? You let us think we were earning them with a few songs and a little entertainment on our part and you were paying them all along. We found out about some of the things you and Dan did for all of us and never said a word to anyone. We were all broke in those days. You and Dan were the only ones with any money. We found out how the bills got paid and who paid them." He seemed to be benefiting from this conversation as much as Marianne. He was saying out loud a lot of what he had kept inside for many years and it made him feel good. Now she wasn't feeling so guilty about asking him for answers.

"Flanagan's Dance Studio was a perfect example," Alan continued. "Dan picked up a five year lease on that place. He worked it out through Bernie Goldman and swore Bernie to secrecy. Bill paid a quarter of the actual cost of that place and Dan picked up the rest because he knew that was all Bill could afford. You knew about that, didn't you?"

"Yes," Marianne admitted, "I knew about it. Dan offered to lend him the money to start the business, but Bill didn't know how he could pay it back so he wouldn't take it. That's when Dan came up with the lease idea."

Alan looked at her over his glasses and made a face. "That's not the way Dan tells it," he said. "You were the one who figured out the lease. Bill didn't find out until almost three years later. By that time the studio was making money and Bill was on the way to being successful. Marge and I owe Dan, too. He put up the money for us to open Custom Costumes. Bernie thinks Dan can walk on water. He spent years knocking himself out on one little deal after another. No one would take a chance on him when it came to big money deals. Then Dan backed him and today Bernie can buy and sell the whole Crew and not put a dent in his bank account. Never once in forty-five years has Dan Shaw said to any of us, "You owe me." They don't make them like him anymore. He's one of a kind, and so are you. That's why we're all glad you're back. It took some time, but it was worth it." He finished the last of his coffee, looked at Marianne and said, "I hope that fills in a lot of the blanks for you."

"It certainly does and I appreciate it," she said. "I have one last question if you don't mind?"

"What is it?" he asked.

"Why wouldn't Dan sing last night?"

Alan bit his bottom lip as he slowly shook his head. "I can't answer that," he told her. "None of us have heard Dan sing a note in over forty years. At first we thought it had something to do with breaking his contract with Broderick, but he wouldn't sing when he was just with us. We all thought for sure he would open up last night. That's why Bernie tried to coax him into it. When it didn't work, we were all disappointed, but we'll keep trying."

As they walked back into the living room Alan remarked that Marianne looked tired.

"I guess I'm not used to all night parties anymore," she said.

"We'll have to rectify that," he commented with a grin.

"How?" she asked.

"We'll probably have to have more of them," he answered. "In the meantime I'll put a bug in Gracie's ear about you being tired. She'll suggest something. She usually finds solutions for life's little problems."

"Thanks Alan," Marianne said, "for everything."

Chapter 26.

Gracie put an arm around Marianne's shoulders as she said, "Every one of us snuck off for an hour or so during the night. You've been so busy you haven't had a chance. You must be exhausted."

"I am kind of tired," Marianne admitted, "but I didn't think it showed. There is so much to catch up on I lost all track of time."

"Go upstairs to the first bedroom on the right," Gracie said. "Get a little sleep and I'll wake you in an hour or so." Marianne welcomed the suggestion. They had been traveling, celebrating and reminiscing since she began this trip with Dan on Friday morning. It was now after two o'clock on Saturday afternoon.

She closed the bedroom door quietly behind her, turned down the bedspread, took off her shoes and sank back on the most comfortable bed in the world. As she closed her eyes she pictured Dan's face. He seems so happy all the time, yet his eyes tell a different story. There's a lot of hurt behind those soft brown eyes. Thanks to Alan she now understood a little more about the in-between years. Dan had been deeply hurt by their separation. She was so wrapped up in her own misery she misjudged him terribly. We really have to talk, she thought, as she drifted off to sleep.

She felt the gentle touch of a hand brush the hair from her forehead. She thought she was dreaming until she felt it again. She blinked her eyes open and saw Dan sitting on the side of the bed.

"You look so peaceful I didn't want to wake you," he said softly. "Are you all right?"

"Oh sure, I'm fine," she answered. "I just needed a quick nap to recharge my battery."

"Can I join you?" he asked.

"Sure," she replied. "Just stay on your own side of the bed."

"I promise," he answered and walked around and sat on the other side, took off his shoes and stretched out beside her. She had not moved. She was lying on her side with her back toward him. He waited a minute hoping she would turn around. When she didn't he put his hand on her shoulder and softly sang.

"I've spent my life looking for you. Finding my way wasn't easy to do.
But I knew there was you all the while and it was worth every mile.
So lay down beside me, love me and hide me, kiss all the hurting of
this world away.
Hold me so close that I feel your heart beat and don't ever wander
away."

She still didn't move so he continued ....

Mornings and evenings all were the same. There was no music till I
heard your name.
But I knew when I saw you smile, now I can rest for awhile.
So lay down beside me, love me and hide me, kiss all the hurting of
this world away.
Hold me so close that I feel your heart beat and don't ever wander
away.

She finally turned toward him and with mock anger said, "Danny, that's not fair — you know I can't sing."

They both laughed and he put his arms around her and kissed her gently. That nice comfortable feeling they shared so many years ago was finally theirs again.

She lay close to his side. His arm was around her and she rested her head on his shoulder. Her eyes were still closed as she said, "This is the most comfortable place in the world." Then reluctantly added, "But something tells me there is a party still going on and we should be part of it."

"You're right," he said, "Gracie sent me up here to wake you, not to join you."

"Foolish woman," Marianne sleepily commented with a contented smile. She opened her eyes, looked at him and asked, "Did anyone ever tell you that you have a beautiful voice? You should go into show business."

"No thanks," he answered, "I did that once and it got me into an awful mess. Now I only sing when I have a good reason.

"Oh," she said and glanced at him from the corner of her eye, "Do you have a good reason?"

"Now I do," he answered.

211

"This sounds interesting," she teased. "Remind me to check into it. Right now I have to get out of this bed and into the bathroom. I need some cold water on my eyes to keep them open for a couple of hours. So will you please let go of me so I can get up?"

"No," he said, "I'm never going to let you go."

"Just temporarily," she said.

The cold water seemed to work. She came back into the bedroom and said it would have been wiser to leave the eyes half closed. Now they were opened so wide she looked as if she had just had a bad scare.

Dan was sitting on the side of the bed, just as he was when she left the room.

"What's the matter, Dan, is something wrong?" she asked.

He reached for her hand and asked her to sit next to him. "Let's talk for a minute before we go downstairs," he said. "We agreed to keep this weekend on the light side and enjoy ourselves. I thought it was a good idea, but now I'm afraid I've been unfair to you. You must be wondering why I haven't told you about California and Jane and how it all came about."

"I have to admit it did cross my mind," Marianne said. "Jen's letters explained a little, Bill filled me in on some and Alan said a few things that surprised me. I thought you would get around to talking about it when you were ready."

"I don't know how to begin," he admitted. "It's a part of my life I wish had never happened and I try to shut it out. You deserve an explanation, or an attempt at one."

Marianne could see how difficult this was for him. "Wait a minute," she said. "Before you say any more let me tell you something. You think you made a mistake, but that was a situation you were trapped into. I know that now. I made a mistake, too, several of them, but mine were my own fault. My wounded pride got in the way of good judgment. I should have trusted you and instead I ran away from you and every one I cared about. I quit my job, walked out on Josh Golden and slammed the door on that part of my life. I was wrong. I was **VERY** wrong. Before you left for California I told you if you ever needed me all you had to do was pick up the phone. I let you down. I wasn't there for you when you did need me. Perhaps if I had been things would have been different for both of us. I'm sorry for that and I don't know how I can ever make it up to you. If you want to talk, Danny, I'm always ready to listen but no explanation is needed — ever."

She could see the tears in his eyes as he looked at her and said, "Marianne, I love you."

"Danny," she answered softly, "I love you, too. I always have." She stood up and looked at him, "Now we better go back downstairs before we both get into trouble."

The short nap revived Marianne and by the time they rejoined the party she was ready to continue the activities. Dan had not had any sleep but the conversation in the bedroom seemed to take a huge weight off his shoulders and raise his spirits considerably.

By eleven o'clock Saturday night the party had diminished to sleepy conversations. The whole Crew had all the singing, dancing and memory raking they could handle for one weekend. Sunday would be here before any of them realized it. Marianne was not looking forward to saying good-bye even though she knew this time it would be different.

From now on good-byes would only be temporary.

Time has a way of catching up with all of us, she thought, as her tired feelings began to surface again. She felt like she had cheated because of the nap earlier in the afternoon.

Dan didn't get a chance to slip away and she knew he was tired, too. They both thought it was time to say good night to the others and head for bed.

Gracie never mentioned sleeping arrangements. She said the front bedroom was ready for company and left the rest to them. It was a beautiful big room with twin beds, a large nightstand between them and an adjoining bathroom. Their clothes had been carefully hung in the closet and the two suitcases placed against the wall next to the bathroom door. Dan left her at the bedroom door and went back downstairs to make arrangements with Bill about Sunday's departure. It gave Marianne a chance to take a quick shower, put on her nightgown and get into bed.

Dan came back, looked at the beds, shook his head and said, "This isn't going to work." He moved the nightstand to the wall by the bathroom door and pushed the beds together. "That's better," he said as he stepped back to admire his handiwork. He seemed satisfied with the new arrangement and went into the bathroom to shower.

He came back into the bedroom in dark blue pajamas and danced an imaginary waltz toward the beds. Marianne watched his performance and wondered what he was going to do next. He reached the foot of the beds and put his hands together as if to pray. Instead, he made a leap for the beds and landed where the beds came together. Neither of them realized both beds were on wheels. The force of his landing caused the bed Marianne was on to go in one direction and the empty bed to go the opposite way. Poor Dan landed on the floor between them.

Marianne was laughing so hard she couldn't even ask him if he was hurt. He sat on the floor between the beds and said, "I can see I'm not going to get a lot of sympathy from you for this one."

"Danny," she said, "I don't think sympathy was really what you were looking for, was it?" She was trying to be serious but the situation was so funny she couldn't control the laughter.

"Well," he admitted, "ten minutes ago it wasn't, now it's a prime concern." By this time he was laughing as hard as she was.

* * * * *

It was almost noon before anyone ventured toward the kitchen. Dan and Marianne were the only two fully dressed. The rest of the Crew were in a wild array of pajamas, robes, nightgowns and anything that was handy. The most popular beverages were Alka-Seltzer and Pepto-Bismol. Food was not a popular item, but sympathy was appreciated and spread lavishly. Dan poured coffee for Marianne and himself. The sound of the liquid hitting the cup caused loud moans from Gracie, Marge, Bill and Jen as all four grabbed their heads with both hands. The beautiful people who played such a big part in this wonderful weekend had been replaced by a disgruntled crowd of sufferers.

Bill watched as Dan poured the coffee. "I can't understand how you two can celebrate longer and stronger than the rest of us and come out looking so good," he said.

Dan shrugged his shoulders and said, "You have to learn to relieve your pent up emotions."

Bill looked across the table at his wife and said, "See Jen, I told you sex cures all kinds of pain."

Jen's reply was a moan that was one decibel above a growl.

Cass and Bernie had not made an appearance yet. Marianne was hoping to see them before she and Dan had to leave. When they finally came in Bernie was wearing pajama pants, a terry cloth robe that didn't go all the way around him, and socks. Cass followed him and to everyone's surprise she was impeccably dressed, right down to perfect makeup. Alan took one look at her and said, "What in hell is with you?"

Cass looked around the table at the group of Sunday morning sufferers and very seriously said, "Today we have to say good-bye to Marianne. Last time she said good-bye we didn't see her for forty years. If she does it again I want her to remember me at my best."

"Cass," Marianne said through the laughter, "I promise it won't be forty years this time."

Good-byes are never easy. Saying it this time was especially difficult because so much was left unsaid. It had been a lighthearted weekend. The Crew had proven themselves to be just as caring as they were forty years ago. Alan was the only one who allowed himself to get serious and that was due solely to Marianne's direct urging.

As departure time caught up with them there were a few tears, lots of hugs, and sincere promises of return visits in the near future. No one really wanted to break up this gathering and it was difficult for Marianne and Dan to leave.

The entire Crew had gathered outside the front entrance of the house to wave good-bye. As Dan backed the car out of the parking area and drove by the front door Marianne had to laugh. Standing at the front entrance to this palatial Connecticut estate were ten well to do, socially prominent people, nine of them in various stages of disarray and impeccably dressed Cass, intent on leaving a good impression. It was quite a sight.

"You said this was going to be a memorable weekend and you were so right. I enjoyed every minute of it," Marianne told him.

"I'm glad," he replied, "I enjoyed it, too. It was something we all needed."

"I still have a million questions," she said.

Dan knew there were serious questions in the back of both of their minds. He knew they would have to be answered sooner or later. He didn't want to look for answers this weekend. He wanted a little more time to prove to Marianne their old love affair was still very much alive. He glanced at her and asked, "What kind of questions?"

She hesitated a minute then had second thoughts about bringing up serious issues. Not now, she thought, the heavy questions can wait. She noticed Dan's happy, contented expression and she didn't want anything to interfere with it. "Oh," she answered casually, "things like, does Gracie talk in her sleep?"

"I'll have to remember to ask Herb," he answered with a chuckle. "We do have some serious questions that need answers. You realize that, don't you?"

"I know we do," she said, "but let's stick to our original agreement and keep this weekend on the light side. We'll do our serious talking next time, OK?"

"It's OK with me," he said, "provided 'next time' is next weekend."

Marianne turned sideways on the seat so she could face him and asked, "Do you really want to come back next weekend?"

"I don't even want to go home," he answered. "I want to hear about everything that happened to you and I want to tell you about everything that happened to me."

"I'd like that, too," she told him and thought for sure he was reading her thoughts.

"Good," he said, "find a place you would like to go, I'll pick you up Saturday morning and we'll spend the weekend filling each other in on what we've done with our lives."

"Wait a minute," she said, "by 'pick me up' do you mean in you airplane?"

"Sure," he answered.

"NOT ON YOUR LIFE" she stated. "There is no way you can talk me into putting one foot in that airplane."

"Don't you trust me?" he asked.

"I have all the faith and trust in the world in you," she told him. "But I refuse to be part of anything that completely separates itself from the earth. With me it's good old terra firma and the more firma the less terror."

216

Dan could see, even though she made a lighthearted remark about the airplane, that Marianne was terrified of flying. We'll have to work on that he thought, but not now, too many other things to clear up first.

"All right," he said, "where would you like to go and how would you like to go there?"

"Why do we have to go anywhere?" she asked. "Why can't we stay home? I have been known to put a meal together in the past. Nothing like the meals at the Prestons, but if you want to be comfortable and talk perhaps the best place is home."

"That's fine with me," he answered. "We won't plan to go anywhere, but we will plan on being together." That suggestion had a nice sound to it, Marianne thought.

The ride home from Connecticut on Sunday seemed a lot quicker than the trip down on Friday. They laughed a lot on the way home. Especially when they remembered the Crew on the front steps as they were leaving.

As he turned the car into the driveway, Dan seemed a little concerned.

"What's the matter?" she asked. "Don't tell me your butterflies are back?"

"No," he answered with a chuckle. "I'm very comfortable with all of your family. I was wondering if you intend to mention anything about the little incident with the beds."

"Would I do a thing like that?" she asked with a big smile as she cast him a sideways glance.

"I suspect you would," he said with a grin as he parked the car in front of the garage and they went into the house together.

"Hi there," Beth greeted them. "How was your reunion?"

"Terrific," Marianne answered. "It couldn't have been better." One funny story followed another until they had relayed all they could remember about the Crew's memorable reunion. There were a few things they felt were just for them and they decided to keep them that way.

The weekend was over. It was time to say good-bye. The ride to the airport was a quiet one. "I hate saying good-bye," he told her. "At least this time we know it's only for a few days."

"Danny," Marianne said, "this has been a fantastic weekend. There were times when I felt like I was twenty years old again. To say I enjoyed it is putting it mildly. I can honestly say that the best part was sharing it with you. You made it all worthwhile."

"I hate leaving you," he said. "We have so much catching up to do." He put his hand on her cheek and turned her face toward him. "I meant it when I said I love you."

"I know you did," she answered softly, "So did I." It's difficult to enjoy a kiss in the front seat of a car when the car has bucket seats with a console in between, but they managed.

Marianne stood on the tarmac next to the airport office and watched as Dan maneuvered the plane into position for take off. Five minutes later he was airborne and on his way home to Long Island. I wish this end of the line was home, she thought, as she walked back to her car. She wondered if anyone at the airport noticed that although she walked straight and steady, her feet never touched the ground.

Chapter 27

Marianne leaned against the chain link fence and watched the plane circle the airport. She had that funny churned up sensation again. It reminded her of the feelings she had when she first met Dan Shaw. It was there when she answered the phone and heard Dan's voice and it was there when she remembered what they had many years ago. She wondered if those feelings could ever be a reality again.

Dan said he would arrive about 8:30 Saturday morning. At 8:26 she watched his plane circle for the approach to the runway. He was right on time. The airport tower blocked her view of the far end of the field and she couldn't see the plane's wheels touch the ground. It was only a minute before the aircraft rolled into sight and turned toward the hangar area. She was fascinated as she watched him maneuver the airplane into the spot the attendant had waiting for him. He's pretty good with that airplane she thought, but not good enough to get me into it.

Dan left the plane and carried his bag to where Marianne was waiting. As he set the bag on the ground next to her, he smiled and asked, "Have you been waiting long?"

"No," she said, "I got here about the same time you did. I watched you circle and come in."

He put his bag in her car and told her he had to stop at the office for a few minutes. He said it was the first time he had used this airport. He liked it better than the one he used on Thanksgiving. The approach was easier, it wasn't as crowded and he liked what he saw so far. He was careful about his plane and wanted to set up a temporary maintenance schedule.

As they drove out of the parking lot he asked about plans for the weekend.

Marianne gave him a surprised look and said, "I thought we were going to stay home and talk."

"That's fine with me," he told her, "if you're sure that's what you want to do."

"I was looking forward to it," she said and glanced at him as she added, "If I had my druthers I'd rather take a trip to Alaska or Hawaii or maybe Bermuda. Since it's already Saturday morning and I have to go to work on Monday, it kind of cuts into the time frame a little. Maybe next time."

"Let me know when you're ready," he invited with a chuckle.

"Don't tempt me," she teased.

"I will, every chance I get," he warned her with a grin. "Do you really want to stay home? Are you sure you don't want to go somewhere?"

"Yes, I really want to stay home, and yes, I'm sure I don't want to go anywhere," she said. "I haven't recovered from last weekend yet. I think we had better take it easy for awhile. Remember, I'm not twenty years old any more."

"I'll try to remember," he assured her with a smile.

The weekend was off to a good start. They were comfortable with each other and wanted some quiet time together. They had a lot to talk about, things they couldn't talk about on the phone. They had forty years to fill in and they hoped most of it could be covered this weekend.

Dan unpacked his bag while Marianne made coffee. She set the cups and saucers on the coffee table in the living room and waited for him to join her on the sofa. She handed him a fresh cup of coffee and said, "OK, we're going to spend this weekend talking – you begin."

"Just like that," he asked with a surprised laugh.

"Sure," she said. "The sooner we get started the sooner we get it over with."

He looked confused and she realized she caught him off guard.

"Where do you want me to start?" he asked.

"I don't care. Start with – I was born and then – if you want to," she told him.

He knew she was trying to make this easy for him and he wondered if it was as difficult for her to talk about the in-between years as it was for him.

"How far did we get when we were reminiscing in Connecticut?" he asked.

"Not very far," she said. "We left off when you went to California.

Dan picked up the conversation from there and continued with his experiences on the West Coast. "I hated everything about California. I was mad at you and I was going to prove to you that you were wrong. I knew what I wanted – I just couldn't sell you on the idea. I didn't understand why you argued with me. I didn't want to let you know how down my spirits were. That's why I didn't call you. You could always tell when something was wrong. I never could hide it from you for long. It's still that way with us. Remember what happened on the phone when you asked me why I called you? I knew you weren't ready for the real reason and I never intended to blurt it out like I did."

He reached for his coffee cup and Marianne noticed a slight tremble in his hand. She wondered if she should stop him, then decided against it.

"Let me get back to what happened in California," he continued. "I hate to think about it or talk about it, but you should know the whole story. Then, maybe we can forget it."

He's got the right idea, she thought. I wish I could help him, but now it's his turn.

Dan took a deep breath and began what he hoped would be the last time he had to dwell on such an unsavory situation. "Steve Broderick told me he scheduled some filming on location in Reno. He said it was a pilot and would be a good break for me and a screen test for Jane Blanchard. I almost refused, but I didn't want him to know I was going back to New York at the end of the month. I thought he would try to talk me out of it and I didn't want to listen to him preach about contracts and other obligations. He said Jane needed someone with stage experience to help her with timing. I fell for the whole line. I thought it was legitimate. He said it was only for studio use, no casting or wardrobe was involved. A camera crew was all we needed. I thought it was odd that we only had one rehearsal and then everything was ready to roll. I figured it was only a test run so it didn't matter that much. At the time I didn't know anything about any press releases."

Marianne could see how difficult this was for him. She wanted to put her arms around him and tell him this didn't matter. He didn't have to prove anything to her, none of this was necessary. Instead, she kept quiet and let him continue.

"Josh Golden called me at the studio. He was furious about the item in Variety. I didn't know anything about the story until he called me. I told him what happened and he figured it out right away. He tried to get back to you and so did I, but you were gone."

He wanted to reach out and hold her. He wanted her to understand that she was the only woman he ever really loved. He wanted to tell her how many nights he couldn't sleep because he wondered where she was and he wanted to tell her how much he still loved her. Not yet, he thought, I have to know how she feels before I can do that.

"Your aunt told us you left after you talked with Josh. We thought you would call back before the day was over. When we didn't hear from you by noon on Sunday I panicked. I called Bill and he said none of the Crew could find you. I flew back to New York on Monday morning. Josh and I went to the police and they said there was nothing they could do. You were not a missing person you left because you wanted to. As far as they were concerned there was no mystery about it. They said you would turn up sooner or later and told us to come back in a week if no one heard from you. Their casual attitude made both of us angry. We found a detective agency in New Jersey and put them to work on it right away. Josh wasn't satisfied with that, he hired another one in New York City."

He turned sideways on the sofa and took her hands in his. "Marianne," he said, "I never experienced feelings like that in all my life. I was afraid you were gone for good and I didn't know what to do. My world was falling apart and no one could do anything to stop it. I was mad at you for leaving, I was angry at me for being so stupid, and I was at the boiling point with Steve Broderick. By then I knew he was behind the whole scheme. I guess I was mad at Jane, too, but I don't remember giving her a second thought. Broderick was the one I wanted to get my hands on."

He explained how the Crew had stepped in and prevented his return to California and how they finally handled the demise of Broderick Enterprises. "As far as Jane was concerned, if she had called it quits on their little ploy I wouldn't have paid any more attention to it. But she didn't. She thought with Broderick out of the picture she wouldn't have to split with anyone, she could keep it all. She had a lawyer serve me with papers for abandonment. I never saw her after we left that Reno chapel. I didn't have anything to abandon."

"After six months with no word from you or no success on the part of the detectives, I was sure you would never come back. Jane wanted a divorce and a financial settlement. I decided not to give her either. The shyster she hired for a lawyer advised her to move into my house in Cincinnati, so I stuck her with it. I always hated that house, anyway. There were provisions, but as long as she stayed within the guidelines she could live there. She could never sell it, or borrow on it. All she could do was live in it, and she had to live in it. That was one of the conditions. She couldn't marry anyone because I wouldn't consent to a divorce. So she was stuck. I'm not usually a vindictive person but this wasn't a usual situation. Steve Broderick and Jane Blanchard were the reason I lost you. I didn't care if it took the rest of my life, I was going to make both of them pay for it."

"I never went back to the studio in California. I never went back to the theater, either. I hated everything about show business. I didn't want to sing anymore. I knew I couldn't put my heart into it so I didn't do it."

Each of Dan's revelations caused Marianne more regret for the way she pushed him into accepting the offer from Broderick Enterprises so many years ago. She could feel his eyes on her as he spoke, but she couldn't look at him. She was almost smothered with guilt. She realized if she had paid more attention to what he wanted, instead of what she wanted for him, none of this would have happened. She knew she couldn't change the past but perhaps she could make up for some of it.

"Herb and Bernie talked me into a dozen things that kept me busy," Dan continued.

"When Bill was ready to start expanding his dance studios it was another chance to do something constructive. Projects came along one right after another. Marge had some good ideas for a costume rental company. When we got the kinks worked out of that it turned into another moneymaker. Julian had taken over the responsibilities of the casting company we bought from Broderick Enterprises. He made it legitimate and successful. There was someone in the Crew who could handle every venture we tried."

Dan put his coffee cup back on the saucer and turned to look at her. "For a good many years I was the only member of the Crew without a partner. I don't feel that way anymore." He leaned back on the sofa and exhaled a deep breath. "There," he said, "You have the story of my life."

223

"I'm glad you told me," Marianne said. "Sometimes it does you good to talk about it one last time. Now do you think you can bury it for good?"

"Do you have any questions?" he asked.

"No questions," she answered as she shook her head.

"You're amazing. I thought you would be full of questions."

"Why?" she asked. "I have no reason to doubt anything you said."

Dan smiled slightly and slowly shook his head. "Marianne, he said softly, "Where have you been all my life?"

"Good question," she replied. "After that awful experience I'm surprised you would want to know. Think back over what you've told me. If I hadn't pushed you into signing with Broderick you wouldn't have had any of those heartaches. I never realized that I set you up for the biggest disappointment in your life. Instead of helping your career, my know-it-all attitude caused you to give it up entirely. Danny, I can never make it up to you, I can only tell you I'm sorry."

"Now wait a minute," he said. "None of this was your fault. Steve Broderick and Jane Blanchard were con artists from the start. Broderick had this set up all arranged before I left New York. Julian warned me about what happened to people who signed with Broderick Enterprises, but I didn't listen."

When he started his explanation it never crossed his mind she would blame herself for his ordeal. Now he was intent on convincing her that she was not to blame. "I should have known that show business was not for me," Dan admitted. "The butterflies in my stomach and the feeling that if things weren't perfect, the audience wouldn't like the performance and I'd fall on my face. Every show had a new audience and I never knew what kind of reaction to expect. The constant demand day after day, always tension, never a let up, it really wasn't for me. I'm glad I tried it, but I'm not unhappy to be out of it."

Marianne was surprised at such an admission. As she thought about it she remembered how he had said several times his career was not the most important thing in his life.

"I've talked about this before," Dan said, "and it always left me feeling empty and miserable. This time it's different. I feel like it finally is over." He took a deep breath and gave a sign of relief. "Now that you know what happened I'm sure we can bury it for good."

"Well, she said, "at least we have accomplished something this weekend, haven't we?"

"Only half of what we intended," he reminded her. "Our conversation so far has all been about what happened to me. I want to know what happened to you."

She wondered how she could ever explain being so thickheaded, so dumb, so wrong and so lonesome. "There really isn't much to tell," she said. "I spent some time in Oregon, came back about a year later, met Bobby, got him drunk enough to get married and stayed married for thirty-two years. That's about it,"

The abrupt, short answer surprised Dan. "Whoa, whoa, hold it," he said. "You lost me after 'met Bobby', start again."

"I'm sorry," she said, "but my life hasn't been that interesting. There isn't that much to tell. There's no Crew involved, no dramatic experiences, just me."

"Marianne," Dan said gently, "YOU are what I want to hear about."

"I'm not a very interesting person. Like I said, there isn't much to tell."

You're interesting to me, Dan thought, and knew if he could help her get started she would pick up the flow on her own. He could feel her anxiety and knew how she felt. He had the same feelings an hour earlier. He gently prompted her to begin by asking, "When did you come back from Oregon and where did you go?"

She didn't want to answer him. Instead she wanted to put those memories back where she had buried them years ago. I can't do that, she thought, he's done his part, now I guess it's my turn.

"I came back to New Jersey the following Spring," she said. "Late April or early May, I'm not sure which. I used up a good part of my savings and I had to find a job. My aunt had moved to Florida while I was in Oregon, so I found a small apartment and started all over again. I thought about going to see Josh, but I was afraid it would involve meeting the Crew and possibly running into you. I didn't want that to happen. At that time I felt like the world's greatest loser."

"I was very brave at one point," she confessed. "I called your Union to see if you were working. They told me you had canceled your contract in California and the last address they had for you was somewhere in Ohio. That shattered my wishful thinking and I was convinced you were happily married and living back home. I couldn't force myself to go back to New York after that – too many memories and too many regrets."

She tried to hide her feelings but every once in a while her voice would falter and a syllable wouldn't come out. She was aggravated at herself for not being able to control it. She tried to cover it up by clearing her throat, changing position on the sofa, or taking a deep breath. She wasn't fooling Dan for a minute. He wanted to remind her those same feelings were his a little earlier, but he decided not to interrupt.

Marianne continued, "One of the girls at the office introduced me to Bobby. He was just getting over a messy divorce and I was trying very hard to get over you. I admit I wasn't being very successful. Neither of us was looking for any sort of commitment. We each had needs to be filled. His were physical and mine were emotional. So we made a deal. If I took care of his physical needs he would take care of my loneliness. I wasn't sure it would work but by that time I was willing to try almost anything. We knew when we married that love was not a factor. We didn't pretend it was. Please don't misunderstand. Bobby was a good man. His biggest problem was alcohol. I knew that when I married him. The optimist that I was, I thought I could change him. I was never successful at that, either. He would never admit he had a problem and he resented any help anyone offered. He didn't go to work drunk, but he never came home sober."

Dan could see that she was close to the breaking point. He was tempted to stop her, but decided to wait.

"I made a commitment and so did Bobby," she said. "We both stuck to our promises. He had his faults, but so did I. He overlooked mine and I disregarded his and somehow the marriage worked. Beth and Tim are living proof of that. He was a good father and he really did love his children. As far as he and I were concerned, we always were honest with each other about our feelings. Never, in all our years together did he say 'I love you' until six months before he died. When he did say it, I didn't know how to answer him. Our marriage was never based on love. I guess after all those years together there was a degree of love involved."

Marianne looked directly at Dan and said, "I thought about you a lot, but I never talked about you to anyone. You were my secret and I kept you locked in my memories. I never shared you with anyone ....and I never stopped loving you."

Dan gently brushed away the tear that ran down her cheek.

"This situation is moving too fast for me," she said as she tried to regain her lost composure. "I never meant to tell you any of that. It's been my secret for a lot of years. I don't know why I've said anything to you now."

"I'm glad you did," he told her. "I was beginning to think this was a one sided love affair." He took the coffee cup from her hand and put it back on the saucer as he moved over on the sofa to sit closer to her. He put his arm around her and no longer tried to hide the feelings he had kept inside for so long. "I've waited forty-three years to hear you say that. Let's not waste any more time. I love you, I always have, and I always will. We have a lot of lost years to make up for and a lot of things that need to be said to each other." He wiped another tear from her cheek and turned her face toward him. "You're everything I ever wanted in this life," he told her as he gently, but firmly kissed her with a passion that had been subdued for over forty years.

Although this weekend was different in many ways it was typical as far as time was concerned. The hours seemed to fly by whenever they were together. This weekend proved to them that there was truth in the adage *Confession is good for the soul.*

Hopes that faded as the years slid by and dreams that neither of them ever imagined could come true now seemed to be within their reach.

It was Sunday again and departure time was closing in. They sat in the car in the airport parking lot and tried to put the separation off as long as possible. They talked about insignificant little things to delay saying good-bye. It was a futile gesture, for time has no mercy.

"We accomplished a lot this weekend," Dan said in an effort to make conversation and not face leaving. "I hope you feel as good about it as I do."

"I'm glad we talked," she admitted. "I said a lot more than I ever intended to, but I think we both needed it. Too bad weekends end so quickly." She glanced at him and wondered if she was going to wake up and find that this was just another dream.

Dan's voice brought her back to reality when he asked, "What would you like to do next weekend?"

"Are you sure you want to come back?" she asked.

"Now I'm more sure than ever," he said, "as long as it's all right with you."

"I was waiting to see if you were going to ask," she said with a chuckle. "It's funny how two people can be so honest with each other on Saturday and beat around the bush so much on Sunday. What's wrong with us?"

"There's nothing wrong," Dan assured her. "I think we're conscious of the mistakes we've made and neither of us wants to let that happen again, so we're overly cautious."

"You're right," she agreed. "I guess we were both being careful. But you know what, Danny, maybe at our age we can afford to take a few chances." She glanced at him from the corner of her eye and asked, "Who's going to criticize? And who cares if they do?"

The surprised look on his face caused her to quickly add, "I've acquired a lot of nerve in my old age, haven't I?"

"Yes you have," he agreed with a laugh, "and I love it"

Chapter 28.

Dan Shaw was aware of the costly mistakes made many years ago. This time he was determined they would not be repeated. Marianne introduced him to her family on Thanksgiving Day. He was impressed by their sincerity and warmth. In some ways they reminded him of the early days of the Crew. It surprised him when he was so openly welcomed without any questions. As he came to know them he began to understand their reasoning. He made Marianne happy. That's what they wanted, too.

She told him she didn't say much to any of her family about their relationship many years ago. She introduced him as an old friend from the past. Someone she knew when she worked for Josh Golden in New York. She didn't tell them how well they knew each other or any of the circumstances surrounding their separation. She said it was difficult to explain something like that to her children. She knew she would have to eventually, but not right now.

Dan had different ideas. He wanted all of them to know how he felt about her. He wanted the whole world to know and he was going to make sure the whole world did. Right now his first concern was to have Marianne's family understand his feeling and his intent.

Dan's arrival on Friday evenings was getting to be a comfortable habit for both of them. Marianne would finish work and head for the airport to pick him up. They didn't make specific plans for each weekend, they didn't need any plans. They enjoyed every hour they could spend together. Sunday evenings were becoming more difficult for it was getting harder to say good-bye.

Dan suggested he come in on Thursday evenings for a while. He said he didn't spend much time in the office on Fridays and anything scheduled could me moved to another time during the week.

"Fine with me," Marianne quickly agreed. "I'd love to have the extra time with you. Just remember, I have to work my regular shift both Thursday and Friday. I don't want to leave you alone all day, but I can't take the time off until I get someone to cover my hours. That may take a week or so."

"I'm sure I can find my way around," he told her. "It won't be as much fun," he added with a grin, "but I'll manage."

"Wait a minute," she said, "Tim doesn't work on Fridays and Beth's husband, Jack, may be able to get some time off, too. Let's see what we can work out."

"Sounds good to me," Dan replied and thought maybe there really is such a thing as mental telepathy.

As Marianne drove to the airport Thursday night she felt sorry for Dan. Tomorrow may be his Baptism of Fire, she thought. Her son, Tim, and her son-in-law, Jack, both jumped at the chance to spend some time with him. They were a little too anxious, she thought.

"You better be prepared for a third degree tomorrow," she warned him as he got in the car.

"Why?" he asked, "is something wrong?"

"No," she replied, "but when I asked the boys if they could spend some time with you tomorrow, they both agreed real quick You better be prepared for lots of questions it looked to me like they were waiting for this opportunity."

"Marianne," Dan calmly replied, "you worry too much. Everything will be fine tomorrow, you'll see." Dan's reassurance took a little of the edge off her worry.

On her way out the door to work on Friday morning Marianne looked back at him and said, "You're on your own, Hon, good luck."

He shook his head, smiled and repeated, "You worry too much."

Dan had fresh coffee waiting when Tim and Jack arrived at the apartment. "Sit down boys," he invited, "I'd like to talk to you for a few minutes before we go anywhere."

They looked at each other and grinned. "On the way over here we were going to flip a coin to see who would get to ask the questions. I guess we can put our money away," Tim said.

Dan explained that the purpose behind his early arrival was to speak with all of them. He watched their reactions as he told them he wanted them to understand how he felt about Marianne. This was not a new thing or a superficial affair, but rather a deep genuine love that first started more than forty years ago. He told them he knew how important she was to them and now he wanted them to know how important she was to him. He felt he owed them an explanation and suggested it be discussed over dinner when their wives could be there, too.

"Good idea," Jack said, "I'm sure Beth will have plenty of questions. I think we should save that discussion until later,"

Tim quickly agreed.

"In that case," Dan said, "we have a whole day ahead of us. What would you like to do?"

"If you don't mind," Tim said, "we would like to see your plane."

"I don't mind," Dan answered and was delighted they were interested in something that was so important to him. "If you would like to we can take a ride and you can see how she handles. Any place in particular you want to go?"

They glanced blankly at each other, shrugged their shoulders and answered, "Anywhere."

* * * * *

The atmosphere at the restaurant was friendly but Dan could sense a little anxiety. He wished Marianne was with him, but felt this was something he had to do on his own. After the waitress took their order for drinks and appetizers the conversation shifted to what he told the boys earlier. He knew this was not going to be easy. He wanted them to know he intended to be around for a long time and to understand what his relationship with Marianne meant to him. He wondered how much he should tell them and decided it would be best to be honest and tell them everything and let them judge for themselves.

"I'm glad we can spend a little time together," he told them. "There are a few things you folks should know. I hesitate to say too much in front of your mother only because it would make her feel uneasy. I don't know how much she has told you about us, so I'll start from the beginning."

He explained that the feelings he and Marianne shared were serious, but not new to either of them. It began more than forty years ago when they were both very young. "I wanted her to marry me then but she put her own happiness aside because she thought my career was more important. It wasn't, but I couldn't convince her of that." He went on to say, through a series of misunderstandings and mix ups they were separated. He mentioned a little about his California experience, but he didn't want them to think he was totally stupid so he only skimmed the edges. He told them of the frantic search by the

Crew, hiring the detectives, and doing everything humanly possible to find Marianne those many years ago.

All four of them looked at him in amazement. This was a side of their mother they knew nothing about. Dan told them how Bill came across the names in the newspaper.

"When I called your Mom, back in August, it opened up a whole new life for me. When we saw each other on Thanksgiving Day we knew right away this was something that was meant to be. We may have gone in different directions for a lot of years, but destiny put us right back together."

He watched the reactions of each of them as he said, "There is a lot I would like to do for your mother. But she is the most independent and stubborn woman I have ever known." He smiled as he added, "That's one of the many reasons I love her."

Tim was the first to speak. "It's hard to believe everything you said. I can't picture my mother in that kind of a role. She doesn't fit the picture. My father was the sociable one. I think Mom spent her life in the kitchen."

"Tim," Beth interrupted impatiently, "He's not interested in Daddy, he's concerned with Mom."

"Wait a minute, Beth," Dan said. "I am interested in your Dad. I never met him, but from the way your mother talks about him he must have been quite a guy." He couldn't tell very much by their facial expressions, but he knew this was a crucial part of the conversation. It was important to let them know he was not trying to be a father to them. He wanted to be their friend.

"I hope I haven't misled you in any way. Please don't think I would ever try to take your Dad's place. No one can do that. That was not my intention at all. We are two completely different people. I can't say I don't envy what he had. He had the greatest wife, and from what I can see, the best family any man could ever hope for." He glanced around the table at each of them. He didn't know what kind of a reaction to expect and although he hoped for positive feedback he wanted them to be honest about their feelings. "I love your mother very much. I'm sure she feels the same way about me – but I'm not sure she will tell you about it – yet."

Beth was the first to speak. "She doesn't have to," she said, as she looked at Dan. "We can all see it. She's been on cloud nine since

Thanksgiving. She talks about you all the time but she never told us the serious side. You know Mom, the serious things she keeps to herself. Since Daddy died we have all watched and worried about her. None of us like the idea of her putting in all those hours at work. One job would have been plenty for anybody, but not for Mom, she has two. No matter how we tried, we couldn't get her to lighten the load. Every time we suggested she slow down she would tell us she liked what she was doing. She said it kept her connected with the outside world without getting involved."

Tim had been toying with a shrimp on the edge of his plate. Finally he looked at his sister and shook his head.

Oh boy, Dan thought, here comes the opposition and the last one I expected it from was Tim. "Is something bothering you, Tim?" Dan asked.

"No matter how I try," Tim said, and looked right at Dan as he very seriously stated, "I just can't picture my mother as a swinger."

Everyone laughed at Tim's dilemma and Dan breathed a huge sigh of relief. "Swinger," he told him, "may not be the right word for it. Your Mom is one of those people who can do almost anything." With a touch of nostalgia he added, "She always was."

Chapter 29

Dan suggested another weekend in Connecticut and Marianne agreed before he could mention an alternative. She knew it could never compare to the first trip, she could only hope that it would come close. Since the Thanksgiving reunion they spent every weekend together. Monday through Friday seemed to drag by and Saturdays couldn't come fast enough for either of them. The anticipation of each one being a little better than the last was never disappointing. Over the years both of them used work to fill a void of loneliness and for many years it served its purpose well. The Thanksgiving reunion in Connecticut focused their thoughts on other matters.

An hour or so into the trip Marianne remembered she had intended to buy a new nightgown before this weekend.

"We can stop when we get to Fairfield," Dan suggested. "That way we won't have to leave the highway, OK?"

"Sure," she agreed.

A mild state of shock set in when she saw the price tags on the nightgowns in the Fairfield shop. It was easy to see these businesses catered to a well to do clientele accustomed to prices that were far beyond her budget.

"Don't worry about it," Dan assured her. "Pick out what you want and put it on my credit card."

She looked at him and frowned, "I can't do that," she said.

"Either you pick it out or I'll pick it out," he told her with a mischievous grin and wiggled his eyebrows up and down like Groucho Marx.

"All right," she finally agreed, "but I want to pay you for it."

"Miss Independence," Dan quipped with a snicker as he shook his head. "We can settle accounts later."

She picked out a light green full length gown with short sleeves. It was exactly what she was looking for and would be a lot more suitable than the baggy sweat suits she was comfortable wearing when she was home. Dan gave the clerk his credit card and walked to the desk for the package. They left the shop and drove the last few miles to the Prestons.

The Flanagans were the only other visitors from New York this weekend and they came by plane instead of driving. Bill and Dan both enjoyed flying and had been piloting their own planes for years. Marianne listened to their flying experiences and began to refer to them as The Long Island Air Force. She was aware of the purpose behind all these stories. Dan Shaw was a man accustomed to getting what he wanted. He was patient, perceptive and skillful in the art of winning. He knew she was terrified of flying and wanted to convert her to his way of thinking. He knew he couldn't force her to do anything, so with the help of the Crew he chose to saturate the atmosphere with the fine characteristics of the airplane. She knew exactly what he was up to and had no doubts he would eventually succeed. In the meantime it was nice to watch such a skilled artist at work.

Two weeks earlier she let him talk her into going on a sight seeing flight over the coast of Massachusetts.

"Just a half hour," he told her, "so you can see what it's like."

The pilot did an excellent job of pointing out several interesting landmarks but it didn't improve her opinion of flying. The hired plane was small, the seats were cramped and the flight was noisy. Marianne had been holding Dan so tight there were bruises from each of her fingers on his arm. Nothing had been mentioned about flying since that trip. She wasn't sure if he decided not to push the issue or if he was waiting for his bruises to heal. Either way, she knew the subject would come up again.

The agenda for the evening consisted of home movies Herb had converted to video tapes. Marianne noticed how time had taken its toll on each individual. A new wrinkle here or there, a few pounds added in noticeable spots and more gray hairs, but mainly the addition of eyeglasses. Almost everyone in the Crew wore glasses, some as a constant and others just for reading. Everyone seemed to be affected, except Cass. She said many years ago that she would never wear them no matter how bad her eyesight was. Bill reminded them of the night, back in the old Ballard Theater days, when Cass had a date with Bernie and asked him to leave his glasses at home. She thought he was "cute" without them. What she didn't realize was that he couldn't see a thing without his glasses, but Bernie could never say "no" to

Cass. He left his glasses at home and showed up at the theater with a seeing eye dog. Cass never mentioned his glasses again.

Another memorable evening, Marianne thought, as they watched events unfold on the big screen. She enjoyed the snug, secure feeling she had as she sat next to Dan on the sofa. Every once in a while a little tightening of his arm around her shoulder let her know he was there and she was uppermost in his mind.

It was close to midnight when the movies ended. Since this was a rest and relax weekend everyone decided to call it a day. The movies were fun but now they were looking for some time alone. They laughed as they remembered the previous experience with the twin beds in the front bedroom. Marianne teased Dan about finding a bed with a safety belt so he wouldn't fall down between them this weekend.

Tonight, Dan got the shower first. She sat on the side of the bed and thought to herself what a comfortable, pleasant house this is. What a wonderful way to spend a lifetime. What a nice feeling to belong somewhere, she thought, and this Crew always makes me feel like I belong with them. Since the holiday reunion in November everyone treated her as if she had never been away.

She could hear Dan singing in the shower, making up the lyrics as he sang. She smiled at the thought of how little it took to make him happy. Her thoughts were interrupted as he came in from the bathroom.

"Your turn," he said and leaned over to kiss her lightly on the cheek.

She ruffled his hair and remarked that his shower robe matched his white hair. She picked up the bag with the new nightgown and went into the bathroom.

She finished her shower and reached for the bag with the nightgown. The gown in the bag was not the one she selected. She chose a light green, full length gown with short sleeves and enough material below the waist to make one guess where she stopped and the gown began. The gown she took from the bag was sheer black lace from shoulders to waist, black satin from waist to thighs, then the lace began again and nothing was left to the imagination.

"WOW!" Marianne commented as she noticed it was at least two sizes too small. Her first thought was that Dan was trying to be funny and had the clerk switch to this show-all creation when he paid for it. She would fix him, she thought, with a grin. If he wants to be funny I'll show him what funny really looks like. She put the black lacy creation on – or at least on as much as she could. Even when she held her breath it was like trying to stuff a sausage. Two can play this little game, she thought, as she struggled to control her breathing.

Even a mild exhale would cause pressure on every seam. She wondered how anyone ever managed to encase themselves in one of these garments and if all the effort was really worth it. She had to wiggle and twist and almost roll the lacy gown on like a stocking. When she was sure she had put as much of herself into it as possible she put her robe on over it and gingerly walked into the bedroom. She had to remember to control her breathing and not to laugh or she would surely come apart at the seams.

Dan had piled the pillows from both beds behind him and was propped up reading a magazine. "I was getting worried," he said. "Is everything all right?"

"Just peachy," she mumbled through clenched teeth as she nodded her head while still trying to control her breathing. It was a real effort to limit breathing and talk at the same time.

"What's the matter?" he asked.

"Did you play a little game with the sales clerk this afternoon, like switching the nightgown I picked out for the one you preferred?" she questioned.

He gave her a puzzled look and wrinkled his brow. He seemed totally confused as he asked, "What do you mean?"

"The nightgown that was in the bag is not the one I picked out," she answered.

"Don't worry about it tonight," he said unconcerned. "We can exchange it tomorrow."

Now Marianne was the one who was confused. "Dan are you sure you didn't switch things around at the store?"

"I'm positive," he said as he sat up and leaned across the other bed to put the pillows back where they belonged.

"Well, if that's the case, I don't think you're quite ready for this," she said as she took off her robe.

Dan's mouth fell open and his eyes got as big as saucers. He tried to straighten up on the bed and those wheels went back into action.

"JEESSUUSS KEEYRHIST!!!!!!!!" he exclaimed, as the beds separated and he landed on the floor between them —again! This time they both doubled over in laughter.

Marianne tried to control herself as she said, "Danny, we have to stop this. If you keep falling down between these beds everyone in this house will think we're into kinky sex."

"If anyone sees that nightgown," he told her, still laughing as hard as she was, "you're going to have one hell of a job trying to convince them we're not."

Neither of them could stop laughing and Marianne was afraid she would split the seams of the scanty nightgown. "I have to get out of this before I ruin it," she told him.

"Good idea," he answered with a chuckle. "You don't need it anyway."

She glanced at him over her shoulder as she headed for the bathroom and said, "Don't get your hopes up, Mr. Shaw. I never travel without my trusty sweat suit."

Dan managed to control his laughter long enough to put the beds back in place when Marianne emerged from the bathroom. The nightgown was so tight she couldn't get it off and she had to ask for his help.

"It will be my pleasure," he said with a big grin.

She leaned forward and he reached over her to pull the gown off over her head. By pulling it evenly from both sides he managed to tug it off a little at a time. He dropped it carefully next to the pajamas he had quickly removed. They stood for a minute and gazed at each other in the shadows cast by the small bedside lamp. He put his arms around her and savored the feeling of oneness.

"This is nothing like it was when we were young," she remarked.

"You're right," he agreed. "Now it's a whole lot better!"

He held her close and kissed the top of her ear. He was gentle and considerate. This, she thought, is the closest to Heaven I'll ever get. Dan knew how to make her feel good. He teased her about having exotic spots. She wondered if there really were such things or was it the touch of this very special man that sent thrills through her whole body. Dan Shaw was the only man in the world who could send her hormones into shock and it happened every time he touched her.

* * * * *

The kitchen was quiet. Dan and Marianne thought they were the first ones up, but they were just the first to come downstairs. A large pot of coffee was ready for breakfast and fresh pastries were on a platter. Dan poured two mugs of coffee and Marianne put out the cream and sugar. They had talked about taking a walk along the shoreline and the tide was out early today. It seemed like an ideal time to go.

Herb came into the kitchen as they were finishing their coffee. "I'm glad you two are here," he said. "I'm afraid I've been lax in my obligations as a host. I apologize."

"What do you mean, Herb" Marianne asked. "You're a perfect host."

"Not this time," he replied as he shook his head. "I forgot to tell you the wheels on those beds have locks on them."

Dan almost choked on his coffee and Marianne burst out laughing. "Better late than never, Herb," she said.

* * * * *

The tide was out, the sand was firm and the beach was beautiful. They set a slow and easy pace as they walked side by side down the shoreline. There was no one else in sight. They felt like they were the only two people in the world. It was warm for February, even though a brisk breeze was blowing in off the water. The cool crisp air left no doubt it was still winter and made their faces tingle from the chill.

"Let's head back to the house and get some breakfast," Dan suggested. "Everyone should be up by now."

Marianne agreed. "I could use some hot coffee," she said.

They reversed their direction and headed back toward the Prestons. They walked hand in hand down the deserted beach as they watched the seagulls glide along on the wintry breeze. It was one of those times when conversation wasn't necessary. The closeness they felt wrapped them in a blanket of togetherness and protected them from interference from the rest of the world.

They walked around the house, crossed the patio and went in through the kitchen door. Gracie had one of Herb's big barbecue aprons on over her silk robe, her sleeves were rolled up past the elbows and she was busy cooking bacon and eggs.

"Your timing is great," she said. "I hope you are going to join us for breakfast. Everything is just about ready."

"We've been out building an appetite," Dan told her.

"Where did you go this early?" Bill asked as he put four more slices of bread in the toaster.

"We took a walk along the beach," Dan answered. "It's a beautiful day and it was a nice walk."

Jen gave them an admiring glance and a smile of approval as she said, "You've done wonders for this old guy since Thanksgiving. The only exercise he ever got was from the house to the car and from the car to the plane. He spent all of his time working. He only took a vacation when we forced him and then he insisted on taking a briefcase full of work with him. It's good to see him finally relaxing a little."

Bill didn't even try to control the smile that danced around the corners of his mouth. "I'd like to know what you are doing that keeps him smiling all the time?" he asked.

Marianne tried to hide the blush that came into her cheeks. "I don't have the foggiest idea what you're talking about," she answered. Just the thought that something she was doing was making Danny a happy man gave her a good feeling. Knowing that the others noticed it made her feel even better.

Herb handed Dan a message sheet from the telephone pad. "You had a call from Joe Fisher at the airport," he said. "He wants you to call him or stop by. The tie downs for your plane are loose and he wants you to check them before he does any repairs."

"OK, Herb, thank you," Dan replied but didn't seem too concerned. "I'll call him after we eat breakfast and we can take a ride down if he wants me to look at them."

Aha, Marianne thought, here comes the airplane routine again. I noticed last night the bruises on his arm are gone. Much to her surprise, nothing more was mentioned about the airplane.

After breakfast, Bill, Herb and Dan went to the airport while Gracie, Jen and Marianne took care of the dishes and cleaned up the kitchen. This was a real break for Marianne. She wanted to talk to both of them, but didn't want to make it too obvious.

Jen made a fresh pot of coffee and the three women made themselves comfortable in the alcove off the main kitchen. They were all quiet for a few minutes. Gracie and Jen knew something was bothering her and wanted to help but didn't want to push her for details. They wanted her to talk to them and trust them as they had all trusted and relied on one another many years ago. Gracie's impatience finally came through and she said, "Marianne, you were quiet and lost in thought last night and again today at breakfast. Can we help you with what ever is on your mind?"

"It might do you good to talk about it," Jen added as she poured fresh coffee for each of them.

"I don't know if anyone can help," Marianne answered as she focused her attention on the cup of coffee in front of her. "I can't remember when I've been happier than I am now. The past few months have been wonderful but they have also created some enormous problems and I'm so confused I don't know what to do."

"Let's break this down and take one problem at a time," Jen suggested. "What's happening with you and Dan?"

"Don't tell us there is nothing happening," Gracie quickly added. "The change in Dan since November is unbelievable. He's happy and singing again, and back to being the Dan Shaw we all knew before that horrible Broderick fiasco."

"What worries us," Jen stated, "is what is going to happen now. You're not going to disappear on us again, I hope." She looked at Marianne and stressed, "That would be a real disaster. Remember, no matter how long you were away you are still just as much a part of this Crew as any one of us."

Marianne tried to control her emotions. She thought she was going to cry and she didn't want to do that.

"This is the most unbelievable situation on the face of the earth. I'm afraid I'm going to wake up and find it was all a dream and I don't know what to do," she confessed. "We know it's not possible, but Dan and I feel like we turned the clock back forty years. Our feelings for each other are just as strong, maybe even stronger now than they were years ago. My problem is the in-between years. They left big scars, physical, mental and emotional. These last couple of years I've dug myself into a comfortable rut, and I'm afraid to climb out. I would love to pull Danny right into my protected little world

241

and make him a part of it, but that wouldn't be fair to him. Right now, I can't make the transition from my world to his. It can't be done overnight. There are too many differences to overcome. We're working on it, but old habits aren't easy to break. If we were twenty years old it wouldn't matter so much. Unfortunately, at our age, time is an important factor and right now it's working against us."

"What can we do to make things easier for you?" Jen asked.

"I don't know," a very confused Marianne answered. How could they help, she wondered, when she didn't know what to do to help herself. "Being able to talk about it with someone who understands, helps considerably," she admitted. "Actually, Dan seems to be coping with it better than I am, or maybe he just hides his feelings better than I do. He's so patient that sometimes I'm ashamed of myself for feeling this way, but I just can't help it. I'm sure it will all work out and I know it will take time. Danny says he's willing to wait for as long as it takes. He says he understands and he doesn't mind. I'm not sure whether he does or not and I don't want to jeopardize the good start we have. So tell me, how do I handle this situation? How do I combine the best of both worlds? How do I keep everyone happy?" She sounded so forlorn in her search for an acceptable solution that Jen and Gracie were glad they encouraged her to talk to them.

"Maybe you're trying too hard," Gracie suggested. "Relax and let things fall into place on their own," she continued. "After all, the only ones you should be worrying about are you and Dan."

"That's easy to say," Marianne replied, "but not so easy to do. You know Dan, he'll go along with anything I want. This time my only interest is to make him happy and now I'm the one who can't cope with the big adjustments."

"Is there a problem with your family?" Jen asked.

"Not at all," Marianne told them. "In fact, Tim and Beth have been telling me the same things you are. The problem is with me. I'm the one who has to accept what's happening. Maybe it's just that I never did believe in fairy tales and that's what this is like."

Jen listened to everything Marianne told them. "Maybe what you two need is some time alone," she suggested. "Every one of your weekends are spent with other people. Why don't you try going away somewhere by yourselves and sorting out whatever is giving you the problem?"

Marianne thought about the suggestion and agreed. "We've been trying so hard to fill in all the past years with everyone we've lost sight of our own needs."

"Jen always was a good problem solver," Gracie said.

"After six kids there isn't a problem in the world we haven't run into one time or another," Jen said with a chuckle. "Problems are always easier to solve if they're someone else's"

Jen's suggestion is a good one," Gracie continued. "Why don't you give it a try? Even if you don't solve anything you'll have a good time. One more word of advice, where ever you go, try to avoid the twin beds. They seem to be a real hazard with you two." Gracie's touch of humor took the serious edge off the conversation and Marianne felt a wave or relief.

"That's the truth," she said with a laugh, but before she could explain the episode with the black lace nightgown, the men returned. I don't want them to get the wrong idea, she thought, I'll have to fill them in later.

"Joe Fisher was off on an errand when we got there," Herb explained. "We couldn't see any problem with the tie downs but Dan wants to check with Joe later."

"Everything looked all right to me," Dan said, "but I'm not a mechanic. "I'll feel better if I check it out with him." He looked over at Marianne and with a sly smile added, "You have some shopping you want to do today don't you?"

She didn't know if he mentioned anything about the nightgown when he was out, so she didn't elaborate on the shopping issue. She grinned back and said, "Yes," and let it go at that.

"Did you ladies make any plans for this afternoon?" Dan asked as he sat down beside Marianne and tucked her hand inside of his.

"Nothing until tonight," Gracie said. "Why?"

"I want to take Marianne for a little ride and show her some of the Connecticut countryside and we have a few things to take care of in town."

"Dan Shaw, you're not kidding us one single bit," Jen said with a smile. "You want her all to yourself. You don't want to share her with us at all."

"Jen," he answered with a grin, "you could always read me like a book."

243

Chapter 30

Dan wanted to see if Joe Fisher had returned and pulled into the parking lot at the airport. If there was a problem with his plane he was sure Joe would have it under control but he wanted to check anyway. They walked around the plane and he explained some of its features to Marianne. She could almost feel his enthusiasm.

"Why don't you sit inside and be comfortable?" he said.

She was astonished that he would suggest such a thing. "Me?" she said as she took a step backwards and pointed to herself. "Inside that airplane? – by myself? – **NO WAY!** I'll wait in the car." Her imagination shifted into high gear as she pictured herself accidentally pushing the wrong button and having this monster machine do an automatic take off with her all alone inside.

Dan seemed to read her thoughts and chuckled as he said, "Do you think I would let you do anything that would hurt you? Come on, be reasonable, it's warm and comfortable in the plane. Listen to the radio and I'll finish up with Joe as quickly as I can. We should be all set in about twenty minutes."

She watched as Joe Fisher opened the door of the airplane, reached inside and snapped a set of steps in place. Why not, she thought, it's on the ground, it's not going anywhere, and it will make Danny happy. She reluctantly agreed to sit in the plane and wait for him to finish his business with the mechanic.

The luxurious interior of what she had always referred to as a "monster machine" surprised her. There were eight oversize plush individual seats, each upholstered in a soft slate blue material. There was plenty of leg room and ample head room. Dan coaxed her into sitting in the copilot's seat.

"Turn on the radio and relax," he suggested.

"**YOU** turn on the radio," she replied. "I'm not touching a thing until you get back."

Dan laughed and pressed one of the many buttons on the complicated instrument panel. He turned it to a station he thought she would enjoy and made sure she was comfortable before he left to join the mechanic waiting outside.

Marianne nervously watched through the window as the two men discussed something near the right wing. They seemed to be in deep conversation and she wondered how long it would take. Dan got in and out of the plane several times. He flipped a few switches and fiddled with some of the dials and buttons on the instrument panel. He wrote down a few figures and left the plane to resume his conversation with Joe.

Marianne was fascinated by the size and splendor of this aircraft. She was amazed at the number of dials and gauges on what she referred to as the dashboard. Dan informed her that in an airplane it was called an instrument panel.

"He has to be pretty sharp to handle a vehicle this complicated all by himself," she said out loud. She smiled as she thought he really is pretty sharp about a lot of things, not just airplanes.

He came back on board and this time sat in the pilot's seat next to her. "How do you like it?" he asked.

"It's fabulous," she answered. He glanced at her through the top corner of his glasses and asked, "Would you like to take a ride?"

"I don't think so," she quickly replied. Looking for an excuse to back up her refusal she added, "You have to start it and get it all warmed up before you can go anywhere."

"That's no problem, Joe had it all warmed up before we got here. He's been checking it out all morning. It's all ready to go." He sounded so eager that she couldn't refuse him again. "How about it?" he asked. "Just fifteen or twenty minutes, OK?"

"Well," she reluctantly conceded, "all right, but just fifteen minutes." She watched Dan's face as the corners of his mouth curled upward and the little lines next to his eyes crinkled together in that special smile of his.

He knew she was still deathly afraid of flying and the only reason she agreed to go was to please him. He couldn't think of any way she could pay him a bigger compliment.

The take off was so smooth Marianne didn't realize they were off the ground until the cars and buildings seemed to shrink to the size of toys. The plane was whisper silent inside and she thought for sure Dan could hear her heart beating. Oh well, she thought, at least it's still pumping.

He pointed out the different sights as they circled the area; the Connecticut Turnpike, the Housatonic River, the Merritt Parkway, the town of Fairfield and the Universities, the city of Bridgeport and even Bridgeport harbor.

"How different everything looks from up here," she said. "How clean and orderly the earth looks from above."

They flew over Long Island sound and then back toward the Connecticut shoreline. The nervous fear Marianne had in the beginning was completely gone now and she was enjoying the ride.

"Look off the tip of the right wing," Dan told her. "The white house with the red roof is the Prestons."

"Wow!" Marianne answered. "I'm really impressed. You're right, Hon, this is beautiful, and you know what, I'm not a bit afraid up here with you. I'm glad you convinced me to try it."

Dan knew if she gave flying a chance she would like it. He also realized she had to find it out for herself.

"It gets better with time," he assured her. "The more you fly the better you like it. After a while you hate to get in the car to go anywhere."

"This is a lot different than the ride we had in Massachusetts," she commented.

"It sure is," he agreed with a laugh. "At least I won't get any bruises on this one, I hope."

"I'm sorry about that," she apologized. "I didn't mean to hurt you. I didn't realize I was holding you so tight. You should learn to fight off my advances," she joked, "and I should learn not to doubt you. So far you've been right about everything."

He glanced at her and had to curb the thoughts he had about a proposal. For now he would be satisfied with one victory at a time.

"We had better go back," Dan said. "You still have some shopping to do and Gracie will have a fit if we're late getting back to the house.'

"OK," she agreed, "but I have to tell you something."

"What's that?" he asked as he banked the plane and got clearance for a landing.

"I forgot to bring the nightgown," she said.

"Good," he answered with a grin. "You can try it on again tonight and we'll see if it fits any better."

246

The landing was just as smooth as the take off, not a single bump and no screeching of brakes. They made a gradual descent until the plane met the runway and seemed to flow along as part of the overall airport picture instead of an intruder from the sky. Dan expertly maneuvered the craft back into the spot where they had first climbed aboard.

Joe opened the cabin door from the outside and snapped the stairs in place. He offered Marianne a hand as he helped her manage the narrow steps.

"How did you like it?" he asked.

"It was fantastic," she said. "I loved it."

"Glad to hear that," Joe remarked as he glanced at Dan who was just coming off the steps. From the corner of her eye Marianne managed to catch the big wink Dan gave him and the "thumbs up" sign with both hands.

Chapter 31

The plane ride in Connecticut with Dan at the controls quickly converted Marianne to air travel. She had doubts about big airliners but wouldn't hesitate to go anywhere with Dan at the controls. To her he seemed to know how to do everything right.

For two months the weekend weather was great and they were taking off for somewhere almost every Friday night. Dan's love for flying was brushing off on her and she found herself enjoying each trip almost as much as he did. Most of the weekend trips were to Dan's home on Long Island. He called it a beach house – she called it a dream house.

Material things were never important to Marianne. The size and elegance of Dan's home was not what affected her. The sharing of something that was entirely his was the important factor. Every room reflected his personality and his likes and needs. She loved being part of it.

She watched him accept, and be accepted by, everyone in the little part of the world she called hers, but she found it difficult to cope with the opulence of his world. He wanted her to be part of every facet of his life. He was anxious to show her his home and wanted her to meet Margaret and John Kiernan, the couple who ran the house for him. He described them as his guardian angels for the past twenty-five years.

Marianne was afraid she would be a misfit and her first trip to Long Island was a challenge. She wanted to be part of everything that was important to him but she wasn't ready to assume the role of Lady Astor just yet, and maybe she never would be.

Dan introduced her to Margaret and John and gave her a guided tour of the house. The first floor had a classic yet comfortable living room, a dining room with an awesome view of the Atlantic Ocean from its enormous windows, a reference library and office area that made it possible for him to do a lot of his work from home and a game room that Dan referred to as his "goof off area." The kitchen was Margaret's domain, and enough to make any cook envious.

"The tour is only half over," he told her. "We still have another whole floor to go."

Halfway up the stairs Dan told her he had something special to show her in his bedroom. Marianne cast a sideways glance at him and raised her eyebrows as she teased, "I'll bet you do." He was surprised at her response but glad to see she could relax so quickly here. He wanted her to feel like this house was home to her, too. If he had his way it would be – very soon.

"You're a real tease, you know that?" he said with a grin.

The master bedroom was to the right at the top of the stairs. Almost an entire wall of glass offered a breathtaking view of the ocean from this magnificent room.

Dan took a small blue ring box from his top dresser drawer. "This has always been my most treasured possession," he said and opened the box to reveal a graduation ring from St. Monica's High School. Marianne had given him her high school ring many years ago when he was in the cast of *Gentlemen Again* and they were in the middle of what they each thought would be a lifelong romance.

When she saw what was in the box she caught her breath and couldn't control the tears that ran down her cheeks. "Oh Danny," was the only comment she could manage as he put his arms around her and she buried her face in his chest.

* * * * *

Marianne wondered if the Kiernans would accept her as part of his household. She wanted them to like her because they were such a big part of Dan's life. She thought they might resent someone else coming into the family circle and she would feel like an outsider. She sat at the kitchen table and slowly sipped her first cup of morning coffee. She watched as Margaret mixed a batch of Dan's favorite muffins. She wanted to talk to her before Dan came downstairs but didn't know how to start the conversation. The muffins were mixed and in the oven and Margaret poured herself a cup of coffee and sat down at the table.

"We know all about you," she told Marianne. "Daniel would sit there, just like you're doing now, and tell us how much fun you had when he was on the Broadway stage. He talked about you all the time. We knew he would find you," she said and sounded as if she really believed it.

249

"You did?" Marianne asked.

"Oh sure," Margaret continued, "John and I have been making novenas to St, Jude to help." As far as Margaret was concerned every problem in the world could be solved by Dan Shaw or one of the other members of the Crew. If that didn't work she called on one of her legion of friendly saints who always seemed to come through for her. She was firmly convinced that since Dan found Marianne again her prayers had been answered.

* * * * *

They arrived on Long Island on Friday night and had no specific plans for the weekend. Early Saturday morning Dan suggested a drive down the coast to visit Josh Golden, then a tour of the old neighborhood of New York City.

As they drove toward Bay Shore, Marianne wondered if this was a good idea. "I don't know if he'll remember me," she said nervously. "What will I say if he doesn't recognize me?"

"Marianne, trust me," Dan said. "Josh will know you and he will be happy to see you. He would recognize you anywhere, anytime, you can bet on it. Every time I see him you're the topic of the conversation."

"You're just saying that to make me feel good," she said.

"No, I'm not. You were always one of Josh's favorite people. How could he forget you?"

"It's been a long time since we've seen each other. I was a lot younger, a lot slimmer and no gray hair," she reminded him.

He knew her doubts were barriers she set up to protect herself from disappointments. "We'll soon find out if he remembers you," he said as he turned the car into the circular driveway to Josh Golden's front door. Dan spoke with Josh's daughter, Shirley, earlier in the day and told her their approximate arrival time. She was sure her father would love to see them. She said not to ring the bell, just knock three times with the brass door knocker and she would have Josh answer the door.

Dan raised the heavy door knocker and tapped three times. Marianne waited directly in front of the door and he stood a little to one side. He wanted to make sure Josh saw her when he opened the door.

The last time she saw Josh was forty-three years ago. He was forty-five then, now he was eighty-eight years old and his health was not good. His wife had divorced him many years ago and now he lived with his daughter and her family. Marianne remembered him as a man of constant motion. He couldn't sit still for more than five minutes and he was always smoking a cigar. Dan warned her that Josh had changed physically after suffering a stroke several years ago. He lost a lot of weight, gained a lot of wrinkles and was forbidden to smoke his precious cigars. He quickly added that Josh would manage to sneak one whenever he thought he could get away with it.

As the door opened Marianne looked at the little man standing there and said, "Hi Josh, remember me?"

Josh took a step backwards, threw his hands in the air and almost shouted, "Oh my God!" Marianne knew instantly that he remembered. "Oh my God!" he repeated. "Shirley come quickly. I died and went to heaven and look who met me at the gate!"

Marianne's nervousness vanished and she had to laugh at his reaction. Josh Golden was the only one who would think of something like that, she thought.

"Are you going to invite me in or do I have to stay out here in the cold?" she asked.

Josh threw the door back so far Marianne thought it would come off its hinges.

"Get in here and tell me, where have you been?" Josh ordered. Then added quickly, "No, better still, give me a hug, a big hug! Then tell me where have you been?"

Marianne complied with the hug request but before she could answer any of Josh's questions he turned to Dan and said, "Shaw, you are a very lucky man. This is the only woman in my life who gave me back more than she took." He still clung to the hug almost as if he was trying to hold on to the good parts of his past. All of a sudden he realized Dan and Marianne were together again. He looked from one to the other and said, "You got married and nobody told me? I'm mad."

"No Josh," Dan said. "We didn't get married yet. I just found her a couple of months ago."

"So what are you waiting for? — She'll run away again," Josh warned him. "Let me call somebody. We'll get it done this afternoon."

"Josh, calm down," Marianne cautioned. "My goodness, you'll have a stroke."

"Not a chance," the older man stated. "I already had one, didn't like it, wouldn't have another."

Josh's physical appearance had changed drastically. He was a lot older, but still as spunky as ever. "I know why you ran away," he said as he shook his finger at Marianne. "But where did you go? I hired detectives, Dan hired detectives. Meshugenuh detectives couldn't find the scent if they were following a ripe skunk. Nobody could find you. We had everybody in this world looking for you."

He was so excited he was trying to put all his questions into one sentence. Every time he paused for a breath he rushed into another question. With each sentence his voice got louder until he was almost shouting. He looked at Marianne and then at Dan and with a happy smile he called out loudly, "Shirley, get me a cigar to celebrate!"

"You don't need a cigar, Josh," Marianne said laughing. "The last time we talked you bit right through your cigar." Josh snapped his attention back to her. "Oh my God! She remembers that, too," he exclaimed. He turned to his daughter and asked, "Shirley, did you hear that?" He sounded like he didn't want her to miss one single syllable of what was said. She couldn't help laughing at her father's reaction to his surprise visitors.

"Papa, if you don't stop shouting you are going to scare them off," she warned.

"Not a chance," Josh answered, still at the same semi-shout decibel level as before. "If I didn't use this tone of voice they would think I was mad at them."

Marianne still had her arm around his frail shoulders. She gave him a little squeeze and said, "Gee, it's good to see you, Josh."

"Good to see me!" he echoed. "Good to see me! Forty years ago it would have been good to see me. Today I look like a prune." He looked from Marianne to Dan as if he was expecting them to disagree with him. "Look at me," he continued, "My pants are too big, my shirt is too big, and my wallet is too small." He remembered he was talking to someone who had made a lot of money for him in the past. He tried

252

to be the convincing salesman he was many years ago. "Kiddo," he said, "you have to come back to work for me. This time it will be different. We split right down the middle – sixty/forty. How about that?" he suggested and quickly added, "We'll be partners!"

Marianne laughed and said, "Josh, sixty/forty is not right down the middle."

"Listen to her," Josh responded with the enthusiasm of someone aching to get back into the business of serious haggling, "already she wants to argue price."

Marianne shook her head and told him he had not changed a bit since she last saw him.

"You're still too much for me," she said. "I would never be able to keep up with you."

"Listen Kiddo," Josh persisted, "I'm not fooling. Say the word and we're back in business."

Josh never called her by name. He always referred to her as "Kiddo." In the old days it was just another nickname. Now she was in her sixties and somehow "Kiddo" didn't seem to fit. Josh was eighty-eight, so from his point of view it fit just fine.

"You don't want to go back to work?" he asked and couldn't believe she would pass up his offer.

"I'm working two jobs now," she told him. "You know, Josh, there are only so many hours in a day."

"Humph," he muttered, "that never stopped you before. You worked two jobs and still had time for hanky-panky with Shaw. Don't tell me you're getting old."

"Not really," she answered, "but now I'm old enough to know what's important. So work can wait and hanky-panky gets priority."

Josh laughed and looked at Dan as he said, "Nothing changes with this woman, does it? After all these years she still puts you first. My God, Shaw, you really are lucky."

"I know I am," Dan answered with a grin.

"Listen to me," Josh directed. "Never in my life did I give you a bum steer. I have a brother-in-law right here in Bay Shore who is a judge. Let me call him. It will take him ten minutes to get here and he can take care of all your problems and tie up the loose ends. He'll have you two married by this afternoon."

253

"Wait a minute, Josh," Marianne said, "I'm not ready for that yet."

He looked at her and couldn't seem to understand her reasoning. "What do you mean, you're not ready? You got a husband?"

"No, I don't have a husband," she answered quickly.

"So what do you mean, you're not ready?" Josh persisted. "You have no husband, he has no wife – he never did have one – what's the hold up?"

"There are other things to be considered," she tried to explain. Josh's compulsive nature wouldn't let him quit. He wanted specific answers and she couldn't give them to him. He would never understand her hesitation and would probably end up using some of his Yiddish words in his frustration with her uncertainty.

"So what's to be considered that all these years haven't taken care of?" he asked impatiently.

Dan could see Marianne's uneasiness with all the questions and he didn't like to see her uncomfortable. He interrupted Josh's questions and said, "We have a few details to straighten out, but it won't take long."

"Keep in mind," Josh said as he looked from one to the other, "I'm eighty-eight years old. If you don't do this soon I might not be able to go to your wedding. I have to be there," he insisted. "Remember, I introduced you to each other. You owe me an invitation."

"You'll be there, Josh," Marianne promised.

The time seemed to fly by as they tried to fill Josh in on Marianne's missing years. Her story was constantly punctured by "whys" from Josh. "Why didn't you call one of us?" or "Why did you pick Oregon?" and "Where in hell is Oregon, anyway?" Some of the questions were finally explained to his satisfaction and Josh came to the conclusion it was impossible to cover everything in one afternoon.

"If I let you off that easy you'll leave out all the good parts," he said. "I want to know everything – then I'll see if it makes any sense."

They had been with Josh for almost three hours. He never ran out of questions. Marianne answered them all, but there was no end in sight. They promised another visit again, real soon. Josh accepted their promise but told them that his curiosity was only temporarily satisfied.

Dan said they were going into the City to stir up a few more memories and visit the rest of the Crew. "It's been a long time since Marianne has been there," he said. "I want to show her what New York City is like today.

"Good idea," Josh said as he turned to Marianne. "Don't forget my offer, Kiddo. A long time ago we made a lot of money for each other and we can do it again." He looked at Dan and with a wink and a grin said, "Remember, Shaw, a new production has a lot of kinks, a return engagement is often better than the original."

As they left Bay Shore they talked about the good times they had in New York City many years ago. Now Dan wanted her to see how things had changed. The streets and avenues they had casually walked so long ago were now the sinkholes of civilization. Time and neglect had desecrated much of the area they enjoyed so often when they were young. He cautioned Marianne to lock the car door and not to roll the window down for any reason. He was uneasy bringing her into this part of the city, but thought it would be safe in the daylight hours. The car stopped at a traffic light and a seedy looking man pounded on Dan's window. "Hey man," he growled in a raspy voice, "Want a good woman?" The rap on the window startled both of them and Dan quickly acknowledged him with, "No thanks, I already have one."

"Thanks a lot," Marianne commented with a chuckle as the light changed and Dan maneuvered the car through the downtown traffic.

"You are a good woman," he said with a grin. "Not like he meant it but definitely the way I mean it." Even though he tried to lighten the atmosphere with a little humor, Marianne couldn't help feel the emptiness left by the devastation of this once friendly neighborhood where most of the inhabitants were struggling performers with dreams of making it big in show business and someday moving uptown. They passed the building where Dan lived when he was in the cast of *Gentlemen Again*. Marianne didn't recognize it until he pointed it out.

"Lots of good memories go with that apartment," Dan reminded her.

"Some of the best memories of my life happened right there," she said. Her attention was focused out the car window but he thought he saw her catch her breath in an attempt to hide her feelings. He

255

wondered what their lives would have been like if one of those "memories" had not been interrupted by a phone call.

As Dan turned the car into a triangular intersection Marianne recognized what had once been Nick's Restaurant, their favorite spot in the City. How times change she thought as she watched a large cross shaped neon sign over the entrance door blink on and off with the words, "Jesus Saves" in big red letters.

When they came to the building that once housed Flanagan's Dance Studio #1 it rekindled many memories of pleasant hours spent there with Bill and Jen. The very successful Flanagan Dance Studio Organization was conceived right there. Its foundation was firmly footed in the turf of lower Manhattan but now it stood desolate and ugly behind an exterior façade of makeshift plywood that was acting as a moat to keep out the dreariness that was all around it. What a shame, Marianne thought.

"Did anyone ever find out where Alan got the piano he showed up with when Bill and Jen moved in there?" she asked.

"I don't think so," Dan replied. "But only because Alan didn't remember himself. He drank too much in those days, not like today. Now he fakes a lot of it."

Marianne was surprised by this comment and said, "Dan Shaw, you're a pretty smart old guy. I thought I was the only one who knew that."

As they traveled through some of the old familiar territory he watched her facial expressions change from nostalgic to disbelief.

"Have you seen enough?" he asked.

"I think I've seen enough to last a lifetime," she told him. "I'm going to try to forget what we saw today. I would rather remember this place the way it was when we were young."

"Nice trick if you can do it," he said. "Now how about a look at the better side of this city?"

"Fine with me," she agreed.

As they drove uptown Marianne recognized some of the famous old familiar landmarks, Macy's, the Empire State Building, Rockefeller Center, St. Patrick's Cathedral and Central Park. The memories came flooding back again as she thought some things never change, they just get overshadowed by time and progress.

The Ballard Theater brought down the curtain for the last time almost twenty years ago. So did many other Broadway theaters. Lou Walter's Latin Quarter was gone, so was Nicky Blair's Carnival and Billy Rose's Diamond Horseshoe.

"Now there's no place in the City that is anything like them," Dan told her.

"In that case, I guess we'll have to make our own fun," Marianne suggested.

"That sounds like a good idea," he agreed.

257

Chapter 32

Julian and Harriet Brice, Alan and Marge Durling and Bernie and Cass Goldman lived within a few blocks of each other. The Brices were the first stop and Julian and Harriet were overjoyed with their unexpected visitors. Dan explained it was a quick trip and they couldn't stay long. He told them about the ride through the old neighborhoods and the sadness felt by its deterioration. Julian was quick to agree and said the deterioration was a negative aspect, but couldn't dim the success of many of the people who began there.

"That's true," Marianne said, "but it tramples right over a lot of good memories and leaves a bitter taste behind."

"Harriet reminds me often that the roots of our Crew are deeply embedded in the terrain of lower Manhattan. Though devastation meets the eye today the core has not been touched. We are all examples of the success that can come from small beginnings," Julian said.

"Julian, you've been cheated out of a pulpit," Marianne teased. Their visit was pleasant but cut short by Dan's reminder there were two more stops before they could head for home. Julian and Harriet raised Marianne's spirits a little but Dan could see she was still disturbed by their earlier tour. He regretted taking her through lower Manhattan, but now was more concerned with taking her mind off it. Bernie and Cass Goldman were ideal candidates for that chore.

They arrived at the exclusive apartment building the Goldmans called home and Marianne was amazed at the luxury all around. The doorman called Cass for permission to allow them entry and quickly directed them to a waiting elevator.

"Wow!" Marianne commented as Dan tucked her arm under his and they crossed the lobby, "Cass really out did herself on this one, didn't she?"

"This is just the tip of the iceberg," Dan told her. "Over the last thirty years Bernie has had some tremendous deals come through for him. He made a fortune, but it hasn't changed these two one bit. Both of them are as nutty as they ever were, you'll see."

Cass greeted them as they got off the elevator. "I'm glad to see you guys," she said in her bubbly fashion. "I called Bernie and he's on his way home." She ushered them across the plush hallway and into the most luxurious apartment Marianne had ever seen. It was ultra modern with a décor of black and white set off by silver amenities.

"This is gorgeous," Marianne said as she looked around the elegant setting. "I don't think I've ever seen anything as impressive."

"It looks nice," Cass agreed, "but you can't sit down anywhere. There's not a comfortable chair in the whole room. I think they were all made for women with tight skirts, skinny legs and small behinds. We only use this area for company." She looked at them and reached for Marianne's hand. "Come on, you guys aren't company, you're family. We'll go back to the real apartment." She took them through the kitchen area and into a whole separate apartment. It was comfortable and casual and extended its own invitation to relax. "Cass, you never stop surprising me," Marianne said. "This is awesome. It's an apartment in an apartment, isn't it?"

"I guess you can say that," Cass agreed. "I was never very comfortable in that setting out front. Bernie says he needs that atmosphere for some of his projects, but it's not for me. When I told him I wasn't happy with it, he put in what made me comfortable. Now I'm happy."

"Do you ever use the front area?" Marianne asked.

"Sometimes," she answered with a shrug of her shoulders, "when I'm trying to act like one of the Rockefellers. I have more fun just walking around out there leaving my fingerprints on all of the silver."

"See," Dan said with a chuckle, "I told you she was still a loveable nut. Nothing has changed with Cass and Bernie."

"He always tells me that," Cass said. "I guess it's a compliment. At least that's the way I always understood it."

"It's definitely a complement, Cass," Dan assured her.

A small red light over the inner apartment door began to blink.

"Bernie's home," Cass said and explained that the blinking light meant the elevator stopped at this floor.

"How do you know it's not for someone else?" Marianne asked.

"There is no one else on this floor," Cass answered.

"That sure narrows it down," Marianne conceded with a laugh.

Bernie's first question was, "Are you guys going to stay for the weekend?"

Dan looked at Marianne as if the thought never occurred to him. "We didn't plan on it. We intended to visit for an hour or so and stop and see Marge and Alan for a little while and then head for home."

He told them about the earlier visit with Josh and the good time they had with him. Dan explained the depressing effect the trip through the old neighborhoods had on both of them.

"Julian and Harriet were a real pleasure," he continued, "but I was counting on you two to put a little fun back in our day."

"That whole area is a mess now," Bernie said. "We ride through once in a while, just for old times sake, but it always hurts. We had a lot of fun there and no matter what happens to it nobody can take away our good memories."

"That's a good philosophy," Dan said. "That was Marianne's idea, too."

Bernie wasn't ready to let them get away so quickly. "I have an idea," he said. "How about if I call Marge and Alan, tell them you're here and see if they can join us for dinner. We can hop a cab and go somewhere right around here. You won't have to worry about parking or anything, OK?"

Dan glanced at Marianne and when she nodded approval he asked Bernie to keep the arrangements simple. "We didn't count on a fancy night out," he said.

"No problem," Bernie assured him. "We'll stick right close to home."

Right close to home turned out to be a small neighborhood restaurant a few blocks from the Goldman's apartment. They were seated at a comfortable table and ordered drinks and appetizers. They decided to wait until Marge and Alan arrived before ordering dinner.

Almost a half hour passed with no sign of the Durlings.

"This is unusual," Bernie said. "Most of the time they get here before we do."

When the Durlings finally did arrive Bernie greeted them by saying, "I thought you said you'd be right over."

"So did I," Alan replied, "but we had a cab driver who couldn't speak English. I think we touched on four of the five boroughs of Manhattan. The only reason he missed Staten Island was because he couldn't find the ferry."

Marge gave him an elbow in the ribs and said, "Alan, don't be such a grouch. The poor man was only trying to make a living."

"He's got a good start on a fat pay from what he made off me tonight," Alan continued "God, do I need a drink!"

It was a rare occasion when Alan got flustered but he was at that stage tonight. Marge explained he was anxious to see them and when the cabby kept going in the wrong direction she almost had to use force to restrain him. Especially when the driver kept smiling and saying yes to everything.

Dinner was wonderful. The food was delicious, the service excellent and the company exceptional. Once Alan's frustrations were put to rest the laughs came a mile a minute. It was close to ten o'clock when they left the restaurant.

"You can't be serious about going home," Alan said. "Not at this hour. This is New York. Things are just getting started now. Besides, what's your hurry? Stick around for awhile and enjoy yourselves."

"We've had a pretty full day," Dan said. "Maybe we had better head for home. We'll be back and do this again soon."

They stood on the sidewalk in front of the restaurant and Alan reached for Dan's arm. He had one more selling point before he was going to let them get away. "I know where there's a jam session tonight," he said. "How long has it been since you went to one?" Before Dan could answer, he continued with his pitch. "Go with us for an hour or so. I'll bet you'll see a lot of people you know. Come on," he coaxed, "you'll have a good time."

"It's tempting," Dan admitted as he looked at Marianne.

She could see it was something he wanted to do and said, "It sounds like fun. Let's go."

The jam session included musicians, singers, dancers and a lot of old timers who felt as if the modern world of entertainment had gone off the track somewhere. These people were real entertainers, doing their own thing, not for pay, just for pleasure.

Marianne watched Dan's reaction to all of this and thought, for someone who hated being on stage he certainly is enjoying himself tonight. She also realized he was right when he said there was a big difference when you performed because you wanted to, and not because you were being paid to entertain people who put out big bucks for tickets.

Alan leaned over toward Marianne and quietly asked, "Do you think Dan will mind if I ask him to sing?"

Marianne looked at him and smiled. "Just look at how he's enjoying himself," she answered. "I think he would love it."

Alan introduced Dan to the audience and Marianne tried to read the expression on his face as he took the microphone. He's a little nervous, she thought, but he'll be fine. Alan started him off with a catchy little tune that got the attention of the audience and helped Dan to relax.

"Let's have another one," and "Don't stop now," could be heard over the applause. Dan looked at Alan who was playing the piano to set the timing for him. The little musician put his hands up, shrugged his shoulders and with a big smile said, "Go for it, Dan."

Dan Shaw never lost his technique. He could put a song over better than anyone. Tonight, he was at his finest. He was singing because he wanted to sing. He was singing with his heart, and it showed. He sang two more songs and the applause was thunderous. Again, he looked at Alan for help, but Alan was enjoying it as much as the audience and all he did was shrug his shoulders again. "Thank you," Dan told the audience, "this has been a real pleasure."

"You're not going to stop now," a man at one of the tables called out.

"Let's give someone else a turn," Dan said.

"Let's not," the man shouted back. "Sing some more."

The rest of the audience was echoing his sentiments and calling for an encore. This reception was unexpected. Dan looked back at Alan and very quietly said, "Help!"

"Dan," Alan reminded him, "this audience is all performers. They know a good thing when they hear it. It sounds to me like they want another song."

Dan turned back to the audience and said "One last song and I want to dedicate this to the lady at the corner table."

He looked right at Marianne and sang, "*I'll be loving you, always. With a love that's true, always.*" The song was a description of his feelings and everyone who heard it could tell he meant every word.

The audience was so quiet you could hear a pin drop on a rug. He finished the song, put the microphone back in its holder and started to walk to the table. All of a sudden the audience came alive. They whistled, shouted and clapped. Everyone was standing. Marianne looked at Cass and Bernie. He had his arm around her and she was snuggled right up against him. She turned and looked at Marge and was surprised to see big tears rolling down her cheeks.

"Boy, he's good," Marge said through her tears.

"He sure is," Marianne agreed as she blinked back a tear of her own.

Dan reached the table and gave her a big hug as he whispered in her ear, "How did I do?"

"Listen to that applause," she said. "I told you a long time ago you were a star!"

Chapter 33

"Have you made any plans for this weekend?" Dan asked.

"Nothing definite," Marianne answered.

"I have a suggestion," he said. "When you come to the airport tomorrow bring a suitcase and don't plan on being home until Sunday."

"Sounds interesting," she said. "What do you have in mind?"

"I'm not going to tell you," he teased. "Trust me, you'll have a good time."

"OK," she said, "I'll see you tomorrow about 5:30."

"I'll be waiting for you," he said.

As she put the receiver back in place Marianne thought about how much she looked forward to each weekend. Being together was such a nice comfortable feeling that even if they never left the house she still couldn't wait for Friday to get here.

The airport was only a twenty minute ride from the office. She drove into the parking lot and saw Dan standing next to the gate. He came over to the car and said, "Lock it up. I'll take your bag and let's go. We have a dinner reservation for nine o'clock."

"Where?" Marianne asked.

"You'll see," he said with a grin.

She buckled the seat belt and watched Dan bring the plane to take-off position. He got his tower clearance and nosed out onto the runway. She wondered if she was getting brave in her old age or if it was the trust she had in Dan that caused her to do things she never would have tried before he came back into her life. Perhaps a little of each, she thought. Dan checked his instrument panel, set the plane on its course and sat back and relaxed. Flying was like second nature to him. It was easier and more comfortable for him to fly than to drive. Strangely enough, Marianne was beginning to feel the same way.

"Now will you tell me where we're going?" she asked.

"No," he teased, "that will spoil the surprise."

"Can I guess?"

"Take three guesses," he said.

"Connecticut," was her first guess.

"Nope," he replied and seemed pleased with himself for keeping the mystery alive.

"New York," was her second guess and she quickly added, "That includes the Flanagans, the Durlings, Brices, Goldmans and Josh, too."

"You're wrong on all of them," Dan said, "and that makes six guesses."

"Wait a minute," she protested, "that was only two, New York and Connecticut."

"You still haven't guessed it," he continued to tease. "You haven't even come close."

"All right, I give up," she conceded. "Where are we going?"

"A quiet little hotel in the country. We can relax and enjoy ourselves and make plans for our vacation."

"Sounds great," she said. "What a good idea."

"We can do whatever we want this weekend. Take a walk in the woods, ride through the countryside, stay in bed for the whole weekend or go out for dinner and a couple of dances. Anything you want to do."

"Anything?" she asked with a mischievous grin.

"Yup," he answered as he reached over and took her hand in his. "Anything," he repeated.

"Wow!" she teased, "I'm going to have to think about this."

"Can I make a suggestion?" he asked.

"No way," she answered, "this is my 'anything' weekend. Save your suggestions for you turn." She looked at him and he put his head back and closed his eyes. "Are you tired?" she asked.

"No," he answered with a chuckle, "I'm testing my powers of mental telepathy."

The hotel sent a car to pick them up at the airport. Their accommodations were beautiful. The first section of the suite was a small but comfortable living room with a sofa, coffee table, several high back upholstered chairs and a big screen television. Against the wall between the living room and the bedroom was a completely stocked bar. Very impressive, she thought, until she saw the bedroom. It was huge! Her whole apartment could fit nicely into this bedroom. Another television was mounted on the wall in the corner so you could watch it comfortably from the bed.

The bath was another example of elegance. The dominant feature was a large round Jacuzzi with three steps going down into it.

"Wow!" Marianne commented, "I could get lost for days in this bathroom."

"We have a reservation for dinner tonight," Dan said, "but I can cancel it if you would rather eat here."

"What do you want to do?" she asked.

He put his arms around her and said, "I just want to make you happy."

"Danny," she said as she returned his hug, "you already have."

She loosened her hug a little and looked up at him. "Would you mind if we cancel the dinner reservation and stay here? I'm tired and you must be, too. Maybe we can relax in the Jacuzzi for awhile, go to bed early and see what tomorrow brings. If you want to go out for dinner and a few dances we can go tomorrow, OK?"

"Fine," he answered with a grin and made a quick remark about the powers of mental telepathy really working for him. "That's what I was hoping you would decide."

"Why don't you order sandwiches and coffee while I unpack our things," she suggested.

"Good idea," he said and reached for the phone.

"Dan, I can't believe the size of this place," she commented. "I've never seen such a big bed."

"At least it doesn't separate in the middle. Maybe I won't fall out of this one," he said with a chuckle.

The waiter arrived with an assortment of small sandwiches, a taste tempting salad and a large pot of coffee. Marianne was glad Dan did the ordering. He certainly knows how to do things right, she thought.

He took a large manila envelope from the inside pocket of his suitcase and spread its contents on the coffee table. "This is information on Alaska. I thought we might look it over together and you can tell me what you want to see and where you want to go. If we need reservations I can take care of them."

"What a good idea," Marianne said, "But let's get something understood about this vacation. Alaska is a wonderful choice and I'm really looking forward to it. It will be the first real vacation of my life. I want you to remember one thing, Danny, the most important part of this whole venture is the company, not the place. I don't care where we go as long as we're together." She liked to watch the corners of his mouth turn up when he smiled.

She picked up the dishes from the coffee table and put them back on the waiter's cart. "Hon, how did you ever find this place?" she asked.

"I didn't find it," he said. "Jen is the one who suggested it. She gave me a half hour lecture about how you and I have to get off by ourselves. It sounded like a good idea and I thought you would like it – so – here we are."

"It is a good idea, and I do like it." She told him. "I think I would like to sit in that tub for half an hour and do nothing but count the bubbles from the Jacuzzi."

"Perfect," Dan agreed. "I'll fill the tub and turn on the Jacuzzi. Wait about fifteen minutes and let the steam circulate and it will really relax you." He got up from the sofa and headed for the bathroom.

"In the right pocket of my suitcase there's a bottle of bath oil. Please dump it in the tub after you fill it, OK?" Marianne asked as she tried to stifle another yawn. "Gee, I must have jet lag or something, I can't stop yawning."

"It's not jet lag, you're just plain tired. We'll fix that," he said with a wink.

Marianne could hear him filling the Jacuzzi and she thought, how did I ever get so lucky? She picked up the Alaska material and began to look through it.

Dan came out of the bathroom and closed the door behind him. "It should take about fifteen minutes to get the room steamy. Then you'll be all set," he said and gave her a satisfied wink. He noticed she was looking through the vacation brochures and asked if there was anything in particular she wanted to see.

"I wish we had enough time to see it all," she said. "The pictures are beautiful. It looks so inviting."

"Why don't you take an additional couple of weeks vacation?" he suggested.

"Not now," she said, "I'm lucky I have three weeks. We'll do what we can and what we miss we can get next time, OK?"

"I guess so," he reluctantly agreed.

Before either of them realized it almost a half hour had passed.

"We better check that bathroom," Marianne said, "It will be so full of steam you won't be able to see in there."

"I'll take care of it," Dan volunteered, as he walked over and opened the bathroom door. "JEESSUUSS KEEYRHIST!!!!!!!!!! How do you stop this thing?" he shouted. Instead of steam he was met by a three foot high sea of bubbles. The Jacuzzi was going full blast and the bubbles were flying all over the bathroom like an explosion.

"Just shut it off," Marianne said.

"Shut it off? How? I can't find the damn tub!" he answered as he gingerly put one stocking foot ahead of the other, like a ballet dancer, in search of the elusive tub.

"Be careful you don't fall," she warned him. With those words of caution ringing in his ears, Dan vanished completely into the sea of bubbles.

"Danny, where are you?" she called.

"Right here," he answered as he stood up in the middle of the tub with bubbles up to his arm pits. "I found the tub and the shut off," he said, as the bubbles flew wildly around his head with every breath he took. He didn't dare move a muscle. Even the slightest movement sent the bubbles on another eruption. "Pfhtt, pfhtt, pfhtt, pfhtt," was all you could hear as he tried to clear the bubbles from his glasses by blowing upward from one side of his mouth and then the other. Even though the Jacuzzi was shut off the bubbles still seemed to multiply. There was no controlling them. They just went flying in every direction.

Marianne was standing in the bathroom doorway almost doubled over in laughter. "Danny, if I only had a camera," she said. "You should see yourself covered with bubbles and they're not doing you much good with all your clothes on."

"How can we get rid of these damn bubbles?" he wanted to know. "I can't even push them down the drain."

"We can try beating them to death with towels, I suppose," she offered, but she was laughing so hard she wasn't much help.

"Do you think I'll get arrested for pollution if I dump them out the window?" he asked. Now he was laughing just as hard.

"I don't think so," she answered, "but I'll bet you will get some real interesting inquiries from downstairs."

"We'll just have to take that chance," he said as he opened the bathroom window and began to push the bubbles out onto the countryside with the aid of a bath towel.

"I never knew bath oil to react like that," he commented.

Marianne still couldn't control her laughter as she told him, "The bath oil is still in the suitcase, that was bubble bath."

"Jeessuuss Keyrhist!" he repeated, as he shook his head. "Here we go again, Frick and Frack back in action for another weekend."

Chapter 34.

Vacation was really here! Marianne fastened her seat belt as Dan received clearance for takeoff from the airport tower. They had followed this routine almost every Friday for the past six months but this weekend was special. They were on their way to Alaska. This was the first part of a three week vacation they had planned with the Flanagans.

The men had a business meeting scheduled for Saturday morning in Chicago.

"I hate to mix business with pleasure," Dan said, "but this is an important meeting for us. We think it's about time to bow out of the Chicago real estate headaches. There are a lot of things we want to do and places we want to go and we can't do any of it if we're constantly called back to settle problems that shouldn't have occurred in the first place."

He glanced at Marianne and hoped the things and places he now had in mind would be something she wanted, too.

The Flanagans were waiting for them at the airport on Long Island. They liked the idea of sharing part of their vacation with Dan and Marianne. Jen was thrilled with the news that Bill was retiring from the Chicago business.

"Now maybe I'll get a chance to have some time with him," she said. "For years I watched his back as he went out the door to one business venture after another. At last we'll be able to enjoy life a little."

Marianne couldn't help wonder what Dan had in mind with all the spare time he was accumulating. Two weeks ago he went to California and withdrew from an active role in Continental Castings.

"It's about time to let the younger guys handle it," he said. "I have other things in mind."

She didn't ask what he meant by 'other things'. I'll wait and see, she thought.

It was a little after eleven Friday night when they reached Chicago. The Saturday morning meeting was scheduled for nine o'clock and the men were confident it would be a short one.

By twelve thirty they were back on their way again. Bill, as copilot, took a good deal of the aircraft responsibilities off Dan and made the long trip a lot easier. A quick stopover in the middle of South Dakota, then on to their second overnight stop in Montana. Dan didn't want to cross the Rocky Mountains at night.

"This is a sight you have to see," he told Marianne as he glanced over his shoulder to wink at his favorite passenger.

A small motel on the outskirts of the Montana airport was the only lodging in the area. The rooms were small and there was nothing luxurious about it. The location was its only advantage. Sparse furnishing consisted of a double bed, a dresser and a chair in each room. Linoleum tiles took the place of carpeting and a few colorful scatter rugs decorated with an Indian motif covered most of the open areas. It was clean, almost to the antiseptic stage. The bathrooms smelled heavily of pine scented disinfectant. The only extras available were two units that boasted of having water beds.

"Can you get seasick on one of these?" Marianne asked with a grin.

"I don't know," Dan answered with a chuckle. "Let's try it and see."

Bill and Jen were laughing at them bouncing up and down on the sides of the bed like a couple of kids. "I think we'll have to keep an eye on these two," Bill said.

"Yes," Jen agreed as she nodded her head, "We might learn a thing or two."

They enjoyed a quick supper at a nearby restaurant and returned to the motel to retire to their "water bed suites" for the night. They were looking forward to an early start and the scenic flight over the beautiful Rocky Mountains.

A few minutes past midnight Marianne woke up for the Kidney Express, her nightly trek to the bathroom. As she put her bare foot on the floor she felt a puddle. She didn't want to wake Dan so she didn't switch on the light. She leaned over the side of the bed and felt around with her hand. The whole floor was wet. She thought the waterbed must have sprung a leak. It didn't affect the comfort of the bed and she hoped it would be all right until morning.

She sat up and waited for her eyes to adjust to the light. The room seemed to be filled with eerie red shadows dancing around the Indian motif of the rugs. It took a minute for her to realize the red glow was from the neon sign in front of the motel. She stood up and with both feet on the wet floor it was like trying to walk on ice. After two steps she slid the rest of the way and crashed into the closed bathroom door. The noise woke Dan.

"Marianne, what's going on? Are you all right?" he asked as he sat up in bed.

"I'm fine," she answered. "There's a little leak in the waterbed and I'm getting a towel to wipe it up. Go back to sleep, I'll take care of it."

"Let me help you," he insisted and hurriedly got out of bed. As soon as his bare feet hit the wet floor he slid across and into Marianne who was laughing hysterically at his struggle to stay upright. The two of them were sitting on the wet floor laughing when Bill knocked on the adjoining door.

"Come in," Dan said but made no effort to get up.

As the door opened, the light from the Flanagan's "waterbed suite" covered them like a spotlight. "I'm afraid to ask what's going on," Bill said, "but you two are making a hell of a racket. Can't you manage to stay in bed one whole night without winding up on the floor?"

Dan and Marianne were laughing so hard they couldn't get back on their feet.

"There was a leak in the waterbed," Marianne said. "I got up to get a towel to wipe it up. I slid, Dan heard me, he got up to help, he slid, and you can see the results."

Bill's attitude quickly turned to concern as he asked, "Are you hurt?" He forgot about the water on the floor, took two steps into the room to help them and wound up on the top of the pile.

"Jeessuuss Keeyrhist!!!!!" Dan exclaimed and looked at Marianne who was still laughing. "Frick and Frack are back in action again," he said with a shake of his head.

Jen stood in the light from the adjoining doorway, surveyed the situation carefully and said, "I'm not setting one foot in that room for any reason. Bill, I'll throw you a rope."

* * * * *

A small airport, south of Seattle, Washington, was their last scheduled stop before Alaska. The Flanagans had reservations for a cruise from Vancouver, British Columbia to Anchorage, Alaska. Dan and Marianne would meet them at the Alaska end of their cruise and they would fly home from there. Bill suggested the cruise would be wonderful therapy for them, too, but Dan had other ideas. He made arrangements to rent a motor home so they could roam around Alaska with no set plans until it was time to meet the Flanagans. They needed this time for themselves and thought this was an ideal way to get it.

The Flanagans left for Vancouver on Monday morning and Dan and Marianne boarded his plane and took off for Haines, Alaska. Perfect weather enhanced their flight and the majestic scenery raised their excitement about this new adventure. Dan was meticulous about his flight plan and careful to make sure things were timed just right. They were scheduled to pick up the motor home anytime after two o'clock that afternoon. They arrived right on schedule and were told the vehicle reserved for them was not available yet. Dan was disappointed and the manager suggested he select one of the smaller models. There were plenty of them available right away.

They looked at the smaller ones, but Dan wasn't satisfied. "These are too small for us," he told the rental agent as he left the vehicle they were trying to talk him into accepting.

"Are you sure?" the agent asked. "It may be a day or two before we have a big one that is ready for the road."

Dan gave him a look that let him know his remarks needed a little more explaining.

"This doesn't usually happen, Mr. Shaw," the manager said. "Our policy is to thoroughly inspect these vehicles before they leave here. Alaska is a big place, lots of open country. We wouldn't want you to break down out there in the wilderness. When we find something wrong it has to be fixed before we allow the vehicle to leave the lot."

"I appreciate your concern, young man," Dan said. "However, it doesn't solve my immediate problem, does it?" Dan Shaw could tell when someone was trying to pull a fast one. He hadn't survived the business world all these years without witnessing almost every trick in the book. "I have a reservation for a specific type of vehicle and that's the one I want. I don't care where you have to go to get it. The vehicle I reserved is the only one I intend to accept. Now, it's your

273

problem, you handle it. I'll be back in one hour and I'll expect everything to be ready."

"Yes sir, but I don't think it can be done," the manager insisted. "You don't seem to understand the situation....."

"I understand the situation a lot better than you think I do," Dan interrupted. "Every rental agency in the world overbooks. The airlines do it, hotels do it, cruise ships do it. You accepted my money for a specific vehicle. I don't want a substitute, I don't want an excuse, I want what I paid for. NOW do we understand each other?"

"I think so, sir" the manager said in a subdued tone. "I'll see what I can do."

"Fine," Dan said, "I'll see you in one hour."

His firm, business like attitude surprised Marianne. She had never seen this side of him. They left the office and walked to the rental car they picked up at the airport. She could see he was upset and she wanted to relieve some of his tension.

"You know Danny, where we are doesn't matter," she told him. "Being together is all we need for a good vacation. If something goes wrong don't let it bother you. Let's laugh at it and have a good time anyway. Remember our reputation for being Frick and Frack. We have a lot to live up to." Her efforts to smooth over the rough spots were not taking the edge off his aggravation.

"Marianne, you counted on this vacation and so did I. I wanted everything to be perfect. It hasn't started out very well, but I'll make it up to you, I promise."

She watched his hands tighten on the steering wheel and the little muscles in his cheeks move up and down as if he wanted to say more but wasn't sure of what to add.

"Ah ha," she said with a touch of mysticism in her voice. "No more Mr. Nice Guy. The dark side of Daniel Shaw finally surfaces. He waited until he lured the sweet young maiden to the wilds of Alaska. Now the other personality shows itself. What will she do? How can she cope with this wilderness monster?" she teased.

Dan looked at her through the top corner of his glasses as the edges of his mouth curled upward in that special smile of his. This time he surprised her. He reached out and grabbed her with both arms and continued the charade. "She will have to give in to his every demand," he said.

"OK, OK, you win," she conceded with a laugh.

"That was the easiest battle I ever won with you," he chuckled. "I should have found this monster years ago."

"Or we should have moved to Alaska," she added.

"Maybe it's still not too late," he said quietly as he started the car and headed into town to find a place to eat.

The vehicle Dan reserved miraculously turned up while they were at the restaurant.

"This is more like it," he commented. "At least we can move around in this one."

"It is nice," Marianne agreed as they went through the motor home together. She wondered if he was going to have a problem driving a vehicle this size. His airplane is a lot bigger than this, she thought, he won't have any trouble.

They traveled north, toward Fairbanks and Marianne was amazed at the spectacular scenery. She had expected Alaska to be covered with snow. Instead the road stretched ahead of them like a dark gray ribbon and at the top of each rise new bursts of fantastic colors met the eye. Lush green trees bordered meadows bursting with wild flowers and in the distance the awesome grandeur of the mountains. No matter where you looked the majestic beauty of the mountains unfolded. Nature, she thought, has a wonderful way of reminding each of us how insignificant we are.

They traveled up the highway and listened to Willie Nelson on the radio singing *On The Road Again*. How fitting, she thought, and laughed as Dan made up his own words to the song. When she asked him to repeat it he couldn't remember what he had sung. They were together, they were happy and both of them knew this was going to be a good vacation.

"Uh oh," Dan said as they rounded a bend and spotted a camper pulled off the side of the road. "Looks like he's in trouble. Maybe we should see if we can help."

He pulled the motor home off the highway near the other vehicle. It was an older model pick up truck with a camper built on the back. Imitation white clapboard sides supported a peaked red roof. A sign over the tiny back door said, *Home Away From Home*. There didn't seem to be anyone around and as Dan walked toward the door he called out loudly, "Anybody here?"

"Just a minute," a muffled voice answered from inside. The tiny door opened and Dan thought he had met his first Leprechaun.

"What do you want?" the little man asked.

"I don't want anything," Dan answered. "I thought you were having trouble and might need some help."

"Nope," the Leprechaun said. "No trouble. Just getting ready for some mountain climbing when you came along."

"Mountain climbing?" Dan said puzzled, as he noticed the pixie like character was in his bare feet and a pair of sweat pants. No further explanation was offered as the Leprechaun came bounding down the steps of the camper and reached out to shake hands.

"Gives you a nice warm feelin' to know we still have some Good Samaritans on the road," he drawled. "My name is Donald (he pronounced it Don-auld) Duncan and it's a pleasure to meet up with you."

Dan returned the handshake and introduced himself.

"This here is my wife Dorothy," (he pronounced it Door-a-thee), Donald said and turned back to the camper. "Come on out Dumplin'."

Dumplin' poked her head out of the tiny camper door and Dan stood wide eyed in surprise. My God! he thought, that woman is huge! They must have built this thing around her. She'll never get out through that little door. But she did, with a series of wiggles and twists she popped out of the camper like the cork out of a bottle. Dan couldn't believe his eyes.

"You travelin' alone?" Donald asked.

"No," Dan said quickly and hurried back to his own vehicle to get Marianne.

"You're not going to believe this," he told her. "You have to see it for yourself, I could never describe it."

He introduced Marianne to the Duncans and Donald promptly inquired, "You and the Mrs. got a mission in mind, or are you just travelin' for the fun of it?"

Dan looked at Marianne, who was standing next to him and biting her bottom lip to keep from laughing. He told the Leprechaun they were heading for Fairbanks to meet friends. "We're behind schedule," he said, "so as long as you folks don't need help we'll be on our way."

"We're headin' for Fairbanks ourselves," Donald said. "Maybe we'll meet up with you again."

Dan didn't answer, just smiled and waved good-bye as he followed Marianne into the motor home.

"Poor little guy looked like he could use some help," Marianne commented.

"Don't be deceived by looks," Dan cautioned as he turned on the ignition and drove back onto the highway. "Don-auld," he mimicked, "has all the characteristics of a real user. He is not as dumb or as helpless as he would like you to believe."

"You saw all that in just the few minutes you were with him?" Marianne asked.

"Sure, that's why I told him we were behind schedule," he said.

Marianne shook her head, smiled and made a remark about him being a smart old guy.

Dan laughed and said, "I may be a smart old guy, but I sure am slow."

"What do you mean 'slow'?" she asked.

"I just realized what Don-auld meant when he said he was getting ready to do some mountain climbing." He chuckled as he told her about Donald's comment when he got out of the camper. "I wondered how he could climb a mountain with no shoes on. He wasn't referring to those mountains," he continued as he pointed to the mountain range in the distance. "He was talking about his wife." He grinned as he glanced over at her and said, "I think I interrupted a love making session in the back of a homemade camper."

Fairbanks was still a long way away but it didn't matter. They were having fun and enjoying every minute of their time together. Hours passed since their meeting with the Duncans and they still laughed every time they thought about the Good Samaritan effort.

Dan suggested they pull into the next service area. "If you want to we can have supper while the camper gets serviced," he said.

"I'm not very hungry," Marianne said. "Besides if we eat out all the time what will we do with all the food in the refrigerator?"

Dan liked the idea of finding a spot off the road by themselves. "Let's get the camper serviced, flush the tanks and get a fresh water supply. Then we can take our time and look for a good spot to camp out for the night," he said. "This vehicle is supposed to survive on its own. Let's find out if it will."

"Good idea," she agreed. "We don't have to be fussy about where we stop. According to this daylight timetable, Fairbanks only has two and a half hours of darkness tonight. Boy, burglars don't stand much of a chance for success up here, do they?" she said.

"Not unless they're quick," Dan answered with a grin.

"Maybe that's why Don-auld Duncan was so busy in the afternoon," Marianne said. "He had his daylight and darkness timetables mixed up."

"That's very possible," Dan agreed as he pulled the camper into the service bay. "Speaking of the Duncans, look in your side view mirror. The lovebirds are pulling in here, too."

"Maybe we got into the bay quick enough so they won't notice us," she said.

"No such luck," he replied. "Here comes Don-auld."

Dan slid the driver's window open as Donald Duncan came alongside.

"Hi neighbor," the little man drawled. "You and the Mrs. stoppin' over tonight?"

"Not tonight," Dan answered. "We're still behind schedule so we're going on ahead."

"Least let me buy you folks a cup of coffee before you go," the Leprechaun offered. "That was a nice gesture, you stoppin' like that today. Wife and I been talkin' about it all afternoon."

Dan and Marianne looked at each other and she gave a slight shrug of her shoulders and said, "Why not if it will make him feel good."

"OK, Donald," Dan told him. "We'll meet you in the coffee shop when we leave the service bay."

The Duncans were a most unusual couple. Donald was just under five feet tall and couldn't have weighed more than one hundred pounds if he stood on the scale with lead weights in every pocket. The most outstanding thing about him was his eyeglasses. Thick lenses set in big round tortoise shell frames covered three quarters of his face. He constantly made sniffing noises and wrinkled his nose in an attempt to keep the glasses somewhere in the area where he could see

278

through them. In spite of his efforts they slipped down and perched on the very tip of his pointed nose.

Dorothy must have tipped the scales at more than three hundred and fifty pounds. A massive thatch of jet black shoulder length curly hair surrounded a pretty face. She had emerald green eyes so big they instantly brought attention to that pretty face. She was amply endowed with the largest breasts Dan and Marianne had ever encountered. Dan said he thought Donald could hide securely between those breasts and the only thing that would show would be his bald head and eyeglasses. After that remark every time Marianne looked at Dorothy all she could picture was Donald's bald head and big eyeglasses protruding from the top of the two huge breasts. By the time they left the coffee shop Dorothy thought Marianne had a wonderful disposition because every time she looked at her, Marianne was smiling.

This vacation was turning into just what Dan and Marianne needed. They traveled when they wanted to, stopped when they felt like it and talked about everything. Much of the past was put to rest and they dared to dream again of a future together. As the years passed they learned the art of patience and realized that impulse is something that fades with youth. They were no longer overshadowed by the demand to succeed. Love never meant sex to either of them. It meant concern, attention and consideration. Sex was a bonus. A kiss never meant a commitment. It was an outward sign of affection. Now they were older and they knew how to listen to what the other was saying. More important, they learned to hear what the other needed.

Marianne glanced over at Dan and realized they had been on the road for several hours. He handled all the driving and she thought he must be tired. "We've been riding for a long time, Hon, maybe we'd better find a place to stop for awhile. We can't wait for the sun to set," she said with a grin. "I don't think it ever does, up here."

Dan put his sunglasses in the visor clip and looked at her. "I think you're right," he said. "These long days are very deceptive and I've been enjoying myself so much I haven't paid any attention to time."

Marianne admired his skill in handling this big, bulky vehicle. Especially when he turned off the main highway and tucked it neatly behind a thick stand of tall evergreens. The trees all around gave them privacy as well as a barrier blocking out most of the highway noise.

"Now that you've done your part," she said, "why don't I make some supper?"

"Fine with me," he answered, "if I can help."

"You can make sure all your gadgets are in place on this machine so we can use the water and electricity and what ever else we need," she suggested. "Two of us in the kitchen will be a pretty tight squeeze."

Dan glanced at her and made a funny little laughing sound. "That should make supper an interesting adventure," he commented and wiggled his eyebrows up and down.

Marianne took fresh salad makings from the refrigerator and put them on the small counter next to the sink. Dan was standing in back of her but close enough for her to smell his after shave. She glanced over her shoulder and said, "Danny you make every day an adventure for me."

He took a step closer to her, put his arms around her waist and rested his chin on her shoulder. He kissed the top of her ear and the side of her neck. His closeness and his gentle touch sent shock waves to her hormones. "Dan Shaw," she said in mock reproach, "cut that out or you won't get any supper."

"What will I get instead?" he asked as he released his hold and turned her around to face him.

She put her arms around his neck and answered, "Probably anything you want."

The tone of his voice went from light and carefree to serious as he looked at her and said, "How can I ever tell you how much I love you? Our love never faded, it just kept right on growing. Words can't describe how I feel. I want to be with you all the time. I want to hold you, and love you, and never let you go."

She studied his deep, brown eyes and put her hands in the soft white hair on the back of his head. "I know how you feel," she told him. "I feel the same way about you."

He held her close to his chest and closed his eyes as if that would block out the loneliness of all those in-between years. "I've kissed you good night every night of my life," he told her, "but it was only in my mind. Now that I found you again I want to be with you forever. No more 'if onlys' or 'what ifs'. I want my good night kiss to be real every night. I don't want to go home on Sundays. I want home to be where you are."

I'm not going to dampen his spirits, Marianne thought. I know I'm not ready for a total commitment yet, but I've already caused him enough grief for a lifetime. Now, I can't say no to him for anything. "That's a reasonable request," she said, "and it's easy enough to handle."

He didn't expect her to give in so quickly and her response surprised him. "Are you finally saying 'yes' to me?" he asked.

She looked at him and for the first time the hurt that she had seen in his eyes had disappeared completely. She tried to explain her answer without putting it back. "You said you don't want to go home on Sundays and I said that was a reasonable request. I know you're not comfortable in the apartment I have now. Maybe we can find one we both like and split expenses. Like Josh says, '60/40 right down the middle'. That way you don't have to go home on Sundays. You can come and go as you please, and I still have a thread of independence left."

"Are you serious?" he asked as if he doubted what he heard.

"Of course I'm serious," she said. "If this is going to work, we both have to give a little. Too much of a good thing can be harmful, too, you know."

"Marianne," he argued, "I've been without you for forty-three years. How can I get too much of you now? That's not possible."

She knew he was right. He could and would make her happy. Now, after a lifetime of disappointments she couldn't make the commitment she knew he wanted. "I can't change everything overnight, Danny. This is not like the old days when I had no one to consider but me. I can't walk away from my family. Even though I'm sure they will agree with you. I like my work. It can't compare to what you've done in your lifetime, but it's my little part of the world. Beth and Tim tell me it's a dull rut, but it's my space. Right now you are the most important part of my life. You put meaning where there was only existence. I love you with all my heart. I always have and nothing will ever change that. I'm afraid if we make this a constant we'll both lose something. Now we look forward to the weekends and each one gets a little better than the one before. I don't want to lose that."

"Why do you think we'll lose it?" he asked.

"I'm afraid to take the chance," she admitted.

He was quiet for a long minute and Marianne hoped she had not diminished any of the old feelings this vacation brought back to both of them. When she looked up at him, he said, "OK, I'll take you up on your suggestion. But remember, it's only a temporary solution. For now, we'll take life one day at a time, but we'll do it together."

Marianne closed her eyes and put her head against the front of his shoulder.

"Dan Shaw," she said as though she was speaking directly to his heart, "I love you."

Chapter 35.

Something woke Marianne but she wasn't sure what it was. She stayed very still and listened. It sounded like a rustling in the trees that surrounded the motor home. Maybe it's an animal, she thought. The sounds continued and seemed to increase. She was getting a little worried. This was strange new territory with different wildlife than what there was in Massachusetts. Suppose it's a bear, she thought. Maybe I better wake Dan.

"Danny," she said softly as she nudged his shoulder.

"What?" he answered sleepily.

She could tell he was not fully awake. "Do bears walk around in the dark?" she asked.

"I suppose so," he said drowsily, "unless they have flashlights."

"Dan, wake up," she said, "I'm serious. I hear all kinds of strange noises outside."

"Don't worry I'll protect you," he said as he put his arm around her and promptly went right back to sleep.

She had to smile at his reaction to her emergency. Oh well, she thought, the door is locked and I'm sure the bear doesn't have a key. She put her head back on his shoulder, closed her eyes and tried to sleep, too.

The early morning hours in Alaska are beautiful. A wispy ground fog had settled in over the motor home and as Marianne glanced out the window she could see it was just starting to shake itself loose from the clutches of the earth. Dan was still asleep and she tried to be quiet as she moved around.

Last night had been one of those few occasions in her life when she wished she could make time stand still. They discussed arrangements for the temporary solution they agreed to and talked about the early days in New York City. They remembered how they helped each other discover what real love was all about. Now it was happening again but this time it was not rushed or impulsive. The pace was slow and easy but appreciated and savored beyond description. She remembered telling Dan nothing could ever be better than the Thanksgiving weekend they spent in Connecticut. Now, she

283

had to correct herself because last night was better. Far better than anything she could ever remember.

She decided not to make coffee. She thought the smell might wake him. She would settle for a glass of juice and sit up front and read until he woke up. As she opened the door of the small refrigerator she glanced out the window. She couldn't believe her eyes. Just visible in the morning haze was the telltale imitation clapboard sides of the camper of Donald and Dorothy Duncan.

"Oh no," she said out loud.

Dan rolled over and propped himself up on one elbow. "What's the matter?" he asked still half asleep.

"Nothing," she said. "I'm sorry I woke you. Go back to sleep."

"Why are you up so early?" he asked and before she could answer he added, "What time is it?"

She sat on the side of the bed and handed him the glass of juice she had poured for herself.

"One question at a time, "she said. "First of all, I got up before you so I could sit here and watch you sleep. You're a pretty good looking old guy even when you're snoring."

"What a way to start the day," he said with a grin and reached for her hand. "If you keep saying things like that I might forget about getting out of bed and pull you back in here with me."

"That sounds exciting but maybe it's not a good idea right now," she answered.

"Why? What's the matter?" he asked.

"We have unexpected company," she told him.

"Did you see a bear?"

"No, not a bear," she said. "Sometime during the night the Duncans pulled in here and parked next to us."

"You're kidding," he exclaimed as he sat up in the bed. "How in hell did they find us out here?"

"I don't know," she said. "They must have trackers blood or something."

"I think Donald has the nose to follow a wallet," Dan commented.

Marianne wondered what time this disastrous duo arrived. There was no other vehicle in sight when Dan pulled the motor home off the road. He picked this spot because it was not very far off the highway yet it was secluded and protected by the trees. It was almost impossible to see the vehicle from the road.

"Danny," Marianne said, "last night we weren't paying attention to anything but each other. Donald could have come freewheeling in here anytime, jammed on his brakes and run into us broadside and I don't think either of us would have been aware of it."

"You're right," he said with a grin. "Last night the Duncans were the farthest thing from my mind. I remember during the night hearing you say something about a bear, but I thought I was dreaming and didn't even wake up. Maybe the Duncans arrived instead of the bear."

The unexpected discovery of Dumplin' and the Wart, as Dan called him, wasn't going to take the glow off their perfect night. They were not going to let it spoil their day, either. Marianne had showered and dressed before Dan was awake. She noticed the shower was running slowly and mentioned it to him when he went into the bathroom. Perhaps the shower head was clogged, she suggested, and thought they should have noticed it when the rental agent went through his extensive demonstration.

They decided to ignore the Duncans as much as possible and do things as they had planned. Marianne cooked breakfast while Dan showered and dressed. As he buttoned the top three buttons of his shirt he remarked there were few smells that could tempt an appetite like bacon cooking in the morning. Unfortunately, that same appetizing smell of bacon drifted toward the Duncans camper and you could see Donald's nose in the air as he followed the scent to their vehicle.

"Mornin' neighbor," he drawled when Marianne answered his knock. "Dumplin' wondered if you might have a little coffee we could borrow. It's the one thing we forgot at the service stop yesterday," he whined as he handed her an empty paper cup.

"Sure," she said and took the cup from him but didn't ask him inside. Donald didn't need an invitation. She turned her back to get the coffee and he bounded inside like a jackrabbit.

"Mighty fine set up you got here," he commented as he looked around the interior of the motor home. "A mite roomier than ours. Our kitchen is our bedroom after dark."

"It's comfortable," Marianne said and tried to keep the conversation at a minimum as she handed him the paper cup full of coffee.

"Dan still sleepin'?" he asked.

"No, Donald, I'm here," Dan answered. "I'm putting my shoes on."

"We're cookin' breakfast outdoors this mornin'," he drawled. Welcome to join us if you like."

"No thank you," Dan answered. "We overslept and we're behind schedule. Our friends will have the police out looking for us if we're late getting to Fairbanks."

"Bacon sure smells good," Donald said as he made sniffing motions with his nose. Marianne wasn't sure if the bacon was causing his reaction or if it was just the fact that his nose constantly made sniffing motions to hold his glasses in place.

"It sure does," Dan agreed. "Marianne is a good cook."

"Bet she's good at a lot of things," Donald commented.

Dan stopped in his tracks and looked straight at the little Wart. "What did you say?" he asked.

"Peers to be a very capable lady," Donald quickly answered. He got the message that Dan was not pleased with his remark. "Thank you for the coffee," he quickly added and left as fast as he came in.

"That little twerp really gets to me," Dan said.

Marianne looked at him and smiled. "Don't pay any attention to him. Eat your breakfast and we'll be on our way."

Donald's visit did manage to dull the glow of their beautiful morning a little. Especially when Dan walked outside to check the turn around area and found that Donald had hooked up to the water tank and electricity of their motor home. The little Wart had rigged special hoses and wires and tapped into their supply. Dan was angry and wanted to pull out and see if he could jerk the camper off the back of the truck.

"With our luck we would probably pull the side out of the motor home," Marianne warned.

"I wish I had a pair of clippers," Dan said. "I'd like to cut the hose right in half and let the Duncans drain all over Alaska."

Marianne looked at him and grinned. "He's not worth the trouble," she said. "Let's just leave him here and be on our way."

As soon as they hit the highway the glow was back. The Duncans were left behind and they were on the road again. The miles flew by and the time flew by. Long daylight hours were deceiving and these happy travelers from the lower forty-eight had a hard time trying to gauge the hour by the position of the sun.

"We've been riding for a long time, we need a break," Marianne suggested.

"Good idea, "Dan agreed. "We'll pull into the next service area and have everything checked. Do you want to keep going or would you rather stay for the night?"

"According to this computer that's been spying on us from the dashboard we have almost four hundred and fifty miles behind us and nearly two hundred to go before we reach Fairbanks," she calculated. "Why don't we take a break for about an hour and walk around while the vehicle gets serviced. If you feel like going farther we can travel for another hour or two."

"Are you sure you're not too tired?" Dan asked.

"I'm not tired," she answered. "I was going to suggest that I drive for awhile. You've done all the driving. You're the one who should be tired."

"Marianne," he said with a smile, "I'm so happy that I haven't given a thought to being tired."

"Well take a minute and think about it now," she said and cast him a mischievous sideways glance. "If I hear any bears tonight I want to be able to wake you up."

He looked at her over the top corner of his glasses and asked, "Do you think you can handle this vehicle?"

"Do you want to see my Teamsters card?" she joked. "You know, Mr. Shaw, there are a few things in my past that I haven't told you about, yet."

"In that case we'll have to pull over early and you can fill me in," he said with a grin.

The beauty, the vastness, and the temptation to explore a little farther were always present. What wasn't always present was the road. The main highway was there, but you couldn't stray very far or you would run out of paved road in a hurry. Last night Dan found a spot he thought was secluded and free from prying eyes, not too far off the road but well out of sight. Even though he had chosen the spot carefully the Duncans managed to find them. That was not going to happen again.

Now, Marianne was driving. Dan knew she was a good driver, but he wasn't quite sure how good.

"Where are you going?" he asked as she turned the motor home off the highway and through a small clearing between the trees. "There's no road here," he said anxiously.

She tightened her grip on the steering wheel and shrugged her shoulders nonchalantly as she replied, "Couple of trips through here and there will be."

He had to admit she could handle this vehicle. He could hardly believe she was making it go where no other vehicle had ever gone. He wondered why he doubted her ability to drive it in the first place. She completely surprised him when they came to a small stream and instead of stopping she drove right through it.

"Jeessuuss Keyrhist!!!!! We'll never get out of here!" he almost shouted and held on to the door frame for support as the bulky vehicle swayed back and forth over the rocky bottom of the little stream.

Marianne laughed and kept it moving until they came to another small clearing. She stopped, pulled straight ahead and finally backed it around until the motor home was facing the path she made getting in.

"There," she said with a satisfied smile, "it's all ready for you to drive it out in the morning."

Dan shook his head as he looked at her and said, "I don't believe you did that." He took off his cap and ran his hand through his hair. "I sat right here and watched and I still don't believe you did that."

"I told you I had a Teamsters card," she said.

"Do you realize you cut your own road through these woods?" he asked.

"Now are you going to ask me why? She questioned.

"No," he said, "but I think you're going to tell me anyway."

She took the keys from the ignition, reached over and handed them to him. "When we picked up this motor home you said you counted on this vacation. Well, you were right when you thought I counted on it, too. Last night was the closest thing to perfection I have ever experienced in my life. It was marred by the Duncans this morning. I knew you were upset, but if you're willing to try again, I defy the Duncans to find us out here."

"Marianne," Dan said with a laugh, "I love you!"

Chapter 36.

These happy travelers had covered a lot of miles in one week. Now they were ready to enjoy some of the creature comforts of a first class hotel. Nothing feels as good as soaking in a hot bath after almost seven hundred miles of roughing it, or watching television on a screen big enough to see and taking full advantage of room service at its best. Marianne suggested they come back in the winter when there were only three and a half hours of daylight — provided the l-o-n-g nights could be like the ones they had just spent in the motor home. Dan laughed when she told him she could understand why the women in Alaska smiled so much and the men all looked pretty satisfied.

"It's all in the priorities," he responded with a satisfied smile of his own.

Alaska is a fascinating place. The old stands next to the new and they seem to bond together against a common predator, the cold Arctic winter. Only one thing is definite about Alaska. It is B-I-G! It is full of youth, energy, open space, wilderness and the spirit of adventure. You feel revitalized. You NEVER feel old.

"Since we're back in civilization, would you like to have dinner in the hotel dining room?" Dan asked.

"Do they serve caribou steaks, moose burgers or whale-on-a-stick?" she asked. "If not let's find some exotic place and do something different, OK?"

There were no caribou steaks or moose burgers, but dinner in the hotel dining room was a pleasant change. Salmon steaks were substituted for the whale-on-a-stick that they joked about earlier.

"I'm sorry I couldn't find something exotic for you," Dan teased. "Maybe tomorrow."

"Well, I'll just keep after you until we locate one of the three," she teased back.

"In the meantime will you settle for a short tour of the Fairbanks area after dinner?" he asked.

"I'd love to if you're not too tired," she said. "These days of endless sunshine are deceiving and I can't keep track of time." She looked across the table at him and continued, "Remember, Mr. Shaw, you're my whole future. I can't take any chances of anything happening to you. So, I'll go along with what you want to do provided you agree to call it a day when you get tired."

"I promise I'll get you home at a reasonable hour," he said.

The first stop on their tour was an authentic turn of the century saloon a few miles out of town. The swinging doors and sawdust on the floor recreated the atmosphere of the Gold Rush Days of the early 1900's. The show was followed by a hot air balloon ride at midnight! They had to remind themselves this was Alaska and midnight was just twelve minutes after the sun set.

They returned to the hotel exhausted and Marianne promised never to use the word 'different' to Dan again. "You have a wild imagination," she told him.

Fairbanks was behind them and they were headed for Anchorage and another phase of this fantastic vacation. Something was bothering Marianne, but she couldn't figure out what it was. She was happier than she had ever been. Dan made her feel alive again. Just thinking about him made her feel good. Yet, something was making her uneasy. Dan could see there was a problem but he couldn't figure it out either. He wondered if he had done or said something that triggered a bad reaction. He tried joking with her and singing the funny little songs they laughed at as they made up their own lyrics. Nothing seemed to help. Finally, he pulled the motor home off the road, turned off the ignition and got up and locked the door from the inside.

"What are you doing?" she asked.

He reached for her hand and said, "Come with me." He walked her back to the rear of the vehicle and as he held tightly to her hand, guided her to the bed and said, "Lay down."

"Are you serious?" she asked as if she didn't believe what was happening.

"Ever since we left the hotel this morning I could tell something was bothering you," he told her. "I've tried every way I can think of to get you to tell me what it is. Nothing seems to work. So, I said to myself, 'self, how can I get this lady to talk to me?' Then I remembered that every one of our problems have been solved when we were flat on our backs. So lie down and talk to me."

By this time his antics had Marianne laughing as she affectionately said, "Dan Shaw, you're a nut," then quickly added, "a very loveable nut."

He sat next to her on the side of the bed with his arm around her and rested her head on his shoulder as he reminded her of the song that worked so well in Connecticut.

> *Come lay down beside me, love me and hide me*
> *Let me kiss all the hurting of this world away.*
> *Let me hold you so close that I feel your heartbeat*
> *And we'll never again wander or stray.*

He tilted her head so he could see her face and asked, "What's the matter, hon?" He could see she was close to tears and he wanted desperately to help her.

"I don't know," she told him as she tried to hold back the tears. "I honestly don't know."

"I'm no expert," he said, "but I think you're homesick. When was the last time you were away from your family for this long?"

"I don't remember," she had to admit, "probably never."

"You keep telling me I'm a smart old guy. Let's see how much of a smart old guy I really am," he said. "We're going to go nonstop to Anchorage, check in to the hotel and you're going to call home. Then, if you're still homesick we'll get the first plane out in the morning." This was not what he planned for this vacation but now he was more concerned about her peace of mind that his own preferences. "If talking to your family solves the problem, tomorrow we'll attack Alaska from another angle."

Dan seemed to pinpoint her problem like a good therapist. Once she realized what was wrong it was a little easier to handle. As they headed back down the highway toward Anchorage he was grateful for the long hours of sunshine. Neither of them realized they had checked out of the hotel so early. Alaska sunrises are as deceptive as midnight sunsets.

They passed the turn for Denali National Park. It was one of the places they intended to visit and Marianne asked if he was sure he didn't want to view Mt. McKinley and see the sights there.

"I don't want to stop today," he said. "I have a couple of other ideas I'll tell you about after you talk to Beth and Tim."

Identifying her problem relieved some of the tension, but now she felt guilty for keeping him from the sights they had planned so carefully to include.

"You're missing the biggest mountain in North America," she reminded him.

He glanced over at her through the top corner of his glasses and said, "I already saw the two biggest mountains on this continent when I met Dumplin' last week." His description of Dumplin's exodus from the Duncan's *Home Away From Home* was priceless and they found themselves laughing at it all over again. He certainly is one of a kind, Marianne thought, as she watched him guide the vehicle through the sporadic bursts of traffic at the stopover areas.

In Anchorage, Dan parked the motor home behind the hotel. They checked in and before they were settled or unpacked he put through the call to Massachusetts. This smart old guy was right again. As soon as Marianne heard the familiar voices of her family the homesick feelings disappeared.

Beth told her mother she had been in touch with two former coworkers who moved to Anchorage a few years ago. She gave Marianne their address and phone number and said they were on vacation now and would be delighted to show Anchorage to any visitors from the lower forty-eight. Marianne could almost see Dan's mental wheels turning when she relayed this news. He was so interested he called Beth back and asked for a little background on them.

Marianne assured him the phone call cured her problems and she was ready to continue their Alaska adventure.

"Good," he said. "Now let me tell you what I have in mind. Beth said her friends are on vacation for the next two weeks and she didn't think they had any plans. I'm going to call them and ask if they would like to use this motor home for the next ten days. They can use it if they can get it to Haines when it's due back. We can meet them there and I'll take care of any other charges and pay for their flight back to Anchorage. If they have other plans, I'll have the hotel get someone to drive it back. I would prefer to see Beth's friends enjoy it rather than let it sit for ten days. Beth says they're reliable so let's see if they are interested."

"What are we going to do in the meantime?" she asked.

"You said you wanted caribou steaks and moose burgers. We're going to find a place where you can get them. We're going to go fishing, watch icebergs drop into the ocean, raft down a river and even find some bears, real bears this time. How does that sound?"

"Fantastic," she answered and he noticed she had regained the enthusiasm that was lost with the bout of homesickness.

Dan phoned the boys and invited them to dinner at the hotel. When they accepted immediately he wondered if Beth told them to expect his call. They proved to be a wealth of information on Anchorage and much of the surrounding area. During dinner they explained how they came to Alaska for a vacation and were so impressed they decided it was where they wanted to live.

"We went home, packed our bags and took the next flight right back here. That was almost four years ago and we've never been sorry we made the move," Peter, the older of the two, told them.

After dinner Dan explained what happened at the rental agency when they arrived in Haines. He didn't want to return the vehicle until it was due. He had already paid the time rental for another ten days. The boys could use it until then, if they would have it back in Haines on time. The two looked at each other and Peter commented, "There has to be a catch to this somewhere."

"The catch is that the motor home has to be back at the rental agency in ten days," Dan told them. "If you would like to use it until then we can meet you at the airport restaurant in Haines at noon one week from Thursday. Do we have a deal?"

"This sounds like one of those offers you can't refuse," Paul, the younger one, said. "You bet we have a deal."

"One more thing," Dan added, and the boys looked at each other as if they knew there was more to this "deal." Dan took a credit card from his wallet and handed it to Peter. "Anything you need for the vehicle charge it on this card. That means all your gas, propane, any service charges, parking or anything to do with the vehicle at all. You have to handle your own entertainment, but everything else is on us, OK?"

They looked at each other and then at him as if they expected someone to shout, "April Fool". Paul looked at Dan and very seriously asked, "Are you with the Mafia?"

"No," Dan assured him with a laugh. "Why do you ask?"

"People don't make offers like this out of the blue," Paul insisted. "I still think there's a catch."

"I have two reasons for making this offer," Dan explained. "First of all, I didn't like the way the rental was handled in the beginning. That manager thought he was going to dump anything he felt was road worthy on us and we would accept it without a peep. I don't do business that way and I don't expect that kind of treatment from people I deal with. The second reason for this offer," he continued, "is because Beth recommended you and I value her opinion. If she says you are reliable you must be. Marianne and I have had enough of the motor home. Now we want to have some fun without the responsibility of the vehicle. If you boys have it, I know you will show up on time and I won't have any more worries about it. You'll be doing me a big favor."

"I wish more people would ask us for favors like this," Peter said.

"Dan, you didn't tell them about the flight back to Anchorage," Marianne reminded him.

"I'll make arrangements for you to fly back to Anchorage from Haines after we return the motor home," he added. "That's part of the package, OK?"

The boys looked at each other again, still not able to believe their luck. "This keeps getting better and better," Paul commented.

After dinner they headed for the hotel parking lot so the boys could look over the motor home.

"WOW!" Paul said. "Looks like a luxury condo on wheels. This is really going first class."

There was a short discussion about who would drive it home. Peter won the decision.

Paul was to follow in their car.

As Dan and Marianne returned to the hotel he put his arm around her shoulders and said, "I think we made a wise choice. The boys will have a good time and they'll show up when they're supposed to. Now, we can relax and have some fun, too."

"What happened to your pioneer spirit?" Marianne asked with a laugh. "What happened to 'Outdoorsey Dan' who came to explore Alaska? All of a sudden you're looking for all the creature comforts. How come?"

"Probably because I'm old enough and smart enough to know what I can handle," he answered with a laugh as they got on the elevator and headed upstairs.

* * * * *

Monday morning was rainy and miserable, not a good vacation day. It looked like activities would be limited for a little while. Dan was optimistic and said he had some planning to do and could use the time. He was sure the rain would be over by the time he had everything settled. She wondered what he was up to and thought there's never a dull moment with this man. Yesterday he said they would attack Alaska from a different angle and she had learned to appreciate the significance of the word "different" when Dan Shaw used it.

He was concerned about Marianne's frame of mind and wanted to make sure the homesick problem was completely solved. He intended to keep her busy and fill the remaining vacation days with plenty of activity. He would plan the days carefully and leave sufficient time at night for the togetherness they both cherished.

The phone rang, Dan answered it and listened intently for several minutes while his caller did the talking. "Sounds good to me," he said. "Send up a copy of the schedule.

Let me understand something, we're not part of a tour group of any kind are we? This has to be independent. If we want to see something else we're free to come and go as we want, am I correct?" After his caller responded, Dan ended the conversation with "Fine," and hung up.

"What are you up to?" Marianne asked as she sat next to him on the small sofa.

"You said you wanted to see Alaska," he answered, "and that's what we're going to do. This afternoon we'll take a plane to Ketchikan, then a boat ride to Juneau and a plane to Glacier Bay. If you like it there we can stay for a couple of days. We'll cruise the bay on Tuesday, walk on a glacier on Wednesday, fish for Halibut on Thursday and be back here to meet Bill and Jen on Friday. How does that sound to you?"

Marianne looked at him and smiled. "Other than that, what do you have planned?"

"That's just the framework," he said. "We can fill the rest of the time any way we want."

By the time they finished breakfast the new itinerary arrived from the hotel office. As if on cue, the rain stopped and the sun pushed the clouds aside. Ketchikan, Sitka and Juneau were visited in true tourist fashion. Quick stops at points of interest, a few souvenirs, then on to the next stop. When they arrived at Glacier Bay, Marianne welcomed the chance to rest. The friendly atmosphere at the Inn with its big comfortable furniture and soft touches of elegance offered a reprieve from the hectic schedule. The unhurried, carefree mood at this pleasant lodge gave them the chance to unwind and enjoy the tranquility that was the perfect ending to a very full day. Dan said they would see Alaska, but he didn't say they would do it all in one day.

Somehow the body clock and the mechanical clock were not in tune with each other. There was no way Marianne could justify going to bed at ten o'clock at night when the sun was still shining, but by ten o'clock they were weary. Dan had planned wisely. The second day of their new schedule was a much slower pace. They cruised the picturesque fjords of Glacier Bay and watched in awe as a huge chunk of ice broke away and fell into the sea, just as Dan had promised. They enjoyed the antics of the harbor seals as they sailed past the boat on ice floats, like little furry hitchhikers on their way to the ocean. They reacted like real tourists and waved to the friendly little creatures as they floated past, almost expecting them to wave back

The days at Glacier Bay were filled with exciting new experiences. They put on special boots to walk on a glacier and made believe they were astronauts walking on the moon. They fished for giant Halibut and watched the incredible display put on by the gigantic whales for the benefit of visitors to their ocean playground. Mother Nature has a sense of humor and some fantastic performers to show spectators that there really is life outside of a shopping mall.

The nights at Glacier Bay were unforgettable. Dan made sure there was always time for each other, sensitive, affectionate periods of quiet rejuvenation for mind and body. It was the ideal way to end each unequaled day.

The Inn was impressive and their stay so satisfying Dan decided to wait until Friday morning before returning to Anchorage. Bill and Jen Flanagan were scheduled to arrive at the hotel between eleven in the morning and one in the afternoon. Arrangements had already been made for them to have an adjoining suite.

"They don't expect us to sit there and wait for them," he said. "No need for us to rush. If we're not there when they get in they'll be there when we get in."

They enjoyed the leisurely pace of the days and the quiet seclusion of the nights at Glacier Bay and neither of them was in a hurry to go back to a hectic sightseeing schedule. Dan seemed especially reluctant to leave.

"I thought you would be anxious to see the Flanagans," Marianne said.

"I am," he replied, "but these last few days have really been nice and I would like to stretch them as far as I can."

"We'll have to put Glacier Bay on our 'places to return to' list," she suggested as she closed the drapes to darken the bedroom.

"We should come back here in the winter," Dan said.

"Why the winter?" she asked.

He looked at her over his glasses and with a sly grin said, "The nights are six months long, remember?"

"Good idea," she agreed with a laugh.

Dan was already in bed. Marianne walked around to her side and got in. As she reached for the covers he stretched his arm across her pillow so that when she laid back down his arm was around her. She turned on her side, put her head on his shoulder and kissed him just below his ear.

"Gee, you smell good," she said.

"Gee, you feel good," he replied.

"This must be love," she told him.

"It is love," he assured her. "It's fascination, affection, devotion, passion, romance, and every other nice thing I can think of," he said as he kissed her and held her close to him. "I love the days I spend with you, but there is nothing that can come close to the nights we've spent together."

She could only respond by whispering, "Danny, I love you."

"I love you, too," he told her between tender kisses. Dan was affectionate, considerate and gentle. Each time they made love it was better than the last. They tried to sustain the feeling and hesitated to let these moments pass. Even in love making their years proved an advantage. Emotions were controlled and enjoyed and passion and affection were prolonged and cherished. They thoroughly enjoyed each other and reached a new level of understanding for their needs and desires. There was no room in their thinking for age barriers. What they could not achieve when they were younger was now attainable with sensitivity and a degree of pleasure and satisfaction neither of them ever realized was possible.

Chapter 37.

Eleven days had passed since Dan and Marianne parted company with Bill and Jen Flanagan. The cruise the Flanagans chose made a few quick stops at major ports but almost all of their sightseeing was done from the deck of the ship. When they reached Anchorage they were ready to see the rest of the land of the midnight sun.

The motor home trip and their stay at Glacier Bay helped Dan and Marianne clear up a lot of their unanswered questions. They had agreed to put the past behind them and were looking forward to what was ahead.

They arrived back at the hotel in Anchorage early Friday afternoon and found the Flanagans had already checked in.

"You two look wonderful," Jen commented.

"Look at this guy," Bill said as he pointed to Dan. "He's still smiling. You must have had one hell of a good time."

Jen put her arm around the back of Bill's waist. "We finally had some time to ourselves," she said affectionately. "I almost forgot how interesting my old guy really is." She looked at Marianne and asked, "How was yours?"

"I can tell you in one word," Marianne answered with a grin, "WOW!"

"Dan," Jen teased, "I think you're blushing."

"It's sunburn," Dan tried to explain self-consciously. "We've been spending a lot of time in the fresh air and sunshine."

"Sure you have," Bill mocked. "Tell us about it."

"All right," Dan answered and began with the trip to Haines from Seattle. Marianne was impressed by how thoroughly he described every detail. He must have enjoyed it to tell it so well, she thought. Dan's account of his first meeting with the Duncans was classic. The Flanagans were amazed that these two had covered so much territory and did so much in such a short time.

Dan explained about the motor home and the arrangements he made with Peter and Paul to take it back to Haines.

Bill thought that was an excellent solution. "I was concerned about how the four of us were going to fit in a motor home. Especially when you two seem to have all kinds of problems staying in bed at night," he teased.

"I think we have that problem solved," Dan told him.

The rest of Friday was spent sharing adventures.

"Somehow you two always manage to get the fun side of things," Jen said. "We had a wonderful time, but mild compared to your trip. You always seem to have all the laughs."

"We're willing to share some with you," Dan told them, "starting tomorrow." He didn't explain any further and left them all wondering what he had planned.

"What's the big secret?" Marianne asked when they were alone.

"You said you wanted caribou steak, whale-on-a-stick or moose burgers. Caribou steak was the only one of the three I could find. So tomorrow we're going to an Eskimo village near Nome to get you one."

"Danny, be serious," she said.

"I am serious," he answered.

"You're incredible!" she commented but made no objection to the plans for the next day.

It didn't surprise the Flanagans that Dan would go to such lengths to satisfy Marianne even though it was something said as a joke. They had been with him through forty years of frustration and now seemed to enjoy his happiness as much as he did.

Marianne was surprised to see that Eskimos lived in houses and not in igloos made of block ice with a small round crawl space for a front door. I've seen too many cartoons, she thought, and looked out the window of the small plane as they approached the village. There weren't many cars and the main street doubled as a runway for the plane. Another cultural defect created by progress, she thought, and wondered what happened to the dog sled, the igloo and the parka.

"No wonder you two have so much fun," Jen commented on the flight back to Anchorage. "You just go ahead and do everything."

Marianne looked at her and said, "believe me, Jen, we've both paid our dues. Now we laugh at life a little and enjoy ourselves a lot. More important, we've learned how to enjoy each other. It was a long time coming but it's a good feeling now."

The Eskimo village trip was followed the next day by a ride on the Alaska Railroad and a visit to Denali National Park and Mt.

McKinley. A helicopter took them over the park to view some of the scenery and the area wildlife.

"Who set up this schedule?" Bill asked when Dan told him they were going to ride a rubber raft down the river in the park.

"The hotel manager put most of it together," Dan told him.

"Next time just pay your bill and you won't have these penalties," Bill suggested as he put on the yellow rain gear to board the raft. Rafting was a first time experience for all of them and they didn't know what to expect. They got completely soaked, laughed a lot and had a wonderful time. Tuesday night they rode the railroad back to Anchorage and fell into bed exhausted by ten o'clock.

Wednesday the Flanagans were ready to collapse. They insisted on a halt to all activities and demanded a day of rest before starting home.

"You two are not on a vacation," Bill commented. "You're on an endurance test. When do you run out of steam?"

Marianne looked at Dan and they laughed as she said, "About ten o'clock every night."

They left the hotel early Thursday morning and headed for their flight to Haines. Peter and Paul were waiting for them in the airport restaurant as planned. The Flanagans were given a tour of the motor home and were impressed at the comforts it offered. It was returned to the rental agency and Dan paid the mileage charges and went back to the airport to say good-bye to the boys as they boarded their flight to Anchorage.

"Remember," Peter said, "Anytime you decide to come back all you have to do is call us."

"We'll be back," Dan told him, "you can count on it."

* * * * *

Vacation was almost over and time once again was proving itself their enemy. No matter how hard they tried they couldn't slow it down. Good thing we build memories Marianne thought. Even time can't take them away.

This vacation had certainly added to their memories. The activity filled days with all their exciting new adventures were the prelude to satisfying nights and recognition of each others needs and desires. Now it was time to put the memories on hold and head for home.

Dan's plane had been stored on the far side of the airport. He and Bill stopped at the office to file their flight plan and pay the storage charges. When they got on board it was like greeting an old friend. The comfortable interior, the plush seats, the "I'm used to this" feeling of this aircraft made Marianne feel guilty that she had so often referred to it as a monster machine. After riding in a hot air balloon, a floatplane, and a helicopter, this was like being back in old familiar territory.

She sat behind Dan and watched him maneuver the plane to take-off position. Bill was acting as copilot and Marianne was fascinated at the synchronization of the two men. They seemed to read each other's thoughts and anticipate the next move. What a fantastic team they make, she thought. She gazed out the window as the plane took off and knew that this was one place she would never forget. The beautiful sights, the wilderness sounds, the new and exciting adventures were left behind but the treasured memories went home with all of them.

The first few days of this vacation they hop scotched across the United States. The journey home was different. Time was catching up with them again and Dan took the most direct route possible even though much of it was over wilderness. The scenery was an artist's fantasy. Forests in every shade of green imaginable, interrupted only by a sporadic splash of azure blue to signify the placid waters of picturesque lakes untouched by the spoilers of civilization.

The first stop was a small airport outside of Quesnel, British Columbia. As always, Dan gave them a perfect landing, no bumps, no jars, no surprises. He proved again how much of a master he is at handling this aircraft. As they coasted to a stop near the airport office, Bill reached across the seat and tapped him on the shoulder. "Nice job," he said.

They had to stay with the plane until the customs officer gave his stamp of approval. No one thought there would be any problems until they learned the customs office was never notified of their arrival. The only customs official available was an elderly gentleman who spoke only French. They had nothing to declare and everyone expected a simple routine procedure.

This inspector had other ideas and was so intent on flaunting his authority he poked in every nook and cranny. No attempt was made to impede his progress as he rummaged through luggage and never put anything back. Marianne and Jen could see that Dan and Bill were getting very angry with this arrogant little bureaucrat. He was more interested in stressing his importance than upholding any law. They were aware of the unwritten rule about not upsetting the customs inspector, but this man was ridiculous.

They watched as he ranted in French and several times threw up his hands in disgust. Finally, Marianne couldn't stand it any longer and looked at Dan and winked. She took him by the arm and walked just far enough away from the plane so the inspector could hear them speaking but couldn't make out what they were saying. In no uncertain terms she rattled off her best French to Dan who put his head down and seemed to be absorbing the brunt of her verbal assault. The fact that one of them did speak the language surprised the customs man and he did a complete about face with his attitude. All of a sudden everything was fine and in proper order. Permission was granted to let them go ahead with their plans. They thanked him for his trouble and took care of their landing fees and refueling charges.

As the inspector left the airport Dan turned to Marianne and asked, "What did you say that got him off our backs so quickly?"

"Nothing that made much sense," she answered with a chuckle. "I rattled off the only two things I remembered from my high school French classes; one Our Father and one Hail Mary."

The Flanagans looked at each other and Bill said, "That was the maddest Hail Mary I ever heard."

The unnecessary delay by the pompous customs inspector wasted almost three hours. An unfamiliar airport in the middle of the Canadian Rockies was not an ideal setting for a take off in clear daylight hours. The safety factor drops substantially when the late afternoon sun casts long shadows that distort the surrounding area. A check with Air Weather warned them of an approaching front and they agreed the best thing to do was stay here for the night and leave early in the morning. The lone occupant of the airport office suggested they check in to a small country inn a few miles to the east of the airport. He made arrangements for them on the office phone and a car was sent to pick them up.

The Inn was a large converted farmhouse with comfortable old fashioned furnishings. The innkeeper, a robust jolly woman in her late fifties greeted her unexpected guests with a pleasant smile and a promise to make their stay enjoyable. She suggested they visit their rooms and freshen up and she would prepare a small supper for them in the dining room. "It will be on the table in one hour," she told them.

Exactly one hour later the four unscheduled guests sat down to a fantastic meal. The small supper consisted of French onion soup, crisp salad with homemade dressing, baked potatoes, chicken breasts sautéed to perfection, broccoli spears crisscrossed with drizzles of tangy cheese and an endless supply of puffy hot rolls that would melt in your mouth.

Homemade ice cream on fresh baked pie along with rich savory coffee completed the meal.

"My only regret is that we didn't get here yesterday," Bill commented as he finished the last bite of his pie.

"My only regret is that I think I put on five pounds," Jen added.

"We'll have to add this to our 'places to return to' list," Marianne suggested, "but without the inspector."

"I don't think the inspector will give us any more trouble," Dan said with a smile. "The last time that swinging door to the kitchen opened I got a good look at the dishwasher. Unless he has an identical twin brother, that arrogant little inspector is also the dishwasher for this establishment."

Friday morning breakfast was as outstanding as supper the night before. "You must start your day with a good meal to travel in comfort," the innkeeper told them as she refilled the platters on the breakfast table. On the trip back to the airport they all agreed the overnight stay was a good decision.

"It's always easier to deal with takeoff problems when you can see what they are," Dan said as he pulled back on the controls and the airplane lifted into the sky. Strong tailwinds gave the journey's progress a real boost. The miles logged up faster than any of them expected. They made a quick stopover at Regina, Saskatchewan, then on to Thunder Bay, Ontario, on the shores of Lake Superior.

This was the last night of their vacation. It was the close of a memorable experience for Dan and Marianne. He enjoyed the fulfillment of forty years of dreams. She had never dared to hope for the excitement and pleasures Dan offered constantly. She wondered why she was so lucky or what she did to deserve the happiness that was now hers on a daily basis. Vacation was behind them but the memories were theirs to enjoy over and over again.

Going from the inn at Quesnel to the hotel at Thunder Bay was like riding a time machine from the old world to the new. Quesnel was old, ornate and comfortable. Position in life was not a factor considered by the innkeeper there. Especially when it was noted the inn's dishwasher was also the local customs inspector.

The hotel at Thunder Bay was new, modern and luxurious. It was built to accommodate uptight executives who wanted to relax and enjoy the better things in life outside of Board Rooms. The higher you were on the corporate ladder the more respect you commanded at Thunder Bay.

Dan Shaw and Bill Flanagan hated this type of situation. Neither of these men suffered from self importance. Bill knew if it started to show with him Jen would bring him down a peg or two by simply asking him to take out the trash. He got the message without further explanation. Dan's situation was different. Marianne never knew his level of importance in the business world. She did not have the slightest idea of what businesses he was affiliated with or how much he was worth. It didn't matter. As far as she was concerned, he was Dan, — her Dan. That was all that was important.

The amenities at Thunder Bay were plentiful. Bright roomy suites with dressing rooms and bathrooms each outfitted with a Jacuzzi. "Just like home," Dan joked and Jen reminded both of them to use it carefully. "No additives in this one, please," she said. "We don't want to walk down the hall and see a stream of bubbles coming out from under your door."

The hotel also had complete health spa facilities, Olympic size pool, sauna, gym and all manner of physical fitness equipment. This health fetish also extended to the dining room and when dinner was served it was portioned into the basic food groups with just enough of each group to sustain a body without adding one single unnecessary calorie. Although the food was excellent there was not enough on the plate to fill a good size cavity. This caused Bill to ask for directions to the nearest McDonald's and Jen to chastise him for not showing a little class. When compared to the "small supper" at Quesnel, Thunder Bay could stand improvement.

After dinner the Flanagans decided to visit the lounge for a few dances and a drink or two. "Maybe they'll have popcorn over there and I can fill up on that," Bill commented.

Dan and Marianne chose to take a walk along the shore line of the inlet. Both of them realized this was the last night of vacation and neither wanted to see this memorable time come to an end. They held hands as they walked at the water's edge for this was a setting for dreamers and a time for making memories.

Breakfast at Thunder Bay was healthy, not very filling, but calorie correct.

"I'm still hungry," Dan said as they boarded his plane.

"We'll have to curb our appetites and have a good meal at the next stop," Marianne suggested. "Unless we're booked into another Health Spa," she added with a grin.

Bill kept looking out the window and finally curiosity got the best of Dan and he asked, "What are you looking for?"

"Here it comes now," Bill answered with a big smile as a car from the Thunder Bay hotel pulled up to the side of the plane. Two packages were handed to him and with a satisfied grin he turned to the others and announced, "Breakfast is here!"

Fruit juice, apples, oranges, bananas and milk were in the first bag. The second had an assortment of unhealthy, fattening, delicious pastries. Jen just happened to have a big thermos of hot coffee in her carry on bag. Now Marianne knew why the Crew referred to them as the Fabulous Flanagans. They were always prepared for any emergency.

"You learn these things when you have six kids," Jen told them.

Dan radioed the tower and informed them that takeoff would be delayed temporarily due to "personal refueling."

Chapter 38

Vacations are wonderful, but Long Island was a welcome sight and it was good to be home. Bill and Jen Flanagan would head for their home and Dan and Marianne would stay at his house Saturday night and leave early Sunday morning for Massachusetts. She was sorry this vacation was over, but remembered the arrangements they had agreed to and knew they no longer had to deal with departures every Sunday.

The Alaska vacation left indelible memories. It was impossible for Marianne to go back to her routine living. She had to make major adjustments and she had to do it quickly. For many years she had focused her attention on work. Now she had different priorities. Work was secondary and Dan was her most important concern. There was nothing routine about her life anymore. They still enjoyed weekends together, but now Dan didn't leave on Sunday night. When he had to focus on business matters he tried to schedule appointments so he could leave in the morning and be back that night. The new arrangement seemed to work well and after the first three weeks both of them seemed comfortable with it.

On Tuesday morning Cass called and asked Dan if he would fly her and Bernie to Montreal on Thursday. Bernie often dealt with diamonds and Dan knew Cass worried about him if he was carrying gems on a commercial airliner. He agreed to take them even though it meant he wouldn't be back until Sunday.

"We didn't have any plans for this weekend," Marianne said. "Enjoy yourself and I'll see you Sunday afternoon."

Saturday morning Dan called and said there had been a change in plans and asked her to pick him up at the airport at noon. It will be a good weekend after all, she thought.

Dan was waiting for her when she pulled into the parking lot at the airport and he didn't look very happy. She knew something was wrong. This was not the carefree, happy man she had greeted at this airport almost every weekend. Today he looked angry and troubled. She had never seen him like this and it worried her.

"What's the matter," she asked.

Dan looked at her, started to answer then checked himself before he said anything. He turned away for a minute, then looked at her again and said, "We have some serious talking to do. We can't talk in the car and we can't discuss this in a restaurant. So let's go home and then we'll talk."

"About what?" she asked.

He wouldn't say any more. "We'll talk when we get home," was all he would say.

"Danny, what happened?" she asked. "What could be this serious? Can't you give me a hint?"

"No," he said firmly, "I can't, but I guarantee you we will get it straightened out before the day is over."

They drove most of the way home in silence. Dan didn't want to talk and Marianne didn't think it was a good idea to push the issue. She wondered if there was something in the past that she should have told him and didn't. She couldn't think of a thing. When she glanced at him the little muscles in his cheeks were jumping up and down as if it was an effort to keep quiet. She could see that he was angry and this was very unusual for him.

Dan closed the apartment door behind him and headed for the living room.

"I'll put on a pot of coffee," Marianne suggested.

"Don't bother with coffee," he said sternly, "Come in here and sit down."

She followed him into the living room and sat next to him on the sofa.

"You called Cass last Tuesday, didn't you?" he asked but it was more of an accusation than a question.

"Yes I did," she answered and wondered how he knew about her phone call.

"You asked her to keep me busy on Friday, didn't you?"

"Yes," she admitted again.

"You went to the hospital on Friday, didn't you?"

"Yes, I did."

"Why didn't you tell me?" he asked and although he still had a stern tone of voice she could tell he was more hurt than angry.

"I didn't say anything because I didn't want you to worry," she said.

"YOU didn't want ME to worry," he exclaimed. "Marianne, I love you. I've earned the right to worry about you. I worry about you all the time. You don't trust me enough to share the real problems, do you?" he asked. Before she could answer he continued, "You should have told me. You should have been honest with me. I don't want to share only the good times I want to share everything. Can't you understand you don't have to carry the burden by yourself anymore. Part of our togetherness is sharing everything. You're not doing that, you're still holding back. You're shutting me out of feelings that I should be part of and I don't like it. I don't want to be a spectator in your life. Your life is my life, too." Once he started talking the words came tumbling out as if he couldn't say them fast enough.

"When I talked to you on the phone Thursday night you never even gave me a hint of what was going on," he continued. "I had to trap Cass into a confession to get the truth. Were you ever going to tell me?"

Again Marianne found herself in a position where she had made a decision regarding Dan and she was wrong. Now all she could do was try to justify her reasoning. She never intended to hurt him or cause him any misery. She was trying to protect him, but it didn't work.

"Sure I was going to tell you. I was going to talk to you as soon as you came back from Montreal. I wanted to make sure everything was all right before I said anything. I couldn't see any sense in causing you needless worry. Now that I know everything is fine, I can tell you all about it."

"Oh," he said, "and if you didn't get the right answers you weren't going to say anything, is that it"

"That's kind of what I had in mind," she admitted. She could see he was still angry, but the anger was overshadowed by the hurt in his voice.

"And how would you have handled it then?" he asked.

"I'm not sure," she said. "I certainly would not have let things continue the way they are going now. I don't know what I would have done. I would have had to find a way to tell you that would cause you the least amount of heartache. After all, I've caused you enough of that in the past, haven't I?"

He tried to explain that their definitions of love varied considerably. Marianne's would protect him from all outside hurt and

310

share only the good times. He wanted to share everything. She accepted him completely, without any restrictions, but rejected any attempts he made to share his material things. He couldn't understand her reasoning and went along with it only because it seemed to please her. Now he was rethinking some of those ideas. They had paid life's dues many times over. Now they should be able to reap some of the rewards. His efforts to make life a little easier for her had been met with her headstrong stubbornness and insistence that she would carry her own share of the load, both expenses and responsibilities. He had proposed marriage many times and each time she found a reason to evade or delay a definite answer. He didn't press the issue, he knew her well enough to know he couldn't force her to do anything. This was a decision he wanted her to make because it was what she wanted, too. She wouldn't consent to a commitment yet she never denied him the love they both treasured. As long as they could be together he was not going to question the circumstances. He would not take a chance on losing her again.

Dan Shaw was accustomed to competition and capable of breaking down any opposition. That was in the business world, where circumstances were usually predictable. Circumstances and everything else about love were totally unpredictable.

He had to create a situation that would prove to her how much they needed each other. She had established a protected little area of her own where she could watch the world go by and not get directly involved. He had no intention of letting her stagnate on the sidelines of life. He had to do something to jolt her out of her comfortable rut or she would continue to let life pass her by.

"Marianne," he said firmly, "Promise me this will never happen again."

"I can't make a promise like that," she said. "I don't know what's in the future. We'll have to wait and see."

"No we won't," he insisted. "If you have a problem I want to know about it. If I have one, you will know about it. If we are going to be successful at this relationship we both have to learn to share, and to share everything."

"You drive a hard bargain, Mr. Shaw," she conceded with a half hearted grin. "I'll try."

311

"There is something else we have to settle, too," he continued. "I'm not comfortable with the arrangement we made for an apartment. We have to talk about that a little more and see if we can come up with a better solution."

"Come on now, we made a deal, remember?" Marianne reminded him.

"I remember," he said, "and I also remember it was a 'temporary solution.' Now we need something permanent. I don't want a 'deal' I want a wife. I want to make a commitment to you and get one from you. I love you, but I have to admit, I don't understand you," he continued in frustration. "It seems to me we had this same argument many years ago. Don't tell me it is going to wind up the same way."

"I don't think it will," she said but her voice gave away the fact that she was worried, too.

"Can you give me one good reason why you're being so damn stubborn now?" he asked.

"Danny, I'm not trying to be stubborn. I'm trying to be realistic. Many years ago we had a lot more in common than we do today. We can't go back to the old days. I'm not the same person I was then.

"Yes you are," he stated firmly.

"No I'm not," she insisted. "The years leave scars and I have some pretty big scars, physical, mental and emotional. I'm not going to make a commitment to you until I can give you one hundred percent. That's why I suggested the temporary solution."

"That's not what I want, Marianne. I want you – scars and all. Neither of us are perfect, neither of us ever will be. I know we have differences, that's part of life. Your differences fascinate me and I want to be part of them. I don't want to change them, that would spoil it. I don't want put offs or conditions. I love you, I want you. I need you. What more can I say?"

Marianne knew he was right in everything he said. She had her own second thoughts about the temporary solution. "Danny," she said, "you're making this very difficult for me."

"I don't want to do that," he told her. "Nor do I want to force you to make a decision. I would rather you did that on your own. I think the best thing for me to do is to go back to New York. This time, you're going to have to call me."

Marianne couldn't say a word as she watched Dan walk out the door. Now she knew exactly how he must have felt those many years ago when he saw his world fall apart.

Their Alaska vacation proved to her how much they needed each other. In spite of setbacks like the Duncans they found real quality time together. It also showed her that Dan Shaw would never be content with second best. He was not a 'do it yourself' person but she had to admit they had not run into a situation that he couldn't handle. She always knew he was capable. What she was looking for was what would make him comfortable.

He preferred everything to be first class. Forty years ago she thought the same way. Nothing short of the best was good enough for her, either. Somehow the in between years had changed all of that and left an indelible mark on her thought process. Do it yourself, stretch it till it fits, and never throw anything away, had all become part of her lifestyle. Old habits are hard to break. She had serious doubts if she could ever again be comfortable if everything was strictly first class. She had tremendous fears of being a misfit in Dan's opulent world.

The loneliness was gone. They had solved that problem for each other. They had a year of memories that filled a void created by forty-three years of separation. No matter what the future brings the memories are forever. No one can erase them, no one can borrow them and no one can change them.

Dan had been gone for almost an hour. Marianne sat at the kitchen table and put her head down on her forearm. How did I ever let this happen again, she thought? How could I have been so stupid? She tried to reason with herself by thinking, at her age she couldn't handle such a drastic change. The affluent, easy living world of Dan Shaw was fine as long as he was by her side but she couldn't expect him to be there every waking minute. The Crew was helpful and supportive, but she couldn't use them as a constant crutch. Fate, she told herself, has me singled out to be an idiot and a workaholic all my life. Her reasoning was interrupted by the front door buzzer. She reached for the release button and pushed it without asking who was there. Probably Tim or Beth, she thought. They seem to posses a sixth sense that tells them when Mom needs a shoulder to cry on. How am I ever going to explain this to either of them, she thought.

There was a soft knock on the apartment door. She opened it and Dan said, "I couldn't leave like this."

"I'm glad you couldn't" she said through the tears, "I didn't want you to go."

"Can we solve our problem?" he asked.

"I have a suggestion," she said, "Let's both go back to New York – and have Josh call the Judge."

She watched Dan's face as the corners of his mouth curled upward and the little lines next to his eyes crinkled together in a happy, pleased smile. He held her in his arms and said, "Marianne, you've just made the rest of my life worth living. I love you."

The End.

About the Author

When I was in school, most females were limited to careers as mothers, secretaries, nurses or teachers. Another option was that you heard "the calling" and chose to become a nun. I never heard the "calling" – even God couldn't shout that loud. I was not going to settle for any delicate female careers. I wanted a lot more out of life. I have been fortunate enough to work in almost every field, except medical. I've gained a wealth of experience and have had a wonderful time doing it.

A college education had always been a goal, but circumstances didn't allow it until I was fifty-one years old. It was one of the smartest things I've ever done. I found some of my best friends in my college years, professors and friends who had faith in me when I didn't have faith in myself. Books have always been my constant companions. Writing was a challenge that tempted me for years, like a fascination that I could never overcome. Articles published in regional magazines and newsletters plus a few years of investigative reporting proved to me how difficult it is to be a successful writer.

Today, I'm older, milder and mellower. My serious years never offered the sense of happiness or feeling of accomplishment that comes with age and experience. I don't like to be classified as "old" but I will admit to having antique value. I have learned not to take life too seriously and that laughter doesn't add to my wrinkles.

Printed in the United States
972100001B